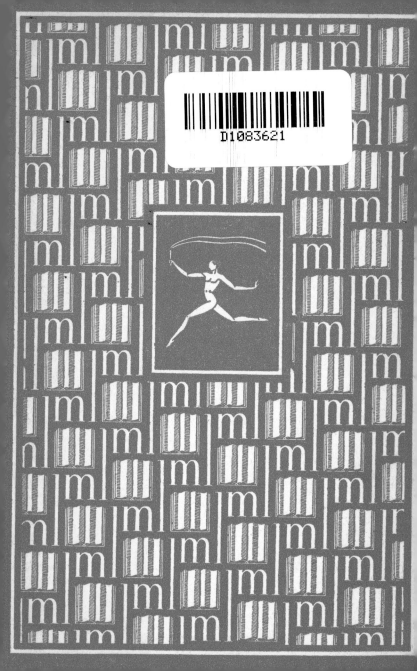

D1083621

BEST RUSSIAN

SHORT STORIES

David Blaylock
October 18, 1956

BEST
RUSSIAN
SHORT
STORIES

COMPILED AND EDITED

BY THOMAS SELTZER

THE MODERN LIBRARY · NEW YORK

Random House IS THE PUBLISHER OF

THE MODERN LIBRARY

BENNETT A. CERF · DONALD S. KLOPFER · ROBERT K. HAAS

Manufactured in the United States of America

By H. Wolff

CONTENTS

Introduction		vii
The Queen of Spades	A. S. Pushkin	3
The Cloak	N. V. Gogol	40
The District Doctor	I. S. Turgenev	82
The Christmas Tree and the Wedding	F. M. Dostoyevsky	96
God Sees the Truth, but Waits	L. N. Tolstoy	107
How a Muzhik Fed Two Officials	M. Y. Saltykov	118
The Shades, a Phantasy	V. G. Korolenko	130
The Signal	V. M. Garshin	165
The Darling	A. P. Chekhov	178
The Bet	A. P. Chekhov	196
Vanka	A. P. Chekhov	206
Hide and Seek	F. Sologub	212
Dethroned	I. N. Potapenko	228
The Servant	S. T. Semyonov	254
One Autumn Night	M. Gorky	263
Her Lover	M. Gorky	276
The Revolutionist	M. P. Artzybashev	284
The Outrage	A. I. Kuprin	298
Lazarus	L. N. Andreyev	320
The Seven That Were Hanged	L. N. Andreyev	347
The Red Laugh	L. N. Andreyev	437
The Gentleman from San Francisco	Ivan Bunin	522

INTRODUCTION

CONCEIVE the joy of a lover of nature who, leaving the art galleries, wanders out among the trees and wild flowers and birds that the pictures of the galleries have sentimentalised. It is some such joy that the man who truly loves the noblest in letters feels when tasting for the first time the simple delights of Russian literature. French and English and German authors, too, occasionally, offer works of lofty, simple naturalness; but the very keynote to the whole of Russian literature is simplicity, naturalness, veraciousness.

Another essentially Russian trait is the quite unaffected conception that the lowly are on a plane of equality with the so-called upper classes. When the Englishman Dickens wrote with his profound pity and understanding of the poor, there was yet a bit of remoteness, perhaps, even, a bit of caricature, in his treatment of them. He showed their sufferings to the rest of the world with a "Behold how the other half lives!" The Russian writes of the poor, as it were, from within, as one of them, with no eye to theatrical effect upon the well-to-do. There is no insistence upon peculiar virtues or vices. The poor are portrayed just as they are, as human beings like the rest of us. A democratic spirit is reflected, breathing a broad humanity, a true universality, an unstudied generosity that proceed not from the intellectual conviction that to understand all is to forgive all, but from an instinctive feeling that no man has the right to set himself up as a judge over another, that one can only observe and record.

In 1834 two short stories appeared, *The Queen of Spades,* by Pushkin, and *The Cloak,* by Gogol. The first was a finishing-off of the old, outgoing style of romanticism, the other was the beginning of the new, the characteristically Russian style. We read Pushkin's *Queen of Spades,* the first story in the volume, and the likelihood is we shall enjoy it greatly. "But why is it Russian?" we ask. The answer is, "It is not Russian." It might have been printed in an American magazine over the name of John Brown. But, now, take the very next story in the volume, *The Cloak.* "Ah," you exclaim, "a genuine Russian story, surely. You cannot palm it off on me over the name of Jones or Smith." Why? Because *The Cloak* for the first time strikes that truly Russian note of deep sympathy with the disinherited. It is not yet wholly free from artificiality, and so is not yet typical of the purely realistic fiction that reached its perfected development in Turgenev and Tolstoy.

Though Pushkin heads the list of those writers who made the literature of their country world-famous, he was still a romanticist, in the universal literary fashion of his day. However, he already gave strong indication of the peculiarly Russian genius for naturalness or realism, and was a true Russian in his simplicity of style. In no sense an innovator, but taking the cue for his poetry from Byron and for his prose from the romanticism current at that period, he was not in advance of his age. He had a revolutionary streak in his nature, as his *Ode to Liberty* and other bits of verse and his intimacy with the Decembrist rebels show. But his youthful fire soon died down, and he found it possible to accommodate himself to the life of a Russian high functionary and courtier under the severe despot Nicholas I, though, to be sure, he always hated that life. For all his flirting with revolutionism, he never displayed great originality or depth of thought. He was simply an extraordinarily gifted author, a perfect versifier, a wondrous lyrist, and a delicious raconteur, endowed with a grace, ease and power of expression that delighted even the exacting artistic sense of Turgenev. To him aptly applies the dictum of Socrates: "Not by wisdom do the poets write poetry, but by a sort of genius and inspiration." I do not mean to convey that as a thinker Pushkin is to be despised. Nevertheless, it is true that he would occupy a lower position in literature did his reputation depend upon his contributions to thought and not upon his value as an artist.

"We are all descended from Gogol's *Cloak*," said a Russian writer. And Dostoyevsky's novel, *Poor People,* which appeared ten years later, is, in a way, merely an extension of Gogol's shorter tale. In Dostoyevsky, indeed, the passion for the common people and the all-embracing, all-penetrating pity for suffering humanity reach their climax. He was a profound psychologist and delved deeply into the human soul, especially in its abnormal and diseased aspects. Between scenes of heart-rending, abject poverty, injustice, and wrong, and the torments of mental pathology, he man-

aged almost to exhaust the whole range of human woe.
And he analysed this misery with an intensity of feeling
and a painstaking regard for the most harrowing details
that are quite upsetting to normally constituted nerves. Yet
all the horrors must be forgiven him because of the motive
inspiring them—an overpowering love and the desire to
induce an equal love in others. It is not horror for horror's
sake, not a literary *tour de force,* as in Poe, but horror for
a high purpose, for purification through suffering, which
was one of the articles of Dostoyevsky's faith.

Following as a corollary from the love and pity for mankind that make a leading element in Russian literature, is
a passionate search for the means of improving the lot of
humanity, a fervent attachment to social ideas and ideals.
A Russian author is more ardently devoted to a cause than
an American short-story writer to a plot. This, in turn, is
but a reflection of the spirit of the Russian people, especially
of the intellectuals. The Russians take literature perhaps
more seriously than any other nation. To them books are
not a mere diversion. They demand that fiction and poetry
be a true mirror of life and be of service to life. A Russian
author, to achieve the highest recognition, must be a thinker
also. He need not necessarily be a finished artist. Everything is subordinated to two main requirements—humanitarian ideals and fidelity to life. This is the secret of the
marvellous simplicity of Russian literary art. Before the
supreme function of literature, the Russian writer stands
awed and humbled. He knows he cannot cover up poverty
of thought, poverty of spirit and lack of sincerity by
rhetorical tricks or verbal cleverness. And if he possesses

the two essential requirements, the simplest language will suffice.

These qualities are exemplified at their best by Turgenev and Tolstoy. They both had a strong social consciousness; they both grappled with the problems of human welfare; they were both artists in the larger sense, that is, in their truthful representation of life. Turgenev was an artist also in the narrower sense—in a keen appreciation of form. Thoroughly Occidental in his tastes, he sought the regeneration of Russia in radical progress along the lines of European democracy. Tolstoy, on the other hand, sought the salvation of mankind in a return to the primitive life and primitive Christian religion.

The very first work of importance by Turgenev, *A Sportsman's Sketches,* dealt with the question of serfdom, and it wielded tremendous influence in bringing about its abolition. Almost every succeeding book of his, from *Rudin* through *Fathers and Sons* to *Virgin Soil,* presented vivid pictures of contemporary Russian society, with its problems, the clash of ideas between the old and the new generations, and the struggles, the aspirations and the thoughts that engrossed the advanced youth of Russia; so that his collected works form a remarkable literary record of the successive movements of Russian society in a period of preparation, fraught with epochal significance, which culminated in the overthrow of Czarism and the inauguration of a new and true democracy, marking the beginning, perhaps, of a radical transformation the world over.

"The greatest writer of Russia." That is Turgenev's estimate of Tolstoy. "A second Shakespeare!" was Flaubert's enthusiastic outburst. The Frenchman's comparison is not wholly illuminating. The one point of resemblance between the two authors is simply in the tremendous magnitude of their genius. Each is a Colossus. Each creates a whole world of characters, from kings and princes and ladies to servants and maids and peasants. But how vastly divergent the angle of approach! Anna Karenina may have all the subtle womanly charm of an Olivia or a Portia, but how different her trials. Shakespeare could not have treated Anna's problems at all. Anna could not have appeared in his pages except as a sinning Gertrude, the mother of Hamlet. Shakespeare had all the prejudices of his age. He accepted the world as it is with its absurd moralities, its conventions and institutions and social classes. A grave-digger is naturally inferior to a lord, and if he is to be presented at all, he must come on as a clown. The people are always a mob, the rabble. Tolstoy is the revolutionist, the iconoclast. He has the completest independence of mind. He utterly refuses to accept established opinions just because they are established. He probes into the right and wrong of things. His is a broad, generous universal democracy, his is a comprehensive sympathy, his an absolute incapacity to evaluate human beings according to station, rank or profession, or any standard but that of spiritual worth. In all this he was a complete contrast to Shakespeare. Each of the two men was like a creature of a higher world, possessed of supernatural endowments. Their omniscience of all things human, their insight into the hiddenmost springs of men's actions appear miraculous. But Shakespeare makes the impression of detachment from his works. The works do not reveal the man; while in Tolstoy the greatness of the man blends with the greatness of the genius. Tolstoy was no mere oracle uttering profundities he wot not of. As the social, religious and moral tracts that he wrote in the latter period of his life are instinct with a literary beauty of which he never could divest himself, and which gave an artistic value even to his sermons, so his earlier novels show a profound concern for the welfare of society, a broad, humanitarian spirit, a bigness of soul that included prince and pauper alike.

Is this extravagant praise? Then let me echo William Dean Howells: "I know very well that I do not speak of Tolstoy's books in measured terms; I cannot."

The Russian writers so far considered have made valuable contributions to the short story; but, with the exception of Pushkin, whose reputation rests chiefly upon his poetry, their best work, generally, was in the field of the long novel. It was the novel that gave Russian literature its pre-eminence. It could not have been otherwise, since Russia is young as a literary nation, and did not come of age until the period at which the novel was almost the only form of literature that counted. If, therefore, Russia was to gain distinction in the world of letters, it could be only through the novel. Of the measure of her success there is perhaps no better testimony than the words of Matthew Arnold, a critic certainly not given to overstatement. "The Russian novel," he wrote in 1887, "has now the vogue, and deserves to have it. . . . The Russian novelist is master of a spell to which the secret of human nature—both what is external and internal, gesture and manner no less than thought and feeling—willingly make themselves known. . . . In that form of imaginative literature, which in our day is the most popular and the most possible, the Russians at the present moment seem to me to hold the field."

With the strict censorship imposed on Russian writers, many of them who might perhaps have contented themselves with expressing their opinions in essays, were driven to conceal their meaning under the guise of satire or allegory; which gave rise to a peculiar genre of literature, a sort of editorial or essay done into fiction, in which the satirist Saltykov, a contemporary of Turgenev and Dostoyevsky, who wrote under the pseudonym of Shchedrin, achieved the greatest success and popularity.

It was not, however, until the concluding quarter of the last century that writers like Korolenko and Garshin arose, who devoted themselves chiefly to the cultivation of the short story. With Anton Chekhov the short story assumed a position of importance alongside the larger works of the great Russian masters. Gorky and Andreyev made the short story do the same service for the active revolutionary period in the last decade of the nineteenth century down to its temporary defeat in 1906 that Turgenev rendered in his series of larger novels for the period of preparation. But very different was the voice of Gorky, the man sprung from the people, the embodiment of all the accumulated wrath and indignation of centuries of social wrong and oppression, from the gentlemanly tones of the cultured artist Turgenev. Like a mighty hammer his blows fell upon the decaying fabric of the old society. His was no longer a feeble, despairing protest. With the strength and confidence of victory he made onslaught upon onslaught on the old institutions until they shook and almost tumbled. And when reaction celebrated its short-lived triumph and gloom settled again upon his country and most of his co-fighters withdrew from the battle in despair, some returning to the old-time Russian mood of hopelessness, passivity and apathy, and some even backsliding into wild orgies of literary debauchery, Gorky never wavered, never lost his faith and hope, never for a moment was untrue to his principles. Now, with the revolution victorious, he has come into his right, one of the most respected, beloved and picturesque figures in the Russian democracy.

Kuprin, the most facile and talented short-story writer next to Chekhov, has, on the whole, kept well to the best literary traditions of Russia, though he has frequently wandered off to extravagant sex themes, for which he seems to display as great a fondness as Artzybashev. Semyonov is a unique character in Russian literature, a peasant who had scarcely mastered the most elementary mechanics of writing when he penned his first story. But that story pleased Tolstoy, who befriended and encouraged him. His tales deal altogether with peasant life in country and city, and have a lifelikeness, an artlessness, a simplicity striking even in a Russian author.

There is a small group of writers detached from the main current of Russian literature who worship at the shrine of beauty and mysticism. Of these Sologub has attained the highest reputation.

Rich as Russia has become in the short story, Anton Chekhov still stands out as the supreme master, one of the greatest short-story writers of the world. He was born in Taganarok, in the Ukraine, in 1860, the son of a peasant serf who succeeded in buying his freedom. Anton Chekhov studied medicine, but devoted himself largely to writing, in which, he acknowledged, his scientific training was of great service. Though he lived only forty-four years, dying of tuberculosis in 1904, his collected works consist of sixteen fair-sized volumes of short stories, and several dramas besides. A few volumes of his works have already appeared in English translation.

Critics, among them Tolstoy, have often compared Chekhov to Maupassant. I find it hard to discover the resemblance. Maupassant holds a supreme position as a short-story writer; so does Chekhov. But there, it seems to me, the likeness ends.

The chill wind that blows from the atmosphere created by the Frenchman's objective artistry is by the Russian commingled with the warm breath of a great human sympathy. Maupassant never tells where his sympathies lie, and you don't know; you only guess. Chekhov does not tell you where his sympathies lie, either, but you know all the same; you don't have to guess. And yet Chekhov is as objective as Maupassant. In the chronicling of facts, conditions, and situations, in the reproduction of characters, he is scrupulously true, hard, and inexorable. But without obtruding his personality, he somehow manages to let you know that he is always present, always at hand. If you laugh, he is there to laugh with you; if you cry, he is there to shed a tear with you; if you are horrified, he is horrified, too. It is a subtle art by which he contrives to make one feel the nearness of himself for all his objectiveness, so subtle that it defies analysis. And yet it constitutes one of the great charms of his tales.

Chekhov's works show an astounding resourcefulness and versatility. There is no monotony, no repetition. Neither in incident nor in character are any two stories alike. The range of Chekhov's knowledge of men and things seems to be unlimited, and he is extravagant in the use of it. Some great idea which many a writer would consider sufficient to expand into a whole novel he disposes of in a story of a few pages. Take, for example, *Vanka*, apparently but a mere episode in the childhood of a nine-year-old boy, while it is really the tragedy of a whole life in its tempting glimpses into a past environment and ominous forebodings of the future—all contracted into the space of four or five pages. Chekhov is lavish with his inventiveness. Apparently, it cost him no effort to invent.

I have used the word inventiveness for lack of a better name. It expresses but lamely the peculiar faculty that distinguishes Chekhov. Chekhov does not really invent. He reveals. He reveals things that no author before him has revealed. It is as though he possessed a special organ which enabled him to see, hear and feel things of which we other mortals did not even dream the existence. Yet when he lays them bare we know that they are not fictitious, not invented, but as real as the ordinary familiar facts of life. This faculty of his playing on all conceivable objects, all conceivable emotions, no matter how microscopic, endows them with life and a soul. By virtue of this power *The Steppe,* an uneventful record of peasants travelling day after day through flat, monotonous fields, becomes instinct with dramatic interest, and its 125 pages seem all too short. And by virtue of the same attribute we follow with breathless suspense the minute description of the declining days of a great scientist, who feels his physical and mental faculties gradually ebbing away. *A Tiresome Story,* Chekhov calls it; and so it would be without the vitality conjured into it by the magic touch of this strange genius.

Divination is perhaps a better term than invention. Chekhov divines the most secret impulses of the soul, scents out what is buried in the subconscious, and brings it up to the surface. Most writers are specialists. They know certain strata of society, and when they venture beyond, their step becomes uncertain. Chekhov's material is only delimited by humanity. He is equally at home everywhere. The peasant, the labourer, the merchant, the priest, the professional man, the scholar, the military officer, and the government functionary, Gentile or Jew, man, woman, or child—Chekhov is intimate with all of them. His characters are sharply defined individuals, not types. In almost all his stories, however short, the men and women and children who play a part in them come out as clear, distinct personalities. Ariadne is as vivid a character as Lilly, the heroine of Sudermann's *Song of Songs;* yet *Ariadne* is but a single story in a volume of stories. Who that has read *The Darling* can ever forget her—the woman who had no separate existence of her own, but thought the thoughts, felt the feelings, and spoke the words of the men she loved? And when there was no man to love any more, she was utterly crushed until she found a child to take care of and to love;

and then she sank her personality in the boy as she had sunk it before in her husbands and lover, became a mere reflection of him, and was happy again.

In the compilation of this volume I have been guided by the desire to give the largest possible representation to the prominent authors of the Russian short story, and to present specimens characteristic of each. At the same time the element of interest has been kept in mind; and in a few instances, as in the case of Korolenko, the selection of the story was made with a view to its intrinsic merit and striking qualities rather than as typifying the writer's art. It was, of course, impossible in the space of one book to exhaust all that is best. But to my knowledge, the present volume is the most comprehensive anthology of the Russian short story in the English language, and gives a fair notion of the achievement in that field. All who enjoy good reading, I have no reason to doubt, will get pleasure from it, and if, in addition, it will prove of assistance to American students of Russian literature, I shall feel that the task has been doubly worth the while.

Korolenko's *Shades* and Andreyev's *Lazarus* first appeared in *Current Opinion,* and Artzybashev's *The Revolutionist* in the *Metropolitan Magazine*. I take pleasure in thanking Mr. Edward J. Wheeler, editor of *Current Opinion,* and Mr. Carl Hovey, editor of the *Metropolitan Magazine,* for permission to reprint them.

Thomas Seltzer

BEST RUSSIAN SHORT STORIES

THE QUEEN OF SPADES

◆◆◆

By *Aleksandr S. Pushkin*

I

THERE WAS A card party at the rooms of Narumov of the Horse Guards. The long winter night passed away imperceptibly, and it was five o'clock in the morning before the company sat down to supper. Those who had won, ate with a good appetite; the others sat staring absently at their empty plates. When the champagne appeared, however, the conversation became more animated, and all took a part in it.

"And how did you fare, Surin?" asked the host.

"Oh, I lost, as usual. I must confess that I am unlucky: I play mirandole, I always keep cool, I never allow anything to put me out, and yet I always lose!"

"And you did not once allow yourself to be tempted to back the red? . . . Your firmness astonishes me."

"But what do you think of Hermann?" said one of the guests, pointing to a young Engineer: "he has never had a card in his hand in his life, he has never in his life laid a wager, and yet he sits here till five o'clock in the morning watching our play."

"Play interests me very much," said Hermann: "but I am not in the position to sacrifice the necessary in the hope of winning the superfluous."

3

"Hermann is a German: he is economical—that is all!" observed Tomsky. "But if there is one person that I cannot understand, it is my grandmother, the Countess Anna Fedotovna."

"How so?" inquired the guests.

"I cannot understand," continued Tomsky, "how it is that my grandmother does not punt."

"What is there remarkable about an old lady of eighty not punting?" said Narumov.

"Then you do not know the reason why?"

"No, really; haven't the faintest idea."

"Oh! then listen. About sixty years ago, my grandmother went to Paris, where she created quite a sensation. People used to run after her to catch a glimpse of the 'Muscovite Venus.' Richelieu made love to her, and my grandmother maintains that he almost blew out his brains in consequence of her cruelty. At that time ladies used to play at faro. On one occasion at the Court, she lost a very considerable sum to the Duke of Orleans. On returning home, my grandmother removed the patches from her face, took off her hoops, informed my grandfather of her loss at the gaming-table, and ordered him to pay the money. My deceased grandfather, as far as I remember, was a sort of house-steward to my grandmother. He dreaded her like fire; but, on hearing of such a heavy loss, he almost went out of his mind; he calculated the various sums she had lost, and pointed out to her that in six months she had spent half a million francs, that neither their Moscow nor Saratov estates were in Paris, and finally refused point blank to pay the debt. My grandmother gave him a box on the ear and slept by herself as a sign of her displeasure. The next day she sent for her husband, hoping that this domestic punishment had produced an effect upon him, but she found him inflexible. For the first time in her life, she entered into reasonings and explanations with him, thinking to be able to convince him by pointing out to him that there are debts and debts, and that there is a great difference between a Prince and a coachmaker. But it was all in vain, my grandfather still remained obdurate. But the matter did not rest there. My grandmother did not know what to do. She had shortly before become acquainted with a very remarkable man. You have heard of Count St. Germain, about whom so many marvellous stories are told. You know that he represented himself as the Wandering Jew, as the discoverer of the elixir of life, of the philosopher's stone, and so forth. Some laughed at him as a charlatan; but Casanova, in his memoirs, says that he was a spy. But be that as it may, St. Germain, in spite of the mystery surrounding him, was a very fascinating person, and was much sought after in the best circles of society. Even to this day my grandmother retains an affectionate recollection of him, and becomes quite angry if any one speaks disrespectfully of him. My grandmother knew that St. Germain had large sums of money at his disposal. She resolved to have recourse to him, and she wrote a letter to him asking him to come to her without delay. The queer old man immediately waited upon her and found her overwhelmed with grief. She described to him in the blackest

colours the barbarity of her husband, and ended by de-
claring that her whole hope depended upon his friendship
and amiability.

"St. Germain reflected.

" 'I could advance you the sum you want,' said he; 'but
I know that you would not rest easy until you had paid me
back, and I should not like to bring fresh troubles upon
you. But there is another way of getting out of your
difficulty: you can win back your money.'

" 'But, my dear Count,' replied my grandmother, 'I tell
you that I haven't any money left.'

" 'Money is not necessary,' replied St. Germain: 'be
pleased to listen to me.'

"Then he revealed to her a secret, for which each of us
would give a good deal . . ."

The young officers listened with increased attention.
Tomsky lit his pipe, puffed away for a moment and then
continued:

"That same evening my grandmother went to Versailles
to the *jeu de la reine*. The Duke of Orleans kept the bank;
my grandmother excused herself in an off-hand manner for
not having yet paid her debt, by inventing some little story,
and then began to play against him. She chose three cards
and played them one after the other: all three won *sonika*,[1]
and my grandmother recovered every farthing that she
had lost."

"Mere chance!" said one of the guests.

"A tale!" observed Hermann.

"Perhaps they were marked cards!" said a third.

[1] Said of a card when it wins or loses in the quickest possible time.

"I do not think so," replied Tomsky gravely.

"What!" said Narumov, "you have a grandmother who knows how to hit upon three lucky cards in succession, and you have never yet succeeded in getting the secret of it out of her?"

"That's the deuce of it!" replied Tomsky: "she had four sons, one of whom was my father; all four were determined gamblers, and yet not to one of them did she ever reveal her secret, although it would not have been a bad thing either for them or for me. But this is what I heard from my uncle, Count Ivan Ilyich, and he assured me, on his honour, that it was true. The late Chaplitzky—the same who died in poverty after having squandered millions— once lost, in his youth, about three hundred thousand roubles—to Zorich, if I remember rightly. He was in despair. My grandmother, who was always very severe upon the extravagance of young men, took pity, however, upon Chaplitzky. She gave him three cards, telling him to play them one after the other, at the same time exacting from him a solemn promise that he would never play at cards again as long as he lived. Chaplitzky then went to his victorious opponent, and they began a fresh game. On the first card he staked fifty thousand rubles and won *sonika;* he doubled the stake and won again, till at last, by pursuing the same tactics, he won back more than he had lost . . .

"But it is time to go to bed: it is a quarter to six already."

And indeed it was already beginning to dawn: the young men emptied their glasses and then took leave of each other.

II

THE OLD Countess A—— was seated in her dressing-room in front of her looking-glass. Three waiting maids stood around her. One held a small pot of rouge, another a box of hair-pins, and the third a tall cap with bright red ribbons. The Countess had no longer the slightest pretensions to beauty, but she still preserved the habits of her youth, dressed in strict accordance with the fashion of seventy years before, and made as long and as careful a toilette as she would have done sixty years previously. Near the window, at an embroidery frame, sat a young lady, her ward.

"Good morning, grandmamma," said a young officer, entering the room. *"Bonjour, Mademoiselle Lise.* Grandmamma, I want to ask you something."

"What is it, Paul?"

"I want you to let me introduce one of my friends to you, and to allow me to bring him to the ball on Friday."

"Bring him direct to the ball and introduce him to me there. Were you at B——'s yesterday?"

"Yes; everything went off very pleasantly, and dancing was kept up until five o'clock. How charming Yeletzkaya was!"

"But, my dear, what is there charming about her? Isn't she like her grandmother, the Princess Daria Petrovna? By the way, she must be very old, the Princess Daria Petrovna."

"How do you mean, old?" cried Tomsky thoughtlessly; "she died seven years ago."

The young lady raised her head and made a sign to the young officer. He then remembered that the old Countess was never to be informed of the death of any of her contemporaries, and he bit his lips. But the old Countess heard the news with the greatest indifference.

"Dead!" said she; "and I did not know it. We were appointed maids of honour at the same time, and when we were presented to the Empress. . . ."

And the Countess for the hundredth time related to her grandson one of her anecdotes.

"Come, Paul," said she, when she had finished her story, "help me to get up. Lizanka, where is my snuff-box?"

And the Countess with her three maids went behind a screen to finish her toilette. Tomsky was left alone with the young lady.

"Who is the gentleman you wish to introduce to the Countess?" asked Lizaveta Ivanovna in a whisper.

"Narumov. Do you know him?"

"No. Is he a soldier or a civilian?"

"A soldier."

"Is he in the Engineers?"

"No, in the Cavalry. What made you think that he was in the Engineers?"

The young lady smiled, but made no reply.

"Paul," cried the Countess from behind the screen, "send me some new novel, only pray don't let it be one of the present day style."

"What do you mean, grandmother?"

"That is, a novel, in which the hero strangles neither his

father nor his mother, and in which there are no drowned bodies. I have a great horror of drowned persons."

"There are no such novels nowadays. Would you like a Russian one?"

"Are there any Russian novels? Send me one, my dear, pray send me one!"

"Good-bye, grandmother: I am in a hurry. . . . Good-bye, Lizaveta Ivanovna. What made you think that Narumov was in the Engineers?"

And Tomsky left the boudoir.

Lizaveta Ivanovna was left alone: she laid aside her work and began to look out of the window. A few moments afterwards, at a corner house on the other side of the street, a young officer appeared. A deep blush covered her cheeks; she took up her work again and bent her head down over the frame. At the same moment the Countess returned completely dressed.

"Order the carriage, Lizaveta," said she; "we will go out for a drive."

Lizaveta arose from the frame and began to arrange her work.

"What is the matter with you, my child, are you deaf?" cried the Countess. "Order the carriage to be got ready at once."

"I will do so this moment," replied the young lady, hastening into the ante-room.

A servant entered and gave the Countess some books from Prince Paul Aleksandrovich.

"Tell him that I am much obliged to him," said the Countess. "Lizaveta! Lizaveta! where are you running to?"

"I am going to dress."

"There is plenty of time my dear. Sit down here. Open the first volume and read to me aloud."

Her companion took the book and read a few lines.

"Louder," said the Countess. "What is the matter with you, my child? Have you lost your voice? Wait—give me that footstool—a little nearer—that will do."

Lizaveta read two more pages. The Countess yawned.

"Put the book down," said she: "what a lot of nonsense! Send it back to Prince Paul with my thanks. . . . But where is the carriage?"

"The carriage is ready," said Lizaveta, looking out into the street.

"How is it that you are not dressed?" said the Countess: "I must always wait for you. It is intolerable, my dear!"

Liza hastened to her room. She had not been there two minutes, before the Countess began to ring with all her might. The three waiting-maids came running in at one door and the valet at another.

"How is it that you cannot hear me when I ring for you?" said the Countess. "Tell Lizaveta Ivanovna that I am waiting for her."

Lizaveta returned with her hat and cloak on.

"At last you are here!" said the Countess. "But why such an elaborate toilette? Whom do you intend to captivate? What sort of weather is it? It seems rather windy."

"No, your Ladyship, it is very calm," replied the valet.

"You never think of what you are talking about. Open the window. So it is: windy and bitterly cold. Unharness the horses. Lizaveta, we won't go out—there was no need for you to deck yourself like that."

"What a life is mine!" thought Lizaveta Ivanovna.

And, in truth, Lizaveta Ivanovna was a very unfortunate creature. "The bread of the stranger is bitter," says Dante, "and his staircase hard to climb." But who can know what the bitterness of dependence is so well as the poor companion of an old lady of quality? The Countess A—— had by no means a bad heart, but she was capricious, like a woman who had been spoilt by the world, as well as being avaricious and egotistical, like all old people who have seen their best days, and whose thoughts are with the past and not the present. She participated in all the vanities of the great world, went to balls, where she sat in a corner, painted and dressed in old-fashioned style, like a deformed but indispensable ornament of the ball-room; all the guests on entering approached her and made a profound bow, as if in accordance with a set ceremony, but after that nobody took any further notice of her. She received the whole town at her house, and observed the strictest etiquette, although she could no longer recognise the faces of people. Her numerous domestics, growing fat and old in her ante-chamber and servants' hall, did just as they liked, and vied with each other in robbing the aged Countess in the most barefaced manner. Lizaveta Ivanovna was the martyr of the household. She made tea, and was reproached with using too much sugar; she read novels aloud to the Countess, and the faults of the author were visited upon her head; she accompanied the Countess in her walks, and was held answerable for the weather or the state of pavement. A salary was attached to the post, but she very rarely received it, although she was expected to dress like everybody else, that is to say, like very few indeed. In society she played the most pitiable rôle. Everybody knew her, and nobody paid her any attention. At balls she danced only when a partner was wanted, and ladies would only take hold of her arm when it was necessary to lead her out of the room to attend to their dresses. She was very self-conscious, and felt her position keenly, and she looked about her with impatience for a deliverer to come to her rescue; but the young men, calculating in their giddiness, honoured her with but very little attention, although Liza-veta Ivanovna was a hundred times prettier than the bare-faced and cold-hearted marriageable girls around whom they hovered. Many a time did she quietly slink away from the glittering but wearisome drawing-room, to go and cry in her own poor little room, in which stood a screen, a chest of drawers, a looking-glass and a painted bedstead, and where a tallow candle burnt feebly in a copper candle-stick.

One morning—this was about two days after the evening party described at the beginning of this story, and a week previous to the scene at which we have just assisted—Lizaveta Ivanovna was seated near the window at her embroidery frame, when, happening to look out into the street, she caught sight of a young Engineer officer, stand-ing motionless with his eyes fixed upon her window. She lowered her head and went on again with her work. About five minutes afterwards she looked out again—the young officer was still standing in the same place. Not being in the habit of coquetting with passing officers, she did not continue to gaze out into the street, but went on sewing for a couple of hours, without raising her head. Dinner was announced. She rose up and began to put her embroidery away, but glancing casually out of the window, she perceived the officer again. This seemed to her very strange. After dinner she went to the window with a certain feeling of uneasiness, but the officer was no longer there—and she thought no more about him.

A couple of days afterwards, just as she was stepping into the carriage with the Countess, she saw him again. He was standing close behind the door, with his face half-concealed by his fur collar, but his dark eyes sparkled beneath his cap. Lizaveta felt alarmed, though she knew not why, and she trembled as she seated herself in the carriage.

On returning home, she hastened to the window—the officer was standing in his accustomed place, with his eyes fixed upon her. She drew back, a prey to curiosity and agitated by a feeling which was quite new to her.

From that time forward not a day passed without the young officer making his appearance under the window at the customary hour, and between him and her there was established a sort of mute acquaintance. Sitting in her place at work, she used to feel his approach; and raising her head, she would look at him longer and longer each day. The young man seemed to be very grateful to her: she saw with the sharp eye of youth, how a sudden flush covered his pale cheeks each time that their glances met. After about a week she commenced to smile at him. . . .

When Tomsky asked permission of his grandmother the Countess to present one of his friends to her, the young girl's heart beat violently. But hearing that Narumov was not an Engineer, she regretted that by her thoughtless question, she had betrayed her secret to the volatile Tomsky.

Hermann was the son of a German who had become a naturalised Russian, and from whom he had inherited a small capital. Being firmly convinced of the necessity of preserving his independence, Hermann did not touch his private income, but lived on his pay, without allowing himself the slightest luxury. Moreover, he was reserved and ambitious, and his companions rarely had an opportunity of making merry at the expense of his extreme parsimony. He had strong passions and an ardent imagination, but his firmness of disposition preserved him from the ordinary errors of young men. Thus, though a gamester at heart, he never touched a card, for he considered his position did not allow him—as he said—"to risk the necessary in the hope of winning the superfluous," yet he would sit for nights together at the card table and follow with feverish anxiety the different turns of the game.

The story of the three cards had produced a powerful impression upon his imagination, and all night long he could think of nothing else. "If," he thought to himself the following evening, as he walked along the streets of St. Petersburg, "if the old Countess would but reveal her secret to me! if she would only tell me the names of the three winning cards. Why should I not try my fortune? I must get introduced to her and win her favour—become her lover. . . . But all that will take time, and she is eighty-seven years old: she might be dead in a week, in a couple of days even! . . . But the story itself: can it really be

true? . . . No! Economy, temperance and industry: those
are my three winning cards; by means of them I shall be
able to double my capital—increase it sevenfold, and
procure for myself ease and independence."

Musing in this manner, he walked on until he found
himself in one of the principal streets of St. Petersburg, in
front of a house of antiquated architecture. The street was
blocked with equipages; carriages one after the other drew
up in front of the brilliantly illuminated doorway. At one
moment there stepped out on to the pavement the well-
shaped little foot of some young beauty, at another the
heavy boot of a cavalry officer, and then the silk stockings
and shoes of a member of the diplomatic world. Furs and
cloaks passed in rapid succession before the gigantic porter
at the entrance.

Hermann stopped. "Who's house is this?" he asked of
the watchman at the corner.

"The Countess A——'s," replied the watchman.

Hermann started. The strange story of the three cards
again presented itself to his imagination. He began walking
up and down before the house, thinking of its owner and
her strange secret. Returning late to his modest lodging,
he could not go to sleep for a long time, and when at last
he did doze off, he could dream of nothing but cards,
green tables, piles of banknotes and heaps of ducats. He
played one card after the other, winning uninterruptedly,
and then he gathered up the gold and filled his pockets
with the notes. When he woke up late the next morning,
he sighed over the loss of his imaginary wealth, and then
sallying out into the town, he found himself once more in

front of the Countess's residence. Some unknown power seemed to have attracted him thither. He stopped and looked up at the windows. At one of these he saw a head with luxuriant black hair, which was bent down probably over some book or an embroidery frame. The head was raised. Hermann saw a fresh complexion and a pair of dark eyes. That moment decided his fate.

III

LIZAVETA IVANOVNA had scarcely taken off her hat and cloak, when the Countess sent for her and again ordered her to get the carriage ready. The vehicle drew up before the door, and they prepared to take their seats. Just at the moment when two footmen were assisting the old lady to enter the carriage, Lizaveta saw her Engineer standing close beside the wheel; he grasped her hand; alarm caused her to lose her presence of mind, and the young man disappeared—but not before he had left a letter between her fingers. She concealed it in her glove, and during the whole of the drive she neither saw nor heard anything. It was the custom of the Countess, when out for an airing in her carriage, to be constantly asking such questions as: "Who was that person that met us just now? What is the name of this bridge? What is written on that signboard?" On this occasion, however, Lizaveta returned such vague and absurd answers, that the Countess became angry with her.

"What is the matter with you, my dear?" she exclaimed. "Have you taken leave of your senses, or what is it? Do you not hear me or understand what I say? . . . Heaven be thanked, I am still in my right mind and speak plainly enough!"

Lizaveta Ivanovna did not hear her. On returning home she ran to her room, and drew the letter out of her glove: it was not sealed. Lizaveta read it. The letter contained a declaration of love; it was tender, respectful, and copied word for word from a German novel. But Lizaveta did not know anything of the German language, and she was quite delighted.

For all that, the letter caused her to feel exceedingly uneasy. For the first time in her life she was entering into secret and confidential relations with a young man. His boldness alarmed her. She reproached herself for her imprudent behaviour, and knew not what to do. Should she cease to sit at the window and, by assuming an appearance of indifference towards him, put a check upon the young officer's desire for further acquaintance with her? Should she send his letter back to him, or should she answer him in a cold and decided manner? There was nobody to whom she could turn in her perplexity, for she had neither female friend nor adviser. . . . At length she resolved to reply to him.

She sat down at her little writing-table, took pen and paper, and began to think. Several times she began her letter, and then tore it up: the way she had expressed herself seemed to her either too inviting or too cold and decisive. At last she succeeded in writing a few lines with which she felt satisfied.

"I am convinced," she wrote, "that your intentions are honourable, and that you do not wish to offend me by any imprudent behaviour, but our acquaintance must not begin in such a manner. I return you your letter, and I hope that I shall never have any cause to complain of this undeserved slight."

The next day, as soon as Hermann made his appearance, Lizaveta rose from her embroidery, went into the drawing-room, opened the ventilator and threw the letter into the street, trusting that the young officer would have the perception to pick it up.

Hermann hastened forward, picked it up and then repaired to a confectioner's shop. Breaking the seal of the envelope, he found inside it his own letter and Lizaveta's reply. He had expected this, and he returned home, his mind deeply occupied with his intrigue.

Three days afterwards, a bright-eyed young girl from a milliner's establishment brought Lizaveta a letter. Lizaveta opened it with great uneasiness, fearing that it was a demand for money, when suddenly she recognised Hermann's hand-writing.

"You have made a mistake, my dear," said she: "this letter is not for me."

"Oh, yes, it is for you," replied the girl, smiling very knowingly. "Have the goodness to read it."

Lizaveta glanced at the letter. Hermann requested an interview.

"It cannot be," she cried, alarmed at the audacious request, and the manner in which it was made. "This letter is certainly not for me."

And she tore it into fragments.

"If the letter was not for you, why have you torn it up?"

said the girl. "I should have given it back to the person who sent it."

"Be good enough, my dear," said Lizaveta, disconcerted by this remark, "not to bring me any more letters for the future, and tell the person who sent you that he ought to be ashamed. . . ."

But Hermann was not the man to be thus put off. Every day Lizaveta received from him a letter, sent now in this way, now in that. They were no longer translated from the German. Hermann wrote them under the inspiration of passion, and spoke in his own language, and they bore full testimony to the inflexibility of his desire and the disordered condition of his uncontrollable imagination. Lizaveta no longer thought of sending them back to him: she became intoxicated with them and began to reply to them, and little by little her answers became longer and more affectionate. At last she threw out of the window to him the following letter:

"This evening there is going to be a ball at the Embassy. The Countess will be there. We shall remain until two o'clock. You have now an opportunity of seeing me alone. As soon as the Countess is gone, the servants will very probably go out, and there will be nobody left but the Swiss, but he usually goes to sleep in his lodge. Come about half-past eleven. Walk straight upstairs. If you meet anybody in the ante-room, ask if the Countess is at home. You will be told 'No,' in which case there will be nothing left for you to do but to go away again. But it is most probable that you will meet nobody. The maidservants will all be together in one room. On leaving the ante-room, turn to the left, and walk straight on until you reach the Countess's bedroom. In the bedroom, behind a screen, you will find two doors: the one on the right leads to a cabinet, which the Countess never enters; the one on the left leads to a corridor, at the end of which is a little winding staircase; this leads to my room."

Hermann trembled like a tiger, as he waited for the appointed time to arrive. At ten o'clock in the evening he was already in front of the Countess's house. The weather was terrible; the wind blew with great violence; the sleety snow fell in large flakes; the lamps emitted a feeble light, the streets were deserted; from time to time a sledge, drawn by a sorry-looking hack, passed by, on the look-out for a belated passenger. Hermann was enveloped in a thick overcoat, and felt neither wind nor snow.

At last the Countess's carriage drew up. Hermann saw two footmen carry out in their arms the bent form of the old lady, wrapped in sable fur, and immediately behind her, clad in a warm mantle, and with her head ornamented with a wreath of fresh flowers, followed Lizaveta. The door was closed. The carriage rolled away heavily through the yielding snow. The porter shut the street-door; the windows became dark.

Hermann began walking up and down near the deserted house; at length he stopped under a lamp, and glanced at his watch: it was twenty minutes past eleven. He remained standing under the lamp, his eyes fixed upon the watch, impatiently waiting for the remaining minutes to pass. At half-past eleven precisely, Hermann ascended the steps of the house, and made his way into the brightly-illuminated vestibule. The porter was not there. Hermann hastily ascended the staircase, opened the door of the ante-room and saw a footman sitting asleep in an antique chair by the side of a lamp. With a light firm step Hermann passed by him. The drawing-room and dining-room were in darkness, but a feeble reflection penetrated thither from the lamp in the ante-room.

Hermann reached the Countess's bedroom. Before a shrine, which was full of old images, a golden lamp was burning. Faded stuffed chairs and divans with soft cushions stood in melancholy symmetry around the room, the walls of which were hung with China silk. On one side of the room hung two portraits painted in Paris by Madame Lebrun. One of these represented a stout, red-faced man of about forty years of age in a bright-green uniform and with a star upon his breast; the other—a beautiful young woman, with an aquiline nose, forehead curls and a rose in her powdered hair. In the corners stood porcelain shepherds and shepherdesses, dining-room clocks from the workshop of the celebrated Lefroy, bandboxes, roulettes, fans and the various playthings for the amusement of ladies that were in vogue at the end of the last century, when Montgolfier's balloons and Mesmer's magnetism were the rage. Hermann stepped behind the screen. At the back of it stood a little iron bedstead; on the right was the door which led to the cabinet; on the left—the other which led to the corridor. He opened the latter, and saw the little winding staircase which led to the room of the poor companion. . . . But he retraced his steps and entered the dark cabinet.

The time passed slowly. All was still. The clock in the drawing-room struck twelve; the strokes echoed through the room one after the other, and everything was quiet again. Hermann stood leaning against the cold stove. He was calm; his heart beat regularly, like that of a man resolved upon a dangerous but inevitable undertaking. One o'clock in the morning struck; then two; and he heard the distant noise of carriage-wheels. An involuntary agitation took possession of him. The carriage drew near and stopped. He heard the sound of the carriage-steps being let down. All was bustle within the house. The servants were running hither and thither, there was a confusion of voices, and the rooms were lit up. Three antiquated chambermaids entered the bedroom, and they were shortly afterwards followed by the Countess who, more dead than alive, sank into a Voltaire armchair. Hermann peeped through a chink. Lizaveta Ivanovna passed closed by him, and he heard her hurried steps as she hastened up the little spiral staircase. For a moment his heart was assailed by something like a pricking of conscience, but the emotion was only transitory, and his heart became petrified as before.

The Countess began to undress before her looking-glass. Her rose-bedecked cap was taken off, and then her powdered wig was removed from off her white and closely-cut hair. Hairpins fell in showers around her. Her yellow satin dress, brocaded with silver, fell down at her swollen feet.

Hermann was a witness of the repugnant mysteries of her toilette; at last the Countess was in her night-cap and dressing-gown, and in this costume, more suitable to her age, she appeared less hideous and deformed.

Like all old people in general, the Countess suffered from sleeplessness. Having undressed, she seated herself at the window in a Voltaire armchair and dismissed her maids. The candles were taken away, and once more the room was left with only one lamp burning in it. The Countess sat there looking quite yellow, mumbling with her flaccid lips and swaying to and fro. Her dull eyes expressed complete vacancy of mind, and, looking at her, one would have thought that the rocking of her body was not a voluntary action of her own, but was produced by the action of some concealed galvanic mechanism.

Suddenly the death-like face assumed an inexplicable expression. The lips ceased to tremble, the eyes became animated: before the Countess stood an unknown man.

"Do not be alarmed, for Heaven's sake, do not be alarmed!" said he in a low but distinct voice. "I have no intention of doing you any harm, I have only come to ask a favour of you."

The old woman looked at him in silence, as if she had not heard what he had said. Hermann thought that she was deaf, and, bending down towards her ear, he repeated what he had said. The aged Countess remained silent as before.

"You can insure the happiness of my life," continued Hermann, "and it will cost you nothing. I know that you can name three cards in order——"

Hermann stopped. The Countess appeared now to understand what he wanted; she seemed as if seeking for words to reply.

"It was a joke," she replied at last: "I assure you it was only a joke."

"There is no joking about the matter," replied Hermann angrily. "Remember Chaplitzky, whom you helped to win."

The Countess became visibly uneasy. Her features expressed strong emotion, but they quickly resumed their former immobility.

"Can you not name me these three winning cards?" continued Hermann.

The Countess remained silent; Hermann continued:

"For whom are you preserving your secret? For your grandsons? They are rich enough without it; they do not know the worth of money. Your cards would be of no use to a spendthrift. He who cannot preserve his paternal inheritance, will die in want, even though he had a demon at his service. I am not a man of that sort; I know the value of money. Your three cards will not be thrown away upon me. Come!" . . .

He paused and tremblingly awaited her reply. The Countess remained silent; Hermann fell upon his knees.

"If your heart has ever known the feeling of love," said he, "if you remember its rapture, if you have ever smiled at the cry of your new-born child, if any human feeling has ever entered into your breast, I entreat you by the feelings of a wife, a lover, a mother, by all that is most sacred in life, not to reject my prayer. Reveal to me your secret. Of what use is it to you? . . . May be it is connected with some terrible sin, with the loss of eternal salvation, with some bargain with the devil. . . . Reflect,—you are old; you have not long to live—I am ready to take your sins upon my soul. Only reveal to me your secret. Remember that the happiness of a man is in your hands, that not only I, but my children, and grandchildren will bless your memory and reverence you as a saint. . . ."

The old Countess answered not a word.

Hermann rose to his feet.

"You old hag!" he exclaimed, grinding his teeth, "then I will make you answer!"

With these words he drew a pistol from his pocket.

At the sight of the pistol, the Countess for the second time exhibited strong emotion. She shook her head and raised her hands as if to protect herself from the shot. . . . then she fell backwards and remained motionless.

"Come, an end to this childish nonsense!" said Hermann, taking hold of her hand. "I ask you for the last time: will you tell me the names of your three cards, or will you not?"

The Countess made no reply. Hermann perceived that she was dead.

IV

LIZAVETA IVANOVNA was sitting in her room, still in her ball dress, lost in deep thought. On returning home, she had hastily dismissed the chambermaid who very reluctantly came forward to assist her, saying that she would undress herself, and with a trembling heart had gone up to her own room, expecting to find Hermann there, but yet hoping not to find him. At the first glance she convinced herself that he was not there, and she thanked her fate for having prevented him keeping the appointment. She sat down without undressing, and began to recall to mind all the circumstances which in so short a time had carried her so far. It was not three weeks since the time when she first saw the young officer from the window—and yet she was already in correspondence with him, and he had succeeded in inducing her to grant him a nocturnal interview! She knew his name only through his having written it at the bottom of some of his letters; she had never spoken to him, had never heard his voice, and had never heard him spoken of until that evening. But, strange to say, that very evening at the ball, Tomsky, being piqued with the young Princess Pauline N——, who, contrary to her usual custom, did not flirt with him, wished to revenge himself by assuming an air of indifference: he therefore engaged Lizaveta Ivanovna and danced an endless mazurka with her. During the whole of the time he kept teasing her about her partiality for Engineer officers; he assured her that he knew far more than she imagined, and some of his jests were so happily aimed, that Lizaveta thought several times that her secret was known to him.

"From whom have you learnt all this?" she asked, smiling.

"From a friend of a person very well known to you," replied Tomsky, "from a very distinguished man."

"And who is this distinguished man?"

"His name is Hermann."

Lizaveta made no reply; but her hands and feet lost all sense of feeling.

"This Hermann," continued Tomsky, "is a man of romantic personality. He has the profile of a Napoleon, and the soul of a Mephistopheles. I believe that he has at least three crimes upon his conscience. . . . How pale you have become!"

"I have a headache . . . But what did this Hermann— or whatever his name is—tell you?"

"Hermann is very much dissatisfied with his friend: he says that in his place he would act very differently . . . I even think that Hermann himself has designs upon you; at least, he listens very attentively to all that his friend has to say about you."

"And where has he seen me?"

"In church, perhaps; or on the parade—God alone knows where. It may have been in your room, while you were asleep, for there is nothing that he——"

Three ladies approaching him with the question: *"oubli ou regret?"* interrupted the conversation, which had become so tantalisingly interesting to Lizaveta.

The lady chosen by Tomsky was the Princess Pauline herself. She succeeded in effecting a reconciliation with him during the numerous turns of the dance, after which he conducted her to her chair. On returning to his place, Tomsky thought no more either of Hermann or Lizaveta. She longed to renew the interrupted conversation, but the mazurka came to an end, and shortly afterwards the old Countess took her departure.

Tomsky's words were nothing more than the customary small talk of the dance, but they sank deep into the soul of the young dreamer. The portrait, sketched by Tomsky, coincided with the picture she had formed within her own mind, and thanks to the latest romances, the ordinary countenance of her admirer became invested with attributes capable of alarming her and fascinating her imagination at the same time. She was now sitting with her bare arms crossed and with her head, still adorned with flowers, sunk upon her uncovered bosom. Suddenly the door opened and Hermann entered. She shuddered.

"Where were you?" she asked in a terrified whisper.

"In the old Countess's bedroom," replied Hermann: "I have just left her. The Countess is dead."

"My God! What do you say?"

"And I am afraid," added Hermann, "that I am the cause of her death."

Lizaveta looked at him, and Tomsky's words found an echo in her soul: "This man has at least three crimes upon his conscience!" Hermann sat down by the window near her, and related all that had happened.

Lizaveta listened to him in terror. So all those passionate letters, those ardent desires, this bold obstinate pursuit—all this was not love! Money—that was what his soul yearned for! She could not satisfy his desire and make him happy! The poor girl had been nothing but the blind tool of a robber, of the murderer of her aged benefactress! . . . She wept bitter tears of agonised repentance. Hermann gazed at her in silence: his heart, too, was a prey to violent emotion, but neither the tears of the poor girl, nor the wonderful charm of her beauty, enhanced by her grief, could produce any impression upon his hardened soul. He felt no pricking of conscience at the thought of the dead old woman. One thing only grieved him: the irreparable loss of the secret from which he had expected to obtain great wealth.

"You are a monster!" said Lizaveta at last.

"I did not wish for her death," replied Hermann: "my pistol was not loaded."

Both remained silent.

The day began to dawn. Lizaveta extinguished her candle: a pale light illumined her room. She wiped her tear-stained eyes and raised them towards Hermann: he was sitting near the window, with his arms crossed and with a fierce frown upon his forehead. In this attitude he bore a striking resemblance to the portrait of Napoleon. This resemblance struck Lizaveta even.

"How shall I get you out of the house?" said she at last. "I thought of conducting you down the secret staircase, but in that case it would be necessary to go through the Countess's bedroom, and I am afraid."

"Tell me how to find this secret staircase—I will go alone."

Lizaveta arose, took from her drawer a key, handed it to Hermann and gave him the necessary instructions. Hermann pressed her cold, limp hand, kissed her bowed head, and left the room.

He descended the winding staircase, and once more entered the Countess's bedroom. The dead old lady sat as if petrified; her face expressed profound tranquillity. Hermann stopped before her, and gazed long and earnestly at her, as if he wished to convince himself of the terrible reality; at last he entered the cabinet, felt behind the tapestry for the door, and then began to descend the dark staircase, filled with strange emotions. "Down this very staircase," thought he, "perhaps coming from the very same room, and at this very same hour sixty years ago, there may have glided, in an embroidered coat, with his hair dressed *à l'oiseau royal* and pressing to his heart his three-cornered hat, some young gallant, who has long been mouldering in the grave, but the heart of his aged mistress has only to-day ceased to beat. . . ."

At the bottom of the staircase Hermann found a door, which he opened with a key, and then traversed a corridor which conducted him into the street.

V

THREE DAYS after the fatal night, at nine o'clock in the morning, Hermann repaired to the Convent of ——, where the last honours were to be paid to the mortal remains of the old Countess. Although feeling no remorse, he could not altogether stifle the voice of conscience, which said to him: "You are the murderer of the old woman!" In spite of his entertaining very little religious belief, he was exceedingly superstitious; and believing that the dead Countess might exercise an evil influence on his life, he resolved to be present at her obsequies in order to implore her pardon.

The church was full. It was with difficulty that Hermann made his way through the crowd of people. The coffin was placed upon a rich catafalque beneath a velvet baldachin. The deceased Countess lay within it, with her hands crossed upon her breast, with a lace cap upon her head and dressed in a white satin robe. Around the catafalque stood the members of her household: the servants in black

caftans, with armorial ribbons upon their shoulders, and
candles in their hands; the relatives—children, grandchildren, and great-grandchildren—in deep mourning.

Nobody wept; tears would have been *une affectation.*
The Countess was so old, that her death could have surprised nobody, and her relatives had long looked upon her
as being out of the world. A famous preacher pronounced
the funeral sermon. In simple and touching words he
described the peaceful passing away of the righteous, who
had passed long years in calm preparation for a Christian
end. "The angel of death found her," said the orator,
"engaged in pious meditation and waiting for the midnight
bridegroom."

The service concluded amidst profound silence. The relatives went forward first to take farewell of the corpse.
Then followed the numerous guests, who had come to
render the last homage to her who for so many years had
been a participator in their frivolous amusements. After
these followed the members of the Countess's household.
The last of these was an old woman of the same age as
the deceased. Two young women led her forward by the
hand. She had not strength enough to bow down to the
ground—she merely shed a few tears and kissed the cold
hand of her mistress.

Hermann now resolved to approach the coffin. He knelt
down upon the cold stones and remained in that position
for some minutes; at last he arose, as pale as the deceased
Countess herself; he ascended the steps of the catafalque
and bent over the corpse. . . . At that moment it seemed to
him that the dead woman darted a mocking look at him

and winked with one eye. Hermann started back, took a false step and fell to the ground. Several persons hurried forward and raised him up. At the same moment Lizaveta Ivanovna was borne fainting into the porch of the church. This episode disturbed for some minutes the solemnity of the gloomy ceremony. Among the congregation arose a deep murmur, and a tall thin chamberlain, a near relative of the deceased, whispered in the ear of an Englishman who was standing near him, that the young officer was a natural son of the Countess, to which the Englishman coldly replied: "Oh!"

During the whole of that day, Hermann was strangely excited. Repairing to an out-of-the-way restaurant to dine, he drank a great deal of wine, contrary to his usual custom, in the hope of deadening his inward agitation. But the wine only served to excite his imagination still more. On returning home, he threw himself upon his bed without undressing, and fell into a deep sleep.

When he woke up it was already night, and the moon was shining into the room. He looked at his watch: it was a quarter to three. Sleep had left him; he sat down upon his bed and thought of the funeral of the old Countess.

At that moment somebody in the street looked in at his window, and immediately passed on again. Hermann paid no attention to this incident. A few moments afterwards he heard the door of his ante-room open. Hermann thought that it was his orderly, drunk as usual, returning from some nocturnal expedition, but presently he heard footsteps that were unknown to him: somebody was walking softly over the floor in slippers. The door opened, and a woman dressed in white, entered the room. Hermann mistook her for his old nurse, and wondered what could bring her there at that hour of the night. But the white woman glided rapidly across the room and stood before him—and Hermann recognised the Countess!

"I have come to you against my wish," she said in a firm voice: "but I have been ordered to grant your request. Three, seven, ace, will win for you if played in succession, but only on these conditions: that you do not play more than one card in twenty-four hours, and that you never play again during the rest of your life. I forgive you my death, on condition that you marry my companion, Lizaveta Ivanovna."

With these words she turned round very quietly, walked with a shuffling gait towards the door and disappeared. Hermann heard the street-door open and shut, and again he saw some one look in at him through the window.

For a long time Hermann could not recover himself. He then rose up and entered the next room. His orderly was lying asleep upon the floor, and he had much difficulty in waking him. The orderly was drunk as usual, and no information could be obtained from him. The street-door was locked. Hermann returned to his room, lit his candle, and wrote down all the details of his vision.

VI

TWO FIXED ideas can no more exist together in the moral world than two bodies can occupy one and the same place in the physical world. "Three, seven, ace," soon drove out of Hermann's mind the thought of the dead Countess.

"Three, seven, ace," were perpetually running through his head and continually being repeated by his lips. If he saw a young girl, he would say: "How slender she is! quite like the three of hearts." If anybody asked: "What is the time?" he would reply: "Five minutes to seven." Every stout man that he saw reminded him of the ace. "Three, seven, ace" haunted him in his sleep, and assumed all possible shapes. The threes bloomed before him in the forms of magnificent flowers, the sevens were represented by Gothic portals, and the aces became transformed into gigantic spiders. One thought alone occupied his whole mind—to make a profitable use of the secret which he had purchased so dearly. He thought of applying for a furlough so as to travel abroad. He wanted to go to Paris and tempt fortune in some of the public gambling-houses that abounded there. Chance spared him all this trouble.

There was in Moscow a society of rich gamesters, presided over by the celebrated Chekalinsky, who had passed all his life at the card-table and had amassed millions, accepting bills of exchange for his winnings and paying his losses in ready money. His long experience secured for him the confidence of his companions, and his open house, his famous cook, and his agreeable and fascinating manners gained for him the respect of the public. He came to St. Petersburg. The young men of the capital flocked to his rooms, forgetting balls for cards, and preferring the emotions of faro to the seductions of flirting. Narumov conducted Hermann to Chekalinsky's residence.

They passed through a suite of magnificent rooms, filled with attentive domestics. The place was crowded. Generals and Privy Counsellors were playing at whist; young men were lolling carelessly upon the velvet-covered sofas, eating ices and smoking pipes. In the drawing-room, at the head of a long table, around which were assembled about a score of players, sat the master of the house keeping the bank. He was a man of about sixty years of age, of a very dignified appearance; his head was covered with silvery-white hair; his full, florid countenance expressed good-nature, and his eyes twinkled with a perpetual smile. Narumov introduced Hermann to him. Chekalinsky shook him by the hand in a friendly manner, requested him not to stand on ceremony, and then went on dealing.

The game occupied some time. On the table lay more than thirty cards. Chekalinsky paused after each throw, in order to give the players time to arrange their cards and note down their losses, listened politely to their requests, and more politely still, put straight the corners of cards that some player's hand had chanced to bend. At last the game was finished. Chekalinsky shuffled the cards and prepared to deal again.

"Will you allow me to take a card?" said Hermann, stretching out his hand from behind a stout gentleman who was punting.

Chekalinsky smiled and bowed silently, as a sign of acquiescence. Narumov laughingly congratulated Hermann on his abjuration of that abstention from cards which he had practised for so long a period, and wished him a lucky beginning.

"Stake!" said Hermann, writing some figures with chalk on the back of his card.

"How much?" asked the banker, contracting the muscles of his eyes; "excuse me, I cannot see quite clearly."

"Forty-seven thousand rubles," replied Hermann.

At these words every head in the room turned suddenly round, and all eyes were fixed upon Hermann.

"He has taken leave of his senses!" thought Narumov.

"Allow me to inform you," said Chekalinsky, with his eternal smile, "that you are playing very high; nobody here has ever staked more than two hundred and seventy-five rubles at once."

"Very well," replied Hermann; "but do you accept my card or not?"

Chekalinsky bowed in token of consent.

"I only wish to observe," said he, "that although I have the greatest confidence in my friends, I can only play against ready money. For my own part, I am quite convinced that your word is sufficient, but for the sake of the order of the game, and to facilitate the reckoning up, I must ask you to put the money on your card."

Hermann drew from his pocket a bank-note and handed it to Chekalinsky, who, after examining it in a cursory manner, placed it on Hermann's card.

He began to deal. On the right a nine turned up, and on the left a three.

"I have won!" said Hermann, showing his card.

A murmur of astonishment arose among the players. Chekalinsky frowned, but the smile quickly returned to his face.

"Do you wish me to settle with you?" he said to Hermann.

"If you please," replied the latter.

Chekalinsky drew from his pocket a number of bank-notes and paid at once. Hermann took up his money and left the table. Narumov could not recover from his astonishment. Hermann drank a glass of lemonade and returned home.

The next evening, he again repaired to Chekalinsky's. The host was dealing. Herman walked up to the table; the punters immediately made room for him. Chekalinsky greeted him with a gracious bow.

Hermann waited for the next deal, took a card and placed upon it his forty-seven thousand rubles, together with his winnings of the previous evening.

Chekalinsky began to deal. A knave turned up on the right, a seven on the left.

Hermann showed his seven.

There was a general exclamation. Chekalinsky was evidently ill at ease, but he counted out the ninety-four thousand rubles and handed them over to Hermann, who pocketed them in the coolest manner possible and immediately left the house.

The next evening Hermann appeared again at the table. Every one was expecting him. The generals and Privy Counsellors left their whist in order to watch such extraordinary play. The young officers quitted their sofas, and even the servants crowded into the room. All pressed round Hermann. The other players left off punting, impatient to see how it would end. Hermann stood at the table and prepared to play alone against the pale, but still smiling Chekalinsky. Each opened a pack of cards. Chekalinsky shuffled. Hermann took a card and covered it with a pile of bank-notes. It was like a duel. Deep silence reigned around.

Chekalinsky began to deal; his hands trembled. On the right a queen turned up, and on the left an ace.

"Ace has won!" cried Hermann, showing his card.

"Your queen has lost," said Chekalinsky, politely.

Hermann started; instead of an ace, there lay before him the queen of spades! He could not believe his eyes, nor could he undertand how he had made such a mistake.

At that moment it seemed to him that the queen of spades smiled ironically and winked her eye at him. He was struck by her remarkable resemblance. . . .

"The old Countess!" he exclaimed, seized with terror.

Chekalinsky gathered up his winnings. For some time, Hermann remained perfectly motionless. When at last he left the table, there was a general commotion in the room.

"Splendidly punted!" said the players. Chekalinsky shuffled the cards afresh, and the game went on as usual.

.   .   .   .

Hermann went out of his mind, and is now confined in room Number 17 of the Obukhov Hospital. He never answers any questions, but he constantly mutters with unusual rapidity: "Three, seven, ace!" "Three, seven, queen!"

Lizaveta Ivanovna has married a very amiable young man, a son of the former steward of the old Countess. He is in the service of the State somewhere, and is in receipt of a good income. Lizaveta is also supporting a poor relative.

Tomsky has been promoted to the rank of captain, and has become the husband of the Princess Pauline.

THE CLOAK

•♦•

By Nikolay V. Gogol

IN THE department of ——, but it is better not to mention the department. The touchiest things in the world are departments, regiments, courts of justice, in a word, all branches of public service. Each individual nowadays thinks all society insulted in his person. Quite recently, a complaint was received from a district chief of police in which he plainly demonstrated that all the imperial institutions were going to the dogs, and that the Czar's sacred name was being taken in vain; and in proof he appended to the complaint a romance, in which the district chief of police is made to appear about once in every ten pages, and sometimes in a downright drunken condition. Therefore, in order to avoid all unpleasantness, it will be better to designate the department in question, as a certain department.

So, in a certain department there was a certain official—not a very notable one, it must be allowed—short of stature, somewhat pock-marked, red-haired, and mole-eyed, with a bald forehead, wrinkled cheeks, and a complexion of the kind known as sanguine. The St. Petersburg climate was responsible for this. As for his official rank—with us Russians the rank comes first—he was what is called a perpetual titular councillor, over which, as is well known, some writers make merry and crack their jokes, obeying the praiseworthy custom of attacking those who cannot bite back.

His family name was Bashmachkin. This name is evidently derived from bashmak (shoe); but, when, at what time, and in what manner, is not known. His father and grandfather, and all the Bashmachkins, always wore boots, which were resoled two or three times a year. His name was Akaky Akakiyevich. It may strike the reader as rather singular and far-fetched; but he may rest assured that it was by no means far-fetched, and that the circumstances were such that it would have been impossible to give him any other.

This was how it came about.

Akaky Akakiyevich was born, if my memory fails me not, in the evening on the 23rd of March. His mother, the wife of a Government official, and a very fine woman, made all due arrangements for having the child baptised. She was lying on the bed opposite the door; on her right stood the godfather, Ivan Ivanovich Eroshkin, a most estimable man, who served as the head clerk of the senate; and the godmother, Arina Semyonovna Bielobrinshkova, the wife of an officer of the quarter, and a woman of rare virtues. They offered the mother her choice of three names, Mokiya, Sossiya, or that the child should be called after the martyr Khozdazat. "No," said the good woman, "all those names are poor." In order to please her, they opened the calendar at another place; three more names appeared, Triphily, Dula, and Varakhasy. "This is awful," said the old woman. "What names! I truly never heard the like. I might have put up with Varadat or Varukh, but not Triphily and Varakhasy!" They turned to another page and found Pavsikakhy and Vakhtisy. "Now I see," said the old woman, "that it is plainly fate. And since such is the case, it will be better to name him after his father. His father's name was Akaky, so let his son's name be Akaky too." In this manner he became Akaky Akakiyevich. They christened the child, whereat he wept, and made a grimace, as though he foresaw that he was to be a titular councillor.

In this manner did it all come about. We have mentioned it in order that the reader might see for himself that it was a case of necessity, and that it was utterly impossible to give him any other name.

When and how he entered the department, and who appointed him, no one could remember. However much the directors and chiefs of all kinds were changed, he was always to be seen in the same place, the same attitude, the same occupation—always the letter-copying clerk—so that it was afterwards affirmed that he had been born in uniform with a bald head. No respect was shown him in the department. The porter not only did not rise from his seat when he passed, but never even glanced at him, any more than if a fly had flown through the reception-room. His superiors treated him in coolly despotic fashion. Some insignificant assistant to the head clerk would thrust a paper under his nose without so much as saying, "Copy," or, "Here's an interesting little case," or anything else agreeable, as is customary amongst well-bred officials. And he took it, looking only at the paper, and not observing who handed it to him, or whether he had the right to do so; simply took it, and set about copying it.

The young officials laughed at and made fun of him, so far as their official wit permitted; told in his presence various stories concocted about him, and about his landlady, an old woman of seventy; declared that she beat him; asked when the wedding was to be; and strewed bits of paper over his head, calling them snow. But Akaky Akakiyevich answered not a word, any more than if there had been no one there besides himself. It even had no effect upon his work. Amid all these annoyances he never made a single mistake in a letter. But if the joking became wholly unbearable, as when they jogged his head, and prevented his attending to his work, he would exclaim:

"Leave me alone! Why do you insult me?"

And there was something strange in the words and the voice in which they were uttered. There was in it something which moved to pity; so much so that one young man, a newcomer, who, taking pattern by the others, had permitted himself to make sport of Akaky, suddenly stopped short, as though all about him had undergone a transformation, and presented itself in a different aspect. Some unseen force repelled him from the comrades whose acquaintance he had made, on the supposition that they were decent, well-bred men. Long afterwards, in his gayest moments, there recurred to his mind the little official with the bald forehead, with his heart-rending words, "Leave me alone! Why do you insult me?" In these moving words, other words resounded—"I am thy brother." And the young man covered his face with his hand; and many a time afterwards, in the course of his life, shuddered at seeing how much inhumanity there is in man, how much savage coarseness is concealed beneath refined, cultured, worldly refinement, and even, O God! in that man whom the world acknowledges as honourable and upright.

It would be difficult to find another man who lived so entirely for his duties. It is not enough to say that Akaky laboured with zeal; no, he laboured with love. In his copying, he found a varied and agreeable employment. Enjoyment was written on his face; some letters were even favourites with him; and when he encountered these, he smiled, winked, and worked with his lips, till it seemed as though each letter might be read in his face, as his pen traced it. If his pay had been in proportion to his zeal, he would, perhaps, to his great surprise, have been made even a councillor of state. But he worked, as his companions, the wits, put it, like a horse in a mill.

However, it would be untrue to say that no attention was paid to him. One director being a kindly man, and desirous of rewarding him for his long service, ordered him to be given something more important than mere copying. So he was ordered to make a report of an already concluded affair, to another department; the duty consisting simply in changing the heading and altering a few words from the first to the third person. This caused him so much toil, that he broke into a perspiration, rubbed his forehead, and finally said, "No, give me rather something to copy." After that they let him copy on forever.

Outside this copying, it appeared that nothing existed for him. He gave no thought to his clothes. His uniform was

not green, but a sort of rusty-meal colour. The collar was
low, so that his neck, in spite of the fact that it was not
long, seemed inordinately so as it emerged from it, like
the necks of the plaster cats which pedlars carry about on
their heads. And something was always sticking to his
uniform, either a bit of hay or some trifle. Moreover, he
had a peculiar knack, as he walked along the street, of
arriving beneath a window just as all sorts of rubbish was
being flung out of it; hence he always bore about on his
hat scraps of melon rinds, and other such articles. Never
once in his life did he give heed to what was going on
every day in the street; while it is well known that his
young brother officials trained the range of their glances till
they could see when any one's trouser-straps came undone
upon the opposite sidewalk, which always brought a mali-
cious smile to their faces. But Akaky Akakiyevich saw in
all things the clean, even strokes of his written lines; and
only when a horse thrust his nose, from some unknown
quarter, over his shoulder, and sent a whole gust of wind
down his neck from his nostrils, did he observe that he was
not in the middle of a line, but in the middle of the street.

On reaching home, he sat down at once at the table,
sipped his cabbage-soup up quickly, and swallowed a bit of
beef with onions, never noticing their taste, and gulping
down everything with flies and anything else which the
Lord happened to send at the moment. When he saw that
his stomach was beginning to swell, he rose from the table
and copied papers which he had brought home. If there
happened to be none, he took copies for himself, for his
own gratification, especially if the document was note-

worthy, not on account of its style, but of its being addressed to some distinguished person.

Even at the hour when the grey St. Petersburg sky had quite disappeared, and all the official world had eaten or dined, each as he could, in accordance with the salary he received and his own fancy; when all were resting from the department jar of pens, running to and fro, for their own and other people's indispensable occupations, and from all the work that an uneasy man makes willingly for himself, rather than what is necessary; when officials hasten to dedicate to pleasure the time which is left to them, one bolder than the rest going to the theatre; another, into the street looking under the bonnets; another wasting his evening in compliments to some pretty girl, the star of a small official circle; another—and this is the common case of all—visiting his comrades on the third or fourth floor, in two small rooms with an ante-room or kitchen, and some pretensions to fashion, such as a lamp or some other trifle which has cost many a sacrifice of dinner or pleasure trip; in a word, at the hour when all officials disperse among the contracted quarters of their friends, to play whist, as they sip their tea from glasses with a kopek's worth of sugar, smoke long pipes, relate at time some bits of gossip which a Russian man can never, under any circumstances, refrain from, and when there is nothing else to talk of, repeat eternal anecdotes about the commandant to whom they had sent word that the tails of the horses on the Falconet Monument had been cut off; when all strive to divert themselves, Akaky Akakiyevich indulged in no kind of diversion. No one could even say that he had seen him at any kind of evening party. Having written to his heart's content, he lay down to sleep, smiling at the thought of the coming day—of what God might send him to copy on the morrow.

Thus flowed on the peaceful life of the man, who, with a salary of four hundred rubles, understood how to be content with his lot; and thus it would have continued to flow on, perhaps, to extreme old age, were it not that there are various ills strewn along the path of life for titular councillors as well as for private, actual, court, and every other species of councillor, even to those who never give any advice or take any themselves.

There exists in St. Petersburg a powerful foe of all who receive a salary of four hundred rubles a year, or thereabouts. This foe is no other than the Northern cold, although it is said to be very healthy. At nine o'clock in the morning, at the very hour when the streets are filled with men bound for the various official departments, it begins to bestow such powerful and piercing nips on all noses impartially, that the poor officials really do not know what to do with them. At an hour when the foreheads of even those who occupy exalted positions ache with the cold, and tears start to their eyes, the poor titular councillors are sometimes quite unprotected. Their only salvation lies in traversing as quickly as possible, in their thin little cloaks, five or six streets, and then warming their feet in the porter's room, and so thawing all their talents and qualifications for official service, which had become frozen on the way.

Akaky Akakiyevich had felt for some time that his back

and shoulders were paining with peculiar poignancy, in spite of the fact that he tried to traverse the distance with all possible speed. He began finally to wonder whether the fault did not lie in his cloak. He examined it thoroughly at home, and discovered that in two places, namely, on the back and shoulders, it had become thin as gauze. The cloth was worn to such a degree that he could see through it, and the lining had fallen into pieces. You must know that Akaky Akakiyevich's cloak served as an object of ridicule to the officials. They even refused it the noble name of cloak, and called it a cape. In fact, it was of singular make, its collar diminishing year by year to serve to patch its other parts. The patching did not exhibit great skill on the part of the tailor, and was, in fact, baggy and ugly. Seeing how the matter stood, Akaky Akakiyevich decided that it would be necessary to take the cloak to Petrovich, the tailor, who lived somewhere on the fourth floor up a dark staircase, and who, in spite of his having but one eye and pock-marks all over his face, busied himself with considerable success in repairing the trousers and coats of officials and others; that is to say, when he was sober and not nursing some other scheme in his head.

It is not necessary to say much about this tailor, but as it is the custom to have the character of each personage in a novel clearly defined there is no help for it, so here is Petrovich the tailor. At first he was called only Grigory, and was some gentleman's serf. He commenced calling himself Petrovich from the time when he received his free papers, and further began to drink heavily on all holidays, at first on the great ones, and then on all church festivals without discrimination, wherever a cross stood in the calendar. On this point he was faithful to ancestral custom; and when quarrelling with his wife, he called her a low female and a German. As we have mentioned his wife, it will be necessary to say a word or two about her. Unfortunately, little is known of her beyond the fact that Petrovich had a wife, who wore a cap and a dress, but could not lay claim to beauty, at least, no one but the soldiers of the guard even looked under her cap when they met her.

Ascending the staircase which led to Petrovich's room— which staircase was all soaked with dish-water and reeked with the smell of spirits which affects the eyes, and is an inevitable adjunct to all dark stairways in St. Petersburg houses—ascending the stairs, Akaky Akakiyevich pondered how much Petrovich would ask, and mentally resolved not to give more than two rubles. The door was open, for the mistress, in cooking some fish, had raised such a smoke in the kitchen that not even the beetles were visible. Akaky Akakiyevich passed through the kitchen unperceived, even by the housewife, and at length reached a room where he beheld Petrovich seated on a large unpainted table, with his legs tucked under him like a Turkish pasha. His feet were bare, after the fashion of tailors as they sit at work; and the first thing which caught the eye was his thumb, with a deformed nail thick and strong as a turtle's shell. About Petrovich's neck hung a skein of silk and thread, and upon his knees lay some old garment. He had been trying unsuccessfully for three minutes to thread his needle, and was enraged at the darkness and even at the thread, growling in a low voice, "It won't go through, the barbarian! You pricked me, you rascal!"

Akaky Akakiyevich was vexed at arriving at the precise moment when Petrovich was angry. He liked to order something of Petrovich when he was a little downhearted, or, as his wife expressed it, "when he had settled himself with brandy, the one-eyed devil!" Under such circumstances Petrovich generally came down in his price very readily, and even bowed and returned thanks. Afterwards, to be sure, his wife would come, complaining that her husband had been drunk, and so had fixed the price too low; but, if only a ten-kopek piece were added then the matter would be settled. But now it appeared that Petrovich was in a sober condition, and therefore rough, taciturn, and inclined to demand, Satan only knows what price. Akaky Akakiyevich felt this, and would gladly have beat a retreat, but he was in for it. Petrovich screwed up his one eye very intently at him, and Akaky Akakiyevich involuntarily said, "How do you do, Petrovich?"

"I wish you a good morning, sir," said Petrovich squinting at Akaky Akakiyevich's hands, to see what sort of booty he had brought.

"Ah! I—to you, Petrovich, this—" It must be known that Akaky Akakiyevich expressed himself chiefly by prepositions, adverbs, and scraps of phrases which had no meaning whatever. If the matter was a very difficult one, he had a habit of never completing his sentences, so that frequently, having begun a phrase with the words, "This, in fact, is quite—" he forgot to go on, thinking he had already finished it.

"What is it?" asked Petrovich, and with his one eye scanned Akaky Akakiyevich's whole uniform from the collar down to the cuffs, the back, the tails and the button-holes, all of which were well known to him, since they were his own handiwork. Such is the habit of tailors; it is the first thing they do on meeting one.

"But I, here, this—Petrovich—a cloak, cloth—here you see, everywhere, in different places, it is quite strong—it is a little dusty and looks old, but it is new, only here in one place it is a little—on the back, and here on one of the shoulders, it is a little worn, yes, here on this shoulder it is a little—do you see? That is all. And a little work—"

Petrovich took the cloak, spread it out, to begin with, on the table, looked at it hard, shook his head, reached out his hand to the window-sill for his snuff-box, adorned with the portrait of some general, though what general is un-known, for the place where the face should have been had been rubbed through by the finger and a square bit of paper had been pasted over it. Having taken a pinch of snuff, Petrovich held up the cloak, and inspected it against the light, and again shook his head. Then he turned it, lining upwards, and shook his head once more. After which he again lifted the general-adorned lid with its bit of pasted paper, and having stuffed his nose with snuff, closed and put away the snuff-box, and said finally, "No, it is impossible to mend it. It is a wretched garment!"

Akaky Akakiyevich's heart sank at these words.

"Why is it impossible, Petrovich?" he said, almost in the pleading voice of a child. "All that ails it is, that it is worn on the shoulders. You must have some pieces——"

"Yes, patches could be found, patches are easily found," said Petrovich, "but there's nothing to sew them to. The thing is completely rotten. If you put a needle to it—see, it will give way."

"Let it give way, and you can put on another patch at once."

"But there is nothing to put the patches on to. There's no use in strengthening it. It is too far gone. It's lucky that it's cloth, for, if the wind were to blow, it would fly away."

"Well, strengthen it again. How this, in fact——"

"No," said Petrovich decisively, "there is nothing to be done with it. It's a thoroughly bad job. You'd better, when the cold winter weather comes on, make yourself some gaiters out of it, because stockings are not warm. The Germans invented them in order to make more money." Petrovich loved on all occasions to have a fling at the Germans. "But it is plain you must have a new cloak."

At the word "new" all grew dark before Akaky Akakiyevich's eyes, and everything in the room began to whirl round. The only thing he saw clearly was the general with the paper face on the lid of Petrovich's snuff-box. "A new one?" said he, as if still in a dream. "Why, I have no money for that."

"Yes, a new one," said Petrovich, with barbarous composure.

"Well, if it came to a new one, how—it——"

"You mean how much would it cost?"

"Yes."

"Well, you would have to lay out a hundred and fifty or more," said Petrovich, and pursed up his lips significantly. He liked to produce powerful effects, liked to stun utterly and suddenly, and then to glance sideways to see what face the stunned person would put on the matter.

"A hundred and fifty rubles for a cloak!" shrieked poor Akaky Akakiyevich, perhaps for the first time in his life, for his voice had always been distinguished for softness.

"Yes, sir," said Petrovich, "for any kind of cloak. If you have a marten fur on the collar, or a silk-lined hood, it will mount up to two hundred."

"Petrovich, please," said Akaky Akakiyevich in a beseeching tone, not hearing, and not trying to hear, Petrovich's words, and disregarding all his "effects," "some repairs, in order that it may wear yet a little longer."

"No, it would only be a waste of time and money," said Petrovich. And Akaky Akakiyevich went away after these words, utterly discouraged. But Petrovich stood for some time after his departure, with significantly compressed lips, and without betaking himself to his work, satisfied that he would not be dropped, and an artistic tailor employed.

Akaky Akakiyevich went out into the street as if in a dream. "Such an affair!" he said to himself. "I did not think it had come to—" and then after a pause, he added, "Well, so it is! see what it has come to at last! and I never imagined that it was so!" Then followed a long silence, after which he exclaimed, "Well, so it is! see what already —nothing unexpected that—it would be nothing—what ₰

strange circumstance!" So saying, instead of going home, he went in exactly the opposite direction without suspecting it. On the way, a chimney-sweep bumped up against him, and blackened his shoulder, and a whole hatful of rubbish landed on him from the top of a house which was building. He did not notice it, and only when he ran against a watchman, who, having planted his halberd beside him, was shaking some snuff from his box into his horny hand, did he recover himself a little, and that because the watchman said, "Why are you poking yourself into a man's very face? Haven't you the pavement?" This caused him to look about him, and turn towards home.

There only, he finally began to collect his thoughts, and to survey his position in its clear and actual light, and to argue with himself, sensibly and frankly, as with a reasonable friend, with whom one can discuss private and personal matters. "No," said Akaky Akakiyevich, "it is impossible to reason with Petrovich now. He is that— evidently, his wife has been beating him. I'd better go to him on Sunday morning. After Saturday night he will be a little cross-eyed and sleepy, for he will want to get drunk, and his wife won't give him any money, and at such a time, a ten-kopek piece in his hand will—he will become more fit to reason with, and then the cloak and that——" Thus argued Akaky Akakiyevich with himself, regained his courage, and waited until the first Sunday, when, seeing from afar that Petrovich's wife had left the house, he went straight to him.

Petrovich's eye was indeed very much askew after

Saturday. His head drooped, and he was very sleepy; but for all that, as soon as he knew what it was a question of, it seemed as though Satan jogged his memory. "Impossible," said he. "Please to order a new one." Thereupon Akaky Akakiyevich handed over the ten-kopek piece. "Thank you, sir. I will drink your good health," said Petrovich. "But as for the cloak, don't trouble yourself about it; it is good for nothing. I will make you a capital new one, so let us settle about it now."

Akaky Akakiyevich was still for mending it, but Petrovich would not hear of it, and said, "I shall certainly have to make you a new one, and you may depend upon it that I shall do my best. It may even be, as the fashion goes, that the collar can be fastened by silver hooks under a flap."

Then Akaky Akakiyevich saw that it was impossible to get along without a new cloak, and his spirit sank utterly. How, in fact, was it to be done? Where was the money to come from? He must have some new trousers, and pay a debt of long standing to the shoemaker for putting new tops to his old boots, and he must order three shirts from the seamstress, and a couple of pieces of linen. In short, all his money must be spent. And even if the director should be so kind as to order him to receive forty-five or even fifty rubles instead of forty, it would be a mere nothing, a mere drop in the ocean towards the funds necessary for a cloak, although he knew that Petrovich was often wrong-headed enough to blurt out some outrageous price, so that even his own wife could not refrain from exclaiming, "Have you lost your senses, you fool?" At one time he would not work at any price, and now it was quite likely that he had named a higher sum than the cloak would cost.

But although he knew that Petrovich would undertake to make a cloak for eighty rubles, still, where was he to get the eighty rubles from? He might possibly manage half. Yes, half might be procured, but where was the other half to come from? But the reader must first be told where the first half came from.

Akaky Akakiyevich had a habit of putting, for every ruble he spent, a groschen into a small box, fastened with lock and key, and with a slit in the top for the reception of money. At the end of every half-year he counted over the heap of coppers, and changed it for silver. This he had done for a long time, and in the course of years, the sum had mounted up to over forty rubles. Thus he had one half on hand. But where was he to find the other half? Where was he to get another forty rubles from? Akaky Akakiyevich thought and thought, and decided that it would be necessary to curtail his ordinary expenses, for the space of one year at least, to dispense with tea in the evening, to burn no candles, and, if there was anything which he must do, to go into his landlady's room, and work by her light. When he went into the street, he must walk as lightly as he could, and as cautiously, upon the stones, almost upon tiptoe, in order not to wear his heels down in too short a time. He must give the laundress as little to wash as possible; and, in order not to wear out his clothes, he must take them off as soon as he got home, and wear only his cotton dressing-gown, which had been long and carefully saved.

To tell the truth, it was a little hard for him at first to accustom himself to these deprivations. But he got used to them at length, after a fashion, and all went smoothly. He even got used to being hungry in the evening, but he made up for it by treating himself, so to say, in spirit, by bearing ever in mind the idea of his future cloak. From that time forth, his existence seemed to become, in some way, fuller, as if he were married, or as if some other man lived in him, as if, in fact, he were not alone, and some pleasant friend had consented to travel along life's path with him, the friend being no other than the cloak, with thick wadding and a strong lining incapable of wearing out. He became more lively, and even his character grew firmer, like that of a man who has made up his mind, and set himself a goal. From his face and gait, doubt and indecision, all hesitating and wavering disappeared of themselves. Fire gleamed in his eyes, and occasionally the boldest and most daring ideas flitted through his mind. Why not, for instance, have marten fur on the collar? The thought of this almost made him absent-minded. Once, in copying a letter, he nearly made a mistake, so that he exclaimed almost aloud, "Ugh!" and crossed himself. Once, in the course of every month, he had a conference with Petrovich on the subject of the cloak, where it would be better to buy the cloth, and the colour, and the price. He always returned home satisfied, though troubled, reflecting that the time would come at last when it could all be bought, and then the cloak made.

The affair progressed more briskly than he had expected. For beyond all his hopes, the director awarded neither forty nor forty-five rubles for Akaky Akakiyevich's share, but sixty. Whether he suspected that Akaky Akakiyevich needed a cloak, or whether it was merely chance, at all events, twenty extra rubles were by this means provided. This circumstance hastened matters. Two or three months more of hunger and Akaky Akakiyevich had accumulated about eighty rubles. His heart, generally so quiet, began to throb. On the first possible day, he went shopping in company with Petrovich. They bought some very good cloth, and at a reasonable rate too, for they had been considering the matter for six months, and rarely let a month pass without their visiting the shops to enquire prices. Petrovich himself said that no better cloth could be had. For lining, they selected a cotton stuff, but so firm and thick, that Petrovich declared it to be better than silk, and even prettier and more glossy. They did not buy the marten fur, because it was, in fact, dear, but in its stead, they picked out the very best of cat-skin, which could be found in the shop, and which might, indeed, be taken for marten at a distance.

Petrovich worked at the cloak two whole weeks, for there was a great deal of quilting; otherwise it would have been finished sooner. He charged twelve rubles for the job, it could not possibly have been done for less. It was all sewed with silk, in small, double seams, and Petrovich went over each seam afterwards with his own teeth, stamping in various patterns.

It was—it is difficult to say precisely on what day, but probably the most glorious one in Akaky Akakiyevich's life, when Petrovich at length brought home the cloak. He brought it in the morning, before the hour when it was necessary to start for the department. Never did a cloak arrive so exactly in the nick of time, for the severe cold had set in, and it seemed to threaten to increase. Petrovich brought the cloak himself as befits a good tailor. On his countenance was a significant expression, such as Akaky Akakiyevich had never beheld there. He seemed fully sensible that he had done no small deed, and crossed a gulf separating tailors who put in linings, and execute repairs, from those who make new things. He took the cloak out of the pocket-handkerchief in which he had brought it. The handkerchief was fresh from the laundress, and he put it in his pocket for use. Taking out the cloak, he gazed proudly at it, held it up with both hands, and flung it skilfully over the shoulders of Akaky Akakiyevich. Then he pulled it and fitted it down behind with his hand, and he draped it around Akaky Akakiyevich without buttoning it. Akaky Akakiyevich, like an experienced man, wished to try the sleeves. Petrovich helped him on with them, and it turned out that the sleeves were satisfactory also. In short, the cloak appeared to be perfect, and most seasonable. Petrovich did not neglect to observe that it was only because he lived in a narrow street, and had no signboard, and had known Akaky Akakiyevich so long, that he had made it so cheaply; but that if he had been in business on the Nevsky Prospect, he would have charged seventy-five rubles for the making alone. Akaky Akakiyevich did not care to argue this point with Petrovich. He paid him, thanked him, and set out at once in his new cloak for the department. Petrovich followed him, and pausing in the street, gazed long at the cloak in the distance, after which he went to one side expressly to run through a crooked alley, and emerge again into the street beyond to gaze once more upon the cloak from another point, namely, directly in front.

Meantime Akaky Akakiyevich went on in holiday mood. He was conscious every second of the time that he had a new cloak on his shoulders, and several times he laughed with internal satisfaction. In fact, there were two advantages, one was its warmth, the other its beauty. He saw nothing of the road, but suddenly found himself at the department. He took off his cloak in the ante-room, looked it over carefully, and confided it to the special care of the attendant. It is impossible to say precisely how it was that every one in the department knew at once that Akaky Akakiyevich had a new cloak, and that the "cape" no longer existed. All rushed at the same moment into the ante-room to inspect it. They congratulated him, and said pleasant things to him, so that he began at first to smile, and then to grow ashamed. When all surrounded him, and said that the new cloak must be "christened," and that he must at least give them all a party, Akaky Akakiyevich lost his head completely, and did not know where he stood, what to answer, or how to get out of it. He stood blushing all over for several minutes, trying to assure them with great simplicity that it was not a new cloak, that it was in fact the old "cape."

At length one of the officials, assistant to the head clerk, in order to show that he was not at all proud, and on good terms with his inferiors, said:

"So be it, only I will give the party instead of Akaky Akakiyevich; I invite you all to tea with me to-night. It just happens to be my name-day too."

The officials naturally at once offered the assistant clerk their congratulations, and accepted the invitation with pleasure. Akaky Akakiyevich would have declined; but all declared that it was discourteous, that it was simply a sin and a shame, and that he could not possibly refuse. Besides, the notion became pleasant to him when he recollected that he should thereby have a chance of wearing his new cloak in the evening also.

That whole day was truly a most triumphant festival for Akaky Akakiyevich. He returned home in the most happy frame of mind, took off his cloak, and hung it carefully on the wall, admiring afresh the cloth and the lining. Then he brought out his old, worn-out cloak, for comparison. He looked at it, and laughed, so vast was the difference. And long after dinner he laughed again when the condition of the "cape" recurred to his mind. He dined cheerfully, and after dinner wrote nothing, but took his ease for a while on the bed, until it got dark. Then he dressed himself lei-surely, put on his cloak, and stepped out into the street.

Where the host lived, unfortunately we cannot say. Our memory begins to fail us badly. The houses and streets in St. Petersburg have become so mixed up in our head that it is very difficult to get anything out of it again in proper form. This much is certain, that the official lived in the best part of the city; and therefore it must have been anything but near to Akaky Akakiyevich's residence. Akaky Aka-kiyevich was first obliged to traverse a kind of wilderness of deserted, dimly-lighted streets. But in proportion as he approached the official's quarter of the city, the streets became more lively, more populous, and more brilliantly illumiated. Pedestrians began to appear; handsomely dressed ladies were more frequently encountered; the men had otter skin collars to their coats; shabby sleigh-men with their wooden, railed sledges stuck over with brass-headed nails, became rarer; whilst on the other hand, more and more drivers in red velvet caps, lacquered sledges and bear-skin coats began to appear, and carriages with rich hammer-cloths flew swiftly through the streets, their wheels scrunching the snow.

Akaky Akakiyevich gazed upon all this as upon a novel sight. He had not been in the streets during the evening for years. He halted out of curiosity before a shop-window, to look at a picture representing a handsome woman, who had thrown off her shoe, thereby baring her whole foot in a very pretty way; whilst behind her the head of a man with whiskers and a handsome moustache peeped through the doorway of another room. Akaky Akakiyevich shook his head, and laughed, and then went on his way. Why did he laugh? Either because he had met with a thing utterly unknown, but for which every one cherishes, nevertheless, some sort of feeling, or else he thought, like many officials, "Well, those French! What is to be said? If they do go in for anything of that sort, why—" But possibly he did not think at all.

Akaky Akakiyevich at length reached the house in which the head clerk's assistant lodged. He lived in fine style. The staircase was lit by a lamp, his apartment being on the second floor. On entering the vestibule, Akaky Akakiyevich beheld a whole row of goloshes on the floor. Among them, in the centre of the room, stood a samovar, hum-

ming and emitting clouds of steam. On the walls hung all
sorts of coats and cloaks, among which there were even
some with beaver collars, or velvet facings. Beyond, the
buzz of conversation was audible, and became clear and
loud, when the servant came out with a trayful of empty
glasses, cream-jugs and sugar-bowls. It was evident that
the officials had arrived long before, and had already finished their first glass of tea.

Akaky Akakiyevich, having hung up his own cloak, entered the inner room. Before him all at once appeared
lights, officials, pipes, and card-tables, and he was bewildered by a sound of rapid conversation rising from all the
tables, and the noise of moving chairs. He halted very awkwardly in the middle of the room, wondering what he
ought to do. But they had seen him. They received him
with a shout, and all thronged at once into the ante-room,
and there took another look at his cloak. Akaky Akakiyevich, although somewhat confused, was frank-hearted, and
could not refrain from rejoicing when he saw how they
praised his cloak. Then, of course, they all dropped him
and his cloak, and returned, as was proper, to the tables set
out for whist.

All this, the noise, the talk, and the throng of people, was
rather overwhelming to Akaky Akakiyevich. He simply
did not know where he stood, or where to put his hands,
his feet, and his whole body. Finally he sat down by the
players, looked at the cards, gazed at the face of one and
another, and after a while began to gape, and to feel that
it was wearisome, the more so, as the hour was already long
past when he usually went to bed. He wanted to take

leave of the host, but they would not let him go, saying that he must not fail to drink a glass of champagne, in honour of his new garment. In the course of an hour, supper, consisting of vegetable salad, cold veal, pastry, confectioner's pies, and champagne, was served. They made Akaky Akakiyevich drink two glasses of champagne, after which he felt things grow livelier.

Still, he could not forget that it was twelve o'clock, and that he should have been at home long ago. In order that the host might not think of some excuse for detaining him, he stole out of the room quickly, sought out, in the anteroom, his cloak, which, to his sorrow, he found lying on the floor, brushed it, picked off every speck upon it, put it on his shoulders, and descended the stairs to the street.

In the street all was still bright. Some petty shops, those permanent clubs of servants and all sorts of folks, were open. Others were shut, but, nevertheless, showed a streak of light the whole length of the door-crack, indicating that they were not yet free of company, and that probably some domestics, male and female, were finishing their stories and conversations, whilst leaving their masters in complete ignorance as to their whereabouts. Akaky Akakiyevich went on in a happy frame of mind. He even started to run, without knowing why, after some lady, who flew past like a flash of lightning. But he stopped short, and went on very quietly as before, wondering why he had quickened his pace. Soon there spread before him those deserted streets which are not cheerful in the daytime, to say nothing of the evening. Now they were even more dim and lonely. The lanterns began to grow rarer, oil, evidently, had been less liberally supplied. Then came wooden houses and fences. Not a soul anywhere; only the snow sparkled in the streets, and mournfully veiled the low-roofed cabins with their closed shutters. He approached the spot where the street crossed a vast square with houses barely visible on its farther side, a square which seemed a fearful desert.

Afar, a tiny spark glimmered from some watchman's-box, which seemed to stand on the edge of the world. Akaky Akakiyevich's cheerfulness diminished at this point in a marked degree. He entered the square, not without an involuntary sensation of fear, as though his heart warned him of some evil. He glanced back, and on both sides it was like a sea about him. "No, it is better not to look," he thought, and went on, closing his eyes. When he opened them, to see whether he was near the end of the square, he suddenly beheld, standing just before his very nose, some bearded individuals of precisely what sort, he could not make out. All grew dark before his eyes, and his heart throbbed.

"Of course, the cloak is mine!" said one of them in a loud voice, seizing hold of his collar. Akaky Akakiyevich was about to shout "Help!" when the second man thrust a fist, about the size of an official's head, at his very mouth, muttering, "Just you dare to scream!"

Akaky Akakiyevich felt them strip off his cloak, and give him a kick. He fell headlong upon the snow, and felt no more.

In a few minutes he recovered consciousness, and rose to his feet, but no one was there. He felt that it was cold in the square, and that his cloak was gone. He began to shout, but his voice did not appear to reach the outskirts of the square. In despair, but without ceasing to shout, he started at a run across the square, straight towards the watch-box, beside which stood the watchman, leaning on his halberd, and apparently curious to know what kind of a customer was running towards him shouting. Akaky Akakiyevich ran up to him, and began in a sobbing voice to shout that he was asleep, and attended to nothing, and did not see when a man was robbed. The watchman replied that he had seen two men stop him in the middle of the square, but supposed that they were friends of his, and that, instead of scolding vainly, he had better go to the police on the morrow, so that they might make a search for whoever had stolen the cloak.

Akaky Akakiyevich ran home and arrived in a state of complete disorder, his hair which grew very thinly upon his temples and the back of his head all tousled, his body, arms and legs, covered with snow. The old woman, who was mistress of his lodgings, on hearing a terrible knocking, sprang hastily from her bed, and, with only one shoe on, ran to open the door, pressing the sleeve of her chemise to her bosom out of modesty. But when she had opened it, she fell back on beholding Akaky Akakiyevich in such a condition. When he told her about the affair, she clasped her hands, and said that he must go straight to the district chief of police, for his subordinate would turn up his nose, promise well, and drop the matter there. The very best thing to do, therefore, would be to go to the district chief, whom she knew, because Finnish Anna, her former cook, was now nurse at his house. She often saw him passing the

house, and he was at church every S*unday*, praying, but at
the same time gazing cheerfully at everybody; so that he
must be a good man, judging from all appearances. Having
listened to this opinion, Akaky Akakiyevich betook himself sadly to his room. And how he spent the night there,
any one who can put himself in another's place may readily
imagine.

Early in the morning, he presented himself at the district chief's, but was told the official was asleep. He went
again at ten and was again informed that he was asleep.
At eleven, and they said, "The superintendent is not at
home." At dinner time, and the clerks in the ante-room
would not admit him on any terms, and insisted upon
knowing his business. So that at last, for once in his life,
Akaky Akakiyevich felt an inclination to show some spirit,
and said curtly that he must see the chief in person, that
they ought not to presume to refuse him entrance, that he
came from the department of justice, and that when he
complained to them, they would see.

The clerks dared make no reply to this, and one of them
went to call the chief, who listened to the strange story of
the theft of the coat. Instead of directing his attention to
the principal points of the matter, he began to question
Akaky Akakiyevich. Why was he going home so late? Was
he in the habit of doing so, or had he been to some disorderly house? So that Akaky Akakiyevich got thoroughly
confused, and left him, without knowing whether the affair
of his cloak was in proper train or not.

All that day, for the first time in his life, he never went
near the department. The next day he made his appear-

ance, very pale, and in his old cape, which had become even more shabby. The news of the robbery of the cloak touched many, although there were some officials present who never lost an opportunity, even such a one as the present, of ridiculing Akaky Akakiyevich. They decided to make a collection for him on the spot, but the officials had already spent a great deal in subscribing for the director's portrait and for some book, at the suggestion of the head of that division, who was a friend of the author; and so the sum was trifling.

One of them, moved by pity, resolved to help Akaky Akakiyevich with some good advice, at least, and told him that he ought not to go to the police, for although it might happen that a police-officer, wishing to win the approval of his superiors, might hunt up the cloak by some means, still, his cloak would remain in the possession of the police if he did not offer legal proof that it belonged to him. The best thing for him, therefore, would be to apply to a certain prominent personage; since this prominent personage, by entering into relation with the proper persons, could greatly expedite the matter.

As there was nothing else to be done, Akaky Akakiyevich decided to go to the prominent personage. What was the exact official position of the prominent personage, remains unknown to this day. The reader must know that the prominent personage had but recently become a prominent personage, having up to that time been only an insignificant person. Moreover, his present position was not considered prominent in comparison with others still more so. But there is always a circle of people to whom what is insignificant in the eyes of others, is important enough. More-over, he strove to increase his importance by sundry de-vices. For instance, he managed to have the inferior officials meet him on the staircase when he entered upon his serv-ice; no one was to presume to come directly to him, but the strictest etiquette must be observed; the collegiate recorder must make a report to the government secretary, the government secretary to the titular councillor, or whatever other man was proper, and all business must come before him in this manner. In Holy Russia, all is thus contami-nated with the love of imitation; every man imitates and copies his superior. They even say that a certain titular councillor, when promoted to the head of some small sepa-rate office, immediately partitioned off a private room for himself, called it the audience chamber, and posted at the door, a lackey with red collar and braid, who grasped the handle of the door, and opened to all comers, though the audience chamber would hardly hold an ordinary writing table.

The manners and customs of the prominent personage were grand and imposing, but rather exaggerated. The main foundation of his system was strictness. "Strictness, strictness, and always strictness!" he generally said; and at the last word he looked significantly into the face of the person to whom he spoke. But there was no necessity for this, for the halfscore of subordinates, who formed the en-tire force of the office, were properly afraid. On catching sight of him afar off, they left their work, and waited, drawn up in line, until he had passed through the room. His ordinary converse with his inferiors smacked of sternness, and consisted chiefly of three phrases: "How dare you?" "Do you know whom you are speaking to?" "Do you realise who is standing before you?"

Otherwise he was a very kind-hearted man, good to his comrades, and ready to oblige. But the rank of general threw him completely off his balance. On receiving any one of that rank, he became confused, lost his way, as it were, and never knew what to do. If he chanced to be amongst his equals, he was still a very nice kind of man, a very good fellow in many respects, and not stupid, but the very moment that he found himself in the society of people but one rank lower than himself, he became silent. And his situation aroused sympathy, the more so, as he felt himself that he might have been making an incomparably better use of his time. In his eyes, there was sometimes visible a desire to join some interesting conversation or group, but he was kept back by the thought, "Would it not be a very great condescension on his part? Would it not be familiar? And would he not thereby lose his importance?" And in consequence of such reflections, he always remained in the same dumb state, uttering from time to time a few monosyllabic sounds, and thereby earning the name of the most wearisome of men.

To this prominent personage Akaky Akakiyevich presented himself, and this at the most unfavourable time for himself, though opportune for the prominent personage. The prominent personage was in his cabinet, conversing very gaily with an old acquaintance and companion of his childhood, whom he had not seen for several years, and who had just arrived, when it was announced to him that a person named Bashmachkin had come. He asked abruptly, "Who is he?"—"Some official," he was informed. "Ah, he can wait! This is no time for him to call," said the important man.

It must be remarked here that the important man lied outrageously. He had said all he had to say to his friend long before, and the conversation had been interspersed for some time with very long pauses, during which they merely slapped each other on the leg, and said, "You think so, Ivan Abramovich!" "Just so, Stepan Varlamovich!" Nevertheless, he ordered that the official should be kept waiting, in order to show his friend, a man who had not been in the service for a long time, but had lived at home in the country, how long officials had to wait in his ante-room.

At length, having talked himself completely out, and more than that, having had his fill of pauses, and smoked a cigar in a very comfortable arm-chair with reclining back, he suddenly seemed to recollect, and said to his secretary, who stood by the door with papers of reports, "So it seems that there is an official waiting to see me. Tell him that he may come in." On perceiving Akaky Akakiyevich's modest mien and his worn uniform, he turned abruptly to him, and said, "What do you want?" in a curt hard voice, which he had practised in his room in private, and before the looking-glass, for a whole week before being raised to his present rank.

Akaky Akakiyevich, who was already imbued with a due amount of fear, became somewhat confused, and as well as his tongue would permit, explained, with a rather more frequent addition than usual of the word "that" that his

cloak was quite new, and had been stolen in the most inhuman manner; that he had applied to him, in order that
he might, in some way, by his intermediation—that he
might enter into correspondence with the chief of police,
and find the cloak.

For some inexplicable reason, this conduct seemed familiar to the prominent personage.

"What, my dear sir!" he said abruptly, "are you not
acquainted with etiquette? To whom have you come?
Don't you know how such matters are managed? You
should first have presented a petition to the office. It would
have gone to the head of the department, then to the chief
of the division, then it would have been handed over to
the secretary, and the secretary would have given it to me."

"But your excellency," said Akaky Akakiyevich, trying
to collect his small handful of wits, and conscious at the
same time that he was perspiring terribly, "I, your excellency, presumed to trouble you because secretaries—are an
untrustworthy race."

"What, what, what!" said the important personage.
"Where did you get such courage? Where did you get such
ideas? What impudence towards their chiefs and superiors
has spread among the young generation!" The prominent
personage apparently had not observed that Akaky Akakiyevich was already in the neighbourhood of fifty. If he
could be called a young man, it must have been in comparison with some one who was seventy. "Do you know to
whom you are speaking? Do you realise who is standing
before you? Do you realise it? Do you realise it, I ask
you!" Then he stamped his foot, and raised his voice to

such a pitch that it would have frightened even a different man from Akaky Akakiyevich.

Akaky Akakiyevich's senses failed him. He staggered, trembled in every limb, and, if the porters had not run in to support him, would have fallen to the floor. They carried him out insensible. But the prominent personage, gratified that the effect should have surpassed his expectations, and quite intoxicated with the thought that his word could even deprive a man of his senses, glanced sideways at his friend in order to see how he looked upon this, and perceived, not without satisfaction, that his friend was in a most uneasy frame of mind, and even beginning on his part, to feel a trifle frightened.

Akaky Akakiyevich could not remember how he descended the stairs, and got into the street. He felt neither his hands nor feet. Never in his life had he been so rated by any high official, let alone a strange one. He went staggering on through the snow-storm, which was blowing in the streets, with his mouth wide open. The wind, in St. Petersburg fashion, darted upon him from all quarters, and down every cross-street. In a twinkling it had blown a quinsy into his throat, and he reached home unable to utter a word. His throat was swollen, and he lay down on his bed. So powerful is sometimes a good scolding!

The next day a violent fever developed. Thanks to the generous assistance of the St. Petersburg climate, the malady progressed more rapidly than could have been expected, and when the doctor arrived, he found, on feeling the sick man's pulse, that there was nothing to be done, except to prescribe a poultice, so that the patient might not be left entirely without the beneficent aid of medicine. But at the same time, he predicted his end in thirty-six hours. After this he turned to the landlady, and said, "And as for you, don't waste your time on him. Order his pine coffin now, for an oak one will be too expensive for him."

Did Akaky Akakiyevich hear these fatal words? And if he heard them, did they produce any overwhelming effect upon him? Did he lament the bitterness of his life?—We know not, for he continued in a delirious condition. Visions incessantly appeared to him, each stranger than the other. Now he saw Petrovich, and ordered him to make a cloak, with some traps for robbers, who seemed to him to be always under the bed; and he cried every moment to the landlady to pull one of them from under his coverlet. Then he inquired why his old mantle hung before him when he had a new cloak. Next he fancied that he was standing before the prominent person, listening to a thorough setting-down and saying, "Forgive me, your excellency!" but at last he began to curse, uttering the most horrible words, so that his aged landlady crossed herself, never in her life having heard anything of the kind from him, and more so, as these words followed directly after the words "your excellency." Later on he talked utter nonsense, of which nothing could be made, all that was evident being that these incoherent words and thoughts hovered ever about one thing, his cloak.

At length poor Akaky Akakiyevich breathed his last. They sealed up neither his room nor his effects, because, in the first place, there were no heirs, and, in the second, there was very little to inherit beyond a bundle of goose-quills, a quire of white official paper, three pairs of socks, two or three buttons which had burst off his trousers, and the mantle already known to the reader. To whom all this fell, God knows. I confess that the person who told me this tale took no interest in the matter. They carried Akaky Akakiyevich out, and buried him.

And St. Petersburg was left without Akaky Akakiyevich, as though he had never lived there. A being disappeared, who was protected by none, dear to none, interesting to none, and who never even attracted to himself the attention of those students of human nature who omit no opportunity of thrusting a pin through a common fly and examining it under the microscope. A being who bore meekly the jibes of the department, and went to his grave without having done one unusual deed, but to whom, nevertheless, at the close of his life, appeared a bright visitant in the form of a cloak, which momentarily cheered his poor life, and upon him, thereafter, an intolerable misfortune descended, just as it descends upon the heads of the mighty of this world!

Several days after his death, the porter was sent from the department to his lodgings, with an order for him to present himself there immediately, the chief commanding it. But the porter had to return unsuccessful, with the answer that he could not come; and to the question, "Why?" replied, "Well, because he is dead! he was buried four days ago." In this manner did they hear of Akaky Akakiyevich's death at the department. And the next day a new official sat in his place, with a handwriting by no means so upright, but more inclined and slanting.

But who could have imagined that this was not really the end of Akaky Akakiyevich, that he was destined to raise a commotion after death, as if in compensation for his utterly insignificant life? But so it happened, and our poor story unexpectedly gains a fantastic ending.

A rumour suddenly spread through St. Petersburg, that a dead man had taken to appearing on the Kalinkin Bridge, and its vicinity, at night in the form of an official seeking a stolen cloak, and that, under the pretext of its being the stolen cloak, he dragged, without regard to rank or calling, every one's cloak from his shoulders, be it cat-skin, beaver, fox, bear, sable, in a word, every sort of fur and skin which men adopted for their covering. One of the department officials saw the dead man with his own eyes, and immediately recognised in him Akaky Akakiyevich. This, however, inspired him with such terror, that he ran off with all his might, and therefore did not scan the dead man closely, but only saw how the latter threatened him from afar with his finger. Constant complaints poured in from all quarters, that the backs and shoulders, not only of titular but even of court councillors, were exposed to the danger of a cold, on account of the frequent dragging off of their cloaks.

Arrangements were made by the police to catch the corpse, alive or dead, at any cost, and punish him as an example to others, in the most severe manner. In this they nearly succeeded, for a watchman, on guard in Kirinshkin Lane, caught the corpse by the collar on the very scene of his evil deeds, when attempting to pull off the frieze cloak of a retired musician. Having seized him by the collar, he summoned, with a shout, two of his comrades, whom he enjoined to hold him fast, while he himself felt for a moment in his boot, in order to draw out his snuff-box, and refresh his frozen nose. But the snuff was of a sort which even a corpse could not endure. The watchman having closed his right nostril with his finger, had no sooner succeeded in holding half a handful up to the left, than the corpse sneezed so violently that he completely filled the eyes of all three. While they raised their hands to wipe them, the dead man vanished completely, so that they positively did not know whether they had actually had him in their grip at all. Thereafter the watchmen conceived such a terror of dead men that they were afraid even to seize the living, and only screamed from a distance. "Hey, there! go your way!" So the dead official began to appear even beyond the Kalinkin Bridge causing no little terror to all timid people.

But we have totally neglected that certain prominent personage who may really be considered as the cause of the fantastic turn taken by this true history. First of all, justice compels us to say, that after the departure of poor, annihilated Akaky Akakiyevich, he felt something like remorse. Suffering was unpleasant to him, for his heart was accessible to many good impulses, in spite of the fact that his rank often prevented his showing his true self. As soon as his friend had left his cabinet, he began to think about poor Akaky Akakiyevich. And from that day forth, poor Akaky Akakiyevich, who could not bear up under an official reprimand, recurred to his mind almost every day. The thought troubled him to such an extent, that a week later he even resolved to send an official to him, to learn whether he really could assist him. And when it was reported to him that Akaky Akakiyevich had died suddenly of fever, he was startled, hearkened to the reproaches of his conscience, and was out of sorts for the whole day.

Wishing to divert his mind in some way and drive away the disagreeable impression, he set out that evening for one of his friends' houses, where he found quite a large party assembled. What was better, nearly every one was of the same rank as himself, so that he need not feel in the least constrained. This had a marvellous effect upon his mental state. He grew expansive, made himself agreeable in conversation, in short, he passed a delightful evening. After supper he drank a couple of glasses of champagne—not a bad recipe for cheerfulness, as every one knows. The champagne inclined him to various adventures, and he determined not to return home, but to go and see a certain well-known lady, of German extraction, Karolina Ivanovna, a lady, it appears, with whom he was on a very friendly footing.

It must be mentioned that the prominent personage was no longer a young man, but a good husband and respected father of a family. Two sons, one of whom was already in the service, and a good-looking, sixteen-year-old daughter, with a slightly arched but pretty little nose, came every morning to kiss his hand and say, *"Bon jour,* papa." His wife, a still fresh and good-looking woman, first gave him her hand to kiss, and then, reversing the procedure, kissed his. But the prominent personage, though perfectly satisfied in his domestic relations, considered it stylish to have a friend in another quarter of the city. This friend was scarcely prettier or younger than his wife; but there are such puzzles in the world, and it is not our place to judge them. So the important personage descended the stairs, stepped into his sledge, said to the coachman, "To Karolina Ivanovna's," and, wrapping himself luxuriously in his warm cloak, found himself in that delightful frame of mind than which a Russian can conceive nothing better, namely, when you think of nothing yourself, yet when the thoughts creep into your mind of their own accord, each more agreeable than the other, giving you no trouble either to drive them away, or seek them. Fully satisfied, he recalled all the gay features of the evening just passed and all the mots which had made the little circle laugh. Many of them he repeated in a low voice, and found them quite as funny as before; so it is not surprising that he should laugh heartily at them. Occasionally, however, he was interrupted by gusts of wind, which, coming suddenly, God knows whence or why, cut his face, drove masses of snow into it, filled out his cloak-collar like a sail, or suddenly blew it over his head with supernatural force, and thus caused him constant trouble to disentangle himself.

Suddenly the important personage felt some one clutch him firmly by the collar. Turning round, he perceived a man of short stature, in an old, worn uniform, and recognised, not without terror, Akaky Akakiyevich. The official's face was white as snow, and looked just like a corpse's. But the horror of the important personage transcended all bounds when he saw the dead man's mouth open, and heard it utter the following remarks, while it breathed upon him the terrible odour of the grave: "Ah, here you are at last! I have you, that—by the collar! I need your cloak. You took no trouble about mine, but reprimanded me. So now give up your own."

The pallid prominent personage almost died of fright. Brave as he was in the office and in the presence of inferiors generally, and although, at the sight of his manly form and appearance, every one said, "Ugh! how much character he has!" at this crisis, he, like many possessed of an heroic exterior, experienced such terror, that, not without cause, he began to fear an attack of illness. He flung his cloak hastily from his shoulders and shouted to his coachman in an unnatural voice, "Home at full speed!" The coachman, hearing the tone which is generally employed at critical moments, and even accompanied by something much more tangible, drew his head down between his shoulders in case of an emergency, flourished his whip, and flew on like an arrow. In a little more than six minutes the prominent personage was at the entrance of his own house. Pale, thoroughly scared, and cloakless, he went home instead of to Karolina Ivanovna's, reached his room somehow or other, and passed the night in the direst distress; so that the next morning over their tea, his daughter said, "You are very pale to-day, papa." But papa remained silent, and said not a word to any one of what had happened to him, where he had been, or where he had intended to go.

This occurrence made a deep impression upon him. He even began to say, "How dare you? Do you realise who is standing before you?" less frequently to the under-officials, and, if he did utter the words, it was only after first having learned the bearings of the matter. But the most noteworthy point was, that from that day forward the apparition of the dead official ceased to be seen. Evidently the prominent personage's cloak just fitted his shoulders. At all events, no more instances of his dragging cloaks from people's shoulders were heard of. But many active and solicitous persons could by no means reassure themselves, and asserted that the dead official still showed himself in distant parts of the city.

In fact, one watchman in Kolomen saw with his own eyes the apparition come from behind a house. But the watchman was not a strong man, so he was afraid to arrest him, and followed him in the dark, until, at length, the apparition looked round, paused, and inquired, "What do you want?" at the same time showing such a fist as is never seen on living men. The watchman said, "Nothing," and turned back instantly. But the apparition was much too tall, wore huge moustaches, and, directing its steps apparently towards the Obukhov Bridge, disappeared in the darkness of the night.

THE DISTRICT DOCTOR

◆◆◆

By *Ivan S. Turgenev*

ONE DAY in autumn on my way back from a remote part of the country I caught cold and fell ill. Fortunately the fever attacked me in the district town at the inn; I sent for the doctor. In half-an-hour the district doctor appeared, a thin, dark-haired man of middle height. He prescribed me the usual sudorific, ordered a mustard-plaster to be put on, very deftly slid a five-ruble note up his sleeve, coughing drily and looking away as he did so, and then was getting up to go home, but somehow fell into talk and remained. I was exhausted with feverishness; I foresaw a sleepless night, and was glad of a little chat with a pleasant companion. Tea was served. My doctor began to converse freely. He was a sensible fellow, and expressed himself with vigour and some humour. Queer things happen in the world: you may live a long while with some people, and be on friendly terms with them, and never once speak openly with them from your soul; with others you have scarcely time to get acquainted, and all at once you are pouring out to him—or he to you—all your secrets, as though you were at confession. I don't know how I gained the confidence of my new friend—anyway, with nothing to

82

lead up to it, he told me a rather curious incident; and here I will report his tale for the information of the indulgent reader. I will try to tell it in the doctor's own words.

"You don't happen to know," he began in a weak and quavering voice (the common result of the use of unmixed Berezov snuff); "you don't happen to know the judge here, Mylov, Pavel Lukich? . . . You don't know him? . . . Well, it's all the same." (He cleared his throat and rubbed his eyes.) "Well, you see, the thing happened, to tell you exactly without mistake, in Lent, at the very time of the thaws. I was sitting at his house—our judge's, you know—playing preference. Our judge is a good fellow, and fond of playing preference. Suddenly" (the doctor made frequent use of this word, suddenly) "they tell me, 'There's a servant asking for you.' I say, 'What does he want?' They say, 'He has brought a note—it must be from a patient.' 'Give me the note,' I say. So it is from a patient—well and good—you understand—it's our bread and butter. . . . But this is how it was: a lady, a widow, writes to me; she says, 'My daughter is dying. Come, for God's sake!' she says, 'and the horses have been sent for you.' . . . Well, that's all right. But she was twenty miles from the town, and it was midnight out of doors, and the roads in such a state, my word! And as she was poor herself, one could not expect more than two silver rubles, and even that problematic; and perhaps it might only be a matter of a roll of linen and a sack of oatmeal in payment. However, duty, you know, before everything: a fellow-creature may be dying. I hand over my cards at once to Kalliopin, the member of the provincial commission, and return home. I look; a wretched little trap was standing at the steps, with peasant's horses, fat—too fat—and their coat as shaggy as felt; and the coachman sitting with his cap off out of respect. Well, I think to myself, 'It's clear, my friend, these patients aren't rolling in riches.' . . . You smile; but I tell you, a poor man like me has to take everything into consideration. . . . If the coachman sits like a prince, and doesn't touch his cap, and even sneers at you behind his beard, and flicks his whip—then you may bet on six rubles. But this case, I saw, had a very different air. However, I think there's no help for it; duty before everything. I snatch up the most necessary drugs, and set off. Will you believe it? I only just managed to get there at all. The road was infernal: streams, snow, watercourses, and the dyke had suddenly burst there—that was the worst of it! However, I arrived at last. It was a little thatched house. There was a light in the windows; that meant they expected me. I was met by an old lady, very venerable, in a cap. 'Save her!' she says; 'she is dying.' I say, 'Pray don't distress yourself— Where is the invalid?' 'Come this way.' I see a clean little room, a lamp in the corner; on the bed a girl of twenty, unconscious. She was in a burning heat, and breathing heavily—it was fever. There were two others girls, her sisters, scared and in tears. 'Yesterday,' they tell me, 'she was perfectly well and had a good appetite; this morning she complained of her head, and this evening, suddenly, you see, like this.' I say again: 'Pray don't be uneasy.' It's a doctor's duty, you know—and I went up to her and bled her, told them to put on a mustard-plaster, and prescribed a mixture. Meantime I looked at her; I looked at her, you

know—there, by God! I had never seen such a face!—she
was a beauty, in a word! I felt quite shaken with pity.
Such lovely features; such eyes! . . . But, thank God! she
became easier; she fell into a perspiration, seemed to come
to her senses, looked round, smiled, and passed her hand
over her face. . . . Her sisters bent over her. They ask,
'How are you?' 'All right,' she says, and turns away. I
looked at her; she had fallen asleep. 'Well,' I say, 'now the
patient should be left alone.' So we all went out on tiptoe;
only a maid remained, in case she was wanted. In the
parlour there was a samovar standing on the table, and a
bottle of rum; in our profession one can't get on without
it. They gave me tea; asked me to stop the night. . . . I
consented: where could I go, indeed, at that time of night?
The old lady kept groaning. 'What is it?' I say; 'she will
live; don't worry yourself; you had better take a little rest
yourself; it is about two o'clock.' 'But will you send to
wake me if anything happens?' 'Yes, yes.' The old lady
went away, and the girls too went to their own room;
they made up a bed for me in the parlour. Well, I went
to bed—but I could not get to sleep, for a wonder! for in
reality I was very tired. I could not get my patient out of
my head. At last I could not put up with it any longer; I
got up suddenly; I think to myself, 'I will go and see how
the patient is getting on.' Her bedroom was next to the
parlour. Well, I got up, and gently opened the door—how
my heart beat! I looked in: the servant was asleep, her
mouth wide open, and even snoring, the wretch! but the
patient lay with her face towards me, and her arms flung
wide apart, poor girl! I went up to her . . . when suddenly

she opened her eyes and stared at me! 'Who is it? who is it?' I was in confusion. 'Don't be alarmed, madam,' I say; 'I am the doctor; I have come to see how you feel.' 'You the doctor?' 'Yes, the doctor; your mother sent for me from the town; we have bled you, madam; now pray go to sleep, and in a day or two, please God! we will set you on your feet again.' 'Ah, yes, yes, doctor, don't let me die. . . . please, please.' 'Why do you talk like that? God bless you!' She is in a fever again, I think to myself; I felt her pulse; yes, she was feverish. She looked at me, and then took me by the hand. 'I will tell you why I don't want to die; I will tell you. . . . Now we are alone; and only, please don't you . . . not to any one . . . Listen. . . .' I bent down; she moved her lips quite to my ear; she touched my cheek with her hair—I confess my head went round—and began to whisper. . . . I could make out nothing of it. . . . Ah, she was delirious! . . . She whispered and whispered, but so quickly, and as if it were not in Russian; at last she finished, and shivering dropped her head on the pillow, and threatened me with her finger: 'Remember, doctor, to no one.' I calmed her somehow, gave her something to drink, waked the servant, and went away."

At this point the doctor again took snuff with exasperated energy, and for a moment seemed stupefied by its effects.

"However," he continued, "the next day, contrary to my expectations, the patient was no better. I thought and thought, and suddenly decided to remain there, even though my other patients were expecting me. . . . And you

know one can't afford to disregard that; one's practice
suffers if one does. But, in the first place, the patient was
really in danger; and secondly, to tell the truth, I felt
strongly drawn to her. Besides, I liked the whole family.
Though they were really badly off, they were singularly, I
may say, cultivated people. . . . Their father had been a
learned man, an author; he died, of course, in poverty, but
he had managed before he died to give his children an excellent education; he left a lot of books too. Either because
I looked after the invalid very carefully, or for some other
reason; anyway, I can venture to say all the household
loved me as if I were one of the family. . . . Meantime the
roads were in a worse state than ever; all communications,
so to say, were cut off completely; even medicine could
with difficulty be got from the town. . . . The sick girl
was not getting better. . . . Day after day, and day after
day . . . but . . . here. . . ." (The doctor made a brief
pause.) "I declare I don't know how to tell you." . . . (He
again took snuff, coughed, and swallowed a little tea.) "I
will tell you without beating about the bush. My patient
. . . how should I say? . . . Well she had fallen in love
with me . . . or, no, it was not that she was in love . . .
however . . . really, how should one say?" (The doctor
looked down and grew red.) "No," he went on quickly,
"in love, indeed! A man should not over-estimate himself.
She was an educated girl, clever and well-read, and I had
even forgotten my Latin, one may say, completely. As to
appearance" (the doctor looked himself over with a smile)
"I am nothing to boast of there either. But God Almighty
did not make me a fool; I don't take black for white; I

know a thing or two; I could see very clearly, for instance that Aleksandra Andreyevna—that was her name—did not feel love for me, but had a friendly, so to say, inclination—a respect or something for me. Though she herself perhaps mistook this sentiment, anyway this was her attitude; you may form your own judgment of it. But," added the doctor, who had brought out all these disconnected sentences without taking breath, and with obvious embarrassment, "I seem to be wandering rather—you won't understand anything like this . . . There, with your leave, I will relate it all in order."

He drank off a glass of tea, and began in a calmer voice.

"Well, then. My patient kept getting worse and worse. You are not a doctor, my good sir; you cannot understand what passes in a poor fellow's heart, especially at first, when he begins to suspect that the disease is getting the upper hand of him. What becomes of his belief in himself? You suddenly grow so timid; it's indescribable. You fancy then that you have forgotten everything you knew, and that the patient has no faith in you, and that other people begin to notice how distracted you are, and tell you the symptoms with reluctance; that they are looking at you suspiciously, whispering . . . Ah! it's horrid! There must be a remedy, you think, for this disease, if one could find it. Isn't this it? You try—no, that's not it! You don't allow the medicine the necessary time to do good . . . You clutch at one thing, then at another. Sometimes you take up a book of medical prescriptions—here it is, you think! Sometimes, by Jove, you pick one out by chance, thinking to leave it to fate. . . . But meantime a fellow-creature's dying, and another doctor would have saved him. 'We must have a consultation,' you say; 'I will not take the responsibility on myself.' And what a fool you look at such times! Well, in time you learn to bear it; it's nothing to you. A man has died—but it's not your fault; you treated him by the rules. But what's still more torture to you is to see blind faith in you, and to feel yourself that you are not able to be of use. Well, it was just this blind faith that the whole of Aleksandra Andreyevna's family had in me; they had forgotten to think that their daughter was in danger. I, too, on my side assure them that it's nothing, but meantime my heart sinks into my boots. To add to our troubles, the roads were in such a state that the coachman was gone for whole days together to get medicine. And I never left the patient's room; I could not tear myself away; I tell her amusing stories, you know, and play cards with her. I watch by her side at night. The old mother thanks me with tears in her eyes; but I think to myself, 'I don't deserve your gratitude.' I frankly confess to you—there is no object in concealing it now—I was in love with my patient. And Aleksandra Andreyevna had grown fond of me; she would not sometimes let any one be in her room but me. She began to talk to me, to ask me questions; where I had studied, how I lived, who are my people, whom I go to see. I feel that she ought not to talk; but to forbid her to—to forbid her resolutely, you know—I could not. Sometimes I held my head in my hands, and asked myself, 'What are you doing, villain?' . . . And she would take my hand and hold it, give me a long, long look, and turn away, sigh, and say, 'How good you are!' Her hands were so feverish, her eyes so large and languid. . . . 'Yes,' she says, 'you are a good, kind man; you are not like our neighbours. . . . No, you are not like that. . . . Why did I not know you till now!' 'Aleksandra Andreyevna, calm yourself,' I say. . . . 'I feel, believe me, I don't know how I have gained . . . but there, calm yourself. . . . All will be right; you will be well again.' And meanwhile I must tell you," continued the doctor, bending forward and raising his eyebrows, "that they associated very little with the neighbours, because the smaller people were not on their level, and pride hindered them from being friendly with the rich. I tell you, they were an exceptionally cultivated family so you know it was gratifying for me. She would only take her medicine from my hands . . . she would lift herself up, poor girl, with my aid, take it, and gaze at me. . . . My heart felt as if it were bursting. And meanwhile she was growing worse and worse, worse and worse, all the time; she will die, I think to myself; she must die. Believe me, I would sooner have gone to the grave myself; and here were her mother and sisters watching me, looking into my eyes . . . and their faith in me was wearing away. 'Well? how is she?' 'Oh, all right, all right!' All right, indeed! My mind was failing me. Well, I was sitting one night alone again by my patient. The maid was sitting there too, and snoring away in full swing; I can't find fault with the poor girl, though! she was worn out too. Aleksandra Andreyevna had felt very unwell all the evening; she was very feverish. Until midnight she kept tossing about; at last she seemed to fall asleep; at least, she lay still without stirring. The lamp was

burning in the corner before the holy image. I sat there,
you know, with my head bent; I even dozed a little. Suddenly it seemed as though some one touched me in the
side; I turned round. . . . Good God! Aleksandra Andrey,
evna was gazing with intent eyes at me . . . her lips parted,
her cheeks seemed burning. 'What is it?' 'Doctor, shall I
die?' 'Merciful Heavens!' 'No, doctor, no; please don't
tell me I shall live . . . don't say so. . . . If you knew. . . .
Listen! for God's sake don't conceal my real position, and
her breath came so fast. 'If I can know for certain that I
must die . . . then I will tell you all—all!' 'Aleksandra
Andreyevna, I beg!' 'Listen; I have not been asleep at all
. . . I have been looking at you a long while. . . . For God's
sake! . . . I believe in you; you are a good man, an honest
man; I entreat you by all that is sacred in the world—tell
me the truth! If you knew how important it is for me. . . .
Doctor, for God's sake tell me. . . . Am I in danger?'
'What can I tell you, Aleksandra Andreyevna pray?' 'For
God's sake, I beseech you!' 'I can't disguise from you,' I
say, 'Aleksandra Andreyevna; you are certainly in danger;
but God is merciful.' 'I shall die, I shall die.' And it seemed
as though she were pleased; her face grew so bright; I was
alarmed. 'Don't be afraid, don't be afraid! I am not frightened of death at all.' She suddenly sat up and leaned on her
elbow. 'Now . . . yes, now I can tell you that I thank you
with my whole heart . . . that you are kind and good—
that I love you! I stare at her, like one possessed; it was
terrible for me, you know. 'Do you hear, I love you!'
'Aleksandra Andreyevna, how have I deserved——' 'No,
no, you don't—you don't understand me.' . . . And suddenly

she stretched out her arms, and taking my head in her hands, she kissed it. . . . Believe me, I almost screamed aloud. . . . I threw myself on my knees, and buried my head in the pillow. She did not speak; her fingers trembled in my hair; I listen; she is weeping. I began to soothe her, to assure her. . . . I really don't know what I did say to her. 'You will wake up the girl,' I say to her; 'Aleksandra Andreyevna, I thank you . . . believe me . . . calm yourself.' 'Enough, enough!' she persisted; 'never mind all of them; let them wake, then; let them come in—it does not matter; I am dying, you see. . . . And what do you fear? why are you afraid? Lift up your head. . . . Or, perhaps, you don't love me; perhaps I am wrong. . . . In that case, forgive me.' 'Aleksandra Andreyevna, what are you saying! . . . I love you, Aleksandra Andreyevna.' She looked straight into my eyes, and opened her arms wide. 'Then take me in your arms.' I tell you frankly, I don't know how it was I did not go mad that night. I feel that my patient is killing herself; I see that she is not fully herself; I understand, too, that if she did not consider herself on the point of death, she would never have thought of me; and, indeed, say what you will, it's hard to die at twenty without having known love; this was what was torturing her; this was why, in despair, she caught at me—do you undersand now? But she held me in her arms, and would not let me go. 'Have pity on me, Aleksandra Andreyevna, and have pity on yourself,' I say. 'Why,' she says; 'what is there to think of? You know I must die.' . . . This she repeated incessantly. . . . . 'If I knew that I should return to life, and be a proper young lady again, I should be ashamed . . . of

'course, ashamed . . . but why now?' 'But who has said you
will die?' 'Oh, no, leave off! you will not deceive me; you
don't know how to lie—look at your face.' . . . 'You shall
live, Aleksandra Andreyevna; I will cure you; we will ask
your mother's blessing . . . we will be united—we will be
happy.' 'No, no, I have your word; I must die . . . you
have promised me . . . you have told me.' . . . It was cruel
for me—cruel for many reasons. And see what trifling
things can do sometimes; it seems nothing at all, but it's
painful. It occurred to her to ask me, what is my name;
not my surname, but my first name. I must needs be so
unlucky as to be called Trifon. Yes, indeed; Trifon Ivanich.
Every one in the house called me doctor. However, there's
no help for it. I say, 'Trifon, madam.' She frowned, shook
her head, and muttered something in French—ah, something unpleasant, of course!—and then she laughed—dis-
agreeably too. Well, I spent the whole night with her in
this way. Before morning I went away, feeling as though
I were mad. When I went again into her room it was daytime, after morning tea. Good God! I could scarcely recognise her; people are laid in their grave looking better than
that. I swear to you, on my honour, I don't understand—
I absolutely don't understand—now, how I lived through
that experience. Three days and nights my patient still
lingered on. And what nights! What things she said to
me! And on the last night—only imagine to yourself—I
was sitting near her, and kept praying to God for one thing
only: 'Take her,' I said, 'quickly, and me with her.' Suddenly the old mother comes unexpectedly into the room. I
had already the evening before told her—the mother—

there was little hope, and it would be well to send for a priest. When the sick girl saw her mother she said: 'It's very well you have come; look at us, we love one another— we have given each other our word.' 'What does she say, doctor? what does she say?' I turned livid. 'She is wandering,' I say; 'the fever.' But she: 'Hush, hush; you told me something quite different just now, and have taken my ring. Why do you pretend? My mother is good—she will forgive—she will understand—and I am dying. . . . I have no need to tell lies; give me your hand.' I jumped up and ran out of the room. The old lady, of course, guessed how it was.

"I will not, however, weary you any longer, and to me too, of course, it's painful to recall all this. My patient passed away the next day. God rest her soul!" the doctor added, speaking quickly and with a sigh. "Before her death she asked her family to go out and leave me alone with her."

" 'Forgive me,' she said; 'I am perhaps to blame towards you . . . my illness . . . but believe me, I have loved no one more than you . . . do not forget me . . . keep my ring.' "

The doctor turned away; I took his hand.

"Ah!" he said, "let us talk of something else, or would you care to play preference for a small stake? It is not for people like me to give way to exalted emotions. There's only one thing for me to think of; how to keep the children from crying and the wife from scolding. Since then, you know, I have had time to enter into lawful wedlock, as they say. . . . Oh . . . I took a merchant's daughter—

seven thousand for her dowry. Her name's Akulina; it goes well with Trifon. She is an ill-tempered woman, I must tell you, but luckily she's asleep all day. . . . Well, shall it be preference?"

We sat down to preference for halfpenny points. Trifon Ivanich won two rubles and a half from me, and went home late, well pleased with his success.

THE CHRISTMAS TREE AND THE WEDDING

By Fiodor M. Dostoyevsky

THE OTHER day I saw a wedding. . . . But no! I would rather tell you about a Christmas tree. The wedding was superb. I liked it immensely. But the other incident was still finer. I don't know why it is that the sight of the wedding reminded me of the Christmas tree. This is the way it happened:

Exactly five years ago, on New Year's Eve, I was invited to a children's ball by a man high up in the business world, who had his connections, his circle of acquaintances, and his intrigues. So it seemed as though the children's ball was merely a pretext for the parents to come together and discuss matters of interest to themselves, quite innocently and casually.

I was an outsider, and, as I had no special matters to air, I was able to spend the evening independently of the others. There was another gentleman present who like myself had just stumbled upon this affair of domestic bliss. He was the first to attract my attention. His appearance was not that of a man of birth or high family. He was tall, rather thin, very serious, and well dressed. Apparently he had no heart for the family festivities. The instant he went off into a corner by himself the smile disappeared from his face, and his thick dark brows knitted into a frown. He knew no one except the host and showed every sign of being bored to death, though bravely sustaining the rôle of thorough enjoyment to the end. Later I learned that he was a provincial, had come to the capital on some important, brain-racking business, had brought a letter of recommendation to our host, and our host had taken him under his protection, not at all *con amore*. It was merely out of politeness that he had invited him to the children's ball.

They did not play cards with him, they did not offer him cigars. No one entered into conversation with him. Possibly they recognised the bird by its feathers from a distance. Thus, my gentleman, not knowing what to do with his hands, was compelled to spend the evening stroking his whiskers. His whiskers were really fine, but he stroked them so assiduously that one got the feeling that the whiskers had come into the world first and afterwards the man in order to stroke them.

There was another guest who interested me. But he was of quite a different order. He was a personage. They called him Julian Mastakovich. At first glance one could tell he was an honoured guest and stood in the same relation to the host as the host to the gentleman of the whiskers. The host and hostess said no end of amiable things to him, were most attentive, wining him, hovering over him, bringing guests up to be introduced, but never leading him to any one else. I noticed tears glisten in our host's eyes when Julian Mastakovich remarked that he had rarely spent such a pleasant evening. Somehow I began to feel uncomfortable in this personage's presence. So, after amusing myself with the children, five of whom, remarkably well-fed young persons, were our host's, I went into a little sitting-room, entirely unoccupied, and seated myself at the end that was a conservatory and took up almost half the room.

The children were charming. They absolutely refused to resemble their elders, notwithstanding the efforts of mothers and governesses. In a jiffy they had denuded the Christmas tree down to the very last sweet and had already succeeded in breaking half of their playthings before they even found out which belonged to whom.

One of them was a particularly handsome little lad, dark-eyed, curly-haired, who stubbornly persisted in aiming at one with his wooden gun. But the child that attracted the greatest attention was his sister, a girl of about eleven, lovely as a Cupid. She was quiet and thoughtful, with large, full, dreamy eyes. The children had somehow offended her, and she left them and walked into the same room that I had withdrawn into. There she seated herself with her doll in a corner.

"Her father is an immensely wealthy business man," the guests informed each other in tones of awe. "Three hundred thousand rubles set aside for her dowry already."

As I turned to look at the group from which I heard this news item issuing, my glance met Julian Mastakovich's. He stood listening to the insipid chatter in an attitude of concentrated attention, with his hands behind his back and his head inclined to one side.

All the while I was quite lost in admiration of the shrewdness our host displayed in the dispensing of the gifts. The little maid of the many-rubled dowry received the handsomest doll, and the rest of the gifts were graded in value according to the diminishing scale of the parents' stations in life. The last child, a tiny chap of ten, thin, red-haired, freckled, came into possession of a small book of nature stories without illustrations or even head and tail pieces. He was the governess's child. She was a poor widow, and her little boy, clad in a sorry-looking little nankeen jacket, looked thoroughly crushed and intimidated. He took the book of nature stories and circled slowly about the children's toys. He would have given anything to play with them. But he did not dare to. You could tell he already knew his place.

I like to observe children. It is fascinating to watch the individuality in them struggling for self-assertion. I could see that the other children's things had tremendous charm for the red-haired boy, especially a toy theatre, in which he was so anxious to take a part that he resolved to fawn upon the other children. He smiled and began to play with them. His one and only apple he handed over to a puffy urchin whose pockets were already crammed with sweets, and he even carried another youngster pickaback—all simply that he might be allowed to stay with the theatre.

But in a few moments an impudent young person fell on him and gave him a pummelling. He did not dare even to cry. The governess came and told him to leave off interfering with the other children's games, and he crept away to the same room the little girl and I were in. She let him sit down beside her, and the two set themselves busily to dressing the expensive doll.

Almost half an hour passed, and I was nearly dozing off, as I sat there in the conservatory half listening to the chatter of the red-haired boy and the dowered beauty, when Julian Mastakovich entered suddenly. He had slipped out of the drawing-room under cover of a noisy scene among the children. From my secluded corner it had not escaped my notice that a few moments before he had been eagerly conversing with the rich girl's father, to whom he had only just been introduced.

He stood still for a while reflecting and mumbling to himself, as if counting something on his fingers.

"Three hundred—three hundred——eleven—twelve—thirteen—sixteen—in five years! Let's say four per cent—five times twelve—sixty, and on these sixty———. Let us assume that in five years it will amount to—well, four hundred. Hm—hm! But the shrewd old fox isn't likely to be satisfied with four per cent. He gets eight or even ten, perhaps. Let's suppose five hundred, five hundred thousand, at least, that's sure. Anything above that for pocket money—hm—"

He blew his nose and was about to leave the room when he spied the girl and stood still. I, behind the plants, escaped his notice. He seemed to me to be quivering with excitement. It must have been his calculations that upset him so. He rubbed his hands and danced from place to place, and kept getting more and more excited. Finally, however, he conquered his emotions and came to a standstill. He cast a determined look at the future bride and wanted to move toward her, but glanced about first. Then, as if with a guilty conscience, he stepped over to the child on tip-toe, smiling, and bent down and kissed her head.

His coming was so unexpected that she uttered a shriek of alarm.

"What are you doing here, dear child?" he whispered, looking around and pinching her cheek.

"We're playing."

"What, with him?" said Julian Mastakovich with a look askance at the governess's child. "You should go into the drawing-room, my lad," he said to him.

The boy remained silent and looked up at the man with wide-open eyes. Julian Mastakovich glanced round again cautiously and bent down over the girl.

"What have you got, a doll, my dear?"

"Yes, sir." The child quailed a little, and her brow wrinkled.

"A doll? And do you know, my dear, what dolls are made of?"

"No, sir," she said weakly, and lowered her head.

"Out of rags, my dear. You, boy, you go back to the drawing-room, to the children," said Julian Mastakovich, looking at the boy sternly.

The two children frowned. They caught hold of each other and would not part.

"And do you know why they gave you the doll?" asked Julian Mastakovich, dropping his voice lower and lower.

"No."

"Because you were a good, very good little girl the whole week."

Saying which, Julian Mastakovich was seized with a paroxysm of agitation. He looked round and said in a tone faint, almost inaudible with excitement and impatience:

"If I come to visit your parents will you love me, my dear?"

He tried to kiss the sweet little creature, but the red-haired boy saw that she was on the verge of tears, and he caught her hand and sobbed out loud in sympathy. That enraged the man.

"Go away! Go away! Go back to the other room, to your playmates."

"I don't want him to. I don't want him to! You go away!" cried the girl. "Let him alone! Let him alone!" She was almost weeping.

There was a sound of footsteps in the doorway. Julian Mastakovich started and straightened up his respectable body. The red-haired boy was even more alarmed. He let go the girl's hand, sidled along the wall, and escaped through the drawing-room into the dining-room.

Not to attract attention, Julian Mastakovich also made for the dining-room. He was red as a lobster. The sight of himself in a mirror seemed to embarrass him. Presumably he was annoyed at his own ardour and impatience. Without due respect to his importance and dignity, his calculations had lured and pricked him to the greedy eagerness of a boy, who makes straight for his object—though this was not as yet an object; it only would be so in five years' time. I followed the worthy man into the dining-room, where I witnessed a remarkable play.

Julian Mastakovich, all flushed with vexation, venom in his look, began to threaten the red-haired boy. The red-haired boy retreated farther and farther until there was no place left for him to retreat to, and he did not know where to turn in his fright.

"Get out of here! What are you doing here? Get out, I say, you good-for-nothing! Stealing fruit, are you? Oh, so, stealing fruit! Get out, you freckle face, go to your likes!"

The frightened child, as a last desperate resort, crawled quickly under the table. His persecutor, completely infuriated, pulled out his large linen handkerchief and used it as a lash to drive the boy out of his position.

Here I must remark that Julian Mastakovich was a somewhat corpulent man, heavy, well-fed, puffy-cheeked, with a paunch and ankles as round as nuts. He perspired and puffed and panted. So strong was his dislike (or was it jealousy?) of the child that he actually began to carry on like a madman.

I laughed heartily. Julian Mastakovich turned. He was utterly confused and for a moment, apparently, quite oblivious of his immense importance. At that moment our host appeared in the doorway opposite. The boy crawled out from under the table and wiped his knees and elbows. Julian Mastakovich hastened to carry his handkerchief, which he had been dangling by the corner, to his nose. Our host looked at the three of us rather suspiciously. But, like a man who knows the world and can readily adjust himself, he seized upon the opportunity to lay hold of his very valuable guest and get what he wanted out of him.

"Here's the boy I was talking to you about," he said, indicating the red-haired child. "I took the liberty of presuming on your goodness in his behalf."

"Oh," replied Julian Mastakovich, still not quite master of himself.

"He's my governess's son," our host continued in a beseeching tone. "She's a poor creature, the widow of an honest official. That's why, if it were possible for you—"

"Impossible, impossible!" Julian Mastakovich cried hastily. "You must excuse me, Philip Alexeyevich, I really cannot. I've made inquiries. There are no vacancies, and there is a waiting list of ten who have a greater right—I'm sorry."

"Too bad," said our host. "He's a quiet, unobtrusive child."

"A very naughty little rascal, I should say," said Julian Mastakovich, wryly "Go away, boy. Why are you here still? Be off with you to the other children."

Unable to control himself, he gave me a sidelong glance. Nor could I control myself. I laughed straight in his face. He turned away and asked our host, in tones quite audible to me, who that odd young fellow was. They whispered to each other and left the room, disregarding me.

I shook with laughter. Then I, too, went to the drawing-room. There the great man, already surrounded by the fathers and mothers and the host and the hostess, had begun to talk eagerly with a lady to whom he had just been introduced. The lady held the rich little girl's hand. Julian Mastakovich went into fulsome praise of her. He waxed ecstatic over the dear child's beauty, her talents, her grace, her excellent breeding, plainly laying himself out to flatter the mother, who listened scarcely able to restrain tears of joy, while the father showed his delight by a gratified smile.

The joy was contagious. Everybody shared in it. Even the

children were obliged to stop playing so as not to disturb the conversation. The atmosphere was surcharged with awe. I heard the mother of the important little girl, touched to her profoundest depths, ask Julian Mastakovich in the choicest language of courtesy, whether he would honour them by coming to see them. I heard Julian Mastakovich accept the invitation with unfeigned enthusiasm. Then the guests scattered decorously to different parts of the room, and I heard them, with veneration in their tones, extol the business man, the business man's wife, the business man's daughter, and, especially, Julian Mastakovich.

"Is he married?" I asked out loud of an acquaintance of mine standing beside Julian Mastakovich.

Julian Mastakovich gave me a venomous look.

"No," answered my acquaintance, profoundly shocked by my—intentional—indiscretion.

.   .   .   .

Not long ago I passed the Church of ——. I was struck by the concourse of people gathered there to witness a wedding. It was a dreary day. A drizzling rain was beginning to come down. I made my way through the throng into the church. The bridegroom was a round, well-fed, pot-bellied little man, very much dressed up. He ran and fussed about and gave orders and arranged things. Finally word was passed that the bride was coming. I pushed through the crowd, and I beheld a marvellous beauty whose first spring was scarcely commencing. But the beauty was pale and sad. She looked distracted. It seemed to me even that her eyes were red from recent weeping. The classic severity of every line of her face imparted a peculiar significance and solemnity to her beauty. But through that severity and solemnity, through the sadness, shone the innocence of a child. There was something inexpressibly naïve, unsettled and young in her features, which, without words, seemed to plead for mercy.

They said she was just sixteen years old. I looked at the bridegroom carefully. Suddenly I recognised Julian Mastakovich, whom I had not seen again in all those five years. Then I looked at the bride again.—Good God! I made my way, as quickly as I could, out of the church. I heard gossiping in the crowd about the bride's wealth—about her dowry of five hundred thousand rubles—so and so much for pocket money.

"Then his calculations were correct," I thought, as I pressed out into the street.

GOD SEES THE TRUTH, BUT WAITS

———◆◆◆———

By Leo N. Tolstoy

IN THE TOWN of Vladimir lived a young merchant named Ivan Dmitrich Aksionov. He had two shops and a house of his own.

Aksionov was a handsome, fair-haired, curly-headed fellow, full of fun, and very fond of singing. When quite a young man he had been given to drink, and was riotous when he had had too much; but after he married he gave up drinking, except now and then.

One summer Aksionov was going to the Nizhny Fair, and as he bade good-bye to his family, his wife said to him, "Ivan Dmitrich, do not start to-day; I have had a bad dream about you."

Aksionov laughed, and said, "You are afraid that when I get to the fair I shall go on a spree."

His wife replied: "I do not know what I am afraid of; all I know is that I had a bad dream. I dreamt you returned from the town, and when you took off your cap I saw that your hair was quite grey."

Aksionov laughed. "That's a lucky sign," said he. "See if I don't sell out all my goods, and bring you some presents from the fair."

So he said good-bye to his family, and drove away.

When he had travelled half-way, he met a merchant whom he knew, and they put up at the same inn for the night. They had some tea together, and then went to bed in adjoining rooms.

It was not Aksionov's habit to sleep late, and, wishing to travel while it was still cool, he aroused his driver before dawn, and told him to put in the horses.

Then he made his way across to the landlord of the inn (who lived in a cottage at the back), paid his bill, and continued his journey.

When he had gone about twenty-five miles, he stopped for the horses to be fed. Aksionov rested awhile in the passage of the inn, then he stepped out into the porch, and, ordering a samovar to be heated, got out his guitar and began to play.

Suddenly a troika drove up with tinkling bells and an official alighted, followed by two soldiers. He came to Aksionov and began to question him, asking him who he was and whence he came. Aksionov answered him fully, and said, "Won't you have some tea with me?" But the official went on cross-questioning him and asking him, "Where did you spend last night? Were you alone, or with a fellow-merchant? Did you see the other merchant this morning? Why did you leave the inn before dawn?"

Aksionov wondered why he was asked all these questions, but he described all that had happened, and then added, "Why do you cross-question me as if I were a thief or a robber? I am travelling on business of my own, and there is no need to question me."

Then the official, calling the soldiers, said, "I am the police-officer of this district, and I question you because the merchant with whom you spent last night has been found with his throat cut. We must search your things."

They entered the house. The soldiers and the police-officer unstrapped Aksionov's luggage and searched it. Suddenly the officer drew a knife out of a bag, crying, "Whose knife is this?"

Aksionov looked, and seeing a blood-stained knife taken from his bag, he was frightened.

"How is it there is blood on this knife?"

Aksionov tried to answer, but could hardly utter a word, and only stammered: "I—don't know—not mine."

Then the police-officer said: "This morning the merchant was found in bed with his throat cut. You are the only person who could have done it. The house was locked from inside, and no one else was there. Here is this blood-stained knife in your bag, and your face and manner betray you! Tell me how you killed him, and how much money you stole?"

Aksionov swore he had not done it; that he had not seen the merchant after they had had tea together; that he had no money except eight thousand rubles of his own, and that the knife was not his. But his voice was broken, his face pale, and he trembled with fear as though he were guilty.

The police-officer ordered the soldiers to bind Aksionov and to put him in the cart. As they tied his feet together and flung him into the cart, Aksionov crossed himself and wept. His money and goods were taken from him, and he was sent to the nearest town and imprisoned there. Enquiries as to his character were made in Vladimir. The merchants and other inhabitants of that town said that in former days he used to drink and waste his time, but that he was a good man. Then the trial came on: he was charged with murdering a merchant from Ryazan, and robbing him of twenty thousand rubles.

His wife was in despair, and did not know what to believe. Her children were all quite small; one was a baby at her breast. Taking them all with her, she went to the town where her husband was in jail. At first she was not allowed to see him; but after much begging, she obtained permission from the officials, and was taken to him. When she saw her husband in prison-dress and in chains, shut up with thieves and criminals, she fell down, and did not come to her senses for a long time. Then she drew her children to her, and sat down near him. She told him of things at home, and asked about what had happened to him. He told her all, and she asked, "What can we do now?"

"We must petition the Czar not to let an innocent man perish."

His wife told him that she had sent a petition to the Czar, but it had not been accepted.

Aksionov did not reply, but only looked downcast.

Then his wife said, "It was not for nothing I dreamt your hair had turned grey. You remember? You should not have started that day." And passing her fingers through his hair, she said: "Vanya dearest, tell your wife the truth; was it not you who did it?"

"So you, too, suspect me!" said Aksionov, and, hiding his face in his hands, he began to weep. Then a soldier came to say that the wife and children must go away; and Aksionov said good-bye to his family for the last time.

When they were gone, Aksionov recalled what had been said, and when he remembered that his wife also had suspected him, he said to himself, "It seems that only God can know the truth; it is to Him alone we must appeal, and from Him alone expect mercy."

And Aksionov wrote no more petitions; gave up all hope, and only prayed to God.

Aksionov was condemned to be flogged and sent to the mines. So he was flogged with a knot, and when the wounds made by the knot were healed, he was driven to Siberia with other convicts.

For twenty-six years Aksionov lived as a convict in Siberia. His hair turned white as snow, and his beard grew long, thin, and grey. All his mirth went; he stooped; he walked slowly, spoke little, and never laughed, but he often prayed.

In prison Aksionov learnt to make boots, and earned a little money, with which he bought *The Lives of the Saints*. He read this book when there was light enough in the prison; and on Sundays in the prison-church he read the lessons and sang in the choir; for his voice was still good.

The prison authorities liked Aksionov for his meekness, and his fellow-prisoners respected him: they called him "Grandfather," and "The Saint." When they wanted to petition the prison authorities about anything, they always made Aksionov their spokesman, and when there were quarrels among the prisoners they came tc him to put things right, and to judge the matter.

No news reached Aksionov from his home, and he did not even know if his wife and children were still alive.

One day a fresh gang of convicts came to the prison. In the evening the old prisoners collected round the new ones and asked them what towns or villages they came from, and what they were sentenced for. Among the rest Aksionov sat down near the newcomers, and listened with downcast air to what was said.

One of the new convicts, a tall, strong man of sixty, with a closely-cropped grey beard, was telling the others what he had been arrested for.

"Well, friends," he said, "'I only took a horse that was tied to a sledge, and I was arrested and accused of stealing. I said I had only taken it to get home quicker, and had then let it go; besides, the driver was a personal friend of mine. So I said, 'It's all right.' 'No,' said they, 'you stole it.' But how or where I stole it they could not say. I once really did something wrong, and ought by rights to have come here long ago, but that time I was not found out. Now I have been sent here for nothing at all. . . . Eh, but it's lies I'm telling you; I've been to Siberia before, but I did not stay long."

"Where are you from?" asked some one.

"From Vladimir. My family are of that town. My name is Makar, and they also call me Semyonich."

Aksionov raised his head and said: "Tell me, Semyonich, do you know anything of the merchants Aksionov of Vladimir? Are they still alive?"

"Know them? Of course I do. The Aksionovs are rich, though their father is in Siberia: a sinner like ourselves, it seems! As for you, Granddad, how did you come here?"

Aksionov did not like to speak of his misfortune. He only sighed, and said, "For my sins I have been in prison these twenty-six years."

"What sins?" asked Makar Semyonich.

But Aksionov only said, "Well, well—I must have deserved it!" He would have said no more, but his companions told the newcomers how Aksionov came to be in Siberia; how some one had killed a merchant, and had put the knife among Aksionov's things, and Aksionov had been unjustly condemned.

When Makar Semyonich heard this, he looked at Aksionov, slapped his own knee, and exclaimed, "Well, this is wonderful! Really wonderful! But how old you've grown, Gran'dad!"

The others asked him why he was so surprised, and where he had seen Aksionov before; but Makar Semyonich did not reply. He only said: "It's wonderful that we should meet here, lads!"

These words made Aksionov wonder whether this man knew who had killed the merchant; so he said, "Perhaps, Semyonich, you have heard of that affair, or maybe you've seen me before?"

"How could I help hearing? The world's full of rumours. But it's a long time ago, and I've forgotten what I heard."

"Perhaps you heard who killed the merchant?" asked Aksionov.

Makar Semyonich laughed, and replied: "It must have

been him in whose bag the knife was found! If some one else hid the knife there, 'He's not a thief till he's caught,' as the saying is. How could any one put a knife into your bag while it was under your head? It would surely have woke you up."

When Aksionov heard these words, he felt sure this was the man who had killed the merchant. He rose and went away. All that night Aksionov lay awake. He felt terribly unhappy, and all sorts of images rose in his mind. There was the image of his wife as she was when he parted from her to go to the fair. He saw her as if she were present; her face and her eyes rose before him; he heard her speak and laugh. Then he saw his children, quite little, as they were at that time: one with a little cloak on, another at his mother's breast. And then he remembered himself as he used to be—young and merry. He remembered how he sat playing the guitar in the porch of the inn where he was arrested, and how free from care he had been. He saw, in his mind, the place where he was flogged, the executioner, and the people standing around; the chains, the convicts, all the twenty-six years of his prison life, and his premature old age. The thought of it all made him so wretched that he was ready to kill himself.

"And it's all that villain's doing!" thought Aksionov. And his anger was so great against Makar Semyonich that he longed for vengeance, even if he himself should perish for it. He kept repeating prayers all night, but could get no peace. During the day he did not go near Makar Semyonich, nor even look at him.

A fortnight passed in this way. Aksionov could not sleep

at night, and was so miserable that he did not know what to do.

One night as he was walking about the prison he noticed some earth that came rolling out from under one of the shelves on which the prisoners slept. He stopped to see what it was. Suddenly Makar Semyonich crept out from under the shelf, and looked up at Aksionov with frightened face. Aksionov tried to pass without looking at him, but Makar seized his hand and told him that he had dug a hole under the wall, getting rid of the earth by putting it into his high-boots, and emptying it out every day on the road when the prisoners were driven to their work.

"Just you keep quiet, old man, and you shall get out too. If you blab, they'll flog the life out of me, but I will kill you first."

Aksionov trembled with anger as he looked at his enemy. He drew his hand away, saying, "I have no wish to escape, and you have no need to kill me; you killed me long ago! As to telling of you—I may do so or not, as God shall direct."

Next day, when the convicts were led out to work, the convoy soldiers noticed that one or other of the prisoners emptied some earth out of his boots. The prison was searched and the tunnel found. The Governor came and questioned all the prisoners to find out who had dug the hole. They all denied any knowledge of it. Those who knew would not betray Makar Semyonich, knowing he would be flogged almost to death. At last the Governor turned to Aksionov whom he knew to be a just man, and said:

"You are a truthful old man; tell me, before God, who dug the hole?"

Makar Semyonich stood as if he were quite unconcerned, looking at the Governor and not so much as glancing at Aksionov. Aksionov's lips and hands trembled, and for a long time he could not utter a word. He thought, "Why should I screen him who ruined my life? Let him pay for what I have suffered. But if I tell, they will probably flog the life out of him, and maybe I suspect him wrongly. And, after all, what good would it be to me?"

"Well, old man," repeated the Governor, "tell me the truth: who has been digging under the wall?"

Aksionov glanced at Makar Semyonich, and said, "I cannot say, your honour. It is not God's will that I should tell! Do what you like with me; I am in your hands."

However much the Governor tried, Aksionov would say no more, and so the matter had to be left.

That night, when Aksionov was lying on his bed and just beginning to doze, some one came quietly and sat down on his bed. He peered through the darkness and recognised Makar.

"What more do you want of me?" asked Aksionov. "Why have you come here?"

Makar Semyonich was silent. So Aksionov sat up and said, "What do you want? Go away, or I will call the guard!"

Makar Semyonich bent close over Aksionov, and whispered, "Ivan Dmitrich, forgive me!"

"What for?" asked Aksionov.

"It was I who killed the merchant and hid the knife

among your things. I meant to kill you too, but I heard a noise outside, so I hid the knife in your bag and escaped out of the window."

Aksionov was silent, and did not know what to say. Makar Semyonich slid off the bed-shelf and knelt upon the ground. "Ivan Dmitrich," said he, "forgive me! For the love of God, forgive me! I will confess that it was I who killed the merchant, and you will be released and can go to your home."

"It is easy for you to talk," said Aksionov, "but I have suffered for you these twenty-six years. Where could I go to now? . . . My wife is dead, and my children have forgotten me. I have nowhere to go. . . ."

Makar Semyonich did not rise, but beat his head on the floor. "Ivan Dmitrich, forgive me!" he cried. "When they flogged me with the knot it was not so hard to bear as it is to see you now . . . yet you had pity on me, and did not tell. For Christ's sake forgive me, wretch that I am!" And he began to sob.

When Aksionov heard him sobbing he, too, began to weep.

"God will forgive you!" said he. "Maybe I am a hundred times worse than you." And at these words his heart grew light, and the longing for home left him. He no longer had any desire to leave the prison, but only hoped for his last hour to come.

In spite of what Aksionov had said, Makar Semyonich confessed his guilt. But when the order for his release came, Aksionov was already dead.

HOW A MUZHIK FED TWO
OFFICIALS

———— ◆◆◆ ————

By. M. Y. Saltykov
(N. Shchedrin)

ONCE UPON a time there were two Officials. They were
both empty-headed, and so they found themselves one day
suddenly transported to an uninhabited isle, as if on a
magic carpet.

They had passed their whole life in a Government Department, where records were kept; had been born there,
bred there, grown old there, and consequently hadn't the
least understanding for anything outside of the Department; and the only words they knew were: "With assurances of the highest esteem, I am your humble servant."

But the Department was abolished, and as the services
of the two Officials were no longer needed, they were given
their freedom. So the retired Officials migrated to Podyacheskaya Street in St. Petersburg. Each had his own home,
his own cook and his pension.

Waking up on the uninhabited isle, they found themselves lying under the same cover. At first, of course, they
couldn't understand what had happened to them, and they
spoke as if nothing extraordinary had taken place.

"What a peculiar dream I had last night, your Excel-

lency," said the one Official. "It seemed to me as if I were
on an uninhabited isle."

Scarcely had he uttered the words, when he jumped to
his feet. The other Official also jumped up.

"Good Lord, what does this mean! Where are we?" they
cried out in astonishment.

They felt each other to make sure that they were no
longer dreaming, and finally convinced themselves of the
sad reality.

Before them stretched the ocean, and behind them was a
little spot of earth, beyond which the ocean stretched again.
They began to cry—the first time since their Department
had been shut down.

They looked at each other, and each noticed that the
other was clad in nothing but his night shirt with his order
hanging about his neck.

"We really should be having our coffee now," observed
the one Official. Then he bethought himself again of the
strange situation he was in and a second time fell to
weeping.

"What are we going to do now?" he sobbed. "Even supposing we were to draw up a report, what good would
that do?"

"You know what, your Excellency," replied the other
Official, "you go to the east and I will go to the west.
Toward evening we will come back here again, and, per-
haps, we shall have found something."

They started to ascertain which was the east and which
was the west. They recalled that the head of their Department had once said to them, "If you want to know where

the east is, then turn your face to the north, and the east will be on your right." But when they tried to find out which was the north, they turned to the right and to the left and looked around on all sides. Having spent their whole life in the Department of Records, their efforts were all in vain.

"To my mind, your Excellency, the best thing to do would be for you to go to the right and me to go to the left," said one Official, who had served not only in the Department of Records, but had also been teacher of hand-writing in the School for Reserves, and so was a little bit cleverer.

So said, so done. The one Official went to the right. He came upon trees bearing all sorts of fruits. Gladly would he have plucked an apple, but they all hung so high that he would have been obliged to climb up. He tried to climb up in vain. All he succeeded in doing was tearing his night shirt. Then he struck upon a brook. It was swarm-ing with fish.

"Wouldn't it be wonderful if we had all this fish in Podyacheskaya Street!" he thought, and his mouth watered. Then he entered woods and found partridges, grouse and hares.

"Good Lord, what an abundance of food!" he cried. His hunger was going up tremendously.

But he had to return to the appointed spot with empty hands. He found the other Official waiting for him.

"Well, Your Excellency, how went it? Did you find any-thing?"

"Nothing but an old number of the *Moscow Gazette,* not another thing."

The Officials lay down to sleep again, but their empty stomachs gave them no rest. They were partly robbed of their sleep by the thought of who was now enjoying their pension, and partly by the recollection of the fruit, fishes, partridges, grouse and hares that they had seen during the day.

"The human pabulum in its original form flies, swims and grows on trees. Who would have thought it your Excellency?" said the one Official.

"To be sure," rejoined the other Official. "I, too, must admit that I had imagined that our breakfast rolls came into the world just as they appear on the table."

"From which it is to be deduced that if we want to eat a pheasant, we must catch it first, kill it, pull its feathers and roast it. But how's that to be done?"

"Yes, how's that to be done?" repeated the other Official.

They turned silent and tried again to fall asleep, but their hunger scared sleep away. Before their eyes swarmed flocks of pheasants and ducks, herds of porklings, and they were all so juicy, done so tenderly and garnished so deliciously with olives, capers and pickles.

"I believe I could devour my own boots now," said the one Official.

"Gloves are not bad either, especially if they have been born quite mellow," said the other Official.

The two Officials stared at each other fixedly. In their glances gleamed an evil-boding fire, their teeth chattered and a dull groaning issued from their breasts. Slowly they crept upon each other and suddenly they burst into a fearful frenzy. There was a yelling and groaning, the rags flew about, and the Official who had been teacher of handwriting bit off his colleague's order and swallowed it. However, the sight of blood brought them both back to their senses.

"God help us!" they cried at the same time. "We certainly don't mean to eat each other up. How could we have come to such a pass as this? What evil genius is making sport of us?"

"We must, by all means, entertain each other to pass the time away, otherwise there will be murder and death," said the one Official.

"You begin," said the other.

"Can you explain why it is that the sun first rises and then sets? Why isn't it the reverse?"

"Aren't you a funny man, your Excellency? You get up first, then you go to your office and work there, and at night you lie down to sleep."

"But why can't one assume the opposite, that is, that one goes to bed, sees all sorts of dream figures, and then gets up?"

"Well, yes, certainly. But when I was still an Official, I always thought this way: 'Now it is dawn, then it will be day, then will come supper, and finally will come the time to go to bed.'"

The word "supper" recalled that incident in the day's doings, and the thought of it made both Officials melancholy, so that the conversation came to a halt.

"A doctor once told me that human beings can sustain themselves for a long time on their own juices," the one Official began again.

"What does that mean?"

"It is quite simple. You see, one's own juices generate other juices, and these in their turn still other juices, and so it goes on until finally all the juices are consumed."

"And then what happens?"

"Then food has to be taken into the system again."

"The devil!"

"No matter what topic the Officials chose, the conversation invariably reverted to the subject of eating; which only increased their appetite more and more. So they decided to give up talking altogether, and, recollecting the *Moscow Gazette* that the one of them had found, they picked it up and began to read it eagerly.

BANQUET GIVEN BY THE MAYOR

"The table was set for one hundred persons. The magnificence of it exceeded all expectations. The remotest provinces were represented at this feast of the gods by the costliest gifts. The golden sturgeon from Sheksna and the silver pheasant from the Caucasian woods held a rendezvous with strawberries so seldom to be had in our latitude in winter. . . ."

"The devil! For God's sake, stop reading, your Excellency. Couldn't you find something else to read about?" cried the other Official in sheer desperation. He snatched the paper from his colleague's hands, and started to read something else.

"Our correspondent in Tula informs us that yesterday a sturgeon was found in the Upa (an event which even the oldest inhabitants cannot recall, and all the more remarkable since they recognised the former police captain in this sturgeon). This was made the occasion for giving a banquet in the club. The prime cause of the banquet was served in a large wooden platter garnished with vinegar pickles. A bunch of parsley stuck out of its mouth. Doctor P—— who acted as toast-master saw to it that everybody present got a piece of the sturgeon. The sauces to go with it were unusually varied and delicate——"

"Permit me, your Excellency, it seems to me you are not so careful either in the selection of reading matter," interrupted the first Official, who secured the *Gazette* again and started to read:

"One of the oldest inhabitants of Viatka has discovered a new and highly original recipe for fish soup. A live codfish (*lota vulgaris*) is taken and beaten with a rod until its liver swells up with anger. . . ."

The Officials' heads drooped. Whatever their eyes fell upon had something to do with eating. Even their own thoughts were fatal. No matter how much they tried to keep their minds off beefsteak and the like, it was all in vain; their fancy returned invariably, with irresistible force, back to that for which they were so painfully yearning.

Suddenly an inspiration came to the Official who had once taught handwriting.

"I have it!" he cried delightedly. "What do you say to this, your Excellency? What do you say to our finding a muzhik?"

"A muzhik, your Excellency? What sort of a muzhik?"

"Why a plain ordinary muzhik. A muzhik like all other muzhiks. He would get the breakfast rolls for us right away, and he could also catch partridges and fish for us."

"Hm, a muzhik. But where are we to fetch one from, if there is no muzhik here?"

"Why shouldn't there be a muzhik here? There are muzhiks everywhere. All one has to do is hunt for them. There certainly must be a muzhik hiding here somewhere so as to get out of working."

This thought so cheered the Officials that they instantly jumped up to go in search of a muzhik.

For a long while they wandered about on the island without the desired result, until finally a concentrated smell of black bread and old sheep skin assailed their nostrils and guided them in the right direction. There under a tree was a colossal muzhik lying fast asleep with his hands under his head. It was clear that to escape his duty to work he had impudently withdrawn to this island. The indignation of the Officials knew no bounds.

"What, lying asleep here, you lazy-bones you!" they raged at him. "It is nothing to you that there are two Officials here who are fairly perishing of hunger. Up, forward, march, work."

The Muzhik rose and looked at the two severe gentlemen standing in front of him. His first thought was to make his escape, but the Officials held him fast.

He had to submit to his fate. He had to work.

First he climbed up on a tree and plucked several dozen of the finest apples for the Officials. He kept a rotten one for himself. Then he turned up the earth and dug out some potatoes. Next he started a fire with two bits of wood that he rubbed against each other. Out of his own hair he made a snare and caught partridges. Over the fire, by this time burning brightly, he cooked so many kinds of food that the question arose in the Officials' minds whether they shouldn't give some to this idler.

Beholding the efforts of the Muzhik, they rejoiced in their hearts. They had already forgotten how the day before they had nearly been perishing of hunger, and all they thought of now was: "What a good thing it is to be an Official. Nothing bad can ever happen to an Official."

"Are you satisfied, gentlemen?" the lazy Muzhik asked.

"Yes, we appreciate your industry," replied the Officials.

"Then you will permit me to rest a little?"

"Go take a little rest, but first make a good strong cord."

The Muzhik gathered wild hemp stalks, laid them in water, beat them and broke them, and toward evening a good stout cord was ready. The Officials took the cord and bound the Muzhik to a tree, so that he should not run away. Then they laid themselves to sleep.

Thus day after day passed, and the Muzhik became so skilful that he could actually cook soup for the Officials in his bare hands. The Officials had become round and well-fed and happy. It rejoiced them that here they needn't spend any money and that in the meanwhile their pensions were accumulating in St. Petersburg.

"What is your opinion, your Excellency," one said to the other after breakfast one day, "is the Story of the

Tower of Babel true? Don't you think it is simply an allegory?"

"By no means, your Excellency, I think it was something that really happened. What other explanation is there for the existence of so many different languages on earth?"

"Then the Flood must really have taken place, too?"

"Certainly, else how would you explain the existence of Antediluvian animals? Besides, the *Moscow Gazette* says——"

They made search for the old number of the *Moscow Gazette,* seated themselves in the shade, and read the whole sheet from beginning to end. They read of festivities in Moscow, Tula, Penza and Riazan, and strangely enough felt no discomfort at the description of the delicacies served.

There is no saying how long this life might have lasted. Finally, however, it began to bore the Officials. They often thought of their cooks in St. Petersburg, and even shed a few tears in secret.

"I wonder how it looks in Podyacheskaya Street now, your Excellency," one of them said to the other.

"Oh, don't remind me of it, your Excellency. I am pining away with homesickness."

"It is very nice here. There is really no fault to be found with this place, but the lamb longs for its mother sheep. And it is a pity, too, for the beautiful uniforms."

"Yes, indeed, a uniform of the fourth class is no joke. The gold embroidery alone is enough to make one dizzy."

Now they began to importune the Muzhik to find some

way of getting them back to Podyacheskaya Street, and strange to say, the Muzhik even knew where Podyacheskaya Street was. He had once drunk beer and mead there, and as the saying goes, everything had run down his beard, alas, but nothing into his mouth. The Officials rejoiced and said: "We are Officials from Podyacheskaya Street."

"And I am one of those men—do you remember?—who sit on a scaffolding hung by ropes from the roofs and paint the outside walls. I am one of those who crawl about on the roofs like flies. That is what I am," replied the Muzhik.

The Muzhik now pondered long and heavily on how to give great pleasure to his Officials, who had been so gracious to him, the lazy-bones, and had not scorned his work. And he actually succeeded in constructing a ship. It was not really a ship, but still it was a vessel that would carry them across the ocean close to Podyacheskaya Street.

"Now, take care, you dog, that you don't drown us," said the Officials, when they saw the raft rising and falling on the waves.

"Don't be afraid. We muzhiks are used to this," said the Muzhik, making all the preparations for the journey. He gathered swan's-down and made a couch for his two Officials, then he crossed himself and rowed off from shore.

How frightened the Officials were on the way, how seasick they were during the storms, how they scolded the coarse Muzhik for his idleness, can neither be told nor described. The Muzhik, however, just kept rowing on and fed his Officials on herring. At last, they caught sight of dear old Mother Neva. Soon they were in the glorious

Catherine Canal, and then, oh joy! they struck the grand Podyacheskaya Street. When the cooks saw their Officials so well-fed, round and so happy, they rejoiced immensely. The Officials drank coffee and rolls, then put on their uniforms and drove to the Pension Bureau. How much money they collected there is another thing that can neither be told nor described. Nor was the Muzhik forgotten. The Officials sent a glass of whiskey out to him and five kopeks.

Now, Muzhik, rejoice.

THE SHADES, A PHANTASY

◆◆◆

By Vladimir G. Korolenko

I

A MONTH and two days had elapsed since the judges, amid the loud acclaim of the Athenian people, had pronounced the death sentence against the philosopher Socrates because he had sought to destroy faith in the gods. What the gadfly is to the horse Socrates was to Athens. The gadfly stings the horse in order to prevent it from dozing off and to keep it moving briskly on its course. The philosopher said to the people of Athens:

"I am your gadfly. My sting pricks your conscience and arouses you when you are caught napping. Sleep not, sleep not, people of Athens; awake and seek the truth!"

The people arose in their exasperation and cruelly demanded to be rid of their gadfly.

"Perchance both of his accusers, Meletus and Anytus, are wrong," said the citizens, on leaving the court after sentence had been pronounced.

"But after all whither do his doctrines tend? What would he do? He has wrought confusion, he overthrows beliefs that have existed since the beginning, he speaks of new virtues which must be recognised and sought for, he

speaks of a Divinity hitherto unknown to us. The blasphemer, he deems himself wiser than the gods! No, 'twere
better we remain true to the old gods whom we know
They may not always be just, sometimes they may flare up
in unjust wrath, and they may also be seized with a wan-
ton lust for the wives of mortals; but did not our ancestors
live with them in the peace of their souls, did not our
forefathers accomplish their heroic deeds with the help of
these very gods? And now the faces of the Olympians have
paled and the old virtue is out of joint. What does it all
lead to? Should not an end be put to this impious wisdom
once for all?"

Thus the citizens of Athens spoke to one another as they
left the place, and the blue twilight was falling. They had
determined to kill the restless gadfly in the hope that the
countenances of the gods would shine again. And yet—
before their souls arose the mild figure of the singular
philosopher. There were some citizens who recalled how
courageously he had shared their troubles and dangers at
Potidæa; how he alone had prevented them from committing the sin of unjustly executing the generals after the
victory over the Arginusæ; how he alone had dared to
raise his voice against the tyrants who had had fifteen
hundred people put to death, speaking to the people on the
market-place concerning shepherds and their sheep.

"Is not he a good shepherd," he asked, "who guards his
flock and watches over its increase? Or is it the work of
the good shepherd to reduce the number of his sheep and
disperse them, and of the good ruler to do the same with
his people? Men of Athens, let us investigate this question!"

And at this question of the solitary, undefended philosopher, the faces of the tyrants paled, while the eyes of the youths kindled with the fire of just wrath and indignation.

Thus, when on dispersing after the sentence the Athenians recalled all these things of Socrates, their hearts were oppressed with heavy doubt.

"Have we not done a cruel wrong to the son of Sophroniscus?"

But then the good Athenians looked upon the harbour and the sea, and in the red glow of the dying day they saw the purple sails of the sharp-keeled ship, sent to the Delian festival, shimmering in the distance on the blue Pontus. The ship would not return until the expiration of a month, and the Athenians recollected that during this time no blood might be shed in Athens, whether the blood of the innocent or the guilty. A month, moreover, has many days and still more hours. Supposing the son of Sophroniscus had been unjustly condemned, who would hinder his escaping from the prison, especially since he had numerous friends to help him? Was it so difficult for the rich Plato, for Æschines and others to bribe the guards? Then the restless gadfly would flee from Athens to the barbarians in Thessaly, or to the Peloponnesus, or, still farther, to Egypt; Athens would no longer hear his blasphemous speeches; his death would not weigh upon the conscience of the worthy citizens, and so everything would end for the best of all.

Thus said many to themselves that evening, while aloud they praised the wisdom of the demos and the heliasts. In secret, however, they cherished the hope that the restless philosopher would leave Athens, fly from the hemlock to the barbarians, and so free the Athenians of his troublesome presence and of the pangs of conscience that smote them for inflicting death upon an innocent man.

Two and thirty times since that evening had the sun risen from the ocean and dipped down into it again. The ship had returned from Delos and lay in the harbour with sadly drooping sails, as if ashamed of its native city. The moon did not shine in the heavens, the sea heaved under a heavy fog, and on the hills lights peered through the obscurity like the eyes of men gripped by a sense of guilt.

The stubborn Socrates did not spare the conscience of the good Athenians.

"We part! You go home and I go to death," he said to the judges after the sentence had been pronounced. "I know not, my friends, which of us chooses the better lot!"

As the time had approached for the return of the ship, many of the citizens had begun to feel uneasy. Must that obstinate fellow really die? And they began to appeal to the consciences of Æschines, Phædo, and other pupils of Socrates, trying to urge them on to further efforts for their master.

"Will you permit your teacher to die?" they asked reproachfully in biting tones. "Or do you grudge the few coins it would take to bribe the guard?"

In vain Crito besought Socrates to take to flight, and complained that the public was upbraiding his disciples with lack of friendship and with avarice. The self-willed philosopher refused to gratify his pupils or the good people of Athens.

"Let us investigate," he said. "If it turns out that I must flee, I will flee; but if I must die, I will die. Let us remember what we once said—the wise man need not fear death, he need fear nothing but falsehood. Is it right to abide by the laws we ourselves have made so long as they are agreeable to us, and refuse to obey those which are disagreeable? If my memory does not deceive me, I believe we once spoke of these things, did we not?"

"Yes, we did," answered his pupil.

"And I think all were agreed as to the answer?"

"Yes."

"But perhaps what is true for others is not true for us?"

"No, truth is alike for all, including ourselves."

"But perhaps when *we* must die and not some one else, truth becomes untruth?"

"No, Socrates, truth remains the truth under all circumstances."

After his pupil had thus agreed to each premise of Socrates in turn, he smiled and drew his conclusion.

"If that is so, my friend, mustn't I die? Or has my head already become so weak that I am no longer in a condition to draw a logical conclusion? Then correct me, my friend, and show my erring brain the right way."

His pupil covered his face with his mantle and turned aside.

"Yes," he said, "now I see you must die."

And on that evening, when the sea tossed hither and thither and roared dully under the load of fog, and the whimsical wind in mournful astonishment gently stirred the sails of the ships; when the citizens meeting on the streets asked one another: "Is he dead?" and their voices timidly betrayed the hope that he was not dead; when the first breath of awakened conscience touched the hearts of the Athenians like the first messenger of the storm; and when, it seemed, the very faces of the gods were darkened with shame—on that evening at the sinking of the sun the self-willed man drank the cup of death!

The wind increased in violence and shrouded the city more closely in the veil of mist, angrily tugging at the sails of the vessels delayed in the harbour. And the Erinyes sang their gloomy songs to the hearts of the citizens and whipped up in their breasts that tempest which was later to overwhelm the denouncers of Socrates.

But in that hour the first stirrings of regret were still uncertain and confused. The citizens found more fault with Socrates than ever because he had not given them the satisfaction of fleeing to Thessaly; they were annoyed with his pupils because in the last days they had walked about in sombre mourning attire, a living reproach to the Athenians; they were vexed with the judges because they had not had the sense and the courage to resist the blind rage of the excited people; they bore even the gods' resentment.

"To you, ye gods, have we brought this sacrifice," spoke many. "Rejoice, ye unsatiable!"

"I know not which of us chooses the better lot!"

Those words of Socrates came back to their memory, those his last words to the judges and to the people gathered in the court. Now he lay in the prison quiet and motionless under his cloak, while over the city hovered mourning, horror, and shame.

Again he became the tormentor of the city, he who was himself no longer accessible to torment. The gadfly had been killed, but it stung the people more sharply than ever —sleep not, sleep not this night, O men of Athens! Sleep not! You have committed an injustice, a cruel injustice, which can never be erased!

II

DURING THOSE sad days Xenophon, the general, a pupil of Socrates, was marching with his Ten Thousand in a distant land, amid dangers, seeking a way of return to his beloved fatherland.

Æschines, Crito, Critobulus, Phædo, and Apollodorus were now occupied with the preparations for the modest funeral.

Plato was burning his lamp and bending over a parchment; the best disciple of the philosopher was busy inscribing the deeds, words, and teachings that marked the end of the sage's life. A thought is never lost, and the truth discovered by a great intellect illumines the way for future generations like a torch in the dark.

There was one other disciple of Socrates. Not long before, the impetuous Ctesippus had been one of the most frivolous and pleasure-seeking of the Athenian youths. He had set up beauty as his sole god, and had bowed before Clinias as its highest exemplar. But since he had become acquainted with Socrates, all desire for pleasure and all light-mindedness had gone from him. He looked on indifferently while others took his place with Clinias. The grace of thought and the harmony of spirit that he found in Socrates seemed a hundred times more attractive than the graceful form and the harmonious features of Clinias. With all the intensity of his stormy temperament he hung on the man who had disturbed the serenity of his virginal soul, which for the first time opened to doubts as the bud of a young oak opens to the fresh winds of spring.

Now that the master was dead, he could find peace neither at his own hearth nor in the oppressive stillness of the streets, nor among his friends and fellow-disciples. The gods of hearth and home and the gods of the people inspired him with repugnance.

"I know not," he said, "whether ye are the best of all the gods to whom numerous generations have burned incense and brought offerings; all I know is that for your sake the blind mob extinguished the clear torch of truth, and for your sake sacrificed the greatest and best of mortals!"

It almost seemed to Ctesippus as though the streets and market-places still echoed with the shrieking of that unjust sentence. And he remembered how it was here that the people clamoured for the execution of the generals who had led them to victory against the Argunisæ, and how Socrates alone had opposed the savage sentence of the judges and the blind rage of the mob. But when Socrates himself needed a champion, no one had been found to defend him with equal strength. Ctesippus blamed himself and his friends, and for that reason he wanted to avoid everybody —even himself, if possible.

That evening he went to the sea. But his grief grew only the more violent. It seemed to him that the mourning daughters of Nereus were tossing hither and thither on the shore bewailing the death of the best of the Athenians and the folly of the frenzied city. The waves broke on the rocky coast with a growl of lament. Their booming sounded like a funeral dirge.

He turned away, left the shore, and went on further without looking before him. He forgot time and space and his own ego, filled only with the afflicting thought of Socrates.

"Yesterday he still was, yesterday his mild words still could be heard. How is it possible that to-day he no longer is? O night, O giant mountain shrouded in mist, O heaving sea moved by your own life, O restless winds that carry the breath of an immeasurable world on your wings, O starry vault flecked with flying clouds—take me to you, disclose to me the mystery of this death, if it is revealed to you! And if ye know not, then grant my ignorant soul your own lofty indifference. Remove from me these torturing questions. I no longer have strength to carry them in my bosom without an answer, without even the hope of an answer. For who shall answer them, now that the lips of Socrates are sealed in eternal silence, and eternal darkness is laid upon his lids?"

Thus Ctesippus cried out to the sea and the mountains, and to the dark night, which followed its invariable course, ceaselessly, invisibly, over the slumbering world. Many hours passed before Ctesippus glanced up and saw whither his steps had unconsciously led him. A dark horror seized his soul as he looked about him.

III

IT SEEMED as if the unknown gods of eternal night had heard his impious prayer. Ctesippus looked about, without being able to recognise the place where he was. The lights of the city had long been extinguished by the darkness. The roaring of the sea had died away in the distance; his anxious soul had even lost the recollection of having heard it. No single sound—no mournful cry of nocturnal bird, nor whirr of wings, nor rustling of trees, nor murmur of a merry stream—broke the deep silence. Only the blind will-o'-the-wisps flickered here and there over rocks, and sheet-lightning, unaccompanied by any sound, flared up and died down against crag-peaks. This brief illumination merely emphasised the darkness; and the dead light disclosed the outlines of dead deserts crossed by gorges like crawling serpents, and rising into rocky heights in a wild chaos.

All the joyous gods that haunt green groves, purling brooks, and mountain valleys seemed to have fled forever from these deserts. Pan alone, the great and mysterious Pan, was hiding somewhere nearby in the chaos of nature, and with mocking glance seemed to be pursuing the tiny ant that a short time before had blasphemously asked to know the secret of the world and of death. Dark, senseless horror overwhelmed the soul of Ctesippus. It is thus that the sea in stormy floodtide overwhelms a rock on the shore.

Was it a dream, was it reality, or was it the revelation of

the unknown divinity? Ctesippus felt that in an instant he would step across the threshold of life, and that his soul would melt into an ocean of unending, inconceivable horror like a drop of rain in the waves of the grey sea on a dark and stormy night. But at this moment he suddenly heard voices that seemed familiar to him, and in the glare of the sheet-lightning his eyes recognised human figures.

IV

ON A ROCKY slope sat a man in deep despair. He had thrown a cloak over his head and was bowed to the ground. Another figure approached him softly, cautiously climbing upward and carefully feeling every step. The first man uncovered his face and exclaimed:

"Is that you I just now saw, my good Socrates? Is that you passing by me in this cheerless place? I have already spent many hours here without knowing when day will relieve the night. I have been waiting in vain for the dawn."

"Yes, I am Socrates, my friend, and you, are you not Elpidias who died three days before me?"

"Yes, I am Elpidias, formerly the richest tanner in Athens, now the most miserable of slaves. For the first time I understand the words of the poet: 'Better to be a slave in this world than a ruler in gloomy Hades.'"

"My friend, if it is disagreeable for you where you are, why don't you move to another spot?"

"O Socrates, I marvel at you—how dare you wander about in this cheerless gloom? I—I sit here overcome with grief and bemoan the joys of a fleeting life."

"Friend Elpidias, like you, I, too, was plunged in this gloom when the light of earthly life was removed from my eyes. But an inner voice told me: 'Tread this new path without hesitation,' and I went."

"But whither do you go, O son of Sophroniscus? Here there is no way, no path, not even a ray of light; nothing but a chaos of rocks, mist, and gloom."

"True. But, my Elpidias, since you are aware of this sad truth, have you not asked yourself what is the most distressing thing in your present situation?"

"Undoubtedly the dismal darkness."

"Then one should seek for light. Perchance you will find here the great law—that mortals must in darkness seek the source of life. Do you not think it is better so to seek than to remain sitting in one spot? *I* think it is, therefore I keep walking. Farewell!"

"Oh, good Socrates, abandon me not! You go with sure steps through the pathless chaos in Hades. Hold out to me but a fold of your mantle——"

"If you think it is better for you, too, then follow me, friend Elpidias."

And the two shades walked on, while the soul of Ctesippus, released by sleep from its mortal envelop, flew after them, greedily absorbing the tones of the clear Socratic speech.

"Are you here, good Socrates?" the voice of the Athenian again was heard. "Why are you silent? Converse shortens the way, and I swear, by Hercules, never did I have to traverse such a horrid way."

"Put questions, friend Elpidias! The question of one

who seeks knowledge brings forth answers and produces conversation."

Elpidias maintained silence for a moment, and then, after he had collected his thoughts, asked:

"Yes, this is what I wanted to say—tell me, my poor Socrates, did they at least give you a good burial?"

"I must confess, friend Elpidias, I cannot satisfy your curiosity."

"I understand, my poor Socrates, it doesn't help you cut a figure. Now with me it was so different! Oh, how they buried me, how magnificently they buried me, my poor fellow-wanderer! I still think with great pleasure of those lovely moments after my death. First they washed me and sprinkled me with well-smelling balsam. Then my faithful Larissa dressed me in garments of the finest weave. The best mourning-women of the city tore their hair from their heads because they had been promised good pay, and in the family vault they placed an amphora—a crater with beautiful, decorated handles of bronze, and, besides, a vial——"

"Stay, friend Elpidias. I am convinced that the faithful Larissa converted her love into several minas. Yet——"

"Exactly ten minas and four drachmas, not counting the drinks for the guests. I hardly think that the richest tanner can come before the souls of his ancestors and boast of such respect on the part of the living."

"Friend Elpidias, don't you think that money would have been of more use to the poor people who are still alive in Athens than to you at this moment?"

"Admit, Socrates, you are speaking in envy," responded

Elpidias, pained. "I am sorry for you, unfortunate Socrates, although, between ourselves, you really deserved your fate. I myself in the family circle said more than once that an end ought to be put to your impious doings, because——"

"Stay, friend, I thought you wanted to draw a conclusion, and I fear you are straying from the straight path. Tell me, my good friend, whither does your wavering thought tend?"

"I wanted to say that in my goodness I am sorry for you. A month ago I myself spoke against you in the assembly, but truly none of us who shouted so loud wanted such a great ill to befall you. Believe me, now I am all the sorrier for you, unhappy philosopher!"

"I thank you. But tell me, my friend, do you perceive a brightness before your eyes?"

"No, on the contrary such darkness lies before me that I must ask myself whether this is not the misty region of Orcus."

"This way, therefore, is just as dark for you as for me?"

"Quite right."

"If I am not mistaken, you are even holding on to the folds of my cloak?"

"Also true."

"Then we are in the same position? You see your ancestors are not hastening to rejoice in the tale of your pompous burial. Where is the difference between us, my good friend?"

"But, Socrates, have the gods enveloped your reason in such obscurity that the difference is not clear to you?"

"Friend, if your situation is clearer to you, then give me

your hand and lead me, for I swear, by the dog, you let me go ahead in this darkness."

"Cease your scoffing, Socrates! Do not make sport, and do not compare yourself, your godless self, with a man who died in his own bed——"

"Ah, I believe I am beginning to understand you. But tell me, Elpidias, do you hope ever again to rejoice in your bed?"

"Oh, I think not."

"And was there ever a time when you did not sleep in it?"

"Yes. That was before I bought goods from Agesilaus at half their value. You see, that Agesilaus is really a deep-dyed rogue——"

"Ah, never mind about Agesilaus! Perhaps he is getting them back from your widow at a quarter their value. Then wasn't I right when I said that you were in possession of your bed only part of the time?"

"Yes, you were right."

"Well, and I, too, was in possession of the bed in which I died part of the time. Proteus, the good guard of the prison, lent it to me for a period."

"Oh, if I had known what you were aiming at with your talk, I wouldn't have answered your wily questions. By Hercules, such profanation is unheard of—he compares himself with me! Why, I could put an end to you with two words, if it came to it——"

"Say them, Elpidias, without fear. Words can scarcely be more destructive to me than the hemlock."

Well, then, that is just what I wanted to say. You unfortunate man, you died by the sentence of the court and had to drink hemlock!"

"But I have known that since the day of my death, even long before. And you, unfortunate Elpidias, tell me what caused your death?"

"Oh, with me it was different, entirely different! You see I got the dropsy in my abdomen. An expensive physician from Corinth was called who promised to cure me for two minas, and he was given half that amount in advance. I am afraid that Larissa in her lack of experience in such things gave him the other half, too——"

"Then the physician did not keep his promise?"

"That's it."

"And you died from dropsy?"

"Ah, Socrates, believe me, three times it wanted to vanquish me, and finally it quenched the flame of my life!"

"Then tell me—did death by dropsy give you great pleasure?"

"Oh, wicked Socrates, don't make sport of me. I told you it wanted to vanquish me three times. I bellowed like a steer under the knife of the slaughterer, and begged the Parcæ to cut the thread of my life as quickly as possible."

"That doesn't surprise me. But from what do you conclude that the dropsy was pleasanter to you than the hemlock to me? The hemlock made an end of me in a moment."

"I see, I fell into your snare again, you crafty sinner! I won't enrage the gods still more by speaking with you, you destroyer of sacred customs."

Both were silent, and quiet reigned. But in a short while Elpidias was again the first to begin a conversation.

"Why are you silent, good Socrates?"

"My friend; didn't you yourself ask for silence?"

"I am not proud, and I can treat men who are worse than I am considerately. Don't let us quarrel."

"I did not quarrel with you, friend Elpidias, and did not wish to say anything to insult you. I am merely accustomed to get at the truth of things by comparisons. My situation is not clear to me. You consider your situation better, and I should be glad to learn why. On the other hand, it would not hurt you to learn the truth, whatever shape it may take."

"Well, no more of this."

"Tell me, are you afraid? I don't think that the feeling I now have can be called fear."

"I am afraid, although I have less cause than you to be at odds with the gods. But don't you think that the gods, in abandoning us to ourselves here in this chaos, have cheated us of our hopes?"

"That depends upon what sort of hopes they were. What did you expect from the gods, Elpidias?"

"Well, well, what did I expect from the gods! What curious questions you ask, Socrates! If a man throughout life brings offerings, and at his death passes away with a pious heart and with all that custom demands, the gods might at least send some one to meet him, at least one of the inferior gods, to show a man the way. . . . But that reminds me. Many a time when I begged for good luck in traffic in hides, I promised Hermes calves——"

"And you didn't have luck?"

"Oh, yes, I had luck, good Socrates, but——"

"I understand, you had no calf."

"Bah! Socrates, a rich tanner and not have calves?"

"Now I understand. You had luck, had calves, but **you** kept them for yourself, and Hermes received nothing."

"You're a clever man. I've often said so. I kept only three of my ten oaths, and I didn't deal differently with the other gods. If the same is the case with you, isn't that the reason, possibly, why we are now abandoned by the gods? To be sure, I ordered Larissa to sacrifice a whole hecatomb after my death."

"But that is Larissa's affair, whereas it was you, friend Elpidias, who made the promises."

"That's true, that's true. But you, good Socrates, could you, godless as you are, deal better with the gods than I who was a god-fearing tanner?"

"My friend, I know not whether I dealt better or worse. At first I brought offerings without having made vows. Later I offered neither calves nor vows."

"What, not a single calf, you unfortunate man?"

"Yes, friend, if Hermes had had to live by my gifts, I am afraid he would have grown very thin."

"I understand. You did not traffic in cattle, so you offered articles of some other trade—probably a mina or so of what the pupils paid you."

"You know, my friend, I didn't ask pay of my pupils, and my trade scarcely sufficed to support me. If the gods reckoned on the sorry remnants of my meals they miscalculated."

"Oh, blasphemer, in comparison with you I can be proud of my piety. Ye Gods, look upon this man! I did deceive you at times, but now and then I shared with you the sur-plus of some fortunate deal. He who gives at all gives much in comparison with a blasphemer who gives nothing. Socrates, I think you had better go on alone! I fear that your company, godless one, damages me in the eyes of the gods."

"As you will, good Elpidias. I swear by the dog no one shall force his company on another. Unhand the fold of my mantle, and farewell. I will go on alone."

And Socrates walked forward with a sure tread, feeling the ground, however, at every step.

But Elpidias behind him instantly cried out:

"Wait, wait, my good fellow-citizen, do not leave an Athenian alone in this horrible place! I was only making fun. Take what I said as a joke, and don't go so quickly. I marvel how you can see a thing in this hellish darkness."

"Friend, I have accustomed my eyes to it."

"That's good. Still I can't approve of your not having brought sacrifices to the gods. No, I can't, poor Socrates, I can't. The honourable Sophroniscus certainly taught you better in your youth, and you yourself used to take part in the prayers. I saw you."

"Yes. But I am accustomed to examine all our motives and to accept only those that after investigation prove to be reasonable. And so a day came on which I said to my-self: 'Socrates, here you are praying to the Olympians. Why are you praying to them?'"

Elpidias laughed.

"Really you philosophers sometimes don't know how to answer the simplest questions. I'm a plain tanner who never in my life studied sophistry, yet I know why I must honour the Olympians."

"Tell me quickly, so that I, too, may know why."

"Why! Ha! Ha! It's too simple, you wise Socrates."

"So much the better if it's simple. But don't keep your wisdom from me. Tell me—why must one honour the gods?"

"Why. Because everybody does it."

"Friend, you know very well that not every one honours the gods. Wouldn't it be more correct to say 'many'?"

"Very well, many."

"But tell me, don't more men deal wickedly than righteously?"

"I think so. You find more wicked people than good people."

"Therefore, if you follow the majority, you ought to deal wickedly and not righteously?"

"What are you saying?"

"I'm not saying it, *you* are. But I think the reason that men reverence the Olympians is not because the majority worship them. We must find another, more rational ground. Perhaps you mean they deserve reverence?"

"Yes, very right."

"Good. But then arises a new question: Why do they deserve reverence?"

"Because of their greatness."

"Ah, that's more like it. Perhaps I will soon be agreeing with you. It only remains for you to tell me wherein their greatness consists. That's a difficult question, isn't it? Let us seek the answer together. Homer says that the impetuous Ares, when stretched flat on the ground by a stone thrown by Pallas Athene, covered with his body the space that can be travelled in seven mornings. You see what an enormous space."

"Is that wherein greatness consists?"

"There you have me, my friend. That raises another question. Do you remember the athlete Theophantes? He towered over the people a whole head's length, whereas Pericles was no larger than you. But whom do we call great, Pericles or Theophantes?"

"I see that greatness does not consist in size of body. In that you're right. I am glad we agree. Perhaps greatness consists in virtue?"

"Certainly."

"I think so, too."

"Well, then, who must bow to whom? The small before the large, or those who are great in virtues before the wicked?"

"The answer is clear."

"I think so, too. Now we will look further into this matter. Tell me truly, did you ever kill other people's children with arrows?"

"It goes without saying, never! Do you think so ill of me?"

"Nor have you, I trust, ever seduced the wives of other men?"

"I was an upright tanner and a good husband. Don't forget that, Socrates, I beg of you!"

"You never became a brute, nor by your lustfulness gave

your faithful Larissa occasion to revenge herself on women whom you had ruined and on their innocent children?"

"You anger me, really, Socrates."

"But perhaps you snatched your inheritance from your father and threw him into prison?"

"Never! Why these insulting questions?"

"Wait, my friend. Perhaps we will both reach a conclusion. Tell me, would you have considered a man great who had done all these things of which I have spoken?"

"No, no, no! I should have called such a man a scoundrel, and lodged public complaint against him with the judges in the market-place."

"Well, Elpidias, why did you not complain in the market-place against Zeus and the Olympians? The son of Cronos carried on war with his own father, and was seized with brutal lust for the daughters of men, while Hera took vengeance upon innocent virgins. Did not both of them convert the unhappy daughter of Inachos into a common cow? Did not Apollo kill all the children of Niobe with his arrows? Did not Callenius steal bulls? Well, then, Elpidias, if it is true that he who has less virtue must do honour to him who has more, then you should not build altars to the Olympians, but they to you."

"Blaspheme not, impious Socrates! Keep quiet! How dare you judge the acts of the gods?"

"Friend, a higher power has judged them. Let us investigate the question. What is the mark of divinity? I think you said, Greatness, which consists in virtue. Now is not this greatness the one divine spark in man? But if we test the greatness of the gods by our small human virtues, and it turns out that that which measures is greater than that which is measured, then it follows that the divine principle itself condemns the Olympians. But, then——"

"What, then?"

"Then, friend Elpidias, they are no gods, but deceptive phantoms, creations of a dream. Is it not so?"

"Ah, that's whither your talk leads, you bare-footed philosopher! Now I see what they said of you is true. You are like that fish that takes men captive with its look. So you took me captive in order to confound my believing soul and awaken doubt in it. It was already beginning to waver in its reverence for Zeus. Speak alone. I won't answer any more."

"Be not wrathful, Elpidias! I don't wish to inflict any evil upon you. But if you are tired of following my arguments to their logical conclusions, permit me to relate to you an allegory of a Milesian youth. Allegories rest the mind, and the relaxation is not unprofitable."

"Speak, if your story is not too long and its purpose is good."

"Its purpose is truth, friend Elpidias, and I will be brief. Once, you know, in ancient times, Miletus was exposed to the attacks of the barbarians. Among the youth who were seized was a son of the wisest and best of all the citizens in the land. His precious child was overtaken by a severe illness and became unconscious. He was abandoned and allowed to lie like worthless booty. In the dead of night he came to his senses. High above him glimmered the stars.

Round about stretched the desert; and in the distance he heard the howl of beasts of prey. He was alone.

"He was entirely alone, and, besides that, the gods had taken from him the recollection of his former life. In vain he racked his brain—it was as dark and empty as the inhospitable desert in which he found himself. But somewhere, far away, behind the misty and obscure figures conjured up by his reason, loomed the thought of his lost home, and a vague realisation of the figure of the best of all men; and in his heart resounded the word 'father.' Doesn't it seem to you that the fate of this youth resembles the fate of all humanity?"

"How so?"

"Do we not all awake to life on earth with a hazy recollection of another home? And does not the figure of the great unknown hover before our souls?"

"Continue, Socrates, I am listening."

"The youth revived, arose, and walked cautiously, seeking to avoid all dangers. When after long wanderings his strength was nearly gone, he discerned a fire in the misty distance which illumined the darkness and banished the cold. A faint hope crept into his weary soul, and the recollections of his father's house again awoke within him. The youth walked toward the light, and cried: 'It is you, my father, it is you!' "

"And was it his father's house?"

"No, it was merely a night lodging of wild nomads. So for many years he led the miserable life of a captive slave, and only in his dreams saw the distant home and rested on his father's bosom. Sometimes with weak hand he endeavoured to lure from dead clay or wood or stone the face and form that ever hovered before him. There even came moments when he grew weary and embraced his own handiwork and prayed to it and wet it with his tears. But the stone remained cold stone. And as he waxed in years the youth destroyed his creations, which already seemed to him a vile defamation of his ever-present dreams. At last fate brought him to a good barbarian, who asked him for the cause of his constant mourning. When the youth confided to him the hopes and longings of his soul, the barbarian, a wise man, said:

" 'The world would be better did such a man and such a country exist as that of which you speak. But by what mark would you recognise your father?'

" 'In my country,' answered the youth, 'they reverenced wisdom and virtue and looked up to my father as to the master.'

" 'Well and good,' answered the barbarian. 'I must assume that a kernel of your father's teaching resides in you. Therefore take up the wanderer's staff, and proceed on your way. Seek perfect wisdom and truth, and when you have found them, cast aside your staff—there will be your home and your father.'

"And the youth went on his way at break of day——"

"Did he find the one whom he sought?"

"He is still seeking. Many countries, cities and men has he seen. He has come to know all the ways by land; he has traversed the stormy seas; he has searched the courses of the stars in heaven by which a pilgrim can direct his course in the limitless deserts. And each time that on his wearisome way an inviting fire lighted up the darkness before his eyes, his heart beat faster and hope crept into his soul. 'That is my father's hospitable house,' he thought.

"And when a hospitable host would greet the tired traveller and offer him the peace and blessing of his hearth, the youth would fall at his feet and say with emotion: 'I thank you, my father! Do you not recognise your son?'

"And many were prepared to take him as their son, for at that time children were frequently kidnapped. But after the first glow of enthusiasm, the youth would detect traces of imperfection, sometimes even of wickedness. Then he would begin to investigate and to test his host with questions concerning justice and injustice. And soon he would be driven forth again upon the cold wearisome way. More than once he said to himself: 'I will remain at this last hearth, I will preserve my last belief. It shall be the home of my father.' "

"Do you know, Socrates, perhaps that would have been the most sensible thing to do."

"So he thought sometimes. But the habit of investigating, the confused dream of a father, gave him no peace. Again and again he shook the dust from his feet; again and again he grasped his staff. Not a few stormy nights found him shelterless. Doesn't it seem to you that the fate of this youth resembles the fate of mankind?"

"Why?"

"Does not the race of man make trial of its childish belief and doubt it while seeking the unknown? Doesn't it fashion the form of its father in wood, stone, custom, and tradition? And then man finds the form imperfect, destroys it, and again goes on his wanderings in the desert of doubt. Always for the purpose of seeking something better——"

"Oh, you cunning sage, now I understand the purpose of your allegory! And I will tell you to your face that if only a ray of light were to penetrate this gloom, I would not put the Lord on trial with unnecessary questions——"

"Friend, the light is already shining," answered Socrates.

V

IT SEEMED as if the words of the philosopher had taken effect. High up in the distance a beam of light penetrated a vapoury envelop and disappeared in the mountains. It was followed by a second and a third. There beyond the darkness luminous genii seemed to be hovering, and a great mystery seemed about to be revealed, as if the breath of life were blowing, as if some great ceremony were in process. But it was still very remote. The shades descended thicker and thicker, foggy clouds rolled into masses, separated, and chased one another endlessly, ceaselessly.

A blue light from a distant peak fell upon a deep ravine; the clouds rose and covered the heavens to the zenith.

The rays disappeared and withdrew to a greater and greater distance, as if fleeing from this vale of shades and horrors. Socrates stood and looked after them sadly. Elpidias peered up at the peak full of dread.

"Look, Socrates! What do you see there on the mountain?"

"Friend," answered the philosopher, "let us investigate

our situation. Since we are in motion, we must arrive some-where, and since earthly existence must have a limit, I be-lieved that this limit is to be found at the parting of two beginnings. In the struggle of light with darkness we at-tain the crown of our endeavours. Since the ability to think has not been taken from us, I believe that it is the will of the divine being who called our power of thinking into existence that we should investigate the goal of our endeav-ours ourselves. Therefore, Elpidias, let us in dignified man-ner go to meet the dawn that lies beyond those clouds."

"Oh, my friend! If that is the dawn, I would rather the long cheerless night had endured forever, for it was quiet and peaceful. Don't you think our time passed tolerably well in instructive converse? And now my soul trembles before the tempest drawing nigh. Say what you will, but there before us are no ordinary shades of the dead night."

Zeus hurled a bolt into the bottomless gulf.

Ctesippus looked up to the peak, and his soul was frozen with horror. Huge sombre figures of the Olympian gods crowded on the mountain in a circle. A last ray shot through the region of clouds and mists, and died away like a faint memory. A storm was approaching now, and the powers of night were once more in the ascendant. Dark figures covered the heavens. In the centre Ctesippus could discern the all-powerful son of Cronos surrounded by a halo. The sombre figures of the older gods encircled him in wrathful excitement. Like flocks of birds winging their way in the twilight, like eddies of dust driven by a hurricane, like autumn leaves lashed by Boreas, numerous minor gods hov-ered in long clouds and occupied the spaces.

When the clouds gradually lifted from the peak and sent down dismal horror to embrace the earth, Ctesippus fell upon his knees. Later, he admitted that in this dreadful moment he forgot all his master's deductions and conclusions. His courage failed him, and terror took possession of his soul.

He merely listened.

Two voices resounded there where before had been silence, the one the mighty and threatening voice of the Godhead, the other the weak voice of a mortal which the wind carried from the mountain slope to the spot where Ctesippus had left Socrates.

"Are you," thus spake the voice from the clouds, "are you the blasphemous Socrates who strives with the gods of heaven and earth? Once there were none so joyous, so immortal, as we. Now, for long we have passed our days in darkness because of the unbelief and doubt that have come upon earth. Never has the mist closed in on us so heavily as since the time your voice resounded in Athens, the city we once so dearly loved. Why did you not follow the commands of your father, Sophroniscus? The good man permitted himself a few little sins, especially in his youth, yet by way of recompense, we frequently enjoyed the smell of his offerings——"

"Stay, son of Cronos, and solve my doubts! Do I understand that you prefer cowardly hypocrisy to searchings for the truth?"

At this question the crags trembled with the shock of a thundering peal. The first breath of the tempest scattered in the distant gorges. But the mountains still trembled, for he who was enthroned upon them still trembled. And in the anxious quiet of the night only distant sighs could be heard.

In the very bowels of the earth the chained Titans seemed to be groaning under the blow of the son of Cronos.

"Where are you now, you impious questioner?" suddenly came the mocking voice of the Olympian.

"I am here, son of Cronos, on the same spot. Nothing but your answer can move me from it. I am waiting."

Thunder bellowed in the clouds like a wild animal amazed at the daring of a Lybian tamer's fearless approach. At the end of a few moments the voice again rolled over the spaces:

"Son of Sophroniscus! Is it not enough that you bred so much scepticism on earth that the clouds of your doubt reached even to Olympus? Indeed, many a time when you were carrying on your discourse in the market-places or in the academies or on the promenades, it seemed to me as if you had already destroyed all the altars on earth, and the dust was rising from them up to us here on the mountain. Even that is not enough! Here before my very face you will not recognise the power of the immortals——"

"Zeus, thou art wrathful. Tell me, who gave me the 'Dæmon' which spoke to my soul throughout my life and forced me to seek the truth without resting?"

Mysterious silence reigned in the clouds.

"Was it not you? You are silent? Then I will investigate the matter. Either this divine beginning emanates from you or from some one else. If from you, I bring it to you as an offering. I offer you the ripe fruit of my life, the flame of the spark of your own kindling! See, son of Cronos, I preserved my gift; in my deepest heart grew the seed that you sowed. It is the very fire of my soul. It burned in those crises when with my own hand I tore the thread of life. Why did you not accept it? Would you have me regard you as a poor master whose age prevents him from seeing that his own pupil obediently follows out his commands? Who are you that would command me to stifle the flame that has illuminated my whole life, ever since it was penetrated by the first ray of sacred thought? The sun says not to the stars: 'Be extinguished that I may rise.' The sun rises and the weak glimmer of the stars is quenched by its far, far stronger light. The day says not to the torch: 'Be extinguished; you interfere with me.' The day breaks, and the torch smokes, but no longer shines. The divinity that I am questing is not you who are afraid of doubt. That divinity is like the day, like the sun, and shines without extinguishing other lights. The god I seek is the god who would say to me: 'Wanderer, give me your torch, you no longer need it, for I am the source of all light. Searcher for truth, set upon my altar the little gift of your doubt, because in me is its solution.' If you are that god, harken to my questions. No one kills his own child, and my doubts are a branch of the eternal spirit whose name is truth."

Round about, the fires of heaven tore the dark clouds, and out of the howling storm again resounded the powerful voice:

"Whither did your doubts tend, you arrogant sage, who renounce humility, the most beautiful adornment of earthly virtues? You abandoned the friendly shelter of credulous simplicity to wander in the desert of doubt. You have seen this dead space from which the living gods have departed. Will you traverse it, you insignificant worm, who crawl in the dust of your pitiful profanation of the gods? Will you vivify the world? Will you conceive the unknown divinity to whom you do not dare to pray? You miserable digger of dung, soiled by the smut of ruined altars, are you perchance the architect who shall build the new temple? Upon what do you base your hopes, you who disavow the old gods and have no new gods to take their place? The eternal night of doubts unsolved, the dead desert, deprived of the living spirit—*this* is your world, you pitiful worm, who gnawed at the living belief which was a refuge for simple hearts, who converted the world into a dead chaos. Now, then, where are you, you insignificant, blasphemous sage?"

Nothing was heard but the mighty storm roaring through the spaces. Then the thunder died away, the wind folded its pinions, and torrents of rain streamed through the darkness, like incessant floods of tears which threatened to devour the earth and drown it in a deluge of unquenchable grief.

It seemed to Ctesippus that the master was overcome, and that the fearless, restless, questioning voice had been silenced forever. But a few moments later it issued again from the same spot.

"Your words, son of Cronos, hit the mark better than your thunderbolts. The thoughts you have cast into my terrified soul have haunted me often, and it has sometimes seemed as if my heart would break under the burden of their unendurable anguish. Yes, I abandoned the friendly shelter of credulous simplicity. Yes, I have seen the spaces from which the living gods have departed enveloped in the night of eternal doubt. But I walked without fear, for my 'Dæmon' lighted the way, the divine beginning of all life. Let us investigate the question. Are not offerings of incense burnt on your altars in the name of Him who gives life? You are stealing what belongs to another! Not you, but that other, is served by credulous simplicity. Yes, you are right, I am no architect. I am not the builder of a new temple. Not to me was it given to raise from the earth to the heavens the glorious structure of the coming faith. I am one who digs dung, soiled by the smut of destruction. But my conscience tells me, son of Cronos, that the work of one who digs dung is also necessary for the future temple. When the time comes for the proud and stately edifice to stand on the purified place, and for the living divinity of the new belief to erect his throne upon it, I, the modest digger of dung, will go to him and say: 'Here am I who restlessly crawled in the dust of disavowal. When surrounded by fog and soot, I had no time to raise my eyes from the ground; my head had only a vague conception of the future building. Will you reject me, you just one, Just, and True, and Great?"

Silence and astonishment reigned in the spaces. Then Socrates raised his voice, and continued:

"The sunbeam falls upon the filthy puddle, and light vapour, leaving heavy mud behind, rises to the sun, melts, and dissolves in the ether. With your sunbeam you touched my dust-laden soul and it aspired to you, Unknown One, whose name is mystery! I sought for you, because you are

Truth; I strove to attain to you, because you are Justice; I loved you, because you are Love; I died for you, because you are the Source of Life. Will you reject me, O Unknown? My torturing doubts, my passionate search for truth, my difficult life, my voluntary death—accept them as a bloodless offering, as a prayer, as a sigh! Absorb them as the immeasurable ether absorbs the evaporating mists! Take them, you whose name I do not know, let not the ghosts of the night I have traversed bar the way to you, to eternal light! Give way, you shades who dim the light of the dawn! I tell you, gods of my people, you are unjust, and where there is no justice there can be no truth, but only phantoms, creations of a dream. To this conclusion have I come, I, Socrates, who sought to fathom all things. Rise, dead mists, I go my way to Him whom I have sought all my life long!"

The thunder burst again—a short, abrupt peal, as if the egis had fallen from the weakened hand of the thunderer. Storm-voices trembled from the mountains, sounding dully in the gorges, and died away in the clefts. In their place resounded other, marvellous tones.

When Ctesippus looked up in astonishment, a spectacle presented itself such as no mortal eyes had ever seen.

The night vanished. The clouds lifted, and godly figures floated in the azure like golden ornaments on the hem of a festive robe. Heroic forms glimmered over the remote crags and ravines, and Elpidias, whose little figure was seen standing at the edge of a cleft in the rocks, stretched his hands toward them, as if beseeching the vanishing gods for a solution of his fate

A mountain-peak now stood out clearly above the mysterious mist, gleaming like a torch over dark blue valleys. The son of Cronos, the thunderer, was no longer enthroned upon it, and the other Olympians too were gone.

Socrates stood alone in the light of the sun under the high heavens.

Ctesippus was distinctly conscious of the pulse-beat of a mysterious life quivering throughout nature, stirring even the tiniest blade of grass.

A breath seemed to be stirring the balmy air, a voice to be sounding in wonderful harmony, an invisible tread to be heard— the tread of the radiant Dawn!

And on the illumined peak a man still stood, stretching out his arms in mute ecstasy, moved by a mighty impulse.

A moment, and all disappeared, and the light of an ordinary day shone upon the awakened soul of Ctesippus. It was like dismal twilight after the revelation of nature that had blown upon him the breath of an unknown life.

In deep silence the pupils of the philosopher listened to the marvellous recital of Ctesippus. Plato broke the silence.

"Let us investigate the dream and its significance," he said.

"Let us investigate it," responded the others.

THE SIGNAL

— ◆◆◆ —

By Vsevolod M. Garshin

SEMYON IVANOV was a track-walker. His hut was ten versts away from a railroad station in one direction and twelve versts away in the other. About four versts away there was a cotton mill that had opened the year before, and its tall chimney rose up darkly from behind the forest. The only dwellings around were the distant huts of the other track-walkers.

Semyon Ivanov's health had been completely shattered. Nine years before he had served right through the war as servant to an officer. The sun had roasted him, the cold frozen him, and hunger famished him on the forced marches of forty and fifty versts a day in the heat and the cold and the rain and the shine. The bullets had whizzed about him, but, thank God! none had struck him.

Semyon's regiment had once been on the firing line. For a whole week there had been skirmishing with the Turks, only a deep ravine separating the two hostile armies; and from morn till eve there had been a steady cross-fire. Thrice daily Semyon carried a steaming samovar and his officer's meals from the camp kitchen to the ravine. The bullets hummed about him and rattled viciously against the rocks. Semyon was terrified and cried sometimes, but still he kept right on. The officers were pleased with him, because he always had hot tea ready for them.

He returned from the campaign with limbs unbroken but crippled with rheumatism. He had experienced no little sorrow since then. He arrived home to find that his father, an old man, and his little four-year-old son had died. Semyon remained alone with his wife. They could not do much. It was difficult to plough with rheumatic arms and legs. They could no longer stay in their village, so they started off to seek their fortune in new places. They stayed for a short time on the line, in Kherson and Donshchina, but nowhere found luck. Then the wife went out to service, and Semyon continued to travel about. Once he happened to ride on an engine, and at one of the stations the face of the station-master seemed familiar to him. Semyon looked at the station-master and the station-master looked at Semyon, and they recognised each other. He had been an officer in Semyon's regiment.

"You are Ivanov?" he said.

"Yes, your Excellency."

"How do you come to be here?"

Semyon told him all.

"Where are you off to?"

"I cannot tell you, sir."

"Idiot! What do you mean by 'cannot tell you?'"

"I mean what I say, your Excellency. There is nowhere for me to go. I must hunt for work, sir."

The station-master looked at him, thought a bit, and

said: "See here, friend, stay here a while at the station. You are married, I think. Where is your wife?"

"Yes, your Excellency, I am married. My wife is at Kursk, in service with a merchant."

"Well, write to your wife to come here. I will give you a free pass for her. There is a position as track-walker open. I will speak to the Chief on your behalf."

"I shall be very grateful to you, your Excellency," replied Semyon.

He stayed at the station, helped in the kitchen, cut firewood, kept the yard clean, and swept the platform. In a fortnight's time his wife arrived, and Semyon went on a hand-trolley to his hut. The hut was a new one and warm, with as much wood as he wanted. There was a little vegetable garden, the legacy of former track-walkers, and there was about half a dessiatin of ploughed land on either side of the railway embankment. Semyon was rejoiced. He began to think of doing some farming, of purchasing a cow and a horse.

He was given all necessary stores—a green flag, a red flag, lanterns, a horn, hammer, screw-wrench for the nuts, a crow-bar, spade, broom, bolts, and nails; they gave him two books of regulations and a time-table of the trains. At first Semyon could not sleep at night and learnt the whole time-table by heart. Two hours before a train was due he would go over his section, sit on the bench at his hut, and look and listen whether the rails were trembling or the rumble of the train could be heard. He even learned the regulations by heart, although he could only read by spelling out each word.

It was summer; the work was not heavy; there was no snow to clear away, and the trains on that line were infrequent. Semyon used to go over his verst twice a day, examine and screw up nuts here and there, keep the bed level, look at the water-pipes, and then go home to his own affairs. There was only one drawback—he always had to get the inspector's permission for the least little thing he wanted to do. Semyon and his wife were even beginning to be bored.

Two months passed, and Semyon commenced to make the acquaintance of his neighbours, the track-walkers on either side of him. One was a very old man, whom the authorities were always meaning to relieve. He scarcely moved out of his hut. His wife used to do all his work. The other track-walker, nearer the station, was a young man, thin, but muscular. He and Semyon met for the first time on the line midway between the huts. Semyon took off his hat and bowed. "Good health to you, neighbour," he said.

The neighbour glanced askance at him. "How do you do?" he replied; then turned around and made off.

Later the wives met. Semyon's wife passed the time of day with her neighbour, but neither did she say much.

On one occasion Semyon said to her: "Young woman, your husband is not very talkative."

The woman said nothing at first, then replied: "But what is there for him to talk about? Every one has his own business. Go your way, and God be with you."

However, after another month or so they became acquainted. Semyon would go with Vasily along the line, sit on the edge of a pipe, smoke, and talk of life. Vasily, for the most part, kept silent, but Semyon talked of his village, and of the campaign through which he had passed.

"I have had no little sorrow in my day," he would say; "and goodness knows I have not lived long. God has not given me happiness, but what He may give, so will it be. That's so, friend Vasily Stepanych."

Vasily Stepanych knocked the ashes out of his pipe against a rail, stood up, and said: "It is not luck which follows us in life, but human beings. There is no crueller beast on this earth than man. Wolf does not eat wolf, but man will readily devour man."

"Come, friend, don't say that; a wolf eats wolf."

"The words came into my mind and I said it. All the same, there is nothing crueller than man. If it were not for his wickedness and greed, it would be possible to live. Everybody tries to sting you to the quick, to bite and eat you up."

Semyon pondered a bit. "I don't know, brother," he said; "perhaps it is as you say, and perhaps it is God's will."

"And perhaps," said Vasily, "it is waste of time for me to talk to you. To put everything unpleasant on God, and sit and suffer, means, brother, being not a man but an animal. That's what I have to say." And he turned and went off without saying good-bye.

Semyon also got up. "Neighbour," he called, "why do you lose your temper?" But his neighbour did not look round, and kept on his way.

Semyon gazed after him until he was lost to sight in the cutting at the turn. He went home and said to his wife: "Arina, our neighbour is a wicked person, not a man."

However, they did not quarrel. They met again and discussed the same topics.

"Ah, friend, if it were not for men we should not be poking in these huts," said Vasily on one occasion.

"And what if we are poking in these huts? It's not so bad. You can live in them."

"Live in them, indeed! Bah, you! . . . You have lived long and learned little, looked at much and seen little. What sort of life is there for a poor man in a hut here or there? The cannibals are devouring you. They are sucking up all your life-blood, and when you become old, they will throw you out just as they do husks to feed the pigs on. What pay do you get?"

"Not much, Vasily Stepanych—twelve rubles."

"And I, thirteen and a half rubles. Why? By the regulations the company should give us fifteen rubles a month with firing and lighting. Who decides that you should have twelve rubles, or I thirteen and a half? Ask yourself! And you say a man can live on that? You understand it is not a question of one and a half rubles or three rubles—even if they paid us each the whole fifteen rubles. I was at the station last month. The director passed through. I saw him. I had that honour. He had a separate coach. He came out and stood on the platform. . . . I shall not stay here long; I shall go somewhere, anywhere, follow my nose."

"But where will you go, Stepanych? Leave well enough

alone. Here you have a house, warmth, a little piece of land. Your wife is a worker."

"Land! You should look at my piece of land. Not a twig on it—nothing. I planted some cabbages in the spring, just when the inspector came along. He said: 'What is this? Why have you not reported this? Why have you done this without permission? Dig them up, roots and all.' He was drunk. Another time he would not have said a word, but this time it struck him. Three rubles fine! . . ."

Vasily kept silent for a while, pulling at his pipe, then added quietly: "A little more and I should have done for him."

"You are hot-tempered."

"No, I am not hot-tempered, but I tell the truth and think. Yes, he will still get a bloody nose from me. I will complain to the Chief. We will seen then!" And Vasily did complain to the Chief.

Once the Chief came to inspect the line. Three days later important personages were coming from St. Petersburg and would pass over the line. They were conducting an inquiry, so that previous to their journey it was necessary to put everything in order. Ballast was laid down, the bed was levelled, the sleepers carefully examined, spikes driven in a bit, nuts screwed up, posts painted, and orders given for yellow sand to be sprinkled at the level crossings. The woman at the neighbouring hut turned her old man out to weed. Semyon worked for a whole week. He put everything in order, mended his kaftan, cleaned and polished his brass plate until it fairly shone. Vasily also worked hard.

The Chief arrived on a trolley, four men working the handles and the levers making the six wheels hum. The trolley travelled at twenty versts an hour, but the wheels squeaked. It reached Semyon's hut, and he ran out and reported in soldierly fashion. All appeared to be in repair.

"Have you been here long?" inquired the Chief.

"Since the second of May, your Excellency."

"All right. Thank you. And who is at hut No. 164?"

The traffic inspector (he was travelling with the Chief on the trolley) replied: "Vasily Spiridov."

"Spiridov, Spiridov. . . . Ah! is he the man against whom you made a note last year?"

"He is."

"Well, we will see Vasily Spiridov. Go on!" The workmen laid to the handles, and the trolley got under way. Semyon watched it, and thought, "There will be trouble between them and my neighbour."

About two hours later he started on his round. He saw some one coming along the line from the cutting. Something white showed on his head. Semyon began to look more attentively. It was Vasily. He had a stick in his hand, a small bundle on his shoulder, and his cheek was bound up in a handkerchief.

"Where are you off to?" cried Semyon.

Vasily came quite close. He was very pale, white as chalk, and his eyes had a wild look. Almost choking, he muttered: "To town—to Moscow—to the head office."

"Head office? Ah, you are going to complain, I suppose. Give it up! Vasily Stepanych, forget it."

"No, mate, I will not forget. It is too late. See! He struck me in the face, drew blood. So long as I live I will not forget. I will not leave it like this!"

Semyon took his hand. "Give it up, Stepanych. I am giving you good advice. You will not better things. . . ."

"Better things! I know myself I shan't better things. You were right about Fate. It would be better for me not to do it, but one must stand up for the right."

"But tell me, how did it happen?"

"How? He examined everything, got down from the trolley, looked into the hut. I knew beforehand that he would be strict, and so I had put everything into proper order. He was just going when I made my complaint. He immediately cried out: 'Here is a Government inquiry coming, and you make a complaint about a vegetable garden. Here are privy councillors coming, and you annoy me with cabbages!' I lost patience and said something—not very much, but it offended him, and he struck me in the face. I stood still; I did nothing, just as if what he did was perfectly all right. They went off; I came to myself, washed my face, and left."

"And what about the hut?"

"My wife is staying there. She will look after things. Never mind about their roads."

Vasily got up and collected himself. "Good-bye, Ivanov. I do not know whether I shall get any one at the office to listen to me."

"Surely you are not going to walk?"

"At the station I will try to get on a freight train, and to-morrow I shall be in Moscow."

The neighbours bade each other farewell. Vasily was absent for some time. His wife worked for him night and day. She never slept, and wore herself out waiting for her husband. On the third day the commission arrived. An engine, luggage-van, and two first-class saloons; but Vasily was still away. Semyon saw his wife on the fourth day. Her face was swollen from crying and her eyes were red.

"Has your husband returned?" he asked. But the woman only made a gesture with her hands, and without saying a word went her way.

Semyon had learnt when still a lad to make flutes out of a kind of reed. He used to burn out the heart of the stalk, make holes where necessary, drill them, fix a mouthpiece at one end, and tune them so well that it was possible to play almost any air on them. He made a number of them in his spare time, and sent them by his friends amongst the freight brakemen to the bazaar in the town. He got two kopeks apiece for them. On the day following the visit of the commission he left his wife at home to meet the six o'clock train, and started off to the forest to cut some sticks. He went to the end of his section—at this point the line made a sharp turn—descended the embankment, and struck into the wood at the foot of the mountain. About half a verst away there was a big marsh, around which splendid reeds for his flutes grew. He cut a whole bundle of stalks and started back home. The sun was already dropping low, and in the dead stillness only the twittering of the birds was audible, and the crackle of the dead wood under his feet. As he walked along rapidly, he fancied he heard the clang of iron striking iron, and he redoubled his pace.

There was no repair going on in his section. What did it mean? He emerged from the woods, the railway embankment stood high before him; on the top a man was squatting on the bed of the line busily engaged in something. Semyon commenced quietly to crawl up towards him. He thought it was some one after the nuts which secure the rails. He watched, and the man got up, holding a crow-bar in his hand. He had loosened a rail, so that it would move to one side. A mist swam before Semyon's eyes; he wanted to cry out, but could not. It was Vasily! Semyon scrambled up the bank, as Vasily with crow-bar and wrench slid headlong down the other side.

"Vasily Stepanych! My dear friend, come back! Give me the crow-bar. We will put the rail back; no one will know. Come back! Save your soul from sin!"

Vasily did not look back, but disappeared into the woods.

Semyon stood before the rail which had been torn up. He threw down his bundle of sticks. A train was due; not a freight, but a passenger-train. And he had nothing with which to stop it, no flag. He could not replace the rail and could not drive in the spikes with his bare hands. It was necessary to run, absolutely necessary to run to the hut for some tools. "God help me!" he murmured.

Semyon started running towards his hut. He was out of breath, but still ran, falling every now and then. He had cleared the forest; he was only a few hundred feet from his hut, not more, when he heard the distant hooter of the factory sound—six o'clock! In two minutes' time No. 7 train was due. "Oh, Lord! Have pity on innocent souls!" In his mind Semyon saw the engine strike against the loosened rail with its left wheel, shiver, careen, tear up and splinter the sleepers—and just there, there was a curve and the embankment seventy feet high, down which the engine would topple—and the third-class carriages would be packed . . . little children. . . . All sitting in the train now, never dreaming of danger. "Oh, Lord! Tell me what to do! . . . No, it is impossible to run to the hut and get back in time."

Semyon did not run on to the hut, but turned back and ran faster than before. He was running almost mechanically, blindly; he did not know himself what was to happen. He ran as far as the rail which had been pulled up; his sticks were lying in a heap. He bent down, seized one without knowing why, and ran on farther. It seemed to him the train was already coming. He heard the distant whistle; he heard the quiet, even tremor of the rails; but his strength was exhausted, he could run no farther, and came to a halt about six hundred feet from the awful spot. Then an idea came into his head, literally like a ray of light. Pulling off his cap, he took out of it a cotton scarf, drew his knife out of the upper part of his boot, and crossed himself, muttering, "God bless me!"

He buried the knife in his left arm above the elbow; the blood spurted out, flowing in a hot stream. In this he soaked his scarf, smoothed it out, tied it to the stick and hung out his red flag.

He stood waving his flag. The train was already in sight. The driver would not see him—would come close up, and a heavy train cannot be pulled up in six hundred feet.

And the blood kept on flowing. Semyon pressed the sides

of the wound together so as to close it, but the blood did not diminish. Evidently he had cut his arm very deep. His head commenced to swim, black spots began to dance before his eyes, and then it became dark. There was a ringing in his ears. He could not see the train or hear the noise. Only one thought possessed him. "I shall not be able to keep standing up. I shall fall and drop the flag; the train will pass over me. Help me, oh Lord!"

All turned black before him, his mind became a blank, and he dropped the flag; but the blood-stained banner did not fall to the ground. A hand seized it and held it high to meet the approaching train. The engineer saw it, shut the regulator, and reversed steam. The train came to a standstill.

People jumped out of the carriages and collected in a crowd. They saw a man lying senseless on the footway, drenched in blood, and another man standing beside him with a blood-stained rag on a stick.

Vasily looked around at all. Then, lowering his head, he said: "Bind me. I tore up a rail!"

THE DARLING

❖❖❖

By Anton P. Chekhov

OLENKA, the daughter of the retired collegiate assessor Plemyanikov, was sitting on the back-door steps of her house doing nothing. It was hot, the flies were nagging and teasing, and it was pleasant to think that it would soon be evening. Dark rain clouds were gathering from the east, wafting a breath of moisture every now and then.

Kukin, who roomed in the wing of the same house, was standing in the yard looking up at the sky. He was the manager of the Tivoli, an open-air theatre.

"Again," he said despairingly. "Rain again. Rain, rain, rain! Every day rain! As though to spite me. I might as well stick my head into a noose and be done with it. It's ruining me. Heavy losses every day!" He wrung his hands, and continued, addressing Olenka: "What a life, Olga Semyonovna! It's enough to make a man weep. He works, he does his best, his very best, he tortures himself, he passes sleepless nights, he thinks and thinks and thinks how to do everything just right. And what's the result? He gives the public the best operetta, the very best pantomime, excellent artists. But do they want it? Have they the least appreciation of it? The public is rude. The public is a great boor. The public wants a circus, a lot of nonsense, a lot of stuff. And there's the weather. Look! Rain almost every evening. It began to rain on the tenth of May, and it's kept it up through the whole of June. It's simply awful. I can't get any audiences, and don't I have to pay rent? Don't I have to pay the actors?"

The next day towards evening the clouds gathered again, and Kukin said with an hysterical laugh:

"Oh, I don't care. Let it do its worst. Let it drown the whole theatre, and me, too. All right, no luck for me in this world or the next. Let the actors bring suit against me and drag me to court. What's the court? Why not Siberia at hard labour, or even the scaffold? Ha, ha, ha!"

It was the same on the third day.

Olenka listened to Kukin seriously, in silence. Sometimes tears would rise to her eyes. At last Kukin's misfortune touched her. She fell in love with him. He was short, gaunt, with a yellow face, and curly hair combed back from his forehead, and a thin tenor voice. His features puckered all up when he spoke. Despair was ever inscribed on his face. And yet he awakened in Olenka a sincere, deep feeling.

She was always loving somebody. She couldn't get on without loving somebody. She had loved her sick father, who sat the whole time in his armchair in a darkened room, breathing heavily. She had loved her aunt, who came from Brianska once or twice a year to visit them. And before that, when a pupil at the progymnasium, she had loved her French teacher. She was a quiet, kind-hearted, compassionate girl, with a soft gentle way about her. And she made a very healthy, wholesome impression. Looking at her full, rosy cheeks, at her soft white neck with the black mole, and at the good naïve smile that always played on her face when something pleasant was said, the men would think, "Not so bad," and would smile too; and the lady visitors, in the middle of the conversation, would suddenly grasp her hand and exclaim, "You darling!" in a burst of delight.

The house, hers by inheritance, in which she had lived from birth, was located at the outskirts of the city on the Gypsy Road, not far from the Tivoli. From early evening till late at night she could hear the music in the theatre and the bursting of the rockets; and it seemed to her that Kukin was roaring and battling with his fate and taking his chief enemy, the indifferent public, by assault. Her heart melted softly, she felt no desire to sleep, and when Kukin returned home towards morning, she tapped on her window-pane, and through the curtains he saw her face and one shoulder and the kind smile she gave him.

He proposed to her, and they were married. And when he had a good look of her neck and her full vigorous shoulders, he clapped his hands and said:

"You darling!"

He was happy. But it rained on their wedding-day, and the expression of despair never left his face.

They got along well together. She sat in the cashier's box, kept the theatre in order, wrote down the expenses, and paid out the salaries. Her rosy cheeks, her kind naïve smile, like a halo around her face, could be seen at the cashier's window, behind the scenes, and in the café. She began to tell her friends that the theatre was the greatest, the most important, the most essential thing in the world, that it was the only place to obtain true enjoyment in and become humanised and educated.

"But do you suppose the public appreciates it?" she asked. "What the public wants is the circus. Yesterday Vanichka and I gave *Faust Burlesqued,* and almost all the boxes were empty. If we had given some silly nonsense, I assure you, the theatre would have been overcrowded. Tomorrow we'll put *Orpheus in Hades* on. Do come."

Whatever Kukin said about the theatre and the actors, she repeated. She spoke, as he did, with contempt of the public, of its indifference to art, of its boorishness. She meddled in the rehearsals, corrected the actors, watched the conduct of the musicians; and when an unfavourable criticism appeared in the local paper, she wept and went to the editor to argue with him.

The actors were fond of her and called her "Vanichka and I" and "the darling." She was sorry for them and lent them small sums. When they bilked her, she never complained to her husband; at the utmost she shed a few tears.

In winter, too, they got along nicely together. They leased a theatre in the town for the whole winter and sublet it for short periods to a Little Russian theatrical company, to a conjuror and to the local amateur players.

Olenka grew fuller and was always beaming with contentment; while Kukin grew thinner and yellower and complained of his terrible losses, though he did fairly well the whole winter. At night he coughed, and she gave him raspberry syrup and lime water, rubbed him with eau de Cologne, and wrapped him up in soft coverings.

"You are my precious sweet," she said with perfect sincerity, stroking his hair. "You are such a dear."

At Lent he went to Moscow to get his company together, and, while without him, Olenka was unable to sleep. She sat at the window the whole time, gazing at the stars. She likened herself to the hens that are also uneasy and unable to sleep when their rooster is out of the coop. Kukin was detained in Moscow. He wrote he would be back during Easter Week, and in his letters discussed arrangements already for the Tivoli. But late one night, before Easter Monday, there was an ill-omened knocking at the wicket-gate. It was like a knocking on a barrel—boom, boom, boom! The sleepy cook ran barefooted, plashing through the puddles, to open the gate.

"Open the gate, please," said some one in a hollow bass voice. "I have a telegram for you."

Olenka had received telegrams from her husband before; but this time, somehow, she was numbed with terror. She opened the telegram with trembling hands and read:

"Ivan Petrovich died suddenly to-day. Awaiting propt orders for wuneral Tuesday."

That was the way the telegram was written—"wuneral" —and another unintelligible word—"propt." The telegram was signed by the manager of the opera company.

"My dearest!" Olenka burst out sobbing. "Vanichka, my dearest, my sweetheart. Why did I ever meet you? Why did I ever get to know you and love you? To whom have you abandoned your poor Olenka, your poor, unhappy Olenka?"

Kukin was buried on Tuesday in the Vagankov Cemetery in Moscow. Olenka returned home on Wednesday; and as soon as she entered her house she threw herself on her bed and broke into such loud sobbing that she could be heard in the street and in the neighbouring yards.

"The darling!" said the neighbours, crossing themselves. "How Olga Semyonovna, the poor darling, is grieving!"

Three months afterwards Olenka was returning home from mass, downhearted and in deep mourning. Beside her walked a man also returning from church. Vasily Pustovalov, the manager of the merchant Babakayev's lumber-yard. He was wearing a straw hat, a white vest with a gold chain, and looked more like a landowner than a business man.

"Everything has its ordained course, Olga Semyonovna," he said sedately, with sympathy in his voice. "And if any one near and dear to us dies, then it means it was God's will and we should remember that and bear it with submission."

He took her to the wicket-gate, said good-bye and went away. After that she heard his sedate voice the whole day; and on closing her eyes she instantly had a vision of his dark beard. She took a great liking to him. And evidently he had been impressed by her, too; for, not long after, an elderly woman, a distant acquaintance, came in to have a cup of coffee with her. As soon as the woman was seated at table she began to speak about Pustovalov—how good he was, what a steady man, and any woman could be glad

to get him as a husband. Three days later Pustovalov himself paid Olenka a visit. He stayed only about ten minutes,
and spoke little, but Olenka fell in love with him, fell in
love so desperately that she did not sleep the whole night
and burned as with fever. In the morning she sent for the
elderly woman. Soon after, Olenka and Pustovalov were
engaged, and the wedding followed.

Pustovalov and Olenka lived happily together. He usually stayed in the lumber-yard until dinner, then went out
on business. In his absence Olenka took his place in the
office until evening, attending to the book-keeping and
despatching the orders.

"Lumber rises twenty per cent every year nowadays,"
she told her customers and acquaintances. "Imagine, we
used to buy wood from our forests here. Now Vasichka
has to go every year to the government of Mogilev to get
wood. And what a tax!" she exclaimed, covering her cheeks
with her hands in terror. "What a tax!"

She felt as if she had been dealing in lumber for ever so
long, that the most important and essential thing in life
was lumber. There was something touching and endearing
in the way she pronounced the words, "beam," "joist,"
"plank," "stave," "lath," "gun-carriage," "clamp." At night
she dreamed of whole mountains of boards and planks,
long, endless rows of wagons conveying the wood somewhere, far, far from the city. She dreamed that a whole
regiment of beams, 36 ft. x 5 in., were advancing in an
upright position to do battle against the lumber-yard; that
the beams and joists and clamps were knocking against

each other, emitting the sharp crackling reports of dry wood, that they were all falling and then rising again, piling on top of each other. Olenka cried out in her sleep, and Pustovalov said to her gently:

"Olenka my dear, what is the matter? Cross yourself."

Her husband's opinions were all hers. If he thought the room was too hot, she thought so too. If he thought business was dull, she thought business was dull. Pustovalov was not fond of amusements and stayed home on holidays; she did the same.

"You are always either at home or in the office," said her friends. "Why don't you go to the theatre or to the circus, darling?"

"Vasichka and I never go to the theatre," she answered sedately. "We have work to do, we have no time for nonsense. What does one get out of going to theatre?"

On Saturdays she and Pustovalov went to vespers, and on holidays to early mass. On returning home they walked side by side with rapt faces, an agreeable smell emanating from both of them and her silk dress rustling pleasantly. At home they drank tea with milk-bread and various jams, and then ate pie. Every day at noontime there was an appetising odour in the yard and outside the gate of cabbage soup, roast mutton, or duck; and, on fast days, of fish. You couldn't pass the gate without being seized by an acute desire to eat. The samovar was always boiling on the office table, and customers were treated to tea and biscuits. Once a week the married couple went to the baths and returned with red faces, walking side by side.

"We are getting along very well, thank God," said Olenka to her friends. "God grant that all should live as well as Vasichka and I."

When Pustovalov went to the government of Mogilev to buy wood, she was dreadfully homesick for him, did not sleep nights, and cried. Sometimes the veterinary surgeon of the regiment, Smirnov, a young man who lodged in the wing of her house, came to see her evenings. He related incidents, or they played cards together. This distracted her. The most interesting of his stories were those of his own life. He was married and had a son; but he had separated from his wife because she had deceived him, and now he hated her and sent her forty rubles a month for his son's support. Olenka sighed, shook her head, and was sorry for him.

"Well, the Lord keep you," she said, as she saw him off to the door by candlelight. "Thank you for coming to kill time with me. May God give you health. Mother in Heaven!" She spoke very sedately, very judiciously, imitating her husband. The veterinary surgeon had disappeared behind the door when she called out after him: "Do you know, Vladimir Platonych, you ought to make up with your wife. Forgive her, if only for the sake of your son. The child understands everything, you may be sure."

When Pustovalov returned, she told him in a low voice about the veterinary surgeon and his unhappy family life; and they sighed and shook their heads, and talked about the boy who must be homesick for his father. Then, by a strange association of ideas, they both stopped before the sacred images, made genuflections, and prayed to God to send them children."

And so the Pustovalovs lived for full six years, quietly and peaceably, in perfect love and harmony. But once in the winter Vasily Andreyich, after drinking some hot tea, went out into the lumber-yard without a hat on his head, caught a cold and took sick. He was treated by the best physicians, but the malady progressed, and he died after an illness of four months. Olenka was again left a widow.

"To whom have you left me, my darling?" she wailed after the funeral. "How shall I live now without you, wretched creature that I am. Pity me, good people, pity me, fatherless and motherless, all alone in the world!"

She went about dressed in black and weepers, and she gave up wearing hats and gloves for good. She hardly left the house except to go to church and to visit her husband's grave. She almost led the life of a nun.

It was not until six months had passed that she took off the weepers and opened her shutters. She began to go out occasionally in the morning to market with her cook. But how she lived at home and what went on there, could only be surmised. It could be surmised from the fact that she was seen in her little garden drinking tea with the veterinarian while he read the paper out loud to her, and also from the fact that once on meeting an acquaintance at the post-office, she said to her:

"There is no proper veterinary inspection in our town. That is why there is so much disease. You constantly hear of people getting sick from the milk and becoming infected by the horses and cows. The health of domestic animals ought really to be looked after as much as that of human beings."

She repeated the veterinarian's words and held the same opinions as he about everything. It was plain that she could not exist a single year without an attachment, and she found her new happiness in the wing of her house. In any one else this would have been condemned; but no one could think ill of Olenka. Everything in her life was so transparent. She and the veterinary surgeon never spoke about the change in their relations. They tried, in fact, to conceal it, but unsuccessfully; for Olenka could have no secrets. When the surgeon's colleagues from the regiment came to see him, she poured tea, and served the supper, and talked to them about the cattle plague, the foot and mouth disease, and the municipal slaughter houses. The surgeon was dreadfully embarrassed, and after the visitors had left, he caught her hand and hissed angrily:

"Didn't I ask you not to talk about what you don't understand? When we doctors discuss things, please don't mix in. It's getting to be a nuisance."

She looked at him in astonishment and alarm, and asked:

"But, Volodichka, what *am* I to talk about?"

And she threw her arms round his neck, with tears in her eyes, and begged him not to be angry. And they were both happy.

But their happiness was of short duration. The veterinary surgeon went away with his regiment to be gone for good, when it was transferred to some distant place almost as far as Siberia, and Olenka was left alone.

Now she was completely alone. Her father had long been dead, and his armchair lay in the attic covered with dust and minus one leg. She got thin and homely, and the people who met her on the street no longer looked at her as they had used to, nor smiled at her. Evidently her best years were over, past and gone, and a new, dubious life was to begin which it were better not to think about.

In the evening Olenka sat on the steps and heard the music playing and the rockets bursting in the Tivoli; but it no longer aroused any response in her. She looked listlessly into the yard, thought of nothing, wanted nothing, and when night came on, she went to bed and dreamed of nothing but the empty yard. She ate and drank as though by compulsion.

And what was worst of all, she no longer held any opinions. She saw and understood everything that went on around her, but she could not form an opinion about it. She knew of nothing to talk about. And how dreadful not to have opinions! For instance, you see a bottle, or you see that it is raining, or you see a muzhik riding by in a wagon. But what the bottle or the rain or the muzhik are for, or what the sense of them all is, you cannot tell—you cannot tell, not for a thousand rubles. In the days of Kukin and Pustovalov and then of the veterinary surgeon, Olenka had had an explanation for everything, and would have given her opinion freely no matter about what. But now there was the same emptiness in her heart and brain as in her yard. It was as galling and bitter as a taste of wormwood.

Gradually the town grew up all around. The Gypsy

Road had become a street, and where the Tivoli and the lumber-yard had been, there were now houses and a row of side streets. How quickly time flies! Olenka's house turned gloomy, the roof rusty, the shed slanting. Dock and thistles overgrew the yard. Olenka herself had aged and grown homely. In the summer she sat on the steps, and her soul was empty and dreary and bitter. When she caught the breath of spring, or when the wind wafted the chime of the cathedral bells, a sudden flood of memories would pour over her, her heart would expand with a tender warmth, and the tears would stream down her cheeks. But that lasted only a moment. Then would come emptiness again, and the feeling, What is the use of living? The black kitten Bryska rubbed up against her and purred softly, but the little creature's caresses left Olenka untouched. That was not what she needed. What she needed was a love that would absorb her whole being, her reason, her whole soul, that would give her ideas, an object in life, that would warm her aging blood. And she shook the black kitten off her skirt angrily, saying:

"Go away! What are you doing here?"

And so day after day, year after year not a single joy, not a single opinion. Whatever Marva, the cook, said was all right.

One hot day in July, towards evening, as the town cattle were being driven by, and the whole yard was filled with clouds of dust, there was suddenly a knocking at the gate. Olenka herself went to open it, and was dumbfounded to behold the veterinarian Smirnov. He had turned grey and was dressed as a civilian. All the old memories flooded into her soul, she could not restrain herself, she burst out crying, and laid her head on Smirnov's breast without saying a word. So overcome was she that she was totally unconscious of how they walked into the house and seated themselves to drink tea.

"My darling!" she murmured, trembling with joy. "Vladimir Platonych, from where has God sent you?"

"I want to settle here for good," he told her. "I have resigned my position and have come here to try my fortune as a free man and lead a settled life. Besides, it's time to send my boy to the gymnasium. He is grown up now. You know, my wife and I have become reconciled."

"Where is she?" asked Olenka.

"At the hotel with the boy. I am looking for lodgings."

"Good gracious, bless you, take my house. Why won't my house do? Oh, dear! Why, I won't ask any rent of you," Olenka burst out in the greatest excitement, and began to cry again. "You live here, and the wing will be enough for me. Oh, Heavens, what a joy!"

The very next day the roof was being painted and the walls whitewashed, and Olenka, arms akimbo, was going about the yard superintending. Her face brightened with her old smile. Her whole being revived and freshened, as though she had awakened from a long sleep. The veterinarian's wife and child arrived. She was a thin, plain woman, with a crabbed expression. The boy Sasha, small for his ten years of age, was a chubby child, with clear blue eyes and dimples in his cheeks. He made for the kitten the instant he entered the yard, and the place rang with his happy laughter.

"Is that your cat, auntie?" he asked Olenka. "When she has little kitties, please give me one. Mamma is awfully afraid of mice."

Olenka chatted with him, gave him tea, and there was a sudden warmth in her bosom and a soft gripping at her heart, as though the boy were her own son.

In the evening, when he sat in the dining-room studying his lessons, she looked at him tenderly and whispered to herself:

"My darling, my pretty. You are such a clever child, so good to look at."

"An island is a tract of land entirely surrounded by water," he recited.

"An island is a tract of land," she repeated—the first idea asseverated with conviction after so many years of silence and mental emptiness.

She now had her opinions, and at supper discussed with Sasha's parents how difficult the studies had become for the children at the gymnasium, but how, after all, a classical education was better than a commercial course, because when you graduated from the gymnasium then the road was open to you for any career at all. If you chose to, you could become a doctor, or, if you wanted to, you could become an engineer.

Sasha began to go to the gymnasium. His mother left on a visit to her sister in Kharkov and never came back. The father was away every day inspecting cattle, and sometimes was gone three whole days at a time, so that Sasha, it seemed to Olenka, was utterly abandoned, was treated as if he were quite superfluous, and must be dying of hunger. So she transferred him into the wing along with herself and fixed up a little room for him there.

Every morning Olenka would come into his room and find him sound asleep with his hand tucked under his cheek, so quiet that he seemed not to be breathing. What a shame to have to wake him, she thought.

"Sashenka," she said sorrowingly, "get up, darling. It's time to go to the gymnasium."

He got up, dressed, said his prayers, then sat down to drink tea. He drank three glasses of tea, ate two large cracknels and half a buttered roll. The sleep was not yet out of him, so he was a little cross.

"You don't know your fable as you should, Sashenka," said Olenka, looking at him as though he were departing on a long journey. "What a lot of trouble you are. You must try hard and learn, dear, and mind your teachers."

"Oh, let me alone, please," said Sasha.

Then he went down the street to the gymnasium, a little fellow wearing a large cap and carrying a satchel on his back. Olenka followed him noiselessly.

"Sashenka," she called.

He looked round and she shoved a date or a caramel into his hand. When he reached the street of the gymnasium, he turned around and said, ashamed of being followed by a tall, stout woman:

"You had better go home, aunt. I can go the rest of the way myself.

She stopped and stared after him until he had disappeared into the school entrance.

Oh, how she loved him! Not one of her other ties had

been so deep. Never before had she given herself so completely, so disinterestedly, so cheerfully as now that her maternal instincts were all aroused. For this boy, who was not hers, for the dimples in his cheeks and for his big cap, she would have given her life, given it with joy and with tears of rapture. Why? Ah, indeed, why?

When she had seen Sasha off to the gymnasium, she returned home quietly, content, serene, overflowing with love. Her face, which had grown younger in the last half year, smiled and beamed. People who met her were pleased as they looked at her.

"How are you, Olga Semyonovna, darling? How are you getting on, darling?"

"The gymnasium course is very hard nowadays," she told at the market. "It's no joke. Yesterday the first class had a fable to learn by heart, a Latin translation, and a problem. How is a little fellow to do all that?"

And she spoke of the teacher and the lessons and the textbooks, repeating exactly what Sasha said about them.

At three o'clock they had dinner. In the evening they prepared the lessons together, and Olenka wept with Sasha over the difficulties. When she put him to bed, she lingered a long time making the sign of the cross over him and muttering a prayer. And when she lay in bed, she dreamed of the far-away, misty future when Sasha would finish his studies and become a doctor or an engineer, have a large house of his own, with horses and a carriage, marry and have children. She would fall asleep still thinking of the same things, and tears would roll down her cheeks from her closed eyes. And the black cat would lie at her side purring: "Mrr, mrr, mrr."

Suddenly there was a loud knocking at the gate. Olenka woke up breathless with fright, her heart beating violently. Half a minute later there was another knock.

"A telegram from Kharkov," she thought, her whole body in a tremble. "His mother wants Sasha to come to her in Kharkov. Oh, great God!"

She was in despair. Her head, her feet, her hands turned cold. There was no unhappier creature in the world, she felt. But another minute passed, she heard voices. It was the veterinarian coming home from the club.

"Thank God," she thought. The load gradually fell from her heart, she was at ease again. And she went back to bed, thinking of Sasha who lay fast asleep in the next room and sometimes cried out in his sleep:

"I'll give it to you! Get away! Quit your scrapping!"

THE BET

◆◆◆

By Anton P. Chekhov

I

IT WAS A DARK autumn night. The old banker was pacing from corner to corner of his study, recalling to his mind the party he gave in the autumn fifteen years before. There were many clever people at the party and much interesting conversation. They talked among other things of capital punishment. The guests, among them not a few scholars and journalists, for the most part disapproved of capital punishment. They found it obsolete as a means of punishment, unfitted to a Christian State and immoral. Some of them thought that capital punishment should be replaced universally by life-imprisonment.

"I don't agree with you," said the host. "I myself have experienced neither capital punishment nor life-imprisonment, but if one may judge *a priori,* then in my opinion capital punishment is more moral and more humane than imprisonment. Execution kills instantly, life-imprisonment kills by degrees. Who is the more humane executioner, one who kills you in a few seconds or one who draws the life out of you incessantly, for years?"

"They're both equally immoral," remarked one of the

guests, "because their purpose is the same, to take away life. The State is not God. It has no right to take away that which it cannot give back, if it should so desire."

Among the company was a lawyer, a young man of about twenty-five. On being asked his opinion, he said:

"Capital punishment and life-imprisonment are equally immoral; but if I were offered the choice between them, I would certainly choose the second. It's better to live somehow than not to live at all."

There ensued a lively discussion. The banker who was then younger and more nervous suddenly lost his temper, banged his fist on the table, and turning to the young lawyer, cried out:

"It's a lie. I bet you two millions you wouldn't stick in a cell even for five years."

"If you mean it seriously," replied the lawyer, "then I bet I'll stay not five but fifteen."

"Fifteen! Done!" cried the banker. "Gentlemen, I stake two millions."

"Agreed. You stake two millions, I my freedom," said the lawyer.

So this wild, ridiculous bet came to pass. The banker, who at that time had too many millions to count, spoiled and capricious, was beside himself with rapture. During supper he said to the lawyer jokingly:

"Come to your senses, young man, before it's too late. Two millions are nothing to me, but you stand to lose three or four of the best years of your life. I say three or four, because you'll never stick it out any longer. Don't forget either, you unhappy man, that voluntary is much heavier than enforced imprisonment. The idea that you have the right to free yourself at any moment will poison the whole of your life in the cell. I pity you."

And now the banker, pacing from corner to corner, recalled all this and asked himself:

"Why did I make this bet? What's the good? The lawyer loses fifteen years of his life and I throw away two millions. Will it convince people that capital punishment is worse or better than imprisonment for life? No, no! all stuff and rubbish. On my part, it was the caprice of a well-fed man; on the lawyer's pure greed of gold."

He recollected further what happened after the evening party. It was decided that the lawyer must undergo his imprisonment under the strictest observation, in a garden wing of the banker's house. It was agreed that during the period he would be deprived of the right to cross the threshold, to see living people, to hear human voices, and to receive letters and newspapers. He was permitted to have a musical instrument, to read books, to write letters, to drink wine and smoke tobacco. By the agreement he could communicate, but only in silence, with the outside world through a little window specially constructed for this purpose. Everything necessary, books, music, wine, he could receive in any quantity by sending a note through the window. The agreement provided for all the minutest details, which made the confinement strictly solitary, and it obliged the lawyer to remain exactly fifteen years from twelve o'clock of November 14th, 1870, to twelve o'clock of November 14th, 1885. The least attempt on his part to violate the conditions, to escape if only for two minutes before the time freed the banker from the obligation to pay him the two millions.

During the first year of imprisonment, the lawyer, as far as it was possible to judge from his short notes, suffered terribly from loneliness and boredom. From his wing day and night came the sound of the piano. He rejected wine and tobacco. "Wine," he wrote, "excites desires, and desires are the chief foes of a prisoner; besides, nothing is more boring than to drink good wine alone," and tobacco spoils the air in his room. During the first year the lawyer was sent books of a light character; novels with a complicated love interest, stories of crime and fantasy, comedies, and so on.

In the second year the piano was heard no longer and the lawyer asked only for classics. In the fifth year, music was heard again, and the prisoner asked for wine. Those who watched him said that during the whole of that year he was only eating, drinking, and lying on his bed. He yawned often and talked angrily to himself. Books he did not read. Sometimes at nights he would sit down to write. He would write for a long time and tear it all up in the morning. More than once he was heard to weep.

In the second half of the sixth year, the prisoner began zealously to study languages, philosophy, and history. He fell on these subjects so hungrily that the banker hardly had time to get books enough for him. In the space of four years about six hundred volumes were bought at his request. It was while that passion lasted that the banker received the following letter from the prisoner: "My dear gaoler, I am writing these lines in six languages. Show them to experts.

Let them read them. If they do not find one single mistake, I beg you to give orders to have a gun fired off in the garden. By the noise I shall know that my efforts have not been in vain. The geniuses of all ages and countries speak in different languages; but in them all burns the same flame. Oh, if you knew my heavenly happiness now that I can understand them!" The prisoner's desire was fulfilled. Two shots were fired in the garden by the banker's order.

Later on, after the tenth year, the lawyer sat immovable before his table and read only the New Testament. The banker found it strange that a man who in four years had mastered six hundred erudite volumes, should have spent nearly a year in reading one book, easy to understand and by no means thick. The New Testament was then replaced by the history of religions and theology.

During the last two years of his confinement the prisoner read an extraordinary amount, quite haphazard. Now he would apply himself to the natural sciences, then he would read Byron or Shakespeare. Notes used to come from him in which he asked to be sent at the same time a book on chemistry, a text-book of medicine, a novel, and some treatise on philosophy or theology. He read as though he were swimming in the sea among broken pieces of wreckage, and in his desire to save his life was eagerly grasping one piece after another.

II

THE BANKER recalled all this, and thought:

"To-morrow at twelve o'clock he receives his freedom.

Under the agreement, I shall have to pay him two millions. If I pay, it's all over with me. I am ruined for ever . . ."

Fifteen years before he had too many millions to count, but now he was afraid to ask himself which he had more of, money or debts. Gambling on the Stock-Exchange, risky speculation, and the recklessness of which he could not rid himself even in old age, had gradually brought his business to decay; and the fearless, self-confident, proud man of business had become an ordinary banker, trembling at every rise and fall in the market.

"That cursed bet," murmured the old man clutching his head in despair. . . . "Why, didn't the man die? He's only forty years old. He will take away my last farthing, marry, enjoy life, gamble on the Exchange, and I will look on like an envious beggar and hear the same words from him every day: 'I'm obliged to you for the happiness of my life. Let me help you.' No, it's too much! The only escape from bankruptcy and disgrace—is that the man should die."

The clock had just struck three. The banker was listening. In the house every one was asleep, and one could hear only the frozen trees whining outside the windows. Trying to make no sound, he took out of his safe the key of the door which had not been opened for fifteen years, put on his overcoat, and went out of the house. The garden was dark and cold. It was raining. A damp, penetrating wind howled in the garden and gave the trees no rest. Though he strained his eyes, the banker could see neither the ground, nor the white statues, nor the garden wing, nor the trees. Approaching the garden wing, he called the watchman twice. There was no answer. Evidently the watchman had taken shelter from the bad weather and was now asleep somewhere in the kitchen or the greenhouse.

"If I have the courage to fulfill my intention," thought the old man, "the suspicion will fall on the watchman first of all."

In the darkness he groped for the steps and the door and entered the hall of the garden-wing, then poked his way into a narrow passage and struck a match. Not a soul was there. Some one's bed, with no bedclothes on it, stood there, and an iron stove loomed dark in the corner. The seals on the door that led into the prisoner's room were unbroken.

When the match went out, the old man, trembling from agitation, peeped into the little window.

In the prisoner's room a candle was burning dimly. The prisoner himself sat by the table. Only his back, the hair on his head and his hands were visible. Open books were strewn about on the table, the two chairs, and on the carpet near the table.

Five minutes passed and the prisoner never once stirred. Fifteen years' confinement had taught him to sit motionless. The banker tapped on the window with his finger, but the prisoner made no movement in reply. Then the banker cautiously tore the seals from the door and put the key into the lock. The rusty lock gave a hoarse groan and the door creaked. The banker expected instantly to hear a cry of surprise and the sound of steps. Three minutes passed and it was as quiet inside as it had been before. He made up his mind to enter.

Before the table sat a man, unlike an ordinary human

being. It was a skeleton, with tight-drawn skin, with long curly hair like a woman's, and a shaggy beard. The colour of his face was yellow, of an earthy shade; the cheeks were sunken, the back long and narrow, and the hand upon which he leaned his hairy head was so lean and skinny that it was painful to look upon. His hair was already silvering with grey, and no one who glanced at the senile emaciation of the face would have believed that he was only forty years old. On the table, before his bended head, lay a sheet of paper on which something was written in a tiny hand.

"Poor devil," thought the banker, "he's asleep and probably seeing millions in his dreams. I have only to take and throw this half-dead thing on the bed, smother him a moment with the pillow, and the most careful examination will find no trace of unnatural death. But, first, let us read what he has written here."

The banker took the sheet from the table and read:

"To-morrow at twelve o'clock midnight, I shall obtain my freedom and the right to mix with people. But before I leave this room and see the sun I think it necessary to say a few words to you. On my own clear conscience and before God who sees me I declare to you that I despise freedom, life, health, and all that your books call the blessings of the world.

"For fifteen years I have diligently studied earthly life. True, I saw neither the earth nor the people, but in your books I drank fragrant wine, sang songs, hunted deer and wild boar in the forests, loved women. . . . And beautiful women, like clouds ethereal, created by the magic of your poets' genius, visited me by night and whispered to me wonderful tales, which made my head drunken. In your books I climbed the summits of Elbruz and Mont Blanc and saw from there how the sun rose in the morning, and in the evening, suffused the sky, the ocean and the mountain ridges with a purple gold. I saw from there how above me lightnings glimmered cleaving the clouds; I saw green forests, fields, rivers, lakes, cities; I heard sirens singing, and the playing of the pipes of Pan; I touched the wings of beautiful devils who came flying to me to speak of God. . . . In your books I cast myself into bottomless abysses, worked miracles, burned cities to the ground, preached new religions, conquered whole countries. . . .

"Your books gave me wisdom. All that unwearying human thought created in the centuries is compressed to a little lump in my skull. I know that I am cleverer than you all.

"And I despise your books, despise all worldly blessings and wisdom. Everything is void, frail, visionary and delusive as a mirage. Though you be proud and wise and beautiful, yet will death wipe you from the face of the earth like the mice underground; and your posterity, your history, and the immortality of your men of genius will be as frozen slag, burnt down together with the terrestrial globe.

"You are mad, and gone the wrong way. You take falsehood for truth and ugliness for beauty. You would marvel if suddenly apple and orange trees should bear frogs and lizards instead of fruit, and if roses should begin to breathe the odour of a sweating horse. So do I marvel at you, who have bartered heaven for earth. I do not want to understand you.

"That I may show you in deed my contempt for that by which you live, I waive the two millions of which I once dreamed as of paradise, and which I now despise. That I may deprive myself of my right to them, I shall come out from here five minutes before the stipulated term, and thus shall violate the agreement."

When he had read, the banker put the sheet on the table, kissed the head of the strange man, and began to weep. He went out of the wing. Never at any other time, not even after his terrible losses on the Exchange, had he felt such contempt for himself as now. Coming home, he lay down on his bed, but agitation and tears kept him a long time from sleeping. . . .

The next morning the poor watchman came running to him and told him that they had seen the man who lived in the wing climb through the window into the garden. He had gone to the gate and disappeared. The banker instantly went with his servants to the wing and established the escape of his prisoner. To avoid unnecessary rumours he took the paper with the renunciation from the table and, on his return, locked it in his safe.

VANKA

• • •

By Anton P. Chekhov

NINE-YEAR-OLD Vanka Zhukov, who had been apprentice to the shoemaker Aliakhin for three months, did not go to bed the night before Christmas. He waited till the master and mistress and the assistants had gone out to an early church-service, to procure from his employer's cupboard a small phial of ink and a penholder with a rusty nib; then, spreading a crumpled sheet of paper in front of him, he began to write.

Before, however, deciding to make the first letter, he looked furtively at the door and at the window, glanced several times at the sombre ikon, on either side of which stretched shelves full of lasts, and heaved a heart-rending sigh. The sheet of paper was spread on a bench, and he himself was on his knees in front of it.

"Dear Grandfather Konstantin Makarych," he wrote, "I am writing you a letter. I wish you a Happy Christmas and all God's holy best. I have no mamma or papa, you are all I have."

Vanka gave a look towards the window in which shone the reflection of his candle, and vividly pictured to himself his grandfather, Konstantin Makarych, who was night watchman at Messrs. Zhivarev. He was a small, lean, unusually lively and active old man of sixty-five, always smiling and blear-eyed. All day he slept in the servants' kitchen or trifled with the cooks. At night, enveloped in an ample sheep-skin coat, he strayed round the domain tapping with his cudgel. Behind him, each hanging its head, walked the old bitch Kashtanka, and the dog Viun, so named because of his black coat and long body and his resemblance to a loach. Viun was an unusually civil and friendly dog, looking as kindly at a stranger as at his masters, but he was not to be trusted. Beneath his deference and humbleness was hid the most inquisitorial maliciousness. No one knew better than he how to sneak up and take a bite at a leg, or slip into the larder or steal a muzhik's chicken. More than once they had nearly broken his hind-legs, twice he had been hung up, every week he was nearly flogged to death, but he always recovered.

At this moment, for certain, Vanka's grandfather must be standing at the gate, blinking his eyes at the bright red windows of the village church, stamping his feet in their high-felt boots, and jesting with the people in the yard; his cudgel will be hanging from his belt, he will be hugging himself with cold, giving a little dry, old man's cough, and at times pinching a servant-girl or a cook.

"Won't we take some snuff?" he asks, holding out his snuff-box to the women. The women take a pinch of snuff, and sneeze.

The old man goes into indescribable ecstasies, breaks into loud laughter, and cries:

"Off with it, it will freeze to your nose!"

He gives his snuff to the dogs, too. Kashtanka sneezes, twitches her nose, and walks away offended. Viun deferentially refuses to sniff and wags his tail. It is glorious weather, not a breath of wind, clear, and frosty; it is a dark night, but the whole village, its white roofs and streaks of smoke from the chimneys, the trees silvered with hoarfrost, and the snowdrifts, you can see it all. The sky scintillates with bright twinkling stars, and the Milky Way stands out so clearly that it looks as if it had been polished and rubbed over with snow for the holidays. . . .

Vanka sighs, dips his pen in the ink, and continues to write:

"Last night I got a thrashing, my master dragged me by my hair into the yard, and belaboured me with a shoemaker's stirrup, because, while I was rocking his brat in its cradle, I unfortunately fell asleep. And during the week, my mistress told me to clean a herring, and I began by its tail, so she took the herring and stuck its snout into my face. The assistants tease me, send me to the tavern for vodka, make me steal the master's cucumbers, and the master beats me with whatever is handy. Food there is none; in the morning it's bread, at dinner, gruel, and in the evening bread again. As for tea or sour-cabbage soup, the master and the mistress themselves guzzle that. They make me sleep in the vestibule, and when their brat cries, I don't sleep at all, but have to rock the cradle. Dear Grandpapa, for Heaven's sake, take me away from here, home to our village, I can't bear this any more. . . . I bow to the ground to you, and will pray to God for ever and ever, take me from here or I shall die. . . ."

The corners of Vanka's mouth went down, he rubbed his eyes with his dirty fist, and sobbed.

"I'll grate your tobacco for you," he continued, "I'll pray to God for you, and if there is anything wrong, then flog me like the grey goat. And if you really think I shan't find work, then I'll ask the manager, for Christ's sake, to let me clean the boots, or I'll go instead of Fedya as underherdsman. Dear Grandpapa, I can't bear this any more, it'll kill me. . . . I wanted to run away to our village, but I have no boots, and I was afraid of the frost, and when I grow up I'll look after you, no one shall harm you, and when you die I'll pray for the repose of your soul, just like I do for mamma Pelagueya.

"As for Moscow, it is a large town, there are all gentlemen's houses, lots of horses, no sheep, and the dogs are not vicious. The children don't come round at Christmas with a star, no one is allowed to sing in the choir, and once I saw in a shop window hooks on a line and fishing rods, all for sale, and for every kind of fish, awfully convenient. And there was one hook which would catch a sheat-fish weighing a pound. And there are shops with guns, like the master's, and I am sure they must cost 100 rubles each. And in the meat-shops there are woodcocks, partridges, and hares, but who shot them or where they come from, the shopman won't say.

"Dear Grandpa, and when the masters give a Christmas tree, take a golden walnut and hide it in my green box.

Ask the young lady, Olga Ignatyevna, for it, say it's for Vanka."

Vanka sighed convulsively, and again stared at the window. He remembered that his grandfather always went to the forest for the Christmas tree, and took his grandson with him. What happy times! The frost crackled, his grandfather crackled, and as they both did, Vanka did the same. Then before cutting down the Christmas tree his grandfather smoked his pipe, took a long pinch of snuff, and made fun of poor frozen little Vanka. . . . The young fir trees, wrapt in hoar-frost, stood motionless, waiting for which of them would die. Suddenly a hare springing from somewhere would dart over the snowdrift. . . . His grandfather could not help shouting:

"Catch it, catch it, catch it! Ah, short-tailed devil!"

When the tree was down, his grandfather dragged it to the master's house, and there they set about decorating it. The young lady, Olga Ignatyevna, Vanka's great friend, busied herself most about it. When little Vanka's mother, Pelagueya, was still alive, and was servant-woman in the house, Olga Ignatyevna used to stuff him with sugar-candy, and, having nothing to do, taught him to read, write, count up to one hundred, and even to dance the quadrille. When Pelagueya died, they placed the orphan Vanka in the kitchen with his grandfather, and from the kitchen he was sent to Moscow to Aliakhin, the shoemaker.

"Come quick, dear Grandpapa," continued Vanka, "I beseech you for Christ's sake take me from here. Have pity on a poor orphan, for here they beat me, and I am frightfully hungry, and so sad that I can't tell you, I cry all the time.

The other day the master hit me on the head with a last; I fell to the ground, and only just returned to life. My life is a misfortune, worse than any dog's. . . . I send greetings to Aliona, to one-eyed Tegor, and the coachman, and don't let any one have my mouth-organ. I remain, your grandson, Ivan Zhukov, dear Grandpapa, do come."

Vanka folded his sheet of paper in four, and put it into an envelope purchased the night before for a kopek. He thought a little, dipped the pen into the ink, and wrote the address:

"The village, to my grandfather." He then scratched his head, thought again, and added: "Konstantin Makarych." Pleased at not having been interfered with in his writing, he put on his cap, and, without putting on his sheep-skin coat, ran out in his shirt-sleeves into the street.

The shopman at the poulterer's, from whom he had inquired the night before, had told him that letters were to be put into post-boxes, and from there they were conveyed over the whole earth in mail troikas by drunken post-boys and to the sound of bells. Vanka ran to the first post-box and slipped his precious letter into the slit.

An hour afterwards, lulled by hope, he was sleeping soundly. In his dreams he saw a stove, by the stove his grandfather sitting with his legs dangling down, barefooted, and reading a letter to the cooks, and Viun walking round the stove wagging his tail.

HIDE AND SEEK

◆◆◆

By Fiodor Sologub

EVERYTHING IN Lelechka's nursery was bright, pretty, and
cheerful. Lelechka's sweet voice charmed her mother.
Lelechka was a delightful child. There was no other such
child, there never had been, and there never would be.
Lelechka's mother, Serafima Aleksandrovna, was sure of
that. Lelechka's eyes were dark and large, her cheeks were
rosy, her lips were made for kisses and for laughter. But
it was not these charms in Lelechka that gave her mother
the keenest joy. Lelechka was her mother's only child. That
was why every movement of Lelechka's bewitched her
mother. It was great bliss to hold Lelechka on her knees
and to fondle her; to feel the little girl in her arms—a thing
as lively and as bright as a little bird.

To tell the truth, Serafima Aleksandrovna felt happy only
in the nursery. She felt cold with her husband.

Perhaps it was because he himself loved the cold—he
loved to drink cold water, and to breathe cold air. He was
always fresh and cool, with a frigid smile, and wherever he
passed cold currents seemed to move in the air.

The Nesletyevs, Sergey Modestovich and Serafima Aleksandrovna, had married without love or calculation, because it was the accepted thing. He was a young man of thirty-five, she a young woman of twenty-five; both were of the same circle and well brought up; he was expected to take a wife, and the time had come for her to take a husband.

It even seemed to Serafima Aleksandrovna that she was in love with her future husband, and this made her happy. He looked handsome and well-bred; his intelligent grey eyes always preserved a dignified expression; and he fulfilled his obligations of a fiancé with irreproachable gentleness.

The bride was also good-looking; she was a tall, dark-eyed, dark-haired girl, somewhat timid but very tactful. He was not after her dowry, though it pleased him to know that she had something. He had connexions, and his wife came of good, influential people. This might, at the proper opportunity, prove useful. Always irreproachable and tactful, Nesletyev got on in his position not so fast that any one should envy him, nor yet so slow that he should envy any one else—everything came in the proper measure and at the proper time.

After their marriage there was nothing in the manner of Sergey Modestovich to suggest anything wrong to his wife. Later, however, when his wife was about to have a child, Sergey Modestovich established connexious elsewhere of a light and temporary nature. Serafima Aleksandrovna found this out, and to her own astonishment, was not particularly hurt; she awaited her infant with a restless anticipation that swallowed every other feeling.

A little girl was born; Serafima Aleksandrovna gave herself up to her. At the beginning she used to tell her husband, with rapture, of all the joyous details of Lelechka's existence. But she soon found that he listened to her without the slightest interest, and only from the habit of politeness. Serafima Aleksandrovna drifted farther and farther away from him. She loved her little girl with the ungratified passion that other women, deceived in their husbands, show their chance young lovers.

"*Mamochka,* let's play *priatki*" (hide and seek), cried Lelechka, pronouncing the *r* like the *l*, so that the word sounded "pliatki."

This charming inability to speak always made Serafima Aleksandrovna smile with tender rapture. Lelechka then ran away, stamping with her plump little legs over the carpets, and hid herself behind the curtains near her bed.

"*Tiu-tiu, mamochka!*" she cried out in her sweet, laughing voice, as she looked out with a single roguish eye.

"Where is my baby girl?" the mother asked, as she looked for Lelechka and made believe that she did not see her.

And Lelechka poured out her rippling laughter in her hiding place. Then she came out a little farther, and her mother, as though she had only just caught sight of her, seized her by her little shoulders and exclaimed joyously: "Here she is, my Lelechka!"

Lelechka laughed long and merrily, her head close to her mother's knees, and all of her cuddled up between her mother' white hands. Her mother's eyes glowed with passionate emotion.

"Now, *mamochka,* you hide," said Lelechka, as she ceased laughing.

Her mother went to hide. Lelechka turned away as though not to see, but watched her *mamochka* stealthily all the time. Mamma hid behind the cupboard, and exclaimed: *"Tiu-tiu,* baby girl!"

Lelechka ran round the room and looked into all the corners, making believe, as her mother had done before, that she was seeking—though she really knew all the time where her *mamochka* was standing.

"Where's my *mamochka?"* asked Lelechka. "She's not here, and she's not here," she kept on repeating, as she ran from corner to corner.

Her mother stood, with suppressed breathing, her head pressed against the wall, her hair somewhat disarranged. A smile of absolute bliss played on her red lips.

The nurse, Fedosya, a good-natured and fine-looking, if somewhat stupid woman, smiled as she looked at her mistress with her characteristic expression, which seemed to say that it was not for her to object to gentlewomen's caprices. She thought to herself: "The mother is like a little child herself—look how excited she is."

Lelechka was getting nearer her mother's corner. Her mother was growing more absorbed every moment by her interest in the game; her heart beat with short quick strokes, and she pressed even closer to the wall, disarranging her hair still more. Lelechka suddenly glanced toward her mother's corner and screamed with joy.

"I've found 'oo," she cried out loudly and joyously, mispronouncing her words in a way that again made her mother happy.

She pulled her mother by her hands to the middle of the room, they were merry and they laughed; and Lelechka again hid her head against her mother's knees, and went on lisping and lisping, without end, her sweet little words, so fascinating yet so awkward.

Sergey Modestovich was coming at this moment toward the nursery. Through the half-closed doors he heard the laughter, the joyous outcries, the sound of romping. He entered the nursery, smiling his genial cold smile; he was irreproachably dressed, and he looked fresh and erect, and he spread round him an atmosphere of cleanliness, freshness and coldness. He entered in the midst of the lively game, and he confused them all by his radiant coldness. Even Fedosya felt abashed, now for her mistress, now for herself. Serafima Aleksandrovna at once became calm and apparently cold—and this mood communicated itself to the little girl, who ceased to laugh, but looked instead, silently and intently, at her father.

Sergey Modestovich gave a swift glance round the room. He liked coming here, where everything was beautifully arranged; this was done by Serafima Aleksandrovna, who wished to surround her little girl, from her very infancy, only with the loveliest things. Serafima Aleksandrovna dressed herself tastefully; this, too, she did for Lelechka, with the same end in view. One thing Sergey Modestovich had not become reconciled to, and this was his wife's almost continuous presence in the nursery.

"It's just as I thought. . . . I knew that I'd find you here," he said with a derisive and condescending smile.

They left the nursery together. As he followed his wife through the door Sergey Modestovich said rather indifferently, in an incidental way, laying no stress on his words: "Don't you think that it would be well for the little girl if she were sometimes without your company? Merely, you see, that the child should feel its own individuality," he explained in answer to Serafima Aleksandrovna's puzzled glance.

"She still so little," said Serafima Aleksandrovna.

"In any case, this is but my humble opinion. I don't insist. It's your kingdom there."

"I'll think it over," his wife answered, smiling, as he did, coldly but genially.

Then they began to talk of something else.

II

NURSE FEDOSYA, sitting in the kitchen that evening, was tell-ing the silent housemaid Darya and the talkative old cook Agathya about the young lady of the house, and how the child loved to play *priatki* with her mother—"She hides her little face, and cries *'tiu--tiu'!*"

"And the mistress herself is like a little one," added Fedosya, smiling.

Agathya listened and shook her head ominously; while her face became grave and reproachful.

"That the mistreess does it, well, that's one thing; but that the young lady does it, that's bad."

"Why?" asked Fedosya with curiosity.

This expression of curiosity gave her face the look of a wooden, roughly-painted doll.

"Yes, that's bad," repeated Agathya with conviction. "Terribly bad!"

"Well?" said Fedosya, the ludicrous expression of curiosity on her face becoming more emphatic.

"She'll hide, and hide, and hide away," said Agathya, in a mysterious whisper, as she looked cautiously toward the door.

"What are you saying?" exclaimed Fedosya, frightened.

"It's the ruth I'm saying, remember my words," Agathya went on with the same assurance and secrecy. "It's the surest sign."

The old woman had invented this sign, quite suddenly, herself; and she was evidently very proud of it.

III

LELECHKA WAS asleep, and Serafima Aleksandrovna was sitting in her own room, thinking with joy and tenderness of Lelechka. Lelechka was in her thoughts, first a sweet, tiny girl, then a sweet, big girl, then again a delightful little girl; and so until the end she remained mamma's little Lelechka.

Serafima Aleksandrovna did not even notice that Fedosya came up to her and paused before her. Fedosya had a worried, frightened look.

"Madam, madam," she said quietly, in a trembling voice.

Serafima Aleksandrovna gave a start. Fedosya's face made her anxious.

"What is it, Fedosya?' she asked with great concern. "Is there anything wrong with Lelechka?"

"No, madam," said Fedosya, as she gesticulated with her hands to reassure her mistress and to make her sit down. "Lelechka is asleep, may God be with her! Only I'd like to say something—you see—Lelechka is always hiding herself —that's not good."

Fedosya looked at her mistress with fixed eyes, which had grown round from fright.

"Why not good?" asked Serafima Aleksandrovna, with vexation, succumbing involuntarily to vague fears.

"I can't tell you how bad it is," said Fedosya, and her face expressed the most decided confidence.

"Please speak in a sensible way," observed Serafima Aleksandrovna dryly. "I understond nothing of what you are saying."

"You see, madam, it's a kind of omen," explained Fedosya abruptly, in a shamefaced way.

"Nonsense!' said Serafima Aleksandrovna.

She did not wish to hear any further as to the sort of omen it was, and what it foreboded. But, somehow, a sense of fear and of sadness crept into her mood, and it was humiliating to feel that an absurd tale should disturb her beloved fancies, and should agitate her so deeply.

"Of course I know that gentlefolk don't believe in omens, but it's a bad omen, madam," Fedosya went on in a doleful voice, "the young lady will hide, and hide. . . ."

Suddenly she burst into tears, sobbing out loudly: "She'll hide, and hide, and hide away, angelic little soul, in a damp grave," she continued, as she wiped her tears with her apron and blew her nose.

"Who told you all this?" asked Serafima Aleksandrovna in an austere low voice.

"Agathya says so, madam," answered Fedosya; "it's she that knows."

"Knows!" exclaimed Serafima Aleksandrovna in irritation, as though she wished to protect herself somehow from this sudden anxiety. "What nonsense! Please don't come to me with any such notions in the future. Now you may go."

Fedosya, dejected, her feelings hurt, left her mistress.

"What nonsense! As though Lelechka could die!" thought Serafima Aleksandrovna to herself, trying to conquer the feeling of coldness and fear which took possession of her at the thought of the possible death of Lelechka. Serafima Aleksandrovna, upon reflection, attributed these women's beliefs in omens to ignorance. She saw clearly that there could be no possible connexion between a child's quite ordinary diversion and the continuation of the child's life. She made a special effort that evening to occupy her mind with other matters, but her thoughts returned involuntarily to the fact that Lelechka loved to hide herself.

When Lelechka was still quite small, and had learned to distinguish between her mother and her nurse, she sometimes, sitting in her nurse's arms, made a sudden roguish grimace, and hid her laughing face in the nurse's shoulder. Then she would look out with a sly glance.

Of late, in those rare moments of the mistress' absence

from the nursery, Fedosya had again taught Lelechka to hide; and when Lelechka's mother, on coming in, saw how lovely the child looked when she was hiding, she herself began to play hide and seek with her tiny daughter.

IV

THE NEXT day Serafima Aleksandrovna, absorbed in her joyous cares for Lelechka, had forgotten Fedosya's words of the day before.

But when she returned to the nursery, after having ordered the dinner, and, she heard Lelechka suddenly cry *"Tiu-tiu!"* from under the table, a feeling of fear suddenly took hold of her. Though she reproached herself at once for this unfounded, superstitious dread, nevertheless she could not enter wholeheartedly into the spirit of Lelechka's favourite game, and she tried to divert Lelechka's attention to something else.

Lelechka was a lovely and obedient child. She eagerly complied with her mother's new wishes. But as she had got into the habit of hiding from her mother in some corner, and of crying out *"Tiu-tiu!"* so even that day she returned more than once to the game.

Serafima Aleksandrovna tried desperately to amuse Lelechka. This was not so easy because restless, threatening thoughts obtruded themselves constantly.

"Why does Lelechka keep on recalling the *tiu-tiu?* Why does she not get tired of the same thing—of eternally closing her eyes, and of hiding her face? Perhaps," thought Serafima Aleksandrovna, "she is not as strongly drawn to the world as other children, who are attracted by many things. If this is so, is it not a sign of organic weakness? Is it not a germ of the unconscious non-desire to live?"

Serafima Aleksandrovna was tormented by presentiments. She felt ashamed of herself for ceasing to play hide and seek with Lelechka before Fedosya. But this game had become agonising to her, all the more agonising because she had a real desire to play it, and because something drew her very strongly to hide herself from Lelechka and to seek out the hiding child. Serafima Aleksandrovna herself began the game once or twice, though she played it with a heavy heart. She suffered as though committing an evil deed with full consciousness.

It was a sad day for Serafima Aleksandrovna.

V

LELECHKA was about to fall asleep. No sooner had she climbed into her little bed, protected by a network on all sides, than her eyes began to close from fatigue. Her mother covered her with a blue blanket. Lelechka drew her sweet little hands from under the blanket and stretched them out to embrace her mother. Her mother bent down. Lelechka, with a tender expression on her sleepy face, kissed her mother and let her head fall on the pillow. As her hands hid themselves under the blanket Lelechka whispered: "The hands *tiu-tiu!*"

The mother's heart seemed to stop—Lelechka lay there so small, so frail, so quiet. Lelechka smiled gently, closed her eyes and said quietly: "The eyes *tiu-tiu!*"

Then even more quietly: "Lelechka *tiu-tiu!*"

With these words she fell asleep, her face pressing the pillow. She seemed so small and so frail under the blanket that covered her. Her mother looked at her with sad eyes.

Serafima Aleksandrovna remained standing over Lelechka's bed a long while, and she kept looking at Lelechka with tenderness and fear.

"I'm a mother: is it possible that I shouldn't be able to protect her?" she thought, as she imagined the various ills that might befall Lelechka.

She prayed long that night, but the prayer did not relieve her sadness.

VI

SEVERAL DAYS passed. Lelechka caught cold. The fever came upon her at night. When Serafima Aleksandrovna, awakened by Fedosya, came to Lelechka and saw her looking so hot, so restless, and so tormented, she instantly recalled the evil omen, and a hopeless despair took possession of her from the first moments.

A doctor was called, and everything was done that is usual on such occasions—but the inevitable happened. Serafima Aleksandrovna tried to console herself with the hope that Lelechka would get well, and would again laugh and play—yet this seemed to her an unthinkable happiness! And Lelechka grew feebler from hour to hour.

All simulated tranquility, so as not to frighten Serafima Aleksandrovna, but their masked faces only made her sad. Nothing made her so unhappy as the reiteration of Fedosy, uttered between sobs: "She hid herself and hid herself, our Lelechka!"

But the thoughts of Serafima Aleksandrovna were confused, and she could not quite grasp what was happening.

Fever was consuming Lelechka, and there were times when she lost consciousness and spoke in delirium. But when she returned to herself she bore her pain and her fatigue with gentle good nature; she smiled feebly at her *mamochka,* so that her *mamochka* should not see how much she suffered. Three days passed, torturing like a nightmare. Lelechka grew quite feeble. She did not know that she was dying.

She glanced at her mother with her dimmed eyes, and lisped in a scarcely audible, hoarse voice: *"Tiu-tiu, mamochka!* Make *tiu-tiu, mamochka!"*

Serafima Aleksandrovna hid her face behind the curtains near Lelechka's bed. How tragic!

"Mamochka!" called Lelechka in an almost inaudible voice.

Lelechka's mother bent over her, and Lelechka, her vision grown still more dim, saw her mother's pale, despairing face for the last time.

"A white *mamochka!"* whispered Lelechka.

Mamochka's white face became blurred, and everything grew dark before Lelechka. She caught the edge of the bedcover feebly with her hands and whispered: *"Tiu-tiu!"*

Something rattled in her throat; Lelechka opened and again closed her rapidly paling lips, and died.

Serafima Aleksandrovna was in dumb despair as she left Lelechka, and went out of the room. She met her husband.

"Lelechka is dead," she said in a quiet, dull voice.

Sergey Modestovich looked anxiously at her pale face. He was struck by the strange stupor in her formerly animated handsome features.

VII

LELECHKA WAS dressed, placed in a little coffin, and carried into the parlour. Serafima Aleksandrovna was standing by the coffin and looking dully at her dead child. Sergey Modestovich went to his wife and, consoling her with cold, empty words, tried to draw her away from the coffin. Serafima Aleksandrovna smiled.

"Go away," she said quietly. "Lelechka is playing. She'll be up in a minute."

"Sima, my dear, don't agitate yourself," said Sergey Modestovich in a whisper. "You must resign yourself to your fate."

"She'll be up in a minute," persisted Serafima Aleksandrovna, her eyes fixed on the dead little girl.

Sergey Modestovich looked around him cautiously: he was afraid of the unseemly and of the ridiculous.

"Sima, don't agitate yourself," he repeated. "This would be a miracle, and miracles do not happen in the nineteenth century."

No sooner had he said these words than Sergey Modestovich felt their irrelevance to what had happened. He was confused and annoyed.

He took his wife by the arm, and cautiously led her away from the coffin. She did not oppose him.

Her face seemed tranquil and her eyes were dry. She
went into the nursery and began to walk round the room,
looking into those places where Lelechka used to hide herself. She walked all about the room, and bent now and
then to look under the table or under the bed, and kept on
repeating cheerfully: "Where is my little one? Where is
my Lelechka?"

After she had walked round the room once she began to
make her quest anew. Fedosya, motionless, with dejected
face, sat in a corner, and looked frightened at her mistress;
then she suddenly burst out sobbing, and she wailed loudly:

"She hid herself, and hid herself, our Lelechka, our angelic little soul!"

Serafima Aleksandrovna trembled, paused, cast a perplexed look at Fedosya, began to weep, and left the nursery
quietly.

VIII

SERGEY MODESTOVICH hurried the funeral. He saw that Serafima Aleksandrovna was terribly shocked by her sudden
misfortune, and as he feared for her reason he thought
she would more readily be diverted and consoled when
Lelechka was buried.

Next morning Serafima Aleksandrovna dressed with particular care—for Lelechka. When she entered the parlour
there were several people between her and Lelechka. The
priest and deacon paced up and down the room; clouds of
blue smoke drifted in the air, and there was a smell of
incense. There was an oppressive feeling of heaviness in

Serafima Aleksandrovna's head as she approached Lelechka. Lelechka lay there still and pale, and smiled pathetically. Serafima Aleksandrovna laid her cheek upon the edge of Lelechka's coffin, and whispered: *"Tiu-tiu,* little one!"

The little one did not reply. Then there was some kind of stir and confusion around Serafima Aleksandrovna; strange, unnecessary faces bent over her, some one held her—and Lelechka was carried away somewhere.

Serafima Aleksandrovna stood up erect, sighed in a lost way, smiled, and called loudly: "Lelechka!"

Lelechka was being carried out. The mother threw herself after the coffin with despairing sobs, but she was held back. She sprang behind the door, through which Lelechka had passed, sat down there on the floor, and as she looked through the crevice, she cried out: "Lelechka, *tiu-tiu!*"

Then she put her head out from behind the door, and began to laugh.

Lelechka was quickly carried away from her mother, and those who carried her seemed to run rather than to walk.

DETHRONED

◆◆◆

By I. N. Potapenko

"WELL?" Captain Zarubkin's wife called out impatiently to her husband, rising from the sofa and turning to face him as he entered.

"He doesn't know anything about it," he replied indifferently, as if the matter were of no interest to him. Then he asked in a businesslike tone: "Nothing for me from the office?"

"Why should I know? Am I your errand boy?"

"How they dilly-dally! If only the package doesn't come too late. It's so important!"

"Idiot!"

"Who's an idiot?"

"You, with your indifference, your stupid egoism."

The captain said nothing. He was neither surprised nor insulted. On the contrary, the smile on his face was as though he had received a compliment. These wifely animadversions, probably oft-heard, by no means interfered with his domestic peace.

"It can't be that the man doesn't know when his wife is coming back home," Mrs. Zarubkin continued excitedly.

228

"She's written to him every day of the four months that she's been away. The postmaster told me so."

"Semyonov! Ho, Semyonov! Has any one from the office been here?"

"I don't know, your Excellency," came in a loud, clear voice from back of the room.

"Why don't you know? Where have you been?"

"I went to Abramka, your Excellency."

"The tailor again?"

"Yes, your Excellency, the tailor Abramka."

The captain spat in annoyance.

"And where is Krynka?"

"He went to market, your Excellency."

"Was he told to go to market?"

"Yes, your Excellency."

The captain spat again.

"Why do you keep spitting? Such vulgar manners!" his wife cried angrily. "You behave at home like a drunken subaltern. You haven't the least consideration for your wife. You are so coarse in your behaviour towards me! Do, please go to your office."

"Semyonov."

"Your Excellency?"

"If the package comes, please have it sent back to the office and say I've gone there. And listen! Some one must always be here. I won't have everybody out of the house at the same time. Do you hear?"

"Yes, your Excellency."

The captain put on his cap to go. In the doorway he turned and addressed his wife.

"Please, Tasya, please don't send all the servants on your errands at the same time. Something important may turn up, and then there's nobody here to attend to it."

He went out, and his wife remained reclining in the sofa corner as if his plea were no concern of hers. But scarcely had he left the house, when she called out:

"Semyonov, come here. Quick!"

A bare-footed unshaven man in dark blue pantaloons and cotton shirt presented himself. His stocky figure and red face made a wholesome appearance. He was the Captain's orderly.

"At your service, your Excellency."

"Listen, Semyonov, you don't seem to be stupid."

"I don't know, your Excellency."

"For goodness' sake drop 'your Excellency.' I am not your superior officer."

"Yes, your Excel—"

"Idiot!"

But the lady's manner toward the servant was far friendlier than toward her husband. Semyonov had it in his power to perform important services for her, while the captain had not come up to her expectations.

"Listen, Semyonov, how do you and the doctor's men get along together? Are you friendly?"

"Yes, your Excellency."

"Intolerable!" cried the lady, jumping up. "Stop using that silly title. Can't you speak like a sensible man?"

Semyonov had been standing in the stiff attitude of attention, with the palms of his hands at the seams of his trousers. Now he suddenly relaxed, and even wiped his nose with his fist.

"That's the way we are taught to do," he said carelessly, with a clownish grin. "The gentlemen, the officers, insist on it."

"Now, tell me, you are on good terms with the doctor's men?"

"You mean Podmar and Shuchok? Of course, we're friends."

"Very well, then go straight to them and try to find out when Mrs. Shaldin is expected back. They ought to know. They must be getting things ready against her return—cleaning her bedroom and fixing it up. Do you understand? But be careful to find out right. And also be very careful not to let on for whom you are finding it out. Do you understand?"

"Of course, I understand."

"Well, then, go. But one more thing. Since you're going out, you may as well stop at Abramka's again and tell him to come here right away. You understand?"

"But his Excellency gave me orders to stay at home," said Semyonov, scratching himself behind his ears.

"Please don't answer back. Just do as I tell you. Go on, now."

"At your service." And the orderly, impressed by the lady's severe military tone, left the room.

Mrs. Zarubkin remained reclining on the sofa for a while. Then she rose and walked up and down the room and finally went to her bedroom, where her two little daughters were playing in their nurse's care. She scolded them a bit and returned to her former place on the couch. Her every movement betrayed great excitement.

. . . .

Tatyana Grigoryevna Zarubkin was one of the most looked-up to ladies of the S—— Regiment and even of the whole town of Chmyrsk, where the regiment was quartered. To be sure, you hardly could say that, outside the regiment, the town could boast any ladies at all. There were very respectable women, decent wives, mothers, daughters and widows of honourable citizens; but they all dressed in cotton and flannel, and on high holidays made a show of cheap Cashmere gowns over which they wore gay shawls with borders of wonderful arabesques. Their hats and other headgear gave not the faintest evidence of good taste. So they could scarcely be dubbed "ladies." They were satisfied to be called "women." Each one of them, almost, had the name of her husband's trade or position tacked to her name—Mrs. Grocer so-and-so, Mrs. Mayor so-and-so, Mrs. Milliner so-and-so, etc. Genuine *ladies* in the Russian society sense had never come to the town before the S—— Regiment had taken up its quarters there; and it goes without saying that the ladies of the regiment had nothing in common, and therefore no intercourse with, the women of the town. They were so dissimilar that they were like creatures of a different species.

There is no disputing that Tatyana Grigoryevna Zarubkin was one of the most looked-up-to of the ladies. She invariably played the most important part at all the regimental affairs—the amateur theatricals, the social evenings, the afternoon teas. If the captain's wife was not to be present, it was a foregone conclusion that the affair would not be a success.

The most important point was that Mrs. Zarubkin had the untarnished reputation of being the best-dressed of all the ladies. She was always the most distinguished looking at the annual ball. Her gown for the occasion, ordered from Moscow, was always chosen with the greatest regard for her charms and defects, and it was always exquisitely beautiful. A new fashion could not gain admittance to the other ladies of the regiment except by way of the captain's wife. Thanks to her good taste in dressing, the stately blonde was queen at all the balls and in all the salons of Chmyrsk. Another advantage of hers was that although she was nearly forty she still looked fresh and youthful, so that the young officers were constantly hovering about her and paying her homage.

November was a very lively month in the regiments' calendar. It was on the tenth of November that the annual ball took place. The ladies, of course, spent their best efforts in preparation for this event. Needless to say that in these arduous activities, Abramka Stiftik, the ladies' tailor, played a prominent rôle. He was the one man in Chmyrsk who had any understanding at all for the subtle art of the feminine toilet. Preparations had begun in his shop in August already. Within the last weeks his modest parlour—furnished with six shabby chairs placed about a round table, and a fly-specked mirror on the wall—the atmosphere heavy with a smell of onions and herring, had been filled from early morning to the evening hours with the most charming and elegant of the fairer sex. There was trying-on and dis·

cussion of styles and selection of material. It was all very nerve-racking for the ladies.

The only one who had never appeared in this parlour was the captain's wife. That had been a thorn in Abramka's flesh. He had spent days and nights going over in his mind how he could rid this lady of the, in his opinion, wretched habit of ordering her clothes from Moscow. For this ball, however, as she herself had told him, she had not ordered a dress but only material from out of town, from which he deduced that he was to make the gown for her. But there was only one week left before the ball, and still she had not come to him. Abramka was in a state of feverishness. He longed once to make a dress for Mrs. Zarubkin. It would add to his glory. He wanted to prove that he understood his trade just as well as any tailor in Moscow, and that it was quite superfluous for her to order her gowns outside of Chmyrsk. He would come out the triumphant competitor of Moscow.

As each day passed and Mrs. Zarubkin did not appear in his shop, his nervousness increased. Finally she ordered a dressing-jacket from him—but not a word said of a ball gown. What was he to think of it?

So, when Semyonov told him that Mrs. Zarubkin was expecting him at her home, it goes without saying that he instantly removed the dozen pins in his mouth, as he was trying on a customer's dress, told one of his assistants to continue with the fitting, and instantly set off to call on the captain's wife. In this case, it was not a question of a mere ball gown, but of the acquisition of the best customer in town.

Although Abramka wore a silk hat and a suit in keeping with the silk hat, still he was careful not to ring at the front entrance, but always knocked at the back door. At another time when the captain's orderly was not in the house—for the captain's orderly also performed the duties of the captain's cook—he might have knocked long and loud. On other occasions a cannon might have been shot off right next to Tatyana Grigoryevna's ears and she would not have lifted her fingers to open the door. But now she instantly caught the sound of the modest knocking and opened the back door herself for Abramka.

"Oh!" she cried delightedly. "You, Abramka!"

She really wanted to address him less familiarly, as was more befitting so dignified a man in a silk hat; but everybody called him "Abramka," and he would have been very much surprised had he been honoured with his full name, Abram Srulevich Stiftik. So she thought it best to address him as the others did.

Mr. "Abramka" was tall and thin. There was always a melancholy expression in his pale face. He had a little stoop, a long and very heavy greyish beard. He had been practising his profession for thirty years. Ever since his apprenticeship he had been called "Abramka," which did not strike him as at all derogatory or unfitting. Even his shingle read: "Ladies' Tailor: Abramka Stiftik"—the most valid proof that he deemed his name immaterial, but that the chief thing to him was his art. As a matter of fact, he had attained, if not perfection in tailoring, yet remarkable skill. To this all the ladies of the S—— Regiment could attest with conviction.

Abramka removed his silk hat, stepped into the kitchen, and said gravely, with profound feeling:

"Mrs. Zarubkin, I am entirely at your service."

"Come into the reception room. I have something very important to speak to you about."

Abramka followed in silence. He stepped softly on tiptoe, as if afraid of waking some one.

"Sit down, Abramka, listen—but give me your word of honour, you won't tell any one?" Tatyana Grigoryevna began, reddening a bit. She was ashamed to have to let the tailor Abramka into her secret, but since there was no getting around it, she quieted herself and in an instant had regained her ease.

"I don't know what you are speaking of, Mrs. Zarubkin," Abramka rejoined. He assumed a somewhat injured manner. "Have you ever heard of Abramka ever blabbling anything out? You certainly know that in my profession—you know everybody has some secret to be kept."

"Oh, you must have misunderstood me, Abramka. What kind of secrets do you mean?"

"Well, one lady is a little bit one-sided, another lady"—he pointed to his breast—"is not quite full enough, another lady has scrawny arms—such things as that have to be covered up or filled out or laced in, so as to look better. That is where our art comes in. But we are in duty bound not to say anything about it."

Tatyana Grigoryevna smiled.

"Well, I can assure you I am all right that way. There is nothing about me that needs to be covered up or filled out."

"Oh, as if I didn't know that! Everybody knows that

Mrs. Zarubkin's figure is perfect," Abramka cried, trying to flatter his new customer.

Mrs. Zarubkin laughed and made up her mind to remember "Everybody knows that Mrs. Zarubkin's figure is perfect." Then she said:

"You know that the ball is to take place in a week."

"Yes, indeed, Mrs. Zarubkin, in only one week; unfortunately, only one week," replied Abramka, sighing.

"But you remember your promise to make my dress for me for the ball this time?"

"Mrs. Zarubkin," Abramka cried, laying his hand on his heart. "Have I said that I was not willing to make it? No, indeed, I said it must be made and made right—for Mrs. Zarubkin, it must be better than for any one else. That's the way I feel about it."

"Splendid! Just what I wanted to know."

"But why don't you show me your material? Why don't you say to me, 'Here, Abramka, here is the stuff, make a dress?' Abramka would work on it day and night."

"Ahem, that's just it—I can't order it. That is where the trouble comes in. Tell me, Abramka, what is the shortest time you need for making the dress? Listen, the very shortest?"

Abramka shrugged his shoulders.

"Well, is a week too much for a ball dress such as you will want? It's got to be sewed, it can't be pasted together. You, yourself, know that, Mrs. Zarubkin."

"But supposing I order it only three days before the ball?"

Abramka started.

"Only three days before the ball? A ball dress? Am I

a god, Mrs. Zarubkin? I am nothing but the ladies' tailor, Abramka Stiftik."

"Well, then you are a nice tailor!" said Tatyana Grigoryevna, scornfully. "In Moscow they made a ball dress for me in two days."

Abramka jumped up as if at a shot, and beat his breast.

"Is that so? Then I say, Mrs. Zarubkin," he cried pathetically, "if they made a ball gown for you in Moscow in two days, very well, then I will make a ball gown for you, if I must, in one day. I will neither eat nor sleep, and I won't let my help off either for one minute. How does that suit you?"

"Sit down, Abramka, thank you very much. I hope I shall not have to put such a strain on you. It really does not depend upon me, otherwise I should have ordered the dress from you long ago."

"It doesn't depend upon you? Then upon whom does it depend?"

"Ahem, it depends upon—but now, Abramka, remember this is just between you and me—it depends upon Mrs. Shaldin."

"Upon Mrs. Shaldin, the doctor's wife? Why she isn't even here."

"That's just it. That is why I have to wait. How is it that a clever man like you, Abramka, doesn't grasp the situation?"

"Hm, hm! Let me see." Abramka racked his brains for a solution of the riddle. How could it be that Mrs. Shaldin, who was away, should have anything to do with Mrs. Zarubkin's order for a gown? No, that passed his comprehension.

"She certainly will get back in time for the ball," said Mrs. Zarubkin, to give him a cue.

"Well, yes."

"And certainly will bring a dress back with her."

"Certainly!"

"A dress from abroad, something we have never seen here —something highly original."

"Mrs. Zarubkin!" Abramka cried, as if a truth of tremendous import had been revealed to him. "Mrs. Zarubkin, I understand. Why certainly! Yes, but that will be pretty hard."

"That's just it."

Abramka reflected a moment, then said:

"I assure you, Mrs. Zarubkin, you need not be a bit uneasy. I will make a dress for you that will be just as grand as the one from abroad. I assure you, your dress will be the most elegant one at the ball, just as it always has been. I tell you, my name won't be Abramka Stiftik if——"

His eager asseverations seemed not quite to satisfy the captain's wife. Her mind was not quite set at ease. She interrupted him.

"But the style, Abramka, the style! You can't possibly guess what the latest fashion is abroad."

"Why shouldn't I know what the latest fashion is, Mrs. Zarubkin? In Kiev I have a friend who publishes fashion-plates. I will telegraph to him, and he will immediately send me pictures of the latest French models. The telegram will cost only eighty cents, Mrs. Zarubkin, and I swear to you I will copy any dress he sends. Mrs. Shaldin can't possibly have a dress like that."

"All very well and good, and that's what we'll do. Still we must wait until Mrs. Shaldin comes back. Don't you see, Abramka, I must have exactly the same style that she has? Can't you see, so that nobody can say that she is in the latest fashion?"

At this point Semyonov entered the room cautiously. He was wearing the oddest-looking jacket and the captain's old boots. His hair was rumpled, and his eyes were shining suspiciously. There was every sign that he had used the renewal of friendship with the doctor's men as a pretext for a booze.

"I had to stand them some brandy, your Excellency," he said saucily, but catching his mistress's threatening look, he lowered his head guiltily.

"Idiot," she yelled at him, "face about. Be off with you to the kitchen."

In his befuddlement, Semyonov had not noticed Abramka's presence. Now he became aware of him, faced about and retired to the kitchen sheepishly.

"What an impolite fellow," said Abramka reproachfully.

"Oh, you wouldn't believe—" said the captain's wife, but instantly followed Semyonov into the kitchen.

Semyonov aware of his awful misdemeanor, tried to stand up straight and give a report.

"She will come back, your Excellency, day after to-morrow toward evening. She sent a telegram."

"Is that true now?"

"I swear it's true. Shuchok saw it himself."

"All right, very good. You will get something for this."

"Yes, your Excellency."

"Silence, you goose. Go on, set the table."

Abramka remained about ten minutes longer with the captain's wife, and on leaving said:

"Let me assure you once again, Mrs. Zarubkin, you needn't worry; just select the style, and I will make a gown for you that the best tailor in Paris can't beat." He pressed his hand to his heart in token of his intention to do everything in his power for Mrs. Zarubkin.

. . . .

It was seven o'clock in the evening. Mrs. Shaldin and her trunk had arrived hardly half an hour before, yet the captain's wife was already there paying a visit; which was a sign of the warm friendship that existed between the two women. They kissed each other and fell to talking. The doctor, a tall man of forty-five, seemed discomfited by the visit, and passed unfriendly side glances at his guest. He had hoped to spend that evening undisturbed with his wife, and he well knew that when the ladies of the regiment came to call upon each other "for only a second," it meant a whole evening of listening to idle talk.

"You wouldn't believe me, dear, how bored I was the whole time you were away, how I longed for you, Natalie Semyonovna. But you probably never gave us a thought."

"Oh, how can you say anything like that. I was thinking of you every minute, every second. If I hadn't been obliged to finish the cure, I should have returned long ago. No matter how beautiful it may be away from home, still the only place to live is among those that are near and dear to you."

These were only the preliminary soundings. They lasted with variations for a quarter of an hour. First Mrs. Shaldin narrated a few incidents of the trip, then Mrs. Zarubkin gave a report of some of the chief happenings in the life of the regiment. When the conversation was in full swing, and the samovar was singing on the table, and the pancakes were spreading their appetising odour, the captain's wide suddenly cried:

"I wonder what the fashions are abroad now. I say, you must have feasted your eyes on them!"

Mrs. Shaldin simply replied with a scornful gesture.

"Other people may like them, but I don't care for them one bit. I am glad we here don't get to see them until a year later. You know, Tatyana Grigoryevna, you sometimes see the ugliest styles."

"Really?" asked the captain's wife eagerly, her eyes gleaming with curiosity. The great moment of complete revelation seemed to have arrived.

"Perfectly hideous, I tell you. Just imagine, you know how nice the plain skirts were. Then why change them? But no, to be in style now, the skirts have to be draped. Why? It is just a sign of complete lack of imagination. And in Lyons they got out a new kind of silk—but that is still a French secret."

"Why a secret? The silk is certainly being worn already?"

"Yes, one does see it being worn already, but when it was first manufactured, the greatest secret was made of it. They were afraid the Germans would imitate. You understand?"

"Oh, but what is the latest style?"

"I really can't explain it to you. All I know is, it is something awful."

"She can't explain! That means she doesn't want to ex-

plain. Oh, the cunning one. What a sly look she has in
her eyes." So thought the captain's wife. From the very
beginning of the conversation, the two warm friends, it
need scarcely be said, were mutually distrustful. Each had
the conviction that everything the other said was to be taken
in the very opposite sense. They were of about the same
age, Mrs. Shaldin possibly one or two years younger than
Mrs. Zarubkin. Mrs. Zarubkin was rather plump, and had
heavy light hair. Her appearance was blooming. Mrs. Shaldin was slim, though well proportioned. She was a brunette
with a pale complexion and large dark eyes. They were
two types of beauty very likely to divide the gentlemen of
the regiment into two camps of admirers. But women are
never content with halves. Mrs. Zarubkin wanted to see
all the officers of the regiment at her feet, and so did Mrs.
Shaldin. It naturally led to great rivalry between the two
women, of which they were both conscious, though they always had the friendliest smiles for each other.

Mrs. Shaldin tried to give a different turn to the conversation.

"Do you think the ball will be interesting this year?"

"Why should it be interesting?" replied the captain's
wife scornfully. "Always the same people, the same old
humdrum jog-trot."

"I suppose the ladies have been besieging our poor
Abramka?"

"I really can't tell you. So far as I am concerned, I have
scarcely looked at what he made for me."

"Hm, how's that? Didn't you order your dress from Moscow again?"

"No, it really does not pay. I am sick of the bother of it all. Why all that trouble? For whom? Our officers don't care a bit how one dresses. They haven't the least taste."

"Hm, there's something back of that," thought Mrs. Shaldin.

The captain's wife continued with apparent indifference:

"I can guess what a gorgeous dress you had made abroad. Certainly in the latest fashion?"

"I?" Mrs. Shaldin laughed innocently. "How could I get the time during my cure to think of a dress? As a matter of fact, I completely forgot the ball, thought of it at the last moment, and bought the first piece of goods I laid my hands on."

"Pink?"

"Oh, no. How can you say pink!"

"Light blue, then?"

"You can't call it exactly light blue. It is a very undefined sort of colour. I really wouldn't know what to call it."

"But it certainly must have some sort of a shade?"

"You may believe me or not if you choose, but really I don't know. It's a very indefinite shade."

"Is it Sura silk?"

"No, I can't bear Sura. It doesn't keep the folds well."

"I suppose it is crêpe de Chine?"

"Heavens, no! Crêpe de Chine is much too expensive for me."

"Then what can it be?"

"Oh, wait a minute, what *is* the name of that goods? You know there are so many funny new names now. They don't make any sense."

"Then show me your dress, dearest. Do please show me your dress."

Mrs. Shaldin seemed to be highly embarrassed.

"I am so sorry I can't. It is way down at the bottom of the trunk. There is the trunk. You see yourself I couldn't unpack it now."

The trunk, close to the wall, was covered with oil cloth and tied tight with heavy cords. The captain's wife devoured it with her eyes. She would have liked to see through and through it. She had nothing to say in reply, because it certainly was impossible to ask her friend, tired out from her recent journey, to begin to unpack right away and take out all her things just to show her her new dress. Yet she could not tear her eyes away from the trunk. There was a magic in it that held her enthralled. Had she been alone she would have begun to unpack it herself, nor even have asked the help of a servant to undo the knots. Now there was nothing left for her but to turn her eyes sorrowfully away from the fascinating object and take up another topic of conversation to which she would be utterly indifferent. But she couldn't think of anything else to talk about. Mrs. Shaldin must have prepared herself beforehand. She must have suspected something. So now Mrs. Zarubkin pinned her last hope to Abramka's inventiveness. She glanced at the clock.

"Dear me," she exclaimed, as if surprised at the lateness of the hour. "I must be going. I don't want to disturb you any longer either, dearest. You must be very tired. I hope you rest well."

She shook hands with Mrs. Shaldin, kissed her and left.

Abramka Stiftik had just taken off his coat and was
doing some ironing in his shirt sleeves, when a peculiar
figure appeared in his shop. It was that of a stocky orderly
in a well-worn uniform without buttons and old galoshes
instead of boots. His face was gloomy-looking and was
covered with a heavy growth of hair. Abramka knew this
figure well. It seemed always just to have been awakened
from the deepest sleep.

"Ah, Shuchok, what do you want?"

"Mrs. Shaldin would like you to call upon her," said
Shuchok. He behaved as if he had come on a terribly serious mission.

"Ah, that's so, your lady has come back. I heard about
it. You see I am very busy. Still you may tell her I am
coming right away. I just want to finish ironing Mrs.
Konopotkin's dress."

Abramka simply wanted to keep up appearances, as always when he was sent for. But his joy at the summons
to Mrs. Shaldin was so great that to the astonishment of
his helpers and Shuchok he left immediately.

He found Mrs. Shaldin alone. She had not slept well the
two nights before and had risen late that morning. Her
husband had left long before for the Military Hospital. She
was sitting beside her open trunk taking her things out very
carefully.

"How do you do, Mrs. Shaldin? Welcome back to
Chmyrsk. I congratulate you on your happy arrival."

"Oh, how do you do, Abramka?" said Mrs. Shaldin delightedly; "we haven't seen each other for a long time, have
we? I was rather homesick for you."

"Oh, Mrs. Shaldin, you must have had a very good time abroad. But what do you need me for? You certainly brought a dress back with you?"

"Abramka always comes in handy," said Mrs. Shaldin jestingly. "We ladies of the regiment are quite helpless without Abramka. Take a seat."

Abramka seated himself. He felt much more at ease in Mrs. Shaldin's home than in Mrs. Zarubkin's. Mrs. Shaldin did not order her clothes from Moscow. She was a steady customer of his. In this room he had many a time circled about the doctor's wife with a yard measure, pins, chalk and scissors, had kneeled down beside her, raised himself to his feet, bent over again and stood puzzling over some difficult problem of dressmaking—how low to cut the dress out at the neck, how long to make the train, how wide the hem, and so on. None of the ladies of the regiment ordered as much from him as Mrs. Shaldin. Her grandmother would send her material from Kiev or the doctor would go on a professional trip to Chernigov and always bring some goods back with him; or sometimes her aunt in Voronesh would make her a gift of some silk.

"Abramka is always ready to serve Mrs. Shaldin first," said the tailor, though seized with a little pang, as if bitten by a guilty conscience.

"Are you sure you are telling the truth? Is Abramka always to be depended upon? Eh, is he?" She looked at him searchingly from beneath drooping lids.

"What a question," rejoined Abramka. His face quivered slightly. His feeling of discomfort was waxing. "Has Abramka ever——"

"Oh, things can happen. But, all right, never mind. I brought a dress along with me. I had to have it made in a great hurry, and there is just a little more to be done on it. Now if I give you this dress to finish, can I be sure that you positively won't tell another soul how it is made?"

"Mrs. Shaldin, oh, Mrs. Shaldin," said Abramka reproachfully. Nevertheless, the expression of his face was not so reassuring as usual.

"You give me your word of honour?"

"Certainly! My name isn't Abramka Stiftik if I——"

"Well, all right, I will trust you. But be careful. You know of whom you must be careful?"

"Who is that, Mrs. Shaldin?"

"Oh, you know very well whom I mean. No, you needn't put your hand on your heart. She was here to see me yesterday and tried in every way she could to find out how my dress is made. But she couldn't get it out of me." Abramka sighed. Mrs. Shaldin seemed to suspect his betrayal. "I am right, am I not? She has not had her dress made yet, has she? She waited to see my dress, didn't she? And she told you to copy the style, didn't she?" Mrs. Shaldin asked with honest naïveté. "But I warn you, Abramka, if you give away the least little thing about my dress, then all is over between you and me. Remember that."

Abramka's hand went to his heart again, and the gesture carried the same sense of conviction as of old.

"Mrs. Shaldin, how can you speak like that?"

"Wait a moment."

Mr. Shaldin left the room. About ten minutes passed

during which Abramka had plenty of time to reflect. How could he have given the captain's wife a promise like that so lightly? What was the captain's wife to him as compared with the doctor's wife? Mrs. Zarubkin had never given him a really decent order—just a few things for the house and some mending. Supposing he were now to perform this great service for her, would that mean that he could depend upon her for the future? Was any woman to be depended upon? She would wear this dress out and go back to ordering her clothes from Moscow again. But *Mrs. Shaldin,* she was very different. He could forgive her having brought this one dress along from abroad. What woman in Russia would have refrained when abroad, from buying a new dress? Mrs. Shaldin would continue to be his steady customer all the same.

The door opened. Abramka rose involuntarily, and clasped his hands in astonishment.

"Well," he exclaimed rapturously, "that is a dress, that is—— My, my!" He was so stunned he could find nothing more to say. And how charming Mrs. Shaldin looked in her wonderful gown! Her tall slim figure seemed to have been made for it. What simple yet elegant lines. At first glance you would think it was nothing more than an ordinary house-gown, but only at first glance. If you looked at it again, you could tell right away that it met all the requirements of a fancy ball-gown. What struck Abramka most was that it had no waist line, that it did not consist of bodice and skirt. That was strange. It was just caught lightly together under the bosom, which it brought out in relief. Draped over the whole was a sort of upper garment

of exquisite old-rose lace embroidered with large silk
flowers, which fell from the shoulders and broadened out
in bold superb lines. The dress was cut low and edged with
a narrow strip of black down around the bosom, around
the bottom of the lace drapery, and around the hem of the
skirt. A wonderful fan of feathers to match the down edging gave the finishing touch.

"Well, how do you like it, Abramka!" asked Mrs. Shaldin
with a triumphant smile.

"Glorious, glorious! I haven't the words at my command.
What a dress! No, I couldn't make a dress like that. And
how beautifully it fits you, as if you had been born in it,
Mrs. Shaldin. What do you call the style?"

"Empire."

"Ampeer?" he queried. "Is that a new style? Well, well,
what people don't think of. Tailors like us might just as
well throw our needles and scissors away."

"Now, listen, Abramka, I wouldn't have shown it to you
if there were not this sewing to be done on it. You are
the only one who will have seen it before the ball. I am not
even letting my husband look at it."

"Oh, Mrs. Shaldin, you can rely upon me as upon a rock.
But after the ball may I copy it?"

"Oh, yes, after the ball copy it as much as you please,
but not now, not for anything in the world."

There were no doubts in Abramka's mind when he left
the doctor's house. He had arrived at his decision. That
superb creation had conquered him. It would be a piece of
audacity on his part, he felt, even to think of imitating such
a gown. Why, it was not a gown. It was a dream, a fan-

tastic vision—without a bodice, without puffs or frills or tawdry trimmings of any sort. Simplicity itself and yet so chic.

Back in his shop he opened the package of fashion-plates that had just arrived from Kiev. He turned the pages and stared in astonishment. What was that? Could he trust his eyes? An Empire gown. There it was, with the broad voluptuous drapery of lace hanging from the shoulders and the edging of down. Almost exactly the same thing as Mrs. Shaldin's.

He glanced up and saw Semyonov outside the window. He had certainly come to fetch him to the captain's wife, who must have ordered him to watch the tailor's movements, and must have learned that he had just been at Mrs. Shaldin's. Semyonov entered and told him his mistress wanted to see him right away.

Abramka slammed the fashion magazine shut as if afraid that Semyonov might catch a glimpse of the new Empire fashion and give the secret away.

"I will come immediately," he said crossly.

He picked up his fashion plates, put the yard measure in his pocket, rammed his silk hat sorrowfully on his head and set off for the captain's house. He found Mrs. Zarubkin pacing the room excitedly, greeted her, but carefully avoided meeting her eyes.

"Well, what did you find out?"

"Nothing, Mrs. Zarubkin," said Abramka dejectedly. "Unfortunately I couldn't find out a thing."

"Idiot! I have no patience with you. Where are the fashion plates?"

"Here, Mrs. Zarubkin."

She turned the pages, looked at one picture after the other, and suddenly her eyes shone and her cheeks reddened.

"Oh, Empire! The very thing. Empire is the very latest. Make this one for me," she cried commandingly.

Abramka turned pale.

"Ampeer, Mrs. Zarubkin? I can't make that Ampeer dress for you," he murmured.

"Why not?" asked the captain's wife, giving him a searching look.

"Because—because—I can't."

"Oh—h—h, you can't? You know why you can't. Because that is the style of Mrs. Shaldin's dress. So that is the reliability you boast so about? Great!"

"Mrs. Zarubkin, I will make any other dress you choose, but it is absolutely impossible for me to make this one."

"I don't need your fashion plates, do you hear me? Get out of here, and don't ever show your face again."

"Mrs. Zarubkin, I——"

"Get out of here," repeated the captain's wife, quite beside herself.

The poor tailor stuck his yard measure, which he had already taken out, back into his pocket and left.

Half an hour later the captain's wife was entering a train for Kiev, carrying a large package which contained material for a dress. The captain had accompanied her to the station with a pucker in his forehead. That was five days before the ball.

.   .   .   .

At the ball two expensive Empire gowns stood out conspicuously from among the more or less elegant gowns which had been finished in the shop of Abramka Stiftik, Ladies' Tailor. The one gown adorned Mrs. Shaldin's figure, the other the figure of the captain's wife.

Mrs. Zarubkin had bought her gown ready made at Kiev, and had returned only two hours before the beginning of the ball. She had scarcely had time to dress. Perhaps it would have been better had she not appeared at this one of the annual balls, had she not taken that fateful trip to Kiev. For in comparison with the make and style of Mrs. Shaldin's dress, which had been bought abroad, hers was like the botched imitation of an amateur.

That was evident to everybody, though the captain's wife had her little group of partisans, who maintained with exaggerated eagerness that she looked extraordinary fascinating in her dress and Mrs. Shaldin still could not rival her. But there was no mistaking it, there was little justice in this contention. Everybody knew better; what was worst of all, Mrs. Zarubkin herself knew better. Mrs. Shaldin's triumph was complete.

The two ladies gave each other the same friendly smiles as always, but one of them was experiencing the fine disdain and the derision of the conqueror, while the other was burning inside with the furious resentment of a dethroned goddess—goddess of the annual ball.

From that time on Abramka cautiously avoided passing the captain's house.

THE SERVANT

◆◆◆

By S. T. Semyonov

I

GERASIM RETURNED to Moscow just at a time when it was hardest to find work, a short while before Christmas, when a man sticks even to a poor job in the expectation of a present. For three weeks the peasant lad had been going about in vain seeking a position.

He stayed with relatives and friends from his village, and although he had not yet suffered great want, it disheartened him that he, a strong young man, should go without work.

Gerasim had lived in Moscow from early boyhood. When still a mere child, he had gone to work in a brewery as bottle-washer, and later as a lower servant in a house. In the last two years he had been in a merchant's employ, and would still have held that position, had he not been summoned back to his village for military duty. However, he had not been drafted. It seemed dull to him in the village, he was not used to the country life, so he decided he would rather count the stones in Moscow than stay there.

Every minute it was getting to be more and more irksome for him to be tramping the streets in idleness. Not a stone did he leave unturned in his efforts to secure any sort of work. He plagued all of his acquaintances, he even

254

held up people on the street and asked them if they knew of a situation—all in vain.

Finally Gerasim could no longer bear being a burden on his people. Some of them were annoyed by his coming to them; and others had suffered unpleasantness from their masters on his account. He was altogether at a loss what to do. Sometimes he would go a whole day without eating.

II

ONE DAY Gerasim betook himself to a friend from his village, who lived at the extreme outer edge of Moscow, near Sokolnik. The man was coachman to a merchant by the name of Sharov, in whose service he had been for many years. He had ingratiated himself with his master, so that Sharov trusted him absolutely and gave every sign of holding him in high favour. It was the man's glib tongue, chiefly, that had gained him his master's confidence. He told on all the servants, and Sharov valued him for it.

Gerasim approached and greeted him. The coachman gave his guest a proper reception, served him with tea and something to eat, and asked him how he was doing.

"Very badly, Yegor Danilych," said Gerasim, "I've been without a job for weeks."

"Didn't you ask your old employer to take you back?"

"I did."

"He wouldn't take you again?"

"The position was filled already."

"That's it. That's the way you young fellows are. You serve your employers so-so, and when you leave your jobs, you usually have muddled up the way back to them. You ought to serve your masters so that they will think a lot of you, and when you come again, they will not refuse you, but rather dismiss the man who has taken your place."

"How can a man do that? In these days there aren't any employers like that, and we aren't exactly angels, either."

"What's the use of wasting words? I just want to tell you about myself. If for some reason or other I should ever have to leave this place and go home, not only would Mr. Sharov, if I came back, take me on again without a word, but he would be glad to, too."

Gerasim sat there downcast. He saw his friend was boasting, and it occurred to him to gratify him.

"I know it," he said. "But it's hard to find men like you, Yegor Danilych. If you were a poor worker, your master would not have kept you twelve years."

Yegor smiled. He liked the praise.

"That's it," he said. "If you were to live and serve as I do, you wouldn't be out of work for months and months."

Gerasim made no reply.

Yegor was summoned to his master.

"Wait a moment," he said to Gerasim. "I'll be right back."

"Very well."

III

YEGOR CAME back and reported that inside of half an hour he would have to have the horses harnessed, ready to drive his master to town. He lighted his pipe and took several turns in the room. Then he came to a halt in front of Gerasim.

"Listen, my boy," he said, "if you want, I'll ask my master to take you as a servant here."

"Does he need a man?"

"We have one, but he's not much good. He's getting old, and it's very hard for him to do the work. It's lucky for us that the neighbourhood isn't a lively one and the police don't make a fuss about things being kept just so, else the old man couldn't manage to keep the place clean enough for them."

"Oh, if you can, then please do say a word for me, Yegor Danilych. I'll pray for you all my life. I can't stand being without work any longer."

"All right, I'll speak for you. Come again to-morrow, and in the meantime take this ten-kopek piece. It may come in handy."

"Thanks, Yegor Danilych. Then you *will* try for me? Please do me the favour."

"All right. I'll try for you."

Gerasim left, and Yegor harnessed up his horses. Then he put on his coachman's habit, and drove up to the front door. Mr. Sharov stepped out of the house, seated himself in the sleigh, and the horses galloped off. He attended to his business in town and returned home. Yegor, observing that his master was in a good humour, said to him:

"Yegor Fiodorych, I have a favour to ask of you."

"What is it?"

"There's a young man from my village here, a good boy. He's without a job."

"Well?"

"Wouldn't you take him?"

"What do I want him for?"

"Use him as man of all work round the place."

"How about Polikarpych?"

"What good is he? It's about time you dismissed him."

"That wouldn't be fair. He has been with me so many years. I can't let him go just so, without any cause."

"Supposing he *has* worked for you for years. He didn't work for nothing. He got paid for it. He's certainly saved up a few dollars for his old age."

"Saved up! How could he? From what? He's not alone in the world. He has a wife to support, and she has to eat and drink also."

"His wife earns money, too, at day's work as charwoman."

"A lot she could have made! Enough for *kvas*."

"Why should you care about Polikarpych and his wife? To tell you the truth, he's a very poor servant. Why should you throw your money away on him? He never shovels the snow away on time, or does anything right. And when it comes his turn to be night watchman, he slips away at least ten times a night. It's too cold for him. You'll see, some day, because of him, you will have trouble with the police. The quarterly inspector will descend on us, and it won't be so agreeable for you to be responsible for Polikarpych."

"Still, it's pretty rough. He's been with me fifteen years. And to treat him that way in his old age—it would be a sin."

"A sin! Why, what harm would you be doing him? He won't starve. He'll go to the almshouse. It will be better for him, too, to be quiet in his old age."

Sharov reflected.

"All right," he said finally. "Bring your friend here. I'll see what I can do."

"Do take him, sir. I'm so sorry for him. He's a good boy, and he's been without work for such a long time. I know he'll do his work well and serve you faithfully. On account of having to report for military duty, he lost his last position. If it hadn't been for that, his master would never have let him go."

IV

THE NEXT evening Gerasim came again and asked:

"Well, could you do anything for me?"

"Something, I believe. First let's have some tea. Then we'll go see my master."

Even tea had no allurements for Gerasim. He was eager for a decision; but under the compulsion of politeness to his host, he gulped down two glasses of tea, and then they betook themselves to Sharov.

Sharov asked Gerasim where he had lived before and what work he could do. Then he told him he was prepared to engage him as a man of all work, and he should come back the next day ready to take the place.

Gerasim was fairly stunned by the great stroke of fortune. So overwhelming was his joy that his legs would scarcely carry him. He went to the coachman's room, and Yegor said to him:

"Well, my lad, see to it that you do your work right, so that I shan't have to be ashamed of you. You know what masters are like. If you go wrong once, they'll be at you forever after with their fault-finding, and never give you peace."

"Don't worry about that, Yegor Danilych."

"Well—well."

Gerasim took leave, crossing the yard to go out by the gate. Polikarpych's rooms gave on the yard, and a broad beam of light from the window fell across Gerasim's way. He was curious to get a glimpse of his future home, but the panes were all frosted over, and it was impossible to peep through. However, he could hear what the people inside were saying.

"What will we do now?" was said in a woman's voice.

"I don't know, I don't know," a man, undoubtedly Polikarpych, replied. "Go begging, I suppose."

"That's all we can do. There's nothing else left," said the woman. "Oh, we poor people, what a miserable life we lead. We work and work from early morning till late at night, day after day, and when we get old, then it's, 'Away with you!'"

"What can we do? Our master is not one of us. It wouldn't be worth the while to say much to him about it. He cares only for his own advantage."

"All the masters are so mean. They don't think of any one but themselves. It doesn't occur to them that we work for them honestly and faithfully for years, and use up our best strength in their service. They're afraid to keep us a year longer, even though we've got all the strength we need to do their work. If we weren't strong enough, we'd go of our own accord."

"The master's not so much to blame as his coachman. Yegor Danilych wants to get a good position for his friend."

"Yes, he's a serpent. He knows how to wag his tongue. You wait, you foul-mouthed beast, I'll get even with you. I'll go straight to the master and tell him how the fellow deceives him, how he steals the hay and fodder. I'll put it down in writing, and he can convince himself how the fellow lies about us all."

"Don't, old woman. Don't sin."

"Sin? Isn't what I said all true? I know to a dot what I'm saying, and I mean to tell it straight out to the master. He should see with his own eyes. Why not? What can we do now anyhow? Where shall we go? He's ruined us, ruined us."

The old woman burst out sobbing.

Gerasim heard all that, and it stabbed him like a dagger. He realised what misfortune he would be bringing the old people, and it made him sick at heart. He stood there a long while, saddened, lost in thought, then he turned and went back into the coachman's room.

"Ah, you forgot something?"

"No, Yegor Danilych." Gerasim stammered out, "I've come—listen—I want to thank you ever and ever so much —for the way you received me—and—and all the trouble you took for me—but—I can't take the place."

"What! What does that mean?"

"Nothing. I don't want the place. I will look for another one for myself."

Yegor flew into a rage.

"Did you mean to make a fool of me, did you, you idiot?
You come here so meek—'Try for me, do try for me'—and
then you refuse to take the place. You rascal, you have dis-
graced me!"

Gerasim found nothing to say in reply. He reddened, and
lowered his eyes. Yegor turned his back scornfully and said
nothing more.

Then Gerasim quietly picked up his cap and left the
coachman's room. He crossed the yard rapidly, went out by
the gate, and hurried off down the street. He felt happy
and lighthearted.

ONE AUTUMN NIGHT

———◆◆◆———

By Maxim Gorky

ONCE IN the autumn I happened to be in a very unpleasant
and inconvenient position. In the town where I had just
arrived and where I knew not a soul, I found myself without a farthing in my pocket and without a night's lodging.

Having sold during the first few days every part of my
costume without which it was still possible to go about, I
passed from the town into the quarter called "Yste," where
were the steamship wharves—a quarter which during the
navigation season fermented with boisterous, laborious life,
but now was silent and deserted, for we were in the last
days of October.

Dragging my feet along the moist sand, and obstinately
scrutinising it with the desire to discover in it any sort of
fragment of food, I wandered alone among the deserted
buildings and warehouses, and thought how good it would
be to get a full meal.

In our present state of culture hunger of the mind is more
quickly satisfied than hunger of the body. You wander
about the streets, you are surrounded by buildings not bad-
looking from the outside and—you may safely say it—not
so badly furnished inside, and the sight of them may excite

within you stimulating ideas about architecture, hygiene, and many other wise and high-flying subjects. You may meet warmly and neatly dressed folks—all very polite, and turning away from you tactfully, not wishing offensively to notice the lamentable fact of your existence. Well, well, the mind of a hungry man is always better nourished and healthier than the mind of the well-fed man; and there you have a situation from which you may draw a very ingenious conclusion in favour of the ill fed.

The evening was approaching, the rain was falling, and the wind blew violently from the north. It whistled in the empty booths and shops, blew into the plastered window-panes of the taverns, and whipped into foam the wavelets of the river which splashed noisily on the sandy shore, casting high their white crests, racing one after another into the dim distance, and leaping impetuously over one another's shoulders. It seemed as if the river felt the proximity of winter, and was running at random away from the fetters of ice which the north wind might well have flung upon her that very night. The sky was heavy and dark; down from it swept incessantly scarcely visible drops of rain, and the melancholy elegy in nature all around me was emphasised by a couple of battered and misshapen willow-trees and a boat, bottom upwards, that was fastened to their roots.

The overturned canoe with its battered keel and the miserable old trees rifled by the cold wind—everything around me was bankrupt, barren, and dead, and the sky flowed with undryable tears. . . . Everything around was waste and gloomy . . . it seemed as if everything were dead, leaving me alone among the living, and for me also a cold death waited.

I was then eighteen years old—a good time!

I walked and walked along the cold wet sand, making my chattering teeth warble in honour of cold and hunger, when suddenly, as I was carefully searching for something to eat behind one of the empty crates, I perceived behind it, crouching on the ground, a figure in woman's clothes dank with the rain and clinging fast to her stooping shoulders. Standing over her, I watched to see what she was doing. It appeared that she was digging a trench in the sand with her hands—digging away under one of the crates.

"Why are you doing that?" I asked, crouching down on my heels quite close to her.

She gave a little scream and was quickly on her legs again. Now that she stood there staring at me, with her wide-open grey eyes full of terror, I perceived that it was a girl of my own age, with a very pleasant face embellished unfortunately by three large blue marks. This spoilt her, although these blue marks had been distributed with a re-markable sense of proportion, one at a time, and all were of equal size—two under the eyes, and one a little bigger on the forehead just over the bridge of the nose. This sym-metry was evidently the work of an artist well inured to the business of spoiling the human physiognomy.

The girl looked at me, and the terror in her eyes gradu-ally died out. . . . She shook the sand from her hands, ad-justed her cotton head-gear, cowered down, and said:

"I suppose you too want something to eat? Dig away

then! My hands are tired. Over there"—she nodded her head
in the direction of a booth—"there is bread for certain . . .
and sausages too. . . . That booth is still carrying on business."

I began to dig. She, after waiting a little and looking at
me, sat down beside me and began to help me.

We worked in silence. I cannot say now whether I
thought at that moment of the criminal code, of morality,
of proprietorship, and all the other things about which, in
the opinion of many experienced persons, one ought to
think every moment of one's life. Wishing to keep as close
to the truth as possible, I must confess that apparently I
was so deeply engaged in digging under the crate that I
completely forgot about everything else except this one
thing: What could be inside that crate?

The evening drew on. The grey, mouldy, cold fog grew
thicker and thicker around us. The waves roared with a
hollower sound than before, and the rain pattered down on
the boards of that crate more loudly and more frequently.
Somewhere or other the night-watchman began springing
his rattle.

"Has it got a bottom or not?" softly inquired my assistant. I did not understand what she was talking about, and
I kept silence.

"I say, has the crate got a bottom? If it has we shall try
in vain to break into it. Here we are digging a trench, and
we may, after all, come upon nothing but solid boards. How
shall we take them off? Better smash the lock; it is a
wretched lock."

Good ideas rarely visit the heads of women, but, as you

see, they do visit them sometimes. I have always valued
good ideas, and have always tried to utilise them as far as
possible.

Having found the lock, I tugged at it and wrenched off
the whole thing. My accomplice immediately stooped down
and wriggled like a serpent into the gaping-open, four cor-
nered cover of the crate whence she called to me approvingly, in a low tone:

"You're a brick!"

Nowadays a little crumb of praise from a woman is
dearer to me than a whole dithyramb from a man, even
though he be more eloquent than all the ancient and modern orators put together. Then, however, I was less amiably
disposed than I am now, and, paying no attention to the
compliment of my comrade, I asked her curtly and anxiously:

"Is there anything?"

In a monotonous tone she set about calculating our dis-
coveries.

"A basketful of bottles—thick furs—a sunshade—an iron
pail."

All this was uneatable. I felt that my hopes had vanished. . . . But suddenly she exclaimed vivaciously:

"Aha! here it is!"

"What?"

"Bread . . . a loaf . . . it's only wet . . . take it!"

A loaf flew to my feet and after it herself, my valiant
comrade. I had already bitten off a morsel, stuffed it in my
mouth, and was chewing it. . . .

"Come, give me some too! . . . And we mustn't stay

here. . . . Where shall we go?" she looked inquiringly about on all sides. . . . It was dark, wet, and boisterous.

"Look! there's an upset canoe yonder . . . let us go there."

"Let us go then!" And off we set, demolishing our booty as we went, and filling our mouths with large portions of it. . . . The rain grew more violent, the river roared; from somewhere or other resounded a prolonged mocking whistle —just as if Someone great who feared nobody was whistling down all earthly institutions and along with them this horrid autumnal wind and us its heroes. This whistling made my heart throb painfully, in spite of which I greedily went on eating, and in this respect the girl, walking on my left hand, kept even pace with me.

"What do they call you?" I asked her—why I know not.

"Natasha," she answered shortly, munching loudly.

I stared at her. My heart ached within me; and then I stared into the mist before me, and it seemed to me as if the inimical countenance of my Destiny was smiling at me enigmatically and coldly.

. . . .

The rain scourged the timbers of the skiff incessantly, and its soft patter induced melancholy thoughts, and the wind whistled as it flew down into the boat's battered bottom through a rift, where some loose splinters of wood were rattling together—a disquieting and depressing sound. The waves of the river were splashing on the shore, and sounded so monotonous and hopeless, just as if they were telling something unbearably dull and heavy, which was boring them into utter disgust, something from which they wanted to run away and yet were obliged to talk about all the same. The sound of the rain blended with their splashing, and a long-drawn sigh seemed to be floating above the overturned skiff—the endless, labouring sigh of the earth, injured and exhausted by the eternal changes from the bright and warm summer to the cold misty and damp autumn. The wind blew continually over the desolate shore and the foaming river—blew and sang its melancholy songs. . . .

Our position beneath the shelter of the skiff was utterly devoid of comfort; it was narrow and damp, tiny cold drops of rain dribbled through the damaged bottom; gusts of wind penetrated it. We sat in silence and shivered with cold. I remembered that I wanted to go to sleep. Natasha leaned her back against the hull of the boat and curled herself up into a tiny ball. Embracing her knees with her hands, and resting her chin upon them, she stared doggedly at the river with wide-open eyes; on the pale patch of her face they seemed immense, because of the blue marks below them. She never moved, and this immobility and silence—I felt it—gradually produced within me a terror of my neighbour. I wanted to talk to her, but I knew not how to begin.

It was she herself who spoke.

"What a cursed thing life is!" she exclaimed plainly, abstractedly, and in a tone of deep conviction.

But this was no complaint. In these words there was too much of indifference for a complaint. This simple soul thought according to her understanding—thought and proceeded to form a certain conclusion which she expressed

aloud, and which I could not confute for fear of contradict-
ing myself. Therefore I was silent, and she, as if she had
not noticed me, continued to sit there immovable.

"Even if we croaked . . . what then . . .?" Natasha began
again, this time quietly and reflectively, and still there was
not one note of complaint in her words. It was plain that
this person, in the course of her reflections on life, was regarding her own case, and had arrived at the conviction
that in order to preserve herself from the mockeries of life,
she was not in a position to do anything else but simply
"croak"—to use her own expression.

The clearness of this line of thought was inexpressibly
sad and painful to me, and I felt that if I kept silence any
longer I was really bound to weep. . . . . And it would have
been shameful to have done this before a woman, especially as she was not weeping herself. I resolved to speak
to her.

"Who was it that knocked you about?" I asked. For the
moment I could not think of anything more sensible or
more delicate.

"Pashka did it all," she answered in a dull and level tone.

"And who is he?"

"My lover. . . . He was a baker."

"Did he beat you often?"

"Whenever he was drunk he beat me. . . . Often!"

And suddenly, turning towards me, she began to talk
about herself, Pashka, and their mutual relations. He was
a baker with red moustaches and played very well on the
banjo. He came to see her and greatly pleased her, for he

was a merry chap and wore nice clean clothes. He had a vest which cost fifteen rubles and boots with dress tops. For these reasons she had fallen in love with him, and he became her "creditor." And when he became her creditor he made it his business to take away from her the money which her other friends gave to her for bonbons, and, getting drunk on this money, he would fall to beating her; but that would have been nothing if he hadn't also begun to "run after" other girls before her very eyes.

"Now, wasn't that an insult? I am not worse than the others. Of course that meant that he was laughing at me, the blackguard. The day before yesterday I asked leave of my mistress to go out for a bit, went to him, and there I found Dimka sitting beside him drunk. And he, too, was half seas over. I said, 'You scoundrel, you!' And he gave me a thorough hiding. He kicked me and dragged me by the hair. But that was nothing to what came after. He spoiled everything I had on—left me just as I am now! How could I appear before my mistress? He spoiled everything . . . my dress and my jacket too—it was quite a new one; I gave a fiver for it . . . and tore my kerchief from my head. . . . Oh, Lord! What will become of me now?" she suddenly whined in a lamentable overstrained voice.

The wind howled, and became ever colder and more boisterous. . . . Again my teeth began to dance up and down, and she, huddled up to avoid the cold, pressed as closely to me as she could, so that I could see the gleam of her eyes through the darkness.

"What wretches all you men are! I'd burn you all in an

oven; I'd cut you in pieces. If any one of you was dying I'd spit in his mouth, and not pity him a bit. Mean skunks! You wheedle and wheedle, you wag your tails like cringing dogs, and we fools give ourselves up to you, and it's all up with us! Immediately you trample us underfoot. . . . Miserable loafers!"

She cursed us up and down, but there was no vigour, no malice, no hatred of these "miserable loafers" in her cursing that I could hear. The tone of her language by no means corresponded with its subject-matter, for it was calm enough, and the gamut of her voice was terribly poor.

Yet all this made a stronger impression on me than the most eloquent and convincing pessimistic books and speeches, of which I had read a good many and which I still read to this day. And this, you see, was because the agony of a dying person is much more natural and violent than the most minute and picturesque descriptions of death.

I felt really wretched—more from cold than from the words of my neighbour. I groaned softly and ground my teeth.

Almost at the same moment I felt two little arms about me—one of them touched my neck and the other lay upon my face—and at the same time an anxious, gentle, friendly voice uttered the question:

"What ails you?"

I was ready to believe that some one else was asking me this and not Natasha, who had just declared that all men were scoundrels, and expressed a wish for their destruction.

But she it was, and now she began speaking quickly, hurriedly.

"What ails you, eh? Are you cold? Are you frozen? Ah, what a one you are, sitting there so silent like a little owl! Why, you should have told me long ago that you were cold. Come . . . lie on the ground . . . stretch yourself out and I will lie . . . there! How's that? Now put your arms round me? . . . tighter! How's that? You shall be warm very soon now. . . . And then we'll lie back to back. . . . The night will pass so quickly, see if it won't. I say . . . have you too been drinking? . . . Turned out of your place, eh? . . . It doesn't matter."

And she comforted me. . . . She encouraged me.

May I be thrice accursed! What a world of irony was in this single fact for me! Just imagine! Here was I, seriously occupied at this very time with the destiny of humanity, thinking of the re-organisation of the social system, of political revolutions, reading all sorts of devilishly-wise books whose abysmal profundity was certainly unfathomable by their very authors—at this very time. I say, I was trying with all my might to make of myself "a potent active social force." It even seemed to me that I had partially accomplished my object; anyhow, at this time, in my ideas about myself, I had got so far as to recognise that I had an exclusive right to exist, that I had the necessary greatness to deserve to live my life, and that I was fully competent to play a great historical part therein. And a woman was now warming me with her body, a wretched, battered, hunted creature, who had no place and no value in life, and whom

I had never thought of helping till she helped me herself, and whom I really would not have known how to help in any way even if the thought of it had occurred to me.

Ah! I was ready to think that all this was happening to me in a dream—in a disagreeable, an oppressive dream.

But, ugh! it was impossible for me to think that, for cold drops of rain were dripping down upon me, the woman was pressing close to me, her warm breath was fanning my face, and—despite a slight odor of vodka—it did me good. The wind howled and raged, the rain smote upon the skiff, the waves splashed, and both of us, embracing each other convulsively, nevertheless shivered with cold. All this was only too real, and I am certain that nobody ever dreamed such an oppressive and horrid dream as that reality.

But Natasha was talking all the time of something or other, talking kindly and sympathetically, as only women can talk. Beneath the influence of her voice and kindly words a little fire began to burn up within me, and something inside my heart thawed in consequence.

Then tears poured from my eyes like a hailstorm, washing away from my heart much that was evil, much that was stupid, much sorrow and dirt which had fastened upon it before that night. Natasha comforted me.

"Come, come, that will do, little one! Don't take on! That'll do! God will give you another chance . . . you will right yourself and stand in your proper place again . . . and it will be all right. . . ."

And she kept kissing me . . . many kisses did she give me . . . burning kisses . . . and all for nothing. . . .

Those were the first kisses from a woman that had ever

been bestowed upon me, and they were the best kisses too, for all the subsequent kisses cost me frightfully dear, and really gave me nothing at all in exchange.

"Come, don't take on so, funny one! I'll manage for you to-morrow if you cannot find a place." Her quiet persuasive whispering sounded in my ears as if it came through a dream. . . .

There we lay till dawn. . . .

And when the dawn came, we crept from behind the skiff and went into the town. . . . Then we took friendly leave of each other and never met again, although for half a year I searched in every hole and corner for that kind Natasha, with whom I spent the autumn night just described.

If she be already dead—and well for her if it were so— may she rest in peace! And if she be alive . . . still I say "Peace to her soul!" And may the consciousness of her fall never enter her soul . . . for that would be a superfluous and fruitless suffering if life is to be lived. . . .

HER LOVER

———◆◆———

By Maxim Gorky

AN ACQUAINTANCE of mine once told me the following story.

When I was a student at Moscow I happened to live alongside one of those ladies whose repute is questionable. She was a Pole and they called her Teresa. She was a tall-ish, powerfully-built brunette, with black, bushy eyebrows and a large coarse face as if carved out by a hatchet—the bestial gleam of her dark eyes, her thick bass voice, her cab-man-like gait and her immense muscular vigour, worthy of a fishwife, inspired me with horror. I lived on the top flight and her garret was opposite to mine. I never left my door open when I knew her to be at home. But this, after all, was a very rare occurrence. Sometimes I chanced to meet her on the staircase or in the yard, and she would smile upon me with a smile which seemed to me to be sly and cynical. Occasionally, I saw her drunk, with bleary eyes, tousled hair, and a particularly hideous grin. On such occasions she would speak to me.

"How d'ye do, Mr. Student!" and her stupid laugh would still further intensify my loathing of her. I should have liked to have changed my quarters in order to have avoided such encounters and greetings; but my little chamber was a nice one, and there was such a wide view from the window, and it was always so quiet in the street below—so I endured.

And one morning I was sprawling on my couch, trying to find some sort of excuse for not attending my class, when the door opened, and the bass voice of Teresa the loathsome resounded from my threshold:

"Good health to you, Mr. Student!"

"What do you want?" I said. I saw that her face was confused and supplicatory. . . . It was a very unusual sort of face for her.

"Sir! I want to beg a favour of you. Will you grant it me?"

I lay there silent, and thought to myself:

"Gracious! . . . Courage, my boy!"

"I want to send a letter home, that's what it is," she said; her voice was beseeching, soft, timid.

"Deuce take you!" I thought; but up I jumped, sat down at my table, took a sheet of paper, and said:

"Come here, sit down, and dictate!"

She came, sat down very gingerly on a chair, and looked at me with a guilty look.

"Well, to whom do you want to write?"

"To Boleslav Kashput, at the town of Svieptziana, on the Warsaw Road. . . ."

"Well, fire away!"

"My dear Boles . . . my darling . . . my faithful lover. May the Mother of God protect thee! Thou heart of gold, why hast thou not written for such a long time to thy sorrowing little dove, Teresa?"

I very nearly burst out laughing. "A sorrowing little

dove!" more than five feet high, with fists a stone and more in weight, and as black a face as if the little dove had lived all its life in a chimney, and had never once washed itself! Restraining myself somehow, I asked:

"Who is this Bolest?"

"Boles, Mr. Student," she said, as if offended with me for blundering over the name, "he is Boles—my young man."

"Young man!"

"Why are you so surprised, sir? Cannot I, a girl have a young man?"

She? A girl? Well!

"Oh, why not?" I said. "All things are possible. And has he been your young man long?"

"Six years."

"Oh, ho!" I thought. "Well, let us write your letter. . . ."

And I tell you plainly that I would willingly have changed places with this Boles if his fair correspondent had been not Teresa but something less than she.

"I thank you most heartily, sir, for your kind services," said Teresa to me, with a curtsey. "Perhaps *I* can show *you* some service, eh?"

"No, I most humbly thank you all the same."

"Perhaps, sir, your shirts or your trousers may want a little mending?"

I felt that this mastodon in petticoats had made me grow quite red with shame, and I told her pretty sharply that I had no need whatever of her services.

She departed.

A week or two passed away. It was evening. I was sitting at my window whistling and thinking of some expedient for enabling me to get away from myself. I was bored; the weather was dirty. I didn't want to go out, and out of sheer ennui I began a course of self-analysis and reflection. This also was dull enough work, but I didn't care about doing anything else. Then the door opened. Heaven be praised! Some one came in.

"Oh, Mr. Student, you have no pressing business, I hope?"

It was Teresa. Humph!

"No. What is it?"

"I was going to ask you, sir, to write me another letter."

"Very well! To Boles, eh?"

"No, this time it is from him."

"Wha-at?"

"Stupid that I am! It is not for me, Mr. Student, I beg your pardon. It is for a friend of mine, that is to say, not a friend but an acquaintance—a man acquaintance. He has a sweetheart just like me here, Teresa. That's how it is. Will you, sir, write a letter to this Teresa?"

I looked at her—her face was troubled, her fingers were trembling. I was a bit fogged at first—and then I guessed how it was.

"Look here, my lady," I said, "there are no Boleses or Teresas at all, and you've been telling me a pack of lies. Don't you come sneaking about me any longer. I have no wish whatever to cultivate your acquaintance. Do you understand?"

And suddenly she grew strangely terrified and distraught; she began to shift from foot to foot without moving from the place, and spluttered comically, as if she wanted to say something and couldn't. I waited to see what would come of all this, and I saw and felt that, apparently, I had made a great mistake in suspecting her of wishing to draw me from the path of righteousness. It was evidently something very different.

. "Mr. Student!" she began, and suddenly, waving her hand, she turned abruptly towards the door and went out. I remained with a very unpleasant feeling in my mind. I listened. Her door was flung violently to—plainly the poor wench was very angry. . . . I thought it over, and resolved to go to her, and, inviting her to come in here, write everything she wanted.

I entered her apartment. I looked round. She was sitting at the table, leaning on her elbows, with her head in her hands.

"Listen to me," I said.

Now, whenever I come to this point in my story, I always feel horribly awkward and idiotic. Well, well!

"Listen to me," I said.

She leaped from her seat, came towards me with flashing eyes, and laying her hands on my shoulders, began to whisper, or rather to hum in her peculiar bass voice:

"Look you, now! It's like this. There's no Boles at all, and there's no Teresa either. But what's that to you? Is it a hard thing for you to draw your pen over paper? Eh? Ah, and *you*, too! Still such a little fair-haired boy! There's nobody at all, neither Boles, nor Teresa, only me. There you have it, and much good may it do you!"

"Pardon me!" said I, altogether flabbergasted by such a reception, "what is it all about? There's no Boles, you say?"

"No. So it is."

"And no Teresa either?"

"And no Teresa. I'm Teresa."

I didn't understand it at all. I fixed my eyes upon her, and tried to make out which of us was taking leave of his or her senses. But she went again to the table, searched about for something, came back to me, and said in an offended tone:

"If it was so hard for you to write to Boles, look, there's your letter, take it! Others will write for me."

I looked. In her hand was my letter to Boles. Phew!

"Listen, Teresa! What is the meaning of all this? Why must you get others to write for you when I have already written it, and you haven't sent it?"

"Sent it where?"

"Why, to this—Boles."

"There's no such person."

I absolutely did not understand it. There was nothing for me but to spit and go. Then she explained.

"What is it?" she said, still offended. "There's no such person, I tell you," and she extended her arms as if she herself did not understand why there should be no such person. "But I wanted him to be. . . . Am I then not a human creature like the rest of them? Yes, yes, I know, I know, of course. . . . Yet no harm was done to any one by my writing to him that I can see. . . ."

"Pardon me—to whom?"

"To Boles, of course."

"But he doesn't exist."

"Alas! alas! But what if he doesn't? He doesn't exist,

but he *might!* I write to him, and it looks as if he did exist. And Teresa—that's me, and he replies to me, and then I write to him again. . . ."

I understood at last. And I felt so sick, so miserable, so ashamed, somehow. Alongside of me, not three yards away, lived a human creature who had nobody in the world to treat her kindly, affectionately, and this human being had invented a friend for herself!

"Look, now! you wrote me a letter to Boles, and I gave it to some one else to read it to me; and when they read it to me I listened and fancied that Boles was there. And I asked you to write me a letter from Boles to Teresa—that is to me. When they write such a letter for me, and read it to me, I feel quite sure that Boles is there. And life grows easier for me in consequence."

"Deuce take you for a blockhead!" said I to myself when I heard this.

And from thenceforth, regularly, twice a week, I wrote a letter to Boles, and an answer from Boles to Teresa. I wrote those answers well. . . . She, of course, listened to them, and wept like anything, roared, I should say, with her bass voice. And in return for my thus moving her to tears by real letters from the imaginary Boles, she began to mend the holes I had in my socks, shirts, and other articles of clothing. Subsequently, about three months after this history began, they put her in prison for something or other. No doubt by this time she is dead.

My acquaintance shook the ash from his cigarette, looked pensively up at the sky, and thus concluded:

Well, well, the more a human creature has tasted of bitter

things the more it hungers after the sweet things of life. And we, wrapped round in the rags of our virtues, and regarding others through the mist of our self-sufficiency, and persuaded of our universal impeccability, do not understand this.

And the whole thing turns out pretty stupidly—and very cruelly. The fallen classes, we say. And who are the fallen classes, I should like to know? They are, first of all, people with the same bones, flesh, and blood and nerves as ourselves. We have been told this day after day for ages. And we actually listen—and the devil only knows how hideous the whole thing is. Or are we completely depraved by the loud sermonising of humanism? In reality, we also are fallen folks, and, so far as I can see, very deeply fallen into the abyss of self-sufficiency and the conviction of our own superiority. But enough of this. It is all as old as the hills—so old that it is a shame to speak of it. Very old indeed—yes, that's what it is!

THE REVOLUTIONIST

◆◆◆

By Mikhaïl P. Artzybashev

I

GABRIEL ANDERSEN, the teacher, walked to the edge of the school garden, where he paused, undecided what to do. Off in the distance, two miles away, the woods hung like bluish lace over a field of pure snow. It was a brilliant day. A hundred tints glistened on the white ground and the iron bars of the garden railing. There was a lightness and transparency in the air that only the days of early spring possess. Gabriel Andersen turned his steps toward the fringe of blue lace for a tramp in the woods.

"Another spring in my life," he said, breathing deep and peering up at the heavens through his spectacles. Andersen was rather given to sentimental poetising. He walked with his hands folded behind him, dangling his cane.

He had gone but a few paces when he noticed a group of soldiers and horses on the road beyond the garden rail. Their drab uniforms stood out dully against the white of the snow, but their swords and horses' coats tossed back the light. Their bowed cavalry legs moved awkwardly on the snow. Andersen wondered what they were doing there. Suddenly the nature of their business flashed upon him. It was an ugly errand they were upon, an instinct rather than his reason told him. Something unusual and terrible was to happen. And the same instinct told him he must conceal himself from the soldiers. He turned to the left quickly, dropped on his knees, and crawled on the soft, thawing, crackling snow to a low haystack, from behind which, by craning his neck, he could watch what the soldiers were doing.

There were twelve of them, one a stocky young officer in a grey cloak caught in prettily at the waist by a silver belt. His face was so red that even at that distance Andersen caught the odd, whitish gleam of his light protruding moustache and eyebrows against the vivid colour of his skin. The broken tones of his raucous voice reached distinctly to where the teacher, listening intently, lay hidden.

"I know what I am about. I don't need anybody's advice," the officer cried. He clapped his arms akimbo and looked down at some one among the group of bustling soldiers. "I'll show you how to be a rebel, you damned skunk."

Andersen's heart beat fast. "Good heavens!" he thought. "Is it possible?" His head grew chill as if struck by a cold wave.

"Officer," a quiet, restrained, yet distinct voice came from among the soldiers, "you have no right—it's for the court to decide—you aren't a judge—it's plain murder, not——"

"Silence!" thundered the officer, his voice choking with rage. "I'll give you a court. Ivanov, go ahead."

He put the spurs to his horse and rode away. Gabriel

Andersen mechanically observed how carefully the horse picked its way, placing its feet daintily as if for the steps of a minuet. Its ears were pricked to catch every sound. There was momentary bustle and excitement among the soldiers. Then they dispersed in different directions, leaving three persons in black behind, two tall men and one very short and frail. Andersen could see the hair of the short one's head. It was very light. And he saw his rosy ears sticking out on each side.

Now he fully understood what was to happen. But it was a thing so out of the ordinary, so horrible, that he fancied he was dreaming.

"It's so bright, so beautiful—the snow, the field, the woods, the sky. The breath of spring is upon everything. Yet people are going to be killed. How can it be? Impossible!" So his thoughts ran in confusion. He had the sensation of a man suddenly gone insane, who finds he sees, hears and feels what he is not accustomed to, and ought not hear, see and feel.

The three men in black stood next to one another hard by the railing, two quite close together, the short one some distance away.

"Officer!" one of them cried in a desperate voice—Andersen could not see which it was—"God sees us! Officer!"

Eight soldiers dismounted quickly, their spurs and sabres catching awkwardly. Evidently they were in a hurry, as if doing a thief's job.

Several seconds passed in silence until the soldiers placed themselves in a row a few feet from the black figures and levelled their guns. In doing so one soldier knocked his cap from his head. He picked it up and put it on again without brushing off the wet snow.

The officer's mount still kept dancing on one spot with his ears pricked, while the other horses, also with sharp ears erect to catch every sound, stood motionless looking at the men in black, their long wise heads inclined to one side.

"Spare the boy at least!" another voice suddenly pierced the air. "Why kill a child, damn you! What has the child done?"

"Ivanov, do what I told you to do," thundered the officer, drowning the other voice. His face turned as scarlet as a piece of red flannel.

There followed a scene savage and repulsive in its gruesomeness. The short figure in black, with the light hair and the rosy ears, uttered a wild shriek in a shrill child's tones and reeled to one side. Instantly it was caught up by two or three soldiers. But the boy began to struggle, and two more soldiers ran up.

"Ow-ow-ow-ow!" the boy cried. "Let me go, let me go! Ow-ow!"

His shrill voice cut the air like the yell of a stuck porkling not quite done to death. Suddenly he grew quiet. Some one must have struck him. An unexpected, oppressive silence ensued. The boy was being pushed forward. Then there came a deafening report. Andersen started back all in a tremble. He saw distinctly, yet vaguely as in a dream, the dropping of two dark bodies, the flash of pale sparks, and a light smoke rising in the clean, bright atmosphere. He saw the soldiers hastily mounting their horses without even glancing at the bodies. He saw them galloping along the muddy road, their arms clanking, their horses' hoofs clattering.

He saw all this, himself now standing in the middle of the road, not knowing when and why he had jumped from behind the haystack. He was deathly pale. His face was covered with dank sweat, his body was aquiver. A physical sadness smote and tortured him. He could not make out the nature of the feeling. It was akin to extreme sickness, though far more nauseating and terrible.

After the soldiers had disappeared beyond the bend toward the woods, people came hurrying to the spot of the shooting, though till then not a soul had been in sight.

The bodies lay at the roadside on the other side of the railing, where the snow was clean, brittle and untrampled and glistened cheerfully in the bright atmosphere. There were three dead bodies, two men and a boy. The boy lay with his long soft neck stretched on the snow. The face of the man next to the boy was invisible. He had fallen face downward in a pool of blood. The third was a big man with a black beard and huge, muscular arms. He lay stretched out to the full length of his big body, his arms extended over a large area of blood-stained snow.

The three men who had been shot lay black against the white snow, motionless. From afar no one could have told the terror that was in their immobility as they lay there at the edge of the narrow road crowded with people.

That night Gabriel Andersen in his little room in the schoolhouse did not write poems as usual. He stood at the window and looked at the distant pale disk of the moon in the misty blue sky, and thought. And his thoughts were confused, gloomy, and heavy as if a cloud had descended upon his brain.

Indistinctly outlined in the dull moonlight he saw the dark railing, the trees, the empty garden. It seemed to him that he beheld them—the three men who had been shot, two grown up, one a child. They were lying there now at the roadside, in the empty, silent field, looking at the far-off cold moon with their dead, white eyes as he with his living eyes.

"The time will come some day," he thought, "when the killing of people by others will be an utter impossibility. The time will come when even the soldiers and officers who killed these three men will realise what they have done and will understand that what they killed them for is just as necessary, important, and dear to them—to the officers and soldiers—as to those whom they killed.

"Yes," he said aloud and solemnly, his eyes moistening, "that time will come. They will understand." And the pale disk of the moon was blotted out by the moisture in his eyes.

A large pity pierced his heart for the three victims whose eyes looked at the moon, sad and unseeing. A feeling of rage cut him as with a sharp knife and took possession of him.

But Gabriel Andersen quieted his heart, whispering

softly, "They know not what they do." And this old and ready phrase gave him the strength to stifle his rage and indignation.

II

THE DAY was as bright and white, but the spring was already advanced. The wet soil smelt of spring. Clear cold water ran everywhere from under the loose, thawing snow. The branches of the trees were springy and elastic. For miles and miles around, the country opened up in clear azure stretches.

Yet the clearness and the joy of the spring day were not in the village. They were somewhere outside the village, where there were no people—in the fields, the woods and the mountains. In the village the air was stifling, heavy and terrible as in a nightmare.

Gabriel Andersen stood in the road near a crowd of dark, sad, absent-minded people and craned his neck to see the preparations for the flogging of seven peasants.

They stood in the thawing snow, and Gabriel Andersen could not persuade himself that they were people whom he had long known and understood. By that which was about to happen to them, the shameful, terrible, ineradicable thing that was to happen to them, they were separated from all the rest of the world, and so were unable to feel what he, Gabriel Andersen, felt, just as he was unable to feel what they felt. Round them were the soldiers, confidently and beautifully mounted on high upon their large steeds, who tossed their wise heads and turned their dappled wooden faces slowly from side to side, looking contemptuously at him, Gabriel Anderson, who was soon to behold this horror, this disgrace, and would do nothing, would not dare to do anything. So it seemed to Gabriel Andersen; and a sense of cold, intolerable shame gripped him as between two clamps of ice through which he could see everything without being able to move, cry out or utter a groan.

They took the first peasant. Gabriel Andersen saw his strange, imploring hopeless look. His lips moved, but no sound was heard, and his eyes wandered. There was a bright gleam in them as in the eyes of a madman. His mind, it was evident, was no longer able to comprehend what was happening.

And so terrible was that face, at once full of reason and of madness, that Andersen felt relieved when they put him face downward on the snow and, instead of the fiery eyes, he saw his bare back glistening—a senseless, shameful, horrible sight.

The large, red-faced soldier in a red cap pushed toward him, looked down at his body with seeming delight, and then cried in a clear voice:

"Well, let her go, with God's blessing!"

Andersen seemed not to see the soldiers, the sky, the horses or the crowd. He did not feel the cold, the terror or the shame. He did not hear the swish of the knout in the air or the savage howl of pain and despair. He only saw the bare back of a man's body swelling up and cov-

ered over evenly with white and purple stripes. Gradually the bare back lost the semblance of human flesh. The
blood oozed and squirted, forming patches, drops and rivu-
lets, which ran down on the white, thawing snow.

Terror gripped the soul of Gabriel Andersen as he
thought of the moment when the man would rise and
face all the people who had seen his body bared out in the
open and reduced to a bloody pulp. He closed his eyes.
When he opened them, he saw four soldiers in uniform
and red hats forcing another man down on the snow, his
back bared just as shamefully, terribly and absurdly—a
ludicrously tragic sight.

Then came the third, the fourth, and so on, to the end.

And Gabriel Andersen stood on the wet, thawing snow,
craning his neck, trembling and stuttering, though he did
not say a word. Dank sweat poured from his body. A
sense of shame permeated his whole being. It was a humiliating feeling, having to escape being noticed so that they
should not catch him and lay him there on the snow and
strip him bare—him, Gabriel Andersen.

The soldiers pressed and crowded, the horses tossed their
heads, the knout swished in the air, and the bare, shamed
human flesh swelled up, tore, ran over with blood, and
curled like a snake. Oaths, wild shrieks rained upon the
village through the clean white air of that spring day.

Andersen now saw five men's faces at the steps of the
town hall, the faces of those men who had already undergone their shame. He quickly turned his eyes away. After
seeing this a man must die, he thought.

III

THERE WERE seventeen of them, fifteen soldiers, a subaltern and a young beardless officer. The officer lay in front of the fire looking intently into the flames. The soldiers were tinkering with the firearms in the wagon.

Their grey figures moved about quietly on the black thawing ground, and occasionally stumbled across the logs sticking out from the blazing fire.

Gabriel Andersen, wearing an overcoat and carrying his cane behind his back, approached them. The subaltern, a stout fellow with a moustache, jumped up, turned from the fire, and looked at him.

"Who are you? What do you want?" he asked excitedly. From his tone it was evident that the soldiers feared everybody in that district, through which they went scattering death, destruction and torture.

"Officer," he said, "there is a man here I don't know."

The officer looked at Andersen without speaking.

"Officer," said Andersen in a thin, strained voice, "my name is Michelson. I am a business man here, and I am going to the village on business. I was afraid I might be mistaken for some one else—you know."

"Then what are you nosing about here for?" the officer said angrily, and turned away.

"A business man," sneered a soldier. "He ought to be searched, this business man ought, so as not to be knocking about at night. A good one in the jaw is what he needs."

"He's a suspicious character, officer," said the subaltern. "Don't you think we'd better arrest him, what?"

"Don't," answered the officer lazily. "I'm sick of them, damn 'em."

Gabriel Andersen stood there without saying anything. His eyes flashed strangely in the dark by the firelight. And it was strange to see his short, substantial, clean, neat figure in the field at night among the soldiers, with his overcoat and cane and glasses glistening in the firelight.

The soldiers left him and walked away. Gabriel Andersen remained standing for a while. Then he turned and left, rapidly disappearing in the darkness.

The night was drawing to a close. The air turned chilly, and the tops of the bushes defined themselves more clearly in the dark. Gabriel Andersen went again to the military post. But this time he hid, crouching low as he made his way under the cover of the bushes. Behind him people moved about quietly and carefully, bending the bushes, silent as shadows. Next to Gabriel, on his right, walked a tall man with a revolver in his hand.

The figure of a soldier on the hill outlined itself strangely, unexpectedly, not where they had been looking for it. It was faintly illumined by the gleam from the dying fire. Gabriel Andersen recognised the soldier. It was the one who had proposed that he should be searched. Nothing stirred in Andersen's heart. His face was cold and motionless, as of a man who is asleep. Round the fire the soldiers lay stretched out sleeping, all except the subaltern, who sat with his head drooping over his knees.

The tall thin man on Andersen's right raised the revolver and pulled the trigger. A momentary blinding flash, a deafening report.

Andersen saw the guard lift his hands and then sit down on the ground clasping his bosom. From all directions short, crackling sparks flashed up which combined into one riving roar. The subaltern jumped up and dropped straight into the fire. Grey soldiers' figures moved about in all directions like apparitions, throwing up their hands and falling and writhing on the black earth. The young officer ran past Andersen, fluttering his hands like some strange, frightened bird. Andersen, as if he were thinking of something else, raised his cane. With all his strength he hit the officer on the head, each blow descending with a dull, ugly thud. The officer reeled in a circle, struck a bush, and sat down after the second blow, covering his head with both hands, as children do. Some one ran up and discharged a revolver as if from Andersen's own hand. The officer sank together in a heap and lunged with great force head foremost on the ground. His legs twitched for a while, then he curled up quietly.

The shots ceased. Black men with white faces, ghostly grey in the dark, moved about the dead bodies of the soldiers, taking away their arms and ammunition.

Andersen watched all this with a cold, attentive stare. When all was over, he went up, took hold of the burned subaltern's legs, and tried to remove the body from the fire. But it was too heavy for him, and he let it go.

IV

ANDERSEN SAT motionless on the steps of the town hall, and thought. He thought of how he, Gabriel Andersen, with

his spectacles, cane, overcoat and poems, had lied and betrayed fifteen men. He thought it was terrible, yet there was
neither pity, shame nor regret in his heart. Were he to be
set free, he knew that he, Gabriel Andersen, with the spectacles and poems, would go straightway and do it again. He
tried to examine himself, to see what was going on inside
his soul. But his thoughts were heavy and confused. For
some reason it was more painful for him to think of the
three men lying on the snow, looking at the pale disk of
the far-off moon with their dead, unseeing eyes, than of the
murdered officer whom he had struck two dry, ugly blows
on the head. Of his own death he did not think. It seemed
to him that he had done with everything long, long ago.
Something had died, had gone out and left him empty, and
he must not think about it.

And when they grabbed him by the shoulder and he rose,
and they quickly led him through the garden where the
cabbages raised their dry heads, he could not formulate a
single thought.

He was conducted to the road and placed at the railing
with his back to one of the iron bars. He fixed his spectacles, put his hands behind him, and stood there with his
neat, stocky body, his head slightly inclined to one side.

At the last moment he looked in front of him and saw
rifle barrels pointing at his head, chest and stomach, and
pale faces with trembling lips. He distinctly saw how one
barrel levelled at his forehead suddenly dropped.

Something strange and incomprehensible, as if no longer
of this world, no longer earthly, passed through Andersen's
mind. He straightened himself to the full height of his

short body and threw back his head in simple pride. A strange indistinct sense of cleanness, strength and pride filled his soul, and everything—the sun and the sky and the people and the field and death—seemed to him insignificant, remote and useless.

The bullets hit him in the chest, in the left eye, in the stomach, went through his clean coat buttoned all the way up. His glasses shivered into bits. He uttered a shriek, circled round, and fell with his face against one of the iron bars, his one remaining eye wide open. He clawed the ground with his outstretched hands as if trying to support himself.

The officer, who had turned green, rushed toward him, and senselessly thrust the revolver against his neck, and fired twice. Andersen stretched out on the ground.

The soldiers left quickly. But Andersen remained pressed flat to the ground. The index finger of his left hand continued to quiver for about ten seconds.

THE OUTRAGE—A TRUE STORY

❖❖❖

By Aleksandr I. Kuprin

It was five o'clock on a July afternoon. The heat was terrible. The whole of the huge stone-built town breathed out heat like a glowing furnace. The glare of the white-walled house was insufferable. The asphalt pavements grew soft and burned the feet. The shadows of the acacias spread over the cobbled road, pitiful and weary. They too seemed hot. The sea, pale in the sunlight, lay heavy and immobile as one dead. Over the streets hung a white dust.

In the foyer of one of the private theatres a small committee of local barristers who had undertaken to conduct the cases of those who had suffered in the last pogrom against the Jews was reaching the end of its daily task. There were nineteen of them, all juniors, young, progressive and conscientious men. The sitting was without formality, and white suits of duck, flannel and alpaca were in the majority. They sat anywhere, at little marble tables, and the chairman stood in front of an empty counter where chocolates were sold in the winter.

The barristers were quite exhausted by the heat which poured in through the windows, with the dazzling sunlight and the noise of the streets. The proceedings went lazily **and** with a certain irritation.

A tall young man with a fair moustache and thin **hair** was in the chair. He was dreaming voluptuously how **he** would be off in an instant on his new-bought bicycle to the bungalow. He would undress quickly, and without waiting to cool, still bathed in sweat, would fling himself into the clear, cold, sweet-smelling sea. His whole body was enervated and tense, thrilled by the thought. Impatiently moving the papers before him, he spoke in a drowsy voice.

"So, Joseph Moritzovich will conduct the case of Rubinchik. . . . Perhaps there is still a statement to be made on the order of the day?"

His youngest colleague, a short, stout Karaite, very black and lively, said in a whisper so that every one could hear: "On the order of the day, the best thing would be iced *kvas*. . . ."

The chairman gave him a stern side-glance, but could not restrain a smile. He sighed and put both his hands on the table to raise himself and declare the meeting closed, when the doorkeeper, who stood at the entrance to the theatre, suddenly moved forward and said: "There are seven people outside, sir. They want to come in."

The chairman looked impatiently round the company.

"What is to be done, gentlemen?"

Voices were heard.

"Next time. *Basta!*"

"Let 'em put it in writing."

"If they'll get it over quickly. . . . Decide it at once."

"Let 'em go to the devil. Phew! It's like boiling pitch."

"Let them in." The chairman gave a sign with his head, annoyed. "Then bring me a Vichy, please. But it must be cold."

The porter opened the door and called down the corridor: "Come in. They say you may."

Then seven of the most surprising and unexpected individuals filed into the foyer. First appeared a full-grown, confident man in a smart suit, of the colour of dry sea-sand, in a magnificent pink shirt with white stripes and a crimson rose in his buttonhole. From the front his head looked like an upright bean, from the side like a horizontal bean. His face was adorned with a strong, bushy, martial moustache. He wore dark blue pince-nez on his nose, on his hands straw-coloured gloves. In his left hand he held a black walking stick with a silver mount, in his right a light blue handkerchief.

The other six produced a strange, chaotic, incongruous impression, exactly as though they had all hastily pooled not merely their clothes, but their hands, feet and heads as well. There was a man with the splendid profile of a Roman senator, dressed in rags and tatters. Another wore an elegant dress waistcoat, from the deep opening of which a dirty Little-Russian shirt leapt to the eye. Here were the unbalanced faces of the criminal type, but looking with a confidence that nothing could shake. All these men, in spite of their apparent youth, evidently possessed a large experience of life, an easy manner, a bold approach, and some hidden, suspicious cunning.

The gentleman in the sandy suit bowed just his head, neatly and easily, and said with a half-question in his voice: "Mr. Chairman?"

"Yes. I am the chairman. What is your business?"

"We—all whom you see before you," the gentleman began in a quiet voice and turned round to indicate his companions, "we come as delegates from the United Rostov-Kharkov-and-Odessa-Nikolayev Association of Thieves."

The barristers began to shift in their seats.

The chairman flung himself back and opened his eyes wide. "Association of *what?*" he said, perplexed.

"The Association of Thieves," the gentleman in the sandy suit coolly repeated. "As for myself, my comrades did me the signal honour of electing me as the spokesman of the deputation."

"Very . . . pleased," the chairman said uncertainly.

"Thank you. All seven of us are ordinary thieves—naturally of different departments. The Association has authorised us to put before your esteemed Committee"—the gentleman again made an elegant bow—"our respectful demand for assistance."

"I don't quite understand . . . quite frankly . . . what is the connection. . . ." The chairman waved his hands helplessly. "However, please go on."

"The matter about which we have the courage and the honour to apply to you, gentlemen, is very clear, very simple, and very brief. It will take only six or seven minutes. I consider it my duty to warn you of this beforehand, in view of the late hour and the 15 degrees that Fahrenheit marks in the shade." The orator expectorated slightly and glanced at his superb gold watch. "You see, in the reports that have lately appeared in the local papers of the melancholy and terrible days of the last pogrom, there have very often been indications that among the instigators of the pogrom who were paid and organised by the police—the dregs of society, consisting of drunkards, tramps, souteneurs, and hooligans from the slums—thieves were also to be found. At first we were silent, but finally we considered ourselves under the necessity of protesting against such an unjust and serious accusation, before the face of the whole of intellectual society. I know well that in the eye of the law we are offenders and enemies of society. But imagine only for a moment, gentlemen, the situation of this enemy of society when he is accused wholesale of an offence which he not only never committed, but which he is ready to resist with the whole strength of his soul. It goes without saying that he will feel the outrage of such an injustice more keenly than a normal, average, fortunate citizen. Now, we declare that the accusation brought against us is utterly devoid of all basis, not merely of fact but even of logic. I intend to prove this in a few words if the honourable committee will kindly listen."

"Proceed," said the chairman.

"Please do . . . Please . . ." was heard from the barristers, now animated.

"I offer you my sincere thanks in the name of all my comrades. Believe me, you will never repent your attention to the representatives of our . . . well, let us say, slippery, but nevertheless difficult, profession. 'So we begin,' as Giraldoni sings in the prologue to *Pagliacci*.

"But first I would ask your permission, Mr. Chairman, to quench my thirst a little. . . . Porter, bring me a lemonade and a glass of English bitter, there's a good fellow. Gentlemen, I will not speak of the moral aspect of our profession nor of its social importance. Doubtless you know better than I the striking and brilliant paradox of Proudhon: *La propriété c'est le vol*—a paradox if you like, but one that has never yet been refuted by the sermons of cowardly bourgeois or fat priests. For instance: a father accumulates a million by energetic and clever exploitation, and leaves it to his son—a rickety, lazy, ignorant, degenerate idiot, a brainless maggot, a true parasite. Potentially a million rubles is a million working days, the absolutely irrational right to labour, sweat, life, and blood of a terrible number of men. Why? What is the ground of reason? Utterly unknown. Then why not agree with the proposition, gentlemen, that our profession is to some extent as it were a correction of the excessive accumulation of values in the hands of individuals, and serves as a protest against all the hardships, abominations, arbitrariness, violence, and negligence of the human personality, against all the monstrosities created by the bourgeois capitalistic organisation of modern society? Sooner or later, this order of things will assuredly be overturned by the social revolution. Property will pass away into the limbo of melancholy memories and with it, alas! we will disappear from the face of the earth, we, *les braves chevaliers d'industrie.*"

The orator paused to take the tray from the hands of the porter, and placed it near to his hand on the table.

"Exuse me, gentlemen. . . . Here, my good man, take

this, . . . and by the way, when you go out shut the door close behind you."

"Very good, your Excellency!" the porter bawled in jest.

The orator drank off half a glass and continued: "However, let us leave aside the philosophical, social, and economic aspects of the question. I do not wish to fatigue your attention. I must nevertheless point out that our profession very closely approaches the idea of that which is called art. Into it enter all the elements which go to form art—vocation, inspiration, fantasy, inventiveness, ambition, and a long and arduous apprenticeship to the science. From it is absent virtue alone, concerning which the great Karamzin wrote with such stupendous and fiery fascination. Gentlemen, nothing is further from my intention than to trifle with you and waste your precious time with idle paradoxes; but I cannot avoid expounding my idea briefly. To an outsider's ear it sounds absurdly wild and ridiculous to speak of the vocation of a thief. However, I venture to assure you that this vocation is a reality. There are men who possess a peculiarly strong visual memory, sharpness and accuracy of eye, presence of mind, dexterity of hand, and above all a subtle sense of touch, who are as it were born into God's world for the sole and special purpose of becoming distinguished card-sharpers. The pickpockets' profession demands extraordinary nimbleness and agility, a terrific certainty of movement, not to mention a ready wit, a talent for observation and strained attention. Some have a positive vocation for breaking open safes: from their tenderest childhood they are attracted by the mysteries of every kind of complicated mechanism—bicycles, sewing machines, clock-work toys and watches. Finally, gentlemen, there are people with an hereditary animus against private property. You may call this phenomenon degeneracy. But I tell you that you cannot entice a true thief, and thief by vocation, into the prose of honest vegetation by any gingerbread reward, or by the offer of a secure position, or by the gift of money, or by a woman's love: because there is here a permanent beauty of risk, a fascinating abyss of danger, the delightful sinking of the heart, the impetuous pulsation of life, the ecstasy! You are armed with the protection of the law, by locks, revolvers, telephones, police and soldiery; but we only by our own dexterity, cunning and fearlessness. We are the foxes, and society—is a chicken-run guarded by dogs. Are you aware that the most artistic and gifted natures in our villages become horse-thieves and poachers? What would you have? Life is so meagre, so insipid, so intolerably dull to eager and high-spirited souls!

"I pass on to inspiration. Gentlemen, doubtless you have had to read of thefts that were supernatural in design and execution. In the headlines of the newspapers they are called 'An Amazing Robbery,' or 'An Ingenious Swindle,' or again 'A Clever Ruse of the Gangsters.' In such cases our bourgeois paterfamilias waves his hands and exclaims: 'What a terrible thing! If only their abilities were turned to good—their inventiveness, their amazing knowledge of human psychology, their self-possession, their fearlessness, their incomparable histrionic powers! What extraordinary benefits they would bring to the country!' But it is well known that the bourgeois paterfamilias was specially devised by Heaven to utter commonplaces and trivialities I myself sometimes—

we thieves are sentimental people, I confess—I myself sometimes admire a beautiful sunset in Aleksandra Park or by
the sea-shore. And I am always certain beforehand that
some one near me will say with infallible *aplomb*: 'Look
at it. If it were put into picture no one would ever believe
it!' I turn round and naturally I see a self-satisfied, full-fed
paterfamilias, who delights in repeating some one else's
silly statement as though it were his own. As for our dear
country, the bourgeois paterfamilias looks upon it as though
it were a roast turkey. If you've managed to cut the best
part of the bird for yourself, eat it quietly in a comfortable
corner and praise God. But he's not really the important
person. I was led away by my detestation of vulgarity and
I apologise for the digression. The real point is that genius
and inspiration, even when they are not devoted to the
service of the Orthodox Church, remain rare and beautiful
things. Progress is a law—and theft too has its creation.

"Finally, our profession is by no means as easy and pleasant as it seems to the first glance. It demands long experience, constant practice, slow and painful apprenticeship. It
comprises in itself hundreds of supple, skilful processes that
the cleverest juggler cannot compass. That I may not give
you only empty words, gentlemen, I will perform a few
experiments before you now. I ask you to have every confidence in the demonstrators. We are all at present in the
enjoyment of legal freedom, and though we are usually
watched, and every one of us is known by face, and our
photographs adorn the albums of all detective departments,
for the time being we are not under the necessity of hiding
ourselves from anybody. If any one of you should recog-

nise any of us in the future under different circumstances, we ask you earnestly always to act in accordance with your professional duties and your obligations as citizens. In grateful return for your kind attention we have decided to declare your property inviolable, and to invest it with a thieves' taboo. However, I proceed to business."

The orator turned round and gave an order: "Sesoi the Great, will you come this way!"

An enormous fellow with a stoop, whose hands reached to his knees, without a forehead or a neck, like a big, fair Hercules, came forward. He grinned stupidly and rubbed his left eyebrow in his confusion.

"Can't do nothin' here," he said hoarsely.

The gentleman in the sandy suit spoke for him, turning to the committee.

"Gentlemen, before you stands a respected member of our association. His specialty is breaking open safes, iron strong boxes, and other receptacles for monetary tokens. In his night work he sometimes avails himself of the electric current of the lighting installation for fusing metals. Unfortunately he has nothing on which he can demonstrate the best items of his repertoire. He will open the most elaborate lock irreproachably. . . . By the way, this door here, it's locked, is it not?"

Every one turned to look at the door, on which a printed notice hung: "Stage Door. Strictly Private."

"Yes, the door's locked, evidently," the chairman agreed.

"Admirable. Sesoi the Great, will you be so kind?"

" 'Tain't nothin' at all," said the giant leisurely.

He went close to the door, shook it cautiously with his

hand, took out of his pocket a small bright instrument, bent down to the keyhole, made some almost imperceptible movements with the tool, suddenly straightened and flung the door wide in silence. The chairman had his watch in his hands. The whole affair took only ten seconds.

"Thank you, Sesoi the Great," said the gentleman in the sandy suit politely. "You may go back to your seat."

But the chairman interrupted in some alarm: "Excuse me. This is all very interesting and instructive, but . . . is it included in your esteemed colleague's profession to be able to lock the door again?"

"Ah, *mille pardons.*" The gentleman bowed hurriedly. "It slipped my mind. Sesoi the Great, would you oblige?"

The door was locked with the same adroitness and the same silence. The esteemed colleague waddled back to his friends, grinning.

"Now I will have the honour to show you the skill of one of our comrades who is in the line of picking pockets in theatres and railway-stations," continued the orator. "He is still very young, but you may to some extent judge from the delicacy of his present work of the heights he will attain by diligence. Yasha!" A swarthy youth in a blue silk blouse and long glacé boots, like a gipsy, came forward with a swagger, fingering the tassels of his belt, and merrily screwing up his big, impudent black eyes with yellow whites.

"Gentlemen," said the gentleman in the sandy suit persuasively, "I must ask if one of you would be kind enough to submit himself to a little experiment. I assure you this will be an exhibition only, just a game."

He looked round over the seated company.

The short plump Karaite, black as a beetle, came forward from his table.

"At your service," he said amusedly.

"Yasha!" The orator signed with his head.

Yasha came close to the solicitor. On his left arm, which was bent, hung a bright-coloured, figured scarf.

"Suppose yer in church or at the bar in one of the halls, —or watchin' a circus," he began in a sugary, fluent voice. "I see straight off—there's a toff. . . . Excuse me, sir. Suppose you're the toff. There's no offence—just means a rich gent, decent enough, but don't know his way about. First— what's he likely to have about 'im? All sorts. Mostly, a ticker and a chain. Whereabouts does he keep 'em? Somewhere in his top vest pocket—here. Others have 'em in the bottom pocket. Just here. Purse—most always in the trousers, except when a greeny keeps it in his jacket. Cigar case. Have a look first what it is—gold, silver—with a monogram. Leather—what decent man'd soil his hands? Cigar case. Seven pockets: here, here, here, up there, there, here and here again. That's right, ain't it? That's how you go to work."

As he spoke the young man smiled. His eyes shone straight into the barrister's. With a quick, dexterous movement of his right hand he pointed to various portions of his clothes.

"Then again you might see a pin here in the tie. However we do not appropriate. Such *gents* nowadays—they hardly ever wear a real stone. Then I comes up to him. I begin straight off to talk to him like a gent: 'Sir, would you be so kind as to give me a light from your cigarette'—or something of the sort. At any rate, I enter into conversation. What's next? I look him straight in the peepers, just like this. Only two of me fingers are at it—just this and this." Yasha lifted two fingers of his right hand on a level with the solicitor's face, the forefinger and the middle finger and moved them about.

"D' you see? With these two fingers I run over the whole pianner. Nothin' wonderful in it: one, two, three—ready. Any man who wasn't stupid could learn easily. That's all it is. Most ordinary business. I thank you."

The pickpocket swung on his heel as if to return to his seat.

"Yasha!" The gentleman in the sandy suit said with meaning weight. "Yasha!" he repeated sternly.

Yasha stopped. His back was turned to the barrister, but he evidently gave his representative an imploring look, because the latter frowned and shook his head.

"Yasha!" he said for the third time, in a threatening tone.

"Huh!" The young thief grunted in vexation and turned to face the solicitor. "Where's your little watch, sir?" he said in a piping voice.

"Oh!" the Karaite brought himself up sharp.

"You see—now you say 'Oh!'" Yasha continued reproachfully. "All the while you were admiring me right hand, I was operatin' yer watch with my left. Just with these two little fingers, under the scarf. That's why we carry a scarf. Since your chain's not worth anything—a present from some *mamselle* and the watch is a gold one, I've left you the chain as a keepsake. Take it," he added with a sigh, holding out the watch.

"But . . . That is clever," the barrister said in confusion. "I didn't notice it at all."

"That's our business," Yasha said with pride.

He swaggered back to his comrades. Meantime the orator took a drink from his glass and continued.

"Now, gentlemen, our next collaborator will give you an exhibition of some ordinary card tricks, which are worked at fairs, on steamboats and railways. With three cards, for instance, an ace, a queen, and a six, he can quite easily. . . . But perhaps you are tired of these demonstrations, gentlemen." . . .

"Not at all. It's extremely interesting," the chairman answered affably. "I should like to ask one question—that is if it is not too indiscreet—what is your own specialty?"

"Mine . . . H'm. . . . No, how could it be an indiscretion? . . . I work the big diamond shops . . . and my other business is banks," answered the orator with a modest smile. "Don't think this occupation is easier than others. Enough that I know four European languages, German, French, English, and Italian, not to mention Polish, Ukrainian and Yiddish. But shall I show you some more experiments, Mr. Chairman?"

The chairman looked at his watch.

"Unfortunately the time is too short," he said. "Wouldn't it be better to pass on to the substance of your business? Besides, the experiments we have just seen have amply convinced us of the talent of your esteemed associates. . . . Am I not right, Isaac Abramovich?"

"Yes, yes . . . absolutely," the Karaite barrister readily confirmed.

"Admirable," the gentleman in the sandy suit kindly agreed. "My dear Count"—he turned to a blond, curly-haired man, with a face like a billiard-maker on a bank-holiday—"put your instruments away. They will not be wanted. I have only a few words more to say, gentlemen. Now that you have convinced yourselves that our art, although it does not enjoy the patronage of high-placed individuals, is nevertheless an art; and you have probably come to my opinion that this art is one which demands many personal qualities besides constant labour, danger, and unpleasant misunderstandings—you will also, I hope, believe that it is possible to become attached to its practice and to love and esteem it, however strange that may appear at first sight. Picture to yourselves that a famous poet of talent, whose tales and poems adorn the pages of our best magazines, is suddenly offered the chance of writing verses at a penny a line, signed into the bargain, as an advertisement for 'Cigarettes Jasmine'—or that a slander was spread about one of you distinguished barristers, accusing you of making a business of concocting evidence for divorce cases, or of writing petitions from the cabmen to the governor in public-houses! Certainly your relatives, friends and acquaintances wouldn't believe it. But the rumour has already done its poisonous work, and you have to live through minutes of torture. Now picture to yourselves that such a disgraceful and vexatious slander, started by God knows whom, begins to threaten not only your good name and your quiet digestion, but your freedom, your health, and even your life!

"This is the position of us thieves, now being slandered by the newspapers. I must explain. There is in existence a class of scum—*passez-moi le mot*—whom we call their 'Mothers' Darlings.' With these we are unfortunately confused. They have neither shame nor conscience, a dissipated riff-raff, mothers' useless darlings, idle, clumsy drones, shop assistants who commit unskilful thefts. He thinks nothing of living on his mistress, a prostitute, like the male mackerel, who always swims after the female and lives on her excrements. He is capable of robbing a child with violence in a dark alley, in order to get a penny; he will kill a man in his sleep and torture an old woman. These men are the pests of our profession. For them the beauties and the traditions of the art have no existence. They watch us real, talented thieves like a pack of jackals after a lion. Suppose I've managed to bring off an important job—we won't mention the fact that I have to leave two-thirds of what I get to the receivers who sell the goods and discount the notes, or the customary subsidies to our incorruptible police—I still have to share out something to each one of these parasites, who have got wind of my job, by accident, hearsay, or a casual glance.

"So we call them *Motients,* which means 'half,' a corruption of *moitié* . . . Original etymology. I pay him only because he knows and may inform against me. And it mostly happens that even when he's got his share he runs off to the police in order to get another dollar. We, honest thieves

. . . Yes, you may laugh, gentlemen, but I repeat it: we honest thieves detest these reptiles. We have another name for them, a stigma of ignominy; but I dare not utter it here out of respect for the place and for my audience. Oh, yes, they would gladly accept an invitation to a pogrom. The thought that we may be confused with them is a hundred times more insulting to us even than the accusation of taking part in a pogrom.

"Gentlemen! While I have been speaking I have often noticed smiles on your faces. I understand you. Our presence here, our application for your assistance, and above all the unexpectedness of such a phenomenon as a systematic organisation of thieves, with delegates who are thieves, and a leader of the deputation, also a thief by profession—it is all so original that it must inevitably arouse a smile. But now I will speak from the depth of my heart. Let us be rid of our outward wrappings, gentlemen, let us speak as men to men.

"Almost all of us are educated, and all love books. We don't only read the adventures of Roqueambole, as the realistic writers say of us. Do you think our hearts did not bleed and our cheeks did not burn from shame, as though we had been slapped in the face, all the time that this unfortunate, disgraceful, accursed, cowardly war lasted? Do you really think that our souls do not flame with anger when our country is lashed with Cossack-whips, and trodden under foot, shot and spit at by mad, exasperated men? Will you not believe that we thieves meet every step towards the liberation to come with a thrill of ecstasy?

"We understand, every one of us—perhaps only a little

less than you barristers, gentlemen—the real sense of the pogroms. Every time that some dastardly event or some ignominious failure has occurred, after executing a martyr in a dark corner of a fortress, or after deceiving public confidence, some one who is hidden and unapproachable gets frightened of the people's anger and diverts its vicious element upon the heads of innocent Jews. Whose diabolical mind invents these pogroms—these titanic blood-lettings, these cannibal amusements for the dark, bestial souls?

"We all see with certain clearness that the last convulsions of the bureaucracy are at hand. Forgive me if I present it imaginatively. There was a people that had a chief temple, wherein dwells a bloodthirsty deity, behind a curtain, guarded by priests. Once fearless hands tore the curtain away. Then all the people saw, instead of a god, a huge, shaggy, voracious spider, like a loathsome cuttlefish. They beat it and shoot at it: it is dismembered already; but still in the frenzy of its final agony it stretches over all the ancient temple its disgusting, clawing tentacles. And the priests, themselves under sentence of death, push into the monster's grasp all whom they can seize in their terrified, trembling fingers.

"Forgive me. What I have said is probably wild and incoherent. But I am somewhat agitated. Forgive me. I continue. We thieves by profession know better than any one else how these pogroms were organised. We wander everywhere: into public houses, markets, tea-shops, doss-houses, public places, the harbour. We can swear before God and man and posterity that we have seen how the police organise the massacres, without shame and almost without concealment. We know them all by face, in uniform or disguise. They invited many of us to take part; but there was none so vile among us as to give even the outward consent that fear might have extorted.

"You know, of course, how the various strata of Russian society behave towards the police? It is not even respected by those who avail themselves of its dark services. But we despise and hate it three, ten times more—not because many of us have been tortured in the detective departments, which are just chambers of horror, beaten almost to death, beaten with whips of ox-hide and of rubber in order to extort a confession or to make us betray a comrade. Yes, we hate them for that too. But we thieves, all of us who have been in prison, have a mad passion for freedom. Therefore we despise our gaolers with all the hatred that a human heart can feel. I will speak for myself. I have been tortured three times by police detectives till I was half dead. My lungs and liver have been shattered. In the mornings I spit blood until I can breathe no more. But if I were told that I will be spared a fourth flogging only by shaking hands with a chief of the detective police, I would refuse to do it!

"And then the newspapers say that we took from these hands Judas-money, dripping with human blood. No, gentlemen, it is a slander which stabs our very soul, and inflicts insufferable pain. Not money, nor threats, nor promises will suffice to make us mercenary murderers of our brethren, nor accomplices with them."

"Never . . . No . . . No . . .," his comrades standing behind him began to murmur.

"I will say more," the thief continued. "Many of us pro-

tected the victims during this pogrom. Our friend, called
Sesoi the Great—you have just seen him, gentlemen—was
then lodging with a Jewish braid-maker on the Moldavanka. With a poker in his hands he defended his landlord
from a great horde of assassins. It is true, Sesoi the Great is
a man of enormous physical strength, and this is well
known to many of the inhabitants of the Moldavanka. But
you must agree, gentlemen, that in these moments Sesoi the
Great looked straight into the face of death. Our comrade
Martin the Miner—this gentleman here"—the orator
pointed to a pale, bearded man with beautiful eyes who was
holding himself in the background—"saved an old Jewess,
whom he had never seen before, who was being pursued by
a crowd of these *canaille*. They broke his head with a crow-
bar for his pains, smashed his arm in two places and splin-
tered a rib. He is only just out of hospital. That is the way
our most ardent and determined members acted. The others
trembled for anger and wept for their own impotence.

"None of us will forget the horrors of those bloody days
and bloody nights lit up by the glare of fires, those sobbing
women, those little children's bodies torn to pieces and left
lying in the street. But for all that not one of us thinks that
the police and the mob are the real origin of the evil. These
tiny, stupid, loathsome vermin are only a senseless fist that
is governed by a vile, calculating mind, moved by a diabolical will.

"Yes, gentlemen," the orator continued, "we thieves have
nevertheless merited your legal contempt. But when you,
noble gentlemen, need the help of clever, brave, obedient
men at the barricades, men who will be ready to meet death

with a song and a jest on their lips for the most glorious word in the world—Freedom—will you cast us off then and order us away because of an inveterate revulsion? Damn it all, the first victim in the French Revolution was a prostitute. She jumped up on to a barricade, with her skirt caught elegantly up into her hand and called out: 'Which of you soldiers will dare to shoot a woman?' Yes, by God." The orator exclaimed aloud and brought down his fist on to the marble table top: "They killed her, but her action was magnificent, and the beauty of her words immortal.

"If you should drive us away on the great day, we will turn to you and say: 'You spotless Cherubim—if human thoughts had the power to wound, kill, and rob man of honour and property, then which of you innocent doves would not deserve the knout and imprisonment for life?' Then we will go away from you and build our own gay, sporting, desperate thieves' barricade, and will die with such united songs on our lips that you will envy us, you who are whiter than snow!

"But I have been once more carried away. Forgive me. I am at the end. You now see, gentlemen, what feelings the newspaper slanders have excited in us. Believe in our sincerity and do what you can to remove the filthy stain which has so unjustly been cast upon us. I have finished."

He went away from the table and joined his comrades. The barristers were whispering in an undertone, very much as the magistrates of the bench at sessions. Then the chairman rose.

"We trust you absolutely, and we will make every effort to clear your association of this most grievous charge. At

the same time my colleagues have authorised me, gentlemen, to convey to you their deep respect for your passionate
feelings as citizens. And for my own part I ask the leader
of the deputation for permission to shake him by the hand."

The two men, both tall and serious, held each other's
hands in a strong, masculine grip.

The barristers were leaving the theatre; but four of them
hung back a little beside the clothes rack in the hall. Isaac
Abramovich could not find his new, smart grey hat anywhere. In its place on the wooden peg hung a cloth cap
jauntily flattened in on either side.

"Yasha!" The stern voice of the orator was suddenly
heard from the other side of the door. "Yasha! It's the last
time I'll speak to you, curse you! . . . Do you hear?"

The heavy door opened wide. The gentleman in the
sandy suit entered. In his hands he held Isaac Abramovich's
hat; on his face was a well-bred smile.

"Gentlemen, for Heaven's sake forgive us—an odd little
misunderstanding. One of our comrades exchanged his hat
by accident. . . . Oh, it is yours! A thousand pardons. Doorkeeper! Why don't you keep an eye on things, my good
fellow, eh? Just give me that cap, there. Once more, I ask
you to forgive me, gentlemen."

With a pleasant bow and the same well-bred smile he
made his way quickly into the street.

LAZARUS

◆◆◆

By L. N. Andreyev

I

WHEN LAZARUS rose from the grave, after three days and nights in the mysterious thraldom of death, and returned alive to his home, it was a long time before any one noticed the evil peculiarities in him that were later to make his very name terrible. His friends and relatives were jubilant that he had come back to life. They surrounded him with tenderness, they were lavish of their eager attentions, spending the greatest care upon his food and drink and the new garments they made for him. They clad him gorgeously in the glowing colours of hope and laughter, and when, arrayed like a bridegroom, he sat at table with them again, ate again, and drank again, they wept fondly and summoned the neighbours to look upon the man miraculously raised from the dead.

The neighbours came and were moved with joy. Strangers arrived from distant cities and villages to worship the miracle. They burst into stormy exclamations, and buzzed around the house of Mary and Martha, like so many bees.

That which was new in Lazarus' face and gestures they explained naturally, as the traces of his severe illness and the shock he had passed through. It was evident that the disintegration of the body had been halted by a miraculous power, but that the restoration had not been complete; that death had left upon his face and body the effect of an artist's unfinished sketch seen through a thin glass. On his temples, under his eyes, and in the hollow of his cheek lay a thick, earthy blue. His fingers were blue, too, and under his nails, which had grown long in the grave, the blue had turned livid. Here and there on his lips and body, the skin, blistered in the grave, had burst open and left reddish glistening cracks, as if covered with a thin, glassy slime. And he had grown exceedingly stout. His body was horribly bloated and suggested the fetid, damp smell of putrefaction. But the cadaverous, heavy odour that clung to his burial garments and, as it seemed, to his very body, soon wore off, and after some time the blue of his hands and face softened, and the reddish cracks of his skin smoothed out, though they never disappeared completely. Such was the aspect of Lazarus in his second life. It looked natural only to those who had seen him buried.

Not merely Lazarus' face, but his very character, it seemed, had changed; though it astonished no one and did not attract the attention it deserved. Before his death Lazarus had been cheerful and careless, a lover of laughter and harmless jest. It was because of his good humour, pleasant and equable, his freedom from meanness and gloom, that he had been so beloved by the Master. Now he was grave and silent; neither he himself jested nor did he laugh at the jests of others; and the words he spoke occasionally were simple, ordinary and necessary words—words as much devoid of sense and depth as are the sounds with which an animal expresses pain and pleasure, thirst and hunger. Such words a man may speak all his life and no one would ever know the sorrows and joys that dwelt within him.

Thus it was that Lazarus sat at the festive table among his friends and relatives—his face the face of a corpse over which, for three days, death had reigned in darkness, his garments gorgeous and festive, glittering with gold, bloody-red and purple; his mien heavy and silent. He was horribly changed and strange, but as yet undiscovered. In high waves, now mild, now stormy, the festivities went on around him. Warm glances of love caressed his face, still cold with the touch of the grave; and a friend's warm hand patted his bluish, heavy hand. And the music played joyous tunes mingled of the sounds of the tympanum, the pipe, the zither and the dulcimer. It was as if bees were humming, locusts buzzing and birds singing over the happy home of Mary and Martha.

II

SOME ONE recklessly lifted the veil. By one breath of an uttered word he destroyed the serene charm, and uncovered the truth in its ugly nakedness. No thought was clearly defined in his mind, when his lips smilingly asked: "Why do you not tell us, Lazarus, what was There?" And all became silent, struck with the question. Only now it seemed to have occurred to them that for three days Lazarus had been dead; and they looked with curiosity, awaiting an answer. But Lazarus remained silent.

"You will not tell us?" wondered the inquirer. "Is it so terrible There?"

Again his thought lagged behind his words. Had it preceded them, he would not have asked the question, for, at the very moment he uttered it, his heart sank with a dread fear. All grew restless; they awaited the words of Lazarus anxiously. But he was silent, cold and severe, and his eyes were cast down. And now, as if for the first time, they perceived the horrible bluishness of his face and the loathsome corpulence of his body. On the table, as if forgotten by Lazarus, lay his livid blue hand, and all eyes were riveted upon it, as though expecting the desired answer from that hand. The musicians still played; then silence fell upon them, too, and the gay sounds died down, as scattered coals are extinguished by water. The pipe became mute, and the ringing tympanum and the murmuring dulcimer; and as though a chord were broken, as though song itself were dying, the zither echoed a trembling broken sound. Then all was quiet.

"You will not?" repeated the inquirer, unable to restrain his babbling tongue. Silence reigned, and the livid blue hand lay motionless. It moved slightly, and the company sighed with relief and raised their eyes. Lazarus, risen from the dead, was looking straight at them, embracing all with one glance, heavy and terrible.

This was on the third day after Lazarus had arisen from the grave. Since then many had felt that his gaze was the gaze of destruction, but neither those who had been forever crushed by it, nor those who in the prime of life (mysterious even as death) had found the will to resist his glance, could ever explain the terror that lay immovable in the depths of his black pupils. He looked quiet and simple. One felt that he had no intention to hide anything, but also no intention to tell anything. His look was cold, as of one who is entirely indifferent to all that is alive. And many careless people who pressed around him, and did not notice him, later learned with wonder and fear the name of this stout, quiet man who brushed against them with his sumptuous, gaudy garments. The sun did not stop shining when he looked, neither did the fountain cease playing, and the Eastern sky remained cloudless and blue as always; but the man who fell under his inscrutable gaze could no longer feel the sun, nor hear the fountain, nor recognise his native sky. Sometimes he would cry bitterly, sometimes tear his hair in despair and madly call for help; but generally it happened that the men thus stricken by the gaze of Lazarus began to fade away listlessly and quietly and pass into a slow death lasting many long years. They died in the presence of everybody, colourless, haggard and gloomy, like trees withering on rocky ground. Those who screamed in madness sometimes came back to life; but the others, never.

"So you will not tell us, Lazarus, what you saw There?" the inquirer repeated for the third time. But now his voice was dull, and a dead, grey weariness looked stupidly from out his eyes. The faces of all present were also covered by the same dead grey weariness like a mist. The guests stared at one another stupidly, not knowing why they had come together or why they sat around this rich table. They stopped talking, and vaguely felt it was time to leave; but they could not overcome the lassitude that spread through their muscles. So they continued to sit there, each one isolated, like little dim lights scattered in the darkness of night.

The musicians were paid to play, and they again took up the instruments, and again played gay or mournful airs. But it was music made to order, always the same tunes, and the guests listened wonderingly. Why was this music necessary, they thought, why was it necessary and what good did it do for people to pull at strings and blow their cheeks into thin pipes, and produce varied and strange-sounding noises?

"How badly they play!" said some one.

The musicians were insulted and left. Then the guests departed one by one, for it was nearing night. And when the quiet darkness enveloped them, and it became easier to breathe, the image of Lazarus suddenly arose before each one in stern splendour. There he stood, with the blue face of a corpse and the raiment of a bridegroom, sumptuous and resplendent, in his eyes that cold stare in the depths of which lurked *The Horrible!* They stood still as if turned into stone. The darkness surrounded them, and in the midst of this darkness flamed up the horrible apparition, the supernatural vision, of the one who for three days had lain under the measureless power of death. Three days he had been dead. Thrice had the sun risen and set—and he had lain dead. The children had played, the water had murmured as it streamed over the rocks, the hot dust had clouded the highway—and he had been dead. And now he was among them again—touched them—looked at them—

looked at them! And through the black rings of his pupils, as through dark glasses, the unfathomable *There* gazed upon humanity.

III

NO ONE took care of Lazarus, and no friends or kindred remained with him. Only the great desert, enfolding the Holy City, came close to the threshold of his abode. It entered his home, and lay down on his couch like a spouse, and put out all the fires. No one cared for Lazarus. One after the other went away, even his sisters, Mary and Martha. For a long while Martha did not want to leave him, for she knew not who would nurse him or take care of him; and she cried and prayed. But one night, when the wind was roaming about the desert, and the rustling cypress trees were bending over the roof, she dressed herself quietly, and quietly went away. Lazarus probably heard how the door was slammed—it had not shut properly and the wind kept knocking it continually against the post —but he did not rise, did not go out, did not try to find out the reason. And the whole night until the morning the cypress trees hissed over his head, and the door swung to and fro, allowing the cold, greedily prowling desert to en ter his dwelling. Everybody shunned him as though he were a leper. They wanted to put a bell on his neck to avoid meeting him. But some one, turning pale, remarked it would be terrible if at night, under the windows, one should happen to hear Lazarus' bell, and all grew pale and assented.

Since he did nothing for himself, he would probably have starved had not his neighbours, in trepidation, saved some food for him. Children brought it to him. They did not fear him, neither did they laugh at him in the innocent cruelty in which children often laugh at unfortunates. They were indifferent to him, and Lazarus showed the same indifference to them. He showed no desire to thank them for their services; he did not try to pat the dark hands and look into the simple shining little eyes. Abandoned to the ravages of time and the desert, his house was falling to ruins, and his hungry, bleating goats had long been scattered among his neighbours. His wedding garments had grown old. He wore them without changing them, as he had donned them on that happy day when the musicians played. He did not see the difference between old and new, between torn and whole. The brilliant colours were burnt and faded; the vicious dogs of the city and the sharp thorns of the desert had rent the fine clothes to shreds.

During the day, when the sun beat down mercilessly upon all living things, and even the scorpions hid under the stones, convulsed with a mad desire to sting, he sat motionless in the burning rays, lifting high his blue face and shaggy wild beard.

While yet the people were unafraid to speak to him, some one had asked him: "Poor Lazarus! Do you find it pleasant to sit so, and look at the sun?" And he answered: "Yes, it is pleasant."

The thought suggested itself to people that the cold of the three days in the grave had been so intense, its darkness so deep, that there was not in all the earth enough

heat or light to warm Lazarus and lighten the gloom of
his eyes; and inquirers turned away with a sigh.

And when the setting sun, flat and purple-red, descended
to earth, Lazarus went into the desert and walked straight
toward it, as though intending to reach it. Always he
walked directly toward the sun, and those who tried to follow him and find out what he did at night in the desert had
indelibly imprinted upon their mind's vision the black silhouette of a tall, stout man against the red background of
an immense disk. The horrors of the night drove them
away, and so they never found out what Lazarus did in the
desert; but the image of the black form against the red was
burned forever into their brains. Like an animal with a
cinder in its eye which furiously rubs its muzzle against its
paws, they foolishly rubbed their eyes; but the impression
left by Lazarus was ineffaceable, forgotten only in death.

There were people living far away who never saw Lazarus and only heard of him. With an audacious curiosity
which is stronger than fear and feeds on fear, with a secret
sneer in their hearts, some of them came to him one day as
he basked in the sun, and entered into conversation with
him. At that time his appearance had changed for the better
and was not so frightful. At first the visitors snapped their
fingers and thought disapprovingly of the foolish inhabitants of the Holy City. But when the short talk came to an
end and they went home, their expression was such that
the inhabitants of the Holy City at once knew their errand
and said: "Here go some more madmen at whom Lazarus
has looked." The speakers raised their hands in silent pity.

Other visitors came, among them brave warriors in clinking armour, who knew not fear, and happy youths who made merry with laughter and song. Busy merchants, jingling their coins, ran in for a while, and proud attendants at the Temple placed their staffs at Lazarus' door. But no one returned the same as he came. A frightful shadow fell upon their souls, and gave a new appearance to the old familiar world.

Those who felt any desire to speak, after they had been stricken by the gaze of Lazarus, described the change that had come over them somewhat like this:

All objects seen by the eye and palpable to the hand became empty, light and transparent, as though they were light shadows in the darkness; and this darkness enveloped the whole universe. It was dispelled neither by the sun, nor by the moon, nor by the stars, but embraced the earth like a mother, and clothed it in a boundless black veil.

Into all bodies it penetrated, even into iron and stone; and the particles of the body lost their unity and became lonely. Even to the heart of the particles it penetrated, and the particles of the particles became lonely.

The vast emptiness which surrounds the universe, was not filled with things seen, with sun or moon or stars; it stretched boundless, penetrating everywhere, disuniting everything, body from body, particle from particle.

In emptiness the trees spread their roots, themselves empty; in emptiness rose phantom temples; palaces and houses—all empty; and in the emptiness moved restless Man, himself empty and light, like a shadow.

There was no more a sense of time; the beginning of all things and their end merged into one. In the very moment

*when a building was being erected and one could hear the
builders striking with their hammers, one seemed already
to see its ruins, and then emptiness where the ruins were.*

*A man was just born, and funeral candles were already
lighted at his head, and then were extinguished; and soon
there was emptiness where before had been the man and
the candles.*

*And surrounded by Darkness and Empty Waste, Man
trembled hopelessly before the dread of the Infinite.*

So spoke those who had a desire to speak. But much
more could probably have been told by those who did not
want to talk, and who died in silence.

IV

AT THAT time there lived in Rome a celebrated sculptor by
the name of Aurelius. Out of clay, marble and bronze he
created forms of gods and men of such beauty that this
beauty was proclaimed immortal. But he himself was not
satisfied, and said there was a supreme beauty that he had
never succeeded in expressing in marble or bronze. "I have
not yet gathered the radiance of the moon," he said; "I have
not yet caught the glare of the sun. There is no soul in
my marble, there is no life in my beautiful bronze." And
when by moonlight he would slowly wander along the
roads, crossing the black shadows of the cypress-trees, his
white tunic flashing in the moonlight, those he met used to
laugh good-naturedly and say: "Is it moonlight that you
are gathering, Aurelius? Why did you not bring some baskets along?"

And he, too, would laugh and point to his eyes and say: "Here are the baskets in which I gather the light of the moon and the radiance of the sun."

And that was the truth. In his eyes shone moon and sun. But he could not transmit the radiance to marble. Therein lay the greatest tragedy of his life. He was a descendant of an ancient race of patricians, had a good wife and children, and except in this one respect, lacked nothing.

When the dark rumour about Lazarus reached him, he consulted his wife and friends and decided to make the long voyage to Judea, in order that he might look upon the man miraculously raised from the dead. He felt lonely in those days and hoped on the way to renew his jaded energies. What they told him about Lazarus did not frighten him. He had meditated much upon death. He did not like it, nor did he like those who tried to harmonise it with life On this side, beautiful life; on the other, mysterious death he reasoned, and no better lot could befall a man than to live—to enjoy life and the beauty of living. And he already had conceived a desire to convince Lazarus of the truth of this view and to return his soul to life even as his body had been returned. This task did not appear impossible, for the reports about Lazarus, fearsome and strange as they were, did not tell the whole truth about him, but only carried a vague warning against something awful.

Lazarus was getting up from a stone to follow in the path of the setting sun, on the evening when the rich Roman, accompanied by an armed slave, approached him, and in a ringing voice called to him: "Lazarus!"

Lazarus saw a proud and beautiful face, made radiant

by fame, and white garments and precious jewels shining in the sunlight. The ruddy rays of the sun lent to the head and face a likeness to dimly shining bronze—that was what Lazarus saw. He sank back to his seat obediently, and wearily lowered his eyes.

"It is true you are not beautiful, my poor Lazarus," said the Roman quietly, playing with his gold chain. "You are even frightful, my poor friend; and death was not lazy the day when you so carelessly fell into its arms. But you are as fat as a barrel, and 'Fat people are not bad,' as the great Cæsar said. I do not understand why people are so afraid of you. You will permit me to stay with you over night? It is late, and I have no abode."

Nobody had ever asked Lazarus to be allowed to pass the night with him.

"I have no bed," said he.

"I am somewhat of a warrior and can sleep sitting," replied the Roman. "We shall make a light."

"I have no light."

"Then we will converse in the darkness like two friends. I suppose you have some wine?"

"I have no wine."

The Roman laughed.

"Now I understand why you are so gloomy and why you do not like your second life. No wine? Well, we shall do without. You know there are words that go to one's head even as Falernian wine."

With a motion of his head he dismissed the slave, and they were alone. And again the sculptor spoke, but it seemed as though the sinking sun had penetrated into his words. They faded, pale and empty, as if trembling on weak feet, as if slipping and falling, drunk with the wine of anguish and despair. And black chasms appeared between the two men—like remote hints of vast emptiness and vast darkness.

"Now I am your guest and you will not ill-treat me, Lazarus!" said the Roman. "Hospitality is binding even upon those who have been three days dead. Three days, I am told, you were in the grave. It must have been cold there . . . and it is from there that you have brought this bad habit of doing without light and wine. I like a light. It gets dark so quickly here. Your eyebrows and forehead have an interesting line: even as the ruins of castles covered with the ashes of an earthquake. But why in such strange, ugly clothes? I have seen the bridegrooms of your country, they wear clothes like that—such ridiculous clothes—such awful garments. . . . Are you a bridegroom?"

Already the sun had disappeared. A gigantic black shadow was approaching fast from the west, as if prodigious bare feet were rustling over the sand. And the chill breezes stole up behind.

"In the darkness you seem even bigger, Lazarus, as though you had grown stouter in these few minutes. Do you feed on darkness, perchance? . . . And I would like a light . . . just a small light . . . just a small light. And I am cold. The nights here are so barbarously cold. . . . If it were not so dark, I should say you were looking at me, Lazarus. Yes, it seems, you are looking. You are looking. *You are looking at me!* . . . I feel it—now you are smiling."

The night had come, and a heavy blackness filled the air.

"How good it will be when the sun rises again to-morrow.
. . . You know I am a great sculptor . . . so my friends
call me. I create, yes, they say I create, but for that day-
light is necessary. I give life to cold marble. I melt the ringing bronze in the fire, in a bright, hot fire. Why did you
touch me with your hand?"

"Come," said Lazarus, "you are my guest." And they
went into the house. And the shadows of the long evening
fell on the earth. . . .

The slave at last grew tired waiting for his master, and
when the sun stood high he came to the house. And he
saw, directly under its burning rays, Lazarus and his
master sitting close together. They looked straight up and
were silent.

The slave wept and cried aloud: "Master, what ails you,
Master!"

The same day Aurelius left for Rome. The whole way
he was thoughtful and silent, attentively examining everything, the people, the ship, and the sea, as though endeav-
ouring to recall something. On the sea a great storm over-
took them, and all the while Aurelius remained on deck
and gazed eagerly at the approaching and falling waves.
When he reached home his family were shocked at the
terrible change in his demeanour, but he calmed them with
the words: "I have found it!"

In the dusty clothes which he had worn during the entire
journey and had not changed, he began his work, and the
marble ringingly responded to the resounding blows of the
hammer. Long and eagerly he worked, admitting no one.
At last, one morning, he announced that the work was

ready, and gave instructions that all his friends, and the severe critics and judges of art, be called together. Then he donned gorgeous garments, shining with gold, glowing with the purple of the byssin.

"Here is what I have created," he said thoughtfully.

His friends looked, and immediately the shadow of deep sorrow covered their faces. It was a thing monstrous, possessing none of the forms familiar to the eye, yet not devoid of a hint of some new unknown form. On a thin tortuous little branch, or rather an ugly likeness of one, lay crooked, strange, unsightly, shapeless heaps of something turned outside in, or something turned inside out— wild fragments which seemed to be feebly trying to get away from themselves. And, accidentally, under one of the wild projections, they noticed a wonderfully sculptured butterfly, with transparent wings, trembling as though with a weak longing to fly.

"Why that wonderful butterfly, Aurelius?" timidly asked some one.

"I do not know," answered the sculptor.

The truth had to be told, and one of his friends, the one who loved Aurelius best, said: "This is ugly, my poor friend. It must be destroyed. Give me the hammer." And with two blows he destroyed the monstrous mass, leaving only the wonderfully sculptured butterfly.

After that Aurelius created nothing. He looked with absolute indifference at marble and at bronze and at his own divine creations, in which dwelt immortal beauty. In the hope of breathing into him once again the old flame of inspiration, with the idea of awakening his dead soul, his

friends led him to see the beautiful creations of others,
but he remained indifferent and no smile warmed his closed
lips. And only after they spoke to him much and long of
beauty, he would reply wearily:

"But all this is—a lie."

And in the daytime, when the sun was shining, he would
go into his rich and beautifully laid-out garden, and finding
a place where there was no shadow, would expose his bare
head and his dull eyes to the glitter and burning heat of
the sun. Red and white butterflies fluttered around; down
into the marble cistern ran splashing water from the
crooked mouth of a blissfully drunken Satyr; but he sat
motionless, like a pale shadow of that other one who, in a
far land, at the very gates of the stony desert, also sat motionless under the fiery sun.

V

AND IT came about finally that Lazarus was summoned to
Rome by the great Augustus.

They dressed him in gorgeous garments as though it had
been ordained that he was to remain a bridegroom to an
unknown bride until the very day of his death. It was as if
an old coffin, rotten and falling apart, were regilded over
and over, and gay tassels were hung on it. And solemnly
they conducted him in gala attire, as though in truth it were
a bridal procession, the runners loudly sounding the
trumpet that the way be made for the ambassadors of the
Emperor. But the roads along which he passed were de-

serted. His entire native land cursed the execrable name of Lazarus, the man miraculously brought to life, and the people scattered at the mere report of his horrible approach. The trumpeters blew lonely blasts, and only the desert answered with a dying echo.

Then they carried him across the sea on the saddest and most gorgeous ship that was ever mirrored in the azure waves of the Mediterranean. There were many people aboard, but the ship was silent and still as a coffin, and the water seemed to moan as it parted before the short curved prow. Lazarus sat lonely, baring his head to the sun, and listening in silence to the splashing of the waters. Further away the seamen and the ambassadors gathered like a crowd of distressed shadows. If a thunderstorm had happened to burst upon them at that time or the wind had overwhelmed the red sails, the ship would probably have perished, for none of those who were on her had strength or desire enough to fight for life. With supreme effort some went to the side of the ship and eagerly gazed at the blue, transparent abyss. Perhaps they imagined they saw a naiad flashing a pink shoulder through the waves, or an insanely joyous and drunken centaur galloping by, splashing up the water with his hoofs. But the sea was deserted and mute, and so was the watery abyss.

Listlessly Lazarus set foot on the streets of the Eternal City, as though all its riches, all the majesty of its gigantic edifices, all the lustre and beauty and music of refined life, were simply the echo of the wind in the desert, or the misty images of hot running sand. Chariots whirled by; the crowd

of strong, beautiful, haughty men passed on, builders of the
Eternal City and proud partakers of its life; songs rang
out; fountains laughed; pearly laughter of women filled the
air, while the drunkard philosophised and the sober ones
smilingly listened; horseshoes rattled on the pavement. And
surrounded on all sides by glad sounds, a fat, heavy man
moved through the centre of the city like a cold spot of
silence, sowing in his path grief, anger and vague, carking
distress. Who dared to be sad in Rome? indignantly demanded frowning citizens; and in two days the swift-
tongued Rome knew of Lazarus, the man miraculously
raised from the grave, and timidly evaded him.

There were many brave men ready to try their strength,
and at their senseless call Lazarus came obediently. The
Emperor was so engrossed with state affairs that he delayed
receiving the visitor, and for seven days Lazarus moved
among the people.

A jovial drunkard met him with a smile on his red lips.
"Drink, Lazarus, drink!" he cried, "Would not Augustus
laugh to see you drink!" And naked, besotted women
laughed, and decked the blue hands of Lazarus with rose-
leaves. But the drunkard looked into the eyes of Lazarus—
and his joy ended forever. Thereafter he was always drunk.
He drank no more, but was drunk all the time, shadowed
by fearful dreams, instead of the joyous reveries that wine
gives. Fearful dreams became the food of his broken spirit.
Fearful dreams held him day and night in the mists of
monstrous fantasy, and death itself was no more fearful
than the apparition of its fierce precursor.

Lazarus came to a youth and his lass who loved each other and were beautiful in their love. Proudly and strongly holding in his arms his beloved one, the youth said, with gentle pity: "Look at us, Lazarus, and rejoice with us. Is there anything stronger than love?"

And Lazarus looked at them. And their whole life they continued to love one another, but their love became mournful and gloomy, even as those cypress trees over the tombs that feed their roots on the putrescence of the grave, and strive in vain in the quiet evening hour to touch the sky with their pointed tops. Hurled by fathomless life-forces into each other's arms, they mingled their kisses with tears, their joy with pain, and only succeeded in realising the more vividly a sense of their slavery to the silent Nothing. Forever united, forever parted, they flashed like sparks, and like sparks went out in boundless darkness.

Lazarus came to a proud sage, and the sage said to him: "I already know all the horrors that you may tell me, Lazarus. With what else can you terrify me?"

Only a few moments passed before the sage realised that the knowledge of the horrible is not the horrible, and that the sight of death is not death. And he felt that in the eyes of the Infinite wisdom and folly are the same, for the Infinite knows them not. And the boundaries between knowledge and igorance, between truth and falsehood, between top and bottom, faded and his shapeless thought was suspended in emptiness. Then he grasped his grey head in his hands and cried out insanely: "I cannot think! I cannot think!"

Thus it was that under the cool gaze of Lazarus, the man miraculously raised from the dead, all that serves to arm life, its sense and its joys, perished. And people began to say it was dangerous to allow him to see the Emperor; that it were better to kill him and bury him secretly, and swear he had disappeared. Swords were sharpened and youths devoted to the welfare of the people announced their readiness to become assassins, when Augustus upset the cruel plans by demanding that Lazarus appear before him.

Even though Lazarus could not be kept away, it was felt that the heavy impression conveyed by his face might be somewhat softened. With that end in view expert painters, barbers and artists were secured who worked the whole night on Lazarus' head. His beard was trimmed and curled. The disagreeable and deadly bluishness of his hands and face was covered up with paint; his hands were whitened, his cheeks rouged. The disgusting wrinkles of suffering that ridged his old face were patched up and painted, and on the smooth surface, wrinkles of good-nature and laughter, and of pleasant, good-humoured cheeriness, were laid on artistically with fine brushes.

Lazarus submitted indifferently to all they did with him, and soon was transformed into a stout, nice-looking old man, for all the world a quiet and good-humoured grandfather of numerous grandchildren. He looked as though the smile with which he told funny stories had not left his lips, as though a quiet tenderness still lay hidden in the corner of his eyes. But the wedding-dress they did not dare to take off; and they could not change his eyes—the dark, terrible eyes from out of which stared the incomprehensible *There*.

VI

LAZARUS was untouched by the magnificence of the imperial apartments. He remained stolidly indifferent, as though he saw no contrast between his ruined house at the edge of the desert and the solid, beautiful palace of stone. Under his feet the hard marble of the floor took on the semblance of the moving sands of the desert, and to his eyes the throngs of gaily dressed, haughty men were as unreal as the emptiness of the air. They looked not into his face as he passed by, fearing to come under the awful bane of his eyes; but when the sound of his heavy steps announced that he had passed, heads were lifted, and eyes examined with timid curiosity the figure of the corpulent, tall, slightly stooping old man, as he slowly passed into the heart of the imperial palace. If death itself had appeared men would not have feared it so much; for hitherto death had been known to the dead only, and life to the living only, and between these two there had been no bridge. But this strange being knew death, and that knowledge of his was felt to be mysterious and cursed. "He will kill our great, divine Augustus," men cried with horror, and they hurled curses after him. Slowly and stolidly he passed them by, penetrating even deeper into the palace.

Cæsar knew already who Lazarus was, and was prepared to meet him. He was a courageous man; he felt his power was invincible, and in the fateful encounter with the man "wonderfully raised from the dead" he refused to lean on other men's weak help. Man to man, face to face, he met Lazarus.

"Do not fix your gaze on me, Lazarus," he commanded. "I have heard that your head is like the head of Medusa, and turns into stone all upon whom you look. But I should like to have a close look at you, and to talk to you before I turn into stone," he added in a spirit of playfulness that concealed his real misgivings.

Approaching him, he examined closely Lazarus' face and his strange festive clothes. Though his eyes were sharp and keen, he was deceived by the skillful counterfeit.

"Well, your appearance is not terrible, venerable sir. But all the worse for men, when the terrible takes on such a venerable and pleasant appearance. Now let us talk."

Augustus sat down, and as much by glance as by words began the discussion. "Why did you not salute me when you entered?"

Lazarus answered indifferently: "I did not know it was necessary."

"You are a Christian?"

"No."

Augustus nodded approvingly. "That is good. I do not like the Christians. They shake the tree of life, forbidding it to bear fruit, and they scatter to the wind its fragrant blossoms. But who are you?"

With some effort Lazarus answered: "I was dead."

"I heard about that. But who are you now?"

Lazarus' answer came slowly. Finally he said again, list-lessly and indistinctly: "I was dead."

"Listen to me, stranger," said the Emperor sharply, giving expression to what had been in his mind before. "My empire is an empire of the living; my people are a people of the living and not of the dead. You are superfluous here. I do not know who you are, I do not know what you have seen There, but if you lie, I hate your lies, and if you tell the truth, I hate your truth. In my heart I feel the pulse of life; in my hands I feel power, and my proud thoughts, like eagles, fly through space. Behind my back, under the protection of my authority, under the shadow of the laws I have created, men live and labour and rejoice. Do you hear this divine harmony of life? Do you hear the war cry that men hurl into the face of the future, challenging it to strife?"

Augustus extended his arms reverently and solemnly cried out: "Blessed art thou, Great Divine Life!"

But Lazarus was silent, and the Emperor continued more severely: "You are not wanted here. Pitiful remnant, half devoured of death, you fill men with distress and aversion to life. Like a caterpillar on the fields, you are gnawing away at the full seed of joy, exuding the slime of despair and sorrow. Your truth is like a rusted sword in the hands of a night assassin, and I shall condemn you to death as an assassin. But first I want to look into your eyes. Mayhap only cowards fear them, and brave men are spurred on to struggle and victory. Then will you merit not death but a reward. Look at me, Lazarus."

At first it seemed to divine Augustus as if a friend were looking at him, so soft, so alluring, so gently fascinating was the gaze of Lazarus. It promised not horror but quiet rest, and the Infinite dwelt there as a fond mistress, a compassionate sister, a mother. And ever stronger grew its gentle embrace, until he felt, as it were, the breath of a mouth hungry for kisses. . . . Then it seemed as if iron bones protruded in a ravenous grip, and closed upon him in an iron band; and cold nails touched his heart, and slowly, slowly sank into it.

"It pains me," said divine Augustus, growing pale; "but look, Lazarus, look!"

Ponderous gates, shutting off eternity, appeared to be slowly swinging open, and through the growing aperture poured in, coldly and calmly, the awful horror of the Infinite. Boundless Emptiness and Boundless Gloom entered like two shadows, extinguishing the sun, removing the ground from under the feet, and the cover from over the head. And the pain in his icy heart ceased.

"Look at me, look at me, Lazarus!" commanded Augustus, staggering. . . .

Time ceased and the beginning of things came perilously near to the end. The throne of Augustus, so recently erected, fell to pieces, and emptiness took the place of the throne and of Augustus. Rome fell silently into ruins. A new city rose in its place, and it too was erased by emptiness. Like phantom giants, cities, kingdoms, and countries swiftly fell and disappeared into emptiness—swallowed up in the black maw of the Infinite. . . .

"Cease," commanded the Emperor. Already the accent

of indifference was in his voice. His arms hung powerless, and his eagle eyes flashed and were dimmed again, struggling against overwhelming darkness.

"You have killed me, Lazarus," he said drowsily.

These words of despair saved him. He thought of the people, whose shield he was destined to be, and a sharp, redeeming pang pierced his dull heart. He thought of them doomed to perish, and he was filled with anguish. First they seemed bright shadows in the gloom of the Infinite. —How terrible! Then they appeared as fragile vessels with life-agitated blood, and hearts that knew both sorrow and great joy.—And he thought of them with tenderness.

And so thinking and feeling, inclining the scales now to the side of life, now to the side of death, he slowly returned to life, to find in its suffering and joy a refuge from the gloom, emptiness and fear of the Infinite.

"No, you did not kill me, Lazarus," said he firmly. "But I will kill you. Go!"

Evening came and divine Augustus partook of food and drink with great joy. But there were moments when his raised arm would remain suspended in the air, and the light of his shining, eager eyes was dimmed. It seemed as if an icy wave of horror washed against his feet. He was vanquished but not killed, and coldly awaited his doom, like a black shadow. His nights were haunted by horror, but the bright days still brought him the joys, as well as the sorrows, of life.

Next day, by order of the Emperor, they burned out Lazarus' eyes with hot irons and sent him home. Even Augustus dared not kill him.

Lazarus returned to the desert and the desert received him with the breath of the hissing wind and the ardour of the glowing sun. Again he sat on the stone with matted beard uplifted; and two black holes, where the eyes had once been, looked dull and horrible at the sky. In the distance the Holy City surged and roared restlessly, but near him all was deserted and still. No one approached the place where Lazarus, miraculously raised from the dead, passed his last days, for his neighbours had long since abandoned their homes. His cursed knowledge, driven by the hot irons from his eyes deep into the brain, lay there in ambush; as if from ambush it might spring out upon men with a thousand unseen eyes. No one dared to look at Lazarus.

And in the evening, when the sun, swollen crimson and growing larger, bent its way toward the west, blind Lazarus slowly groped after it. He stumbled against stones and fell; corpulent and feeble, he rose heavily and walked on; and against the red curtain of sunset his dark form and outstretched arms gave him the semblance of a cross.

It happened once that he went and never returned. Thus ended the second life of Lazarus, who for three days had been in the mysterious thraldom of death and then was miraculously raised from the dead.

THE SEVEN THAT WERE HANGED

◆◆◆

By L. N. Andreyev

I

"AT ONE O'CLOCK IN THE AFTERNOON, YOUR
EXCELLENCY!"

As THE Minister was a very fat man, predisposed to apoplexy, and as it was necessary therefore to spare him every dangerous emotion, they took the minutest precautions in warning him that a serious attempt upon his life had been planned. When they saw that he received the news calmly, they gave him the details: the attempt was to be made the next day, at the moment when His Excellency was to leave the house to go to make his report. A few terrorists, armed with revolvers and bombs, whom a police spy had betrayed and who were now being watched by the police, were to meet near the steps at one o'clock in the afternoon, and await the Minister's exit. There the criminals would be arrested.

"Pardon me," interrupted the Minister in surprise. "How do they know that I am to go to present my report at one o'clock in the afternoon, when I learned it myself only two days ago?"

The commander of the body-guard made a vague gesture signifying ignorance.

"At one o'clock in the afternoon, Your Excellency!"

Astonished, and at the same time satisfied with the police who had managed the affair so well, the Minister shook his head; a disdainful smile appeared on his thick red lips; quickly he made all the necessary preparations to pass the night in another palace; in no way did he wish to embarrass the police. His wife and children also were removed from the dangerous premises.

As long as the lights gleamed in this new residence, and while his familiars bustled about him expressing their indignation, the Minister felt a sensation of agreeable excitement. It seemed to him that he had just received, or was about to receive, a great and unexpected reward. But the friends went away, and the lights were put out. The intermittent and fantastic glare of the arc-lights in the street fell upon the ceiling and the walls, penetrating through the high windows, symbolizing, as it were, the fragility of all bolts and walls, the vanity of all supervision. Then, in the silence and the solitude of a strange chamber, the dignitary was seized with an unspeakable terror.

He was afflicted with a kidney trouble. Every violent emotion caused his face, feet, and hands to swell, and made him appear heavier, more massive. Now, like a heap of bloated flesh that made the bed-springs bend, he suffered the anguish of the sick as he felt his face puff up and become, as it were, something foreign to his body. His thought recurred obstinately to the cruel fate that his enemies were preparing for him. He evoked one after the other all the horrible attempts of recent date, in which bombs had been thrown against persons as noble as himself and bearing even higher titles, tearing their bodies into a thousand shreds, hurling their brains against foul brick walls, and knocking their teeth from their jaws. And, at these recollections, it seemed to him that his diseased body was another man's body suffering from the fiery shock of the explosion. He pictured to himself his arms detached from his shoulders, his teeth broken, his brain crushed. His legs, stretched out in the bed, grew numb and motionless, the feet pointing upward, like those of a dead man. He breathed noisily, coughing occasionally, to avoid all resemblance to a corpse: he moved about, that he might hear the sound of the metallic springs, the rustling of the silk coverlet. And, to prove that he was really alive, he exclaimed in a loud and clear voice:

"Brave fellows! Brave fellows!"

These words of praise were for the police, the gendarmes, the soldiers, all those who protected his life and had prevented the assassination. But in vain did he stir about, lavish his praise, and smile at the discomfiture of the terrorists; he could not yet believe that he was saved. It seemed to him that the death evoked for him by the anarchists, and which existed in their thought, was already there and would remain there, refusing to go away until the assassins should be seized, deprived of their bombs, and lodged safely in prison. There it stood, in the corner yonder, declining to leave, and unable to leave, like an obedient soldier placed on guard by an unknown will.

"At one o'clock in the afternoon, Your Excellency!" This phrase came back to him continually, uttered in all tones, now joyously and ironically, now irritably, now obstinately and stupidly. One would have said that a hundred phonographs had been placed in the chamber, and were crying one after the other, with the idiotic persistence of machines:

"At one o'clock in the afternoon, Your Excellency!"

And this "one o'clock in the afternoon" of the next day, which so short a time before was in no way to be distinguished from other hours, had taken on a menacing importance; it had stepped out of the clock-dial, and was beginning to live a distinct life, stretching itself like an immense black curtain, to divide life into two parts. Before it and after it no other hour existed; it alone, presumptuous and obsessing, was entitled to a special life.

Grinding his teeth, the Minister raised himself in his bed to a sitting posture. It was positively impossible for him to sleep.

Pressing his bloated hands against his face, he pictured to himself with terrifying clearness how he would have risen on the morrow if he had been left in ignorance; he would have taken his coffee, and dressed. And neither he, nor the Swiss who would have helped him on with his fur coat, or the valet who would have served his coffee, would have understood the uselessness of breakfasting and dressing, when a few moments later everything would be annihilated by the explosion. . . . The Swiss opens the door. . . . And it is he, this good and thoughtful Swiss, with the blue eyes, and the open countenance, and the numerous military decorations—he it is who opens the terrible door with his own hands. . . .

"Ah!" suddenly exclaimed the Minister aloud; slowly he removed his hands from his face. Gazing far before him into the darkness with a fixed and attentive look, he stretched out his hand to turn on the light. Then he arose, and in his bare feet walked around the strange chamber so unfamiliar to him; finding another light, he turned that on also. The room became bright and agreeable; there was only the disordered bed and the fallen coverlet to indicate a terror that had not yet completely disappeared.

Clad in a night-shirt, his beard in a tangle, a look of irritation on his face, the Minister resembled those old people who are tormented by asthma and insomnia. One would have said that the death prepared for him by others had stripped him bare, had torn him from the luxury with which he was surrounded. Without dressing he threw himself into an arm-chair, his eyes wandered to the ceiling.

"Imbeciles!" he cried in a contemptuous tone of conviction.

"Imbeciles!" And he was speaking of the policemen whom but a few moments before he had called "brave fellows," and who, through excess of zeal, had told him all the details of the attack that had been planned.

"Evidently," he thought with lucidity, "I am afraid now because I have been warned and because I know. But, if I had been left in ignorance, I should have taken my coffee quietly. And then, evidently, this death. . . . But am I then so afraid of death? I have a kidney trouble; some day I must die of it, and yet I am not afraid, because I don't know when. And these imbeciles say to me: 'At one o'clock in the afternoon, Your Excellency!' They thought that I would be glad to know about it! . . . Instead of that, death has placed himself in the corner yonder, and does not go away! He does not go away, because I have that fixed idea! To die is not so terrible; the terrible thing is to know that one is going to die. It would be quite impossible for a man to live if he knew the hour and day of his death with absolute certainty. And yet these idiots warn me: 'At one o'clock in the afternoon, Your Excellency!' "

Recently he had been ill, and the doctors had told him that he was going to die and should make his final arrangements. He had refused to believe them; and, in fact, he did not die. Once, in his youth, it had happened to him to get beyond his depth; he had decided to put an end to his existence; he had loaded his revolver, written some letters, and even fixed the hour of his suicide; then, at the last moment, he had reconsidered. And always, at the supreme moment, something unexpected may happen; consequently no man can know when he will die.

"At one o'clock in the afternoon, Your Excellency!" these amiable idiots had said to him. They had informed him only because his death had been plotted; and yet he was terrified simply to learn the hour when it might have occurred. He admitted that they would kill him some day or another, but it would not be the next day . . . it would not be the next day, and he could sleep quietly, like an immortal being. . . . The imbeciles! They did not know what a gulf they had dug in saying, with stupid amiability: "At one o'clock in the afternoon, Your Excellency!"

From the bitter anguish that shot through his heart, the Minister understood that he would know neither sleep, nor rest, nor joy, until this black and accursed hour, thus detached from the course of time, had passed. It was enough in itself to annihilate the light and enwrap the man in the opaque darkness of fear. Now that he was awake, the fear of death permeated his entire body, filtered into his bones, exuded from every pore.

Already the Minister had ceased to think of the assassins of the morrow: they had disappeared, forgotten in the multitude of inauspicious things that surrounded his life. He feared the unexpected, the inevitable: an attack of apoplexy, a laceration of the heart, the rupture of a little artery suddenly made powerless to resist the flow of blood and splitting like a glove on swollen hands.

His thick, short neck frightened him; he dared not look at his swollen fingers, full of some fatal fluid. And though, just before, in the darkness, he had been compelled to stir in order to avoid resemblance to a corpse, now, under this bright, cold, hostile, frightful light, it seemed to him horrible, impossible, to move even to light a cigarette or ring for a servant. His nerves were at a tension. With red and upturned eyes and burning head, he stifled.

Suddenly, in the darkness of the sleeping house, the electric bell just under the ceiling, among the dust and spiders' webs, became animate. Its little metallic tongue beat hurriedly against its sonorous edge. It stopped for a moment, and then began to ring again in a continuous and terrifying fashion.

People came running. Here and there lamps were lighted on the walls and chandeliers—too few of them for intense illumination, but enough to create shadows. On every hand appeared these shadows: they arose in the corners and stretched out upon the ceiling, fastening upon all projections and running along the walls. It was difficult to understand where all these taciturn, monstrous, and innumerable shadows could have kept themselves before—mute souls of mute things.

A thick and trembling voice said something indistinguishable. Then they telephoned to the doctor: the Minister was ill. His Excellency's wife was summoned also.

II

SENTENCED TO BE HANGED

THE PREDICTIONS of the police were realized. Four terrorists, three men and one woman, carrying bombs, revolvers, and infernal machines, were taken in front of the steps of the residence; a fifth accomplice was arrested at her dwelling, where the implements had been manufactured and the conspiracy planned. A large quantity of dynamite and many weapons were found there. All five were very young: the eldest of the men was twenty-eight, the younger of the women nineteen. They were tried in the fortress where they had been imprisoned after their arrest; they were tried quickly and secretly, as was the custom at that merciless epoch.

Before the court all five were calm, but serious and thoughtful; their contempt for the judges was so great that they did not care to emphasize their fearlessness by a useless smile or a pretense of gaiety. They were just tranquil enough to protect their souls and the deep gloom of their agony from the malevolent gaze of strangers. Some

questions they refused to answer, some they answered simply, briefly, precisely, as if they were speaking, not to
judges, but to statisticians desirous of completing tables of
figures. Three of them, one woman and two men, gave
their real names; two refused to disclose their identity,
which remained unknown to the court. In everything that
happened they manifested that distant and attenuated curiosity peculiar to people seriously ill or possessed by a single
all-powerful idea. They cast swift glances, seized upon an
interesting word in its flight, and went back to their
thoughts, resuming them at the exact point where they
had dropped them.

The accused placed nearest the judges had given his name
as Sergey Golovin, a former officer, son of a retired colonel.
He was very young, with broad shoulders, and so robust
that neither the prison or the expectation of certain death
had been able to dim the color of his cheeks or the expression of happy innocence in his blue eyes. Throughout the
trial he twisted his thick and blond beard, to which he had
not yet become accustomed, and gazed steadily at the window, knitting his brows.

It was the latter part of winter, that period into which,
among snowstorms and gray, cold days, the approaching
spring projects sometimes, as a forerunner, a warm and
luminous day, or even a single hour, so passionately young
and sparkling that the sparrows in the street become mad
with joy and men seem intoxicated. Now, through the
upper window, still covered with the dust of the previous
summer, a very odd and beautiful sky was to be seen; at
the first glance it seemed a thick and milky gray; then,

upon a second examination, it appeared to be covered with azure stains, of an ever-deepening blue, a blue pure and infinite. And because it did not strip itself suddenly, but modestly draped itself in the transparent veil of clouds, it became charming, like one's *fiancée*. Sergey Golovin looked at the sky, pulled at his mustache, winked now one and now the other of his eyes behind the long, heavy eye-lashes, and reflected profoundly on nobody knows what. Once, even, his fingers moved rapidly, and an expression of naïve joy appeared upon his face; but he looked around him, and his joy was extinguished like a live coal upon which one steps. Almost instantaneously, almost without transition, the redness of his cheeks gave place to a corpse-like pallor; a fine hair painfully pulled out was pressed as in a vice between his bloodless finger-ends. But the joy of life and of the spring was still stronger. A few minutes later the young face resumed its naïve expression and sought again the sky of spring.

Toward the sky also looked an unknown young girl, surnamed Musya. She was younger than Golovin, but seemed his elder because of the severity, the gravity, of her proud and loyal eyes. The delicate neck and slender arms alone revealed that intangible something which is youth itself, and which sounded so distinctly in the pure harmonious voice that resembled a costly instrument in perfect tune. Musya was very pale, of that passionate pallor peculiar to those who burn with an inner, radiant, and powerful fire. She scarcely stirred; from time to time only, with a gesture that was hardly visible, she felt for a deep trace in the third finger of her right hand—the trace of a ring recently removed. She looked at the sky with calmness and indifference; she looked at it simply because everything in this commonplace and dirty hall was hostile to her and seemed to scrutinize her face. This bit of blue sky was the only pure and true thing upon which she could look with confidence.

The judges pitied Sergey Golovin and hated Musya.

Musya's neighbor, motionless also, with hands folded between his knees and somewhat of affectation in his pose, was an unknown surnamed Werner. If one can bolt a face as one bolts a heavy door, the unknown had bolted his as if it were a door of iron. He gazed steadily at the floor, and it was impossible to tell whether he was calm or deeply moved, whether he was thinking of something or listening to the testimony of the policemen. He was rather short of stature; his features were fine and noble. He gave the impression of an immense and calm force, of a cold and audacious valor. The very politeness with which he uttered his clear and curt replies seemed dangerous on his lips. On the backs of the other prisoners the customary cloak seemed a ridiculous costume; on him it was not even noticeable, so foreign was the garment to the man. Although Werner had been armed only with a poor revolver, while the others carried bombs and infernal machines, the judges looked upon him as the leader, and treated him with a certain respect, with the same brevity which he employed toward them.

In his neighbor, Vasily Kashirin, a frightful moral struggle was going on between the intolerable terror of death and the desperate desire to subdue this fear and conceal it from the judges. Ever since the prisoners had been taken to court in the morning, he had been stifling under the hurried beating of his heart. Drops of sweat appeared continually on his brow; his hands were moist and cold; his damp and icy shirt, sticking to his body, hindered his movements. By a superhuman effort of the will he kept his fingers from trembling, and maintained the firmness and moderation of his voice and the tranquillity of his gaze. He saw nothing around him; the sound of the voice that he heard seemed to reach him through a fog, and it was in a fog also that he stiffened himself in a desperate effort to answer firmly and aloud. But, as soon as he had spoken, he forgot the questions, as well as his own phrases; the silent and terrible struggle began again. And upon his person death was so in evidence that the judges turned their eyes away from him. It was as difficult to determine his age as that of a rotting corpse. According to his papers he was only twenty-three. Once or twice Werner touched him gently on the knee, and each time he answered briefly:

"It's nothing!"

His hardest moment was when he suddenly felt an irresistible desire to utter inarticulate cries, like a hunted beast. Then he gave Werner a slight push; without raising his eyes, the latter answered in a low voice:

"It's nothing, Vasya. It will soon be over!"

Consumed by anxiety, Tanya Kovalchuk, the fifth terrorist, sheltered her comrades with a maternal look. She was still very young; her cheeks seemed as highly colored as those of Sergey Golovin; and yet she seemed to be the mother of all the accused, so full of tender anxiety and infinite love were her looks, her smile, her fear. The progress of the trial did not interest her. She listened to her comrades simply to see if their voices trembled, if they were afraid, if they needed water.

But she could not look at Vasya; his anguish was too intense; she contented herself with cracking her plump fingers. At Musya and Werner she gazed with proud and respectful admiration, her face then wearing a grave and serious expression. As for Sergey Golovin, she continually tried to attract his attention by her smile.

"The dear comrade, he is looking at the sky. Look, look!" thought she, as she observed the direction of his eyes.

"And Vasya? My God! My God! . . . What can be done to comfort him? If I speak to him, perhaps it will make matters worse; suppose he should begin to weep?"

Like a peaceful pool reflecting every wandering cloud, her amiable and clear countenance showed all the feelings and all the thoughts, however fleeting, of her four comrades. She forgot that she was on trial too and would be hanged; her indifference to this was absolute. It was in her dwelling that the bombs and dynamite had been found; strange as it may seem, she had received the police with pistol shots, and had wounded one of them in the head.

The trial ended toward eight o'clock, just as the day was drawing to its close. Little by little, in the eyes of Sergey and Musya, the blue sky disappeared; without reddening, without smiling, it grew dim gently as on a summer evening, becoming grayish, and suddenly cold and wintry. Golovin heaved a sigh, stretched himself, and raised his eyes toward the window, where the chilly darkness of the night was already making itself manifest; still pulling his beard, he began to examine the judges, the soldiers, and their weapons, exchanging a smile with Tanya Kovalchuk. As for Musya, when the sun had set completely, she did not lower her gaze to the ground, but directed it toward a corner where a spider's web was swaying gently in the invisible current of warm air from the stove; and thus she remained until the sentence had been pronounced.

After the verdict, the condemned said their farewells to their lawyers, avoiding their disconcerted, pitying, and confused looks; then they grouped themselves for a moment near the door, and exchanged short phrases.

"It's nothing, Vasya! All will soon be over!" said Werner.

"But there is nothing the matter with me, brother!" answered Kashirin, in a strong, quiet, and almost joyous voice. In fact, his face had taken on a slight color, no longer resembling that of a corpse.

"The devil take them! They have hanged us all just the same!" swore Golovin naïvely.

"It was to have been expected," answered Werner, without agitation.

"To-morrow the final judgment will be rendered, and they will put us all in the same cell," said Tanya, to console her comrades. "We shall remain together until the execution."

Silently, and with a resolute air, Musya started off.

III

"I MUST NOT BE HANGED"

A FORTNIGHT before the affair of the terrorists, in the same court, but before other judges, Ivan Yanson, a peasant, had been tried and sentenced to be hanged.

Ivan Yanson had been hired as a farm-hand by a well-to-do farmer, and was distinguished in no way from the other poor devils of his class. He was a native of Wesenberg, in Esthonia; for some years he had been advancing gradually toward the capital, passing from one farm to another. He had very little knowledge of Russian. As there were none of his countrymen living in the neighborhood, and as his employer was a Russian, named Lazaref, Yanson remained silent for almost two years. He said hardly a word to either man or beast. He led the horse to water and harnessed it without speaking to it, walking about it lazily, with short hesitating steps. When the horse began to run, Yanson did not say a word, but beat it cruelly with his enormous whip. Drink transformed his cold and wicked obstinacy into fury. The hissing of the lash and the regular and painful sound of his wooden shoes on the floor of the shed could be heard even at the farmhouse. To punish him for torturing the horse the farmer at first beat Yanson, but, not succeeding in correcting him, he gave it up.

Once or twice a month Yanson got drunk, especially when he took his master to the station. His employer once on board the train, Yanson drove a short distance away, and waited until the train had started.

Then he returned to the station, and got drunk at the buffet. He came back to the farm on the gallop, a distance of seven miles, beating the unfortunate beast unmercifully, giving it its head, and singing and shouting incomprehensible phrases in Esthonian. Sometimes silent, with set teeth, impelled by a whirlwind of indescribable fury, suffering, and enthusiasm, he was like a blind man in his mad career;

he did not see the passers-by, he did not insult them, uphill and down he maintained his furious gait.

His master would have discharged him, but Yanson did not demand high wages, and his comrades were no better than he.

One day he received a letter written in Esthonian; but, as he did not know how to read or write, and as no one about him knew this language, Yanson threw it into the muck-heap with savage indifference, as if he did not understand that it brought him news from his native country. Probably needing a woman, he tried also to pay court to the girl employed on the farm. She repulsed him, for he was short and puny, and covered with hideous freckles; after that, he let her alone.

But, though he spoke little, Yanson listened continually. He listened to the desolate snow-covered fields, containing hillocks of frozen manure that resembled a series of little tombs heaped up by the snow; he listened to the bluish and limpid distance, the sonorous telegraph-poles. He alone knew what the fields and telegraph-poles were saying. He listened also to the conversation of men, the stories of murder, pillage, fire.

One night, in the village, the little church-bell began to ring in a feeble and lamentable way; flames appeared. Malefactors from nobody knew where were pillaging the neighboring farm. They killed the owner and his wife, and set fire to the house. This caused a feeling of anxiety on the farm where Yanson lived: day and night the dogs were loose; the master kept a gun within reach of his bed.

He wished also to give an old weapon to Yanson, but the latter, after examining it, shook his head and refused it. The farmer did not understand that Yanson had more confidence in the efficacy of his Finnish knife than in this rusty old machine.

"It would kill me myself!" said he.

"You are only an imbecile, Ivan!"

And one winter evening, when the other farm-hand had gone to the station, this same Ivan Yanson, who was afraid of a gun, committed robbery and murder, and made an attempt at rape. He did it with an astonishing simplicity. After shutting the servant in the kitchen, lazily, like a man almost dead with sleep, he approached his master from behind, and stabbed him several times in the back. The master fell unconscious; his wife began to cry and to run about the chamber. Showing his teeth, and holding his knife in his hand, Yanson began to ransack trunks and drawers. He found the money; then, as if he had just seen the master's wife for the first time, he threw himself upon her to rape her, without the slightest premeditation. But he happened to drop his knife; and, as the woman was the stronger, she not only resisted Yanson, but half strangled him. At this moment the farmer recovered his senses, and the servant broke in the kitchen-door and came in. Yanson fled. They took him an hour later, squatting in the corner of the shed, and scratching matches which continually went out. He was trying to set fire to the farm.

A few days later the farmer died. Yanson was tried and sentenced to death. In the court one would have said that he did not understand what was going on; he viewed the large imposing hall without curiosity, and explored his nose with a shrunken finger that nothing disgusted. Only those who had seen him at church on Sunday could have guessed that he had done something in the way of making a toilet; he wore a knitted cravat of dirty red; in spots his hair was smooth and dark; in others it consisted of light thin locks, like wisps of straw on an uncultivated and devastated field.

When the sentence of death by hanging was pronounced, Yanson suddenly showed emotion. He turned scarlet, and began to untie and tie his cravat, as if it were choking him. Then he waved his arms without knowing why, and declared to the presiding judge, who had read the sentence:

"She has said that I must be hanged."

" 'She'? Who?" asked the presiding judge, in a deep bass voice.

Yanson pointed at the presiding judge with his finger, and, looking at him furtively, answered angrily:

"You!"

"Well?"

Again Yanson turned his eyes toward one of the judges, in whom he divined a friend, and repeated:

"She has said that I must be hanged. I must not be hanged."

"Take away the accused."

But Yanson still had time to repeat, in a grave tone of conviction:

"I must not be hanged."

And with his outstretched finger and irritated face, to which he tried in vain to give an air of gravity, he seemed so stupid that the guard, in violation of orders, said to him in an undertone as he led him away:

"Well, you are a famous imbecile, you are!"

"I must not be hanged!" repeated Yanson, obstinately.

They shut him up again in the cell in which he had passed a month, and to which he had become accustomed, as he had become accustomed to everything: to blows, to brandy, to the desolate and snow-covered country sown with rounded hillocks resembling tombs. It even gave him pleasure to see his bed again, and his grated window, and to eat what they gave him; he had taken nothing since morning. The disagreeable thing was what had happened in court, about which he knew not what to think. He had no idea at all of what death by hanging was like.

The guard said to him, in a tone of remonstrance:

"Well, brother, there you are, hanged!"

"And when will they hang me?" asked Yanson, in a tone of incredulity. The guard reflected.

"Ah! wait, brother; you must have companions; they do not disturb themselves for a single individual, and especially for a little fellow like you."

"Then, when?" insisted Yanson.

He was not offended that they did not want to take the trouble to hang him all alone; he did not believe in this excuse, and thought they simply wanted to put off the execution, and then pardon him.

"When? When?" resumed the guard. "It is not a question of hanging a dog, which one takes behind a shed and dispatches with a single blow! Is that what you would like, imbecile?"

"Why, no, I would not like it!" said Yanson suddenly, with a joyous grimace. " 'Twas she that said I must be hanged, but I, I do not want to be hanged!"

And, for the first time in his life perhaps, he began to laugh—a grinning and stupid laugh, but terribly gay. He seemed like a goose beginning to quack. The guard looked at Yanson in astonishment, and then knitted his brows: this stupid gaiety on the part of a man who was to be executed insulted the prison, the gallows itself, and made them ridiculous. And suddenly it seemed to the old guard, who had passed all his life in prison and considered the laws of the gaol as those of nature, that the prison and all of life were a sort of mad-house in which he, the guard, was the chief madman.

"The devil take you!" said he, spitting on the ground. "Why do you show your teeth? This is no wine-hop!"

"And I, I do not want to be hanged! Ha! ha! ha!"

Yanson laughed always.

"Satan!" replied the guard, crossing himself.

All the evening Yanson was calm, and even joyous. He repeated the phrase that he had uttered: "I must not be hanged," and so convincing, so irrefutable was it that he had no occasion for anxiety. He had long since forgotten his crime; sometimes he simply regretted that he had not succeeded in raping the woman. Soon he thought no more about the matter.

Every morning Yanson asked when he would be hanged, and every morning the guard answered him angrily:

"You have time enough." And he went out quickly, before Yanson began to laugh.

Thanks to this invariable exchange of words, Yanson persuaded himself that the execution would never take place; for whole days he lay upon his bed, dreaming vaguely of the desolate and snow-covered fields, of the buffet at the railway station, and also of things farther away and more luminous. He was well fed in prison, he took on flesh.

"She would love me now," he said to himself, thinking of his master's wife. "Now I am as big as her husband."

He had only one desire—to drink brandy and course madly over the roads with his horse at full gallop.

When the terrorists were arrested, the whole prison learned of it. One day, when Yanson put his customary question, the guard answered him abruptly, in an irritated voice:

"It will be soon. In a week, I think."

Yanson turned pale; the gaze of his glassy eyes became so thick that he seemed as if asleep.

"You are joking?" he asked.

"Formerly you could not await the time, to-day you say that I am joking. No jokes are tolerated here. It is you who like jokes, but we do not tolerate them," replied the guard with dignity; then he went out.

When evening came, Yanson had grown thin. His skin, which had become smooth again for a few days, was con-

tracted into a thousand little wrinkles. He took no notice
of anything; his movements were made slowly, as if every
toss of the head, every gesture of the arm, every step, were
a difficult undertaking, that must first be deeply studied.
During the night Yanson lay on his camp-bed, but his eyes
did not close; they remained open until morning.

"Ah!" exclaimed the guard, on seeing him the next day.

With the satisfaction of the *savant* who has made a new
and a successful experiment, he examined the condemned
man attentively and without haste; now everything was
proceeding in the usual fashion. Satan was covered with
shame, the sanctity of the prison and of the gallows was re-
established. Indulgent, and even full of sincere pity, the
old man asked:

"Do you want to see someone?"

"Why?"

"To say good-bye, of course . . . to your mother, for instance, or to your brother."

"I must not be hanged," said Yanson in a low voice, casting a glance sidewise at the gaoler. "I do not want to be
hanged."

The guard looked at him, without saying a word.

Yanson was a little calmer in the evening. The day was
so ordinary, the cloudy winter sky shone in so usual a
fashion, so familiar was the sound of steps and conversations in the corridor, that he ceased to believe in the execution. Formerly the night had been to him simply the
moment of darkness, the time for sleep. But now he was
conscious of its mysterious and menacing essence. To dis-

believe in death one must see and hear about one the customary course of life: steps, voices, light. And now everything seemed extraordinary to him; this silence, these shades, that seemed to be already the shades of death; already he felt the approach of inevitable death; in bewilderment he climbed the first steps of the gibbet.

The day, the night, brought him alternations of hope and fear; and so things went until the evening when he felt, or understood, that the inevitable death would come three days later, at sunrise.

He had never thought of death; for him it had no shape. But now he felt plainly that it had entered his cell, and was groping about in search of him. To escape it he began to run.

The room was so small that the corners seemed to push him back toward the centre. He could not hide himself anywhere. Several times he struck the walls with his body; once he hurled himself against the door. He staggered and fell, with his face upon the ground; he felt the grasp of death upon him. Glued to the floor, his face touching the dirty black asphalt. Yanson screamed with terror until help came. When they had lifted him up, seated him on his bed, and sprinkled him with cold water, he did not dare open both eyes. He half opened one, perceived an empty and luminous corner of his cell, and began again to scream.

But the cold water had its effect. The guard, moreover, always the same old man, slapped Yanson several times on the head in a fatherly fashion. This sensation of life drove out the thought of death. Yanson slept deeply the rest of the night. He lay on his back, with mouth open, snoring loud and long. Between his half-closed eyelids appeared a whitish, flat, and dead eye, without a pupil.

Then day, night, voices, steps, the cabbage soup, everything became for him one continuous horror that plunged him into a state of wild astonishment. His weak mind could not reconcile the monstrous contradiction between, on the one hand, the bright light and odor of the cabbage, and, on the other, the fact that two days later he must die. He thought of nothing; he did not even count the hours; he was simply the prey of a dumb terror in presence of this contradiction that bewildered his brain: to-day life, to-morrow death. He ate nothing, he slept no more; he sat timidly all night long on a stool, with his legs crossed under him, or else he walked up and down his cell with furtive steps. He appeared to be in a state of open-mouthed astonishment; before taking the most common-place article into his hands he would examine it suspiciously.

The gaolers ceased to pay attention to him. His was the ordinary condition of the condemned man, resembling, according to his gaoler who had not experienced it himself, that of an ox felled by a club.

"He is stunned; now he will feel nothing more until the moment of death," said the guard, examining him with his experienced eye. "Ivan, do you hear? Ho there, Ivan!"

"I must not be hanged!" answered Yanson, in a colorless voice; his lower jaw had dropped.

"If you had not killed, they would not hang you," reproachfully said the chief gaoler, a highly important young man, wearing a decoration. "To steal, you have killed, and you do not want to be hanged!"

"I do not want to be hanged!" replied Yanson.

"Well, you don't have to want to; that's your affair. But, instead of talking nonsense, you would do better to dispose of your possessions. You surely must have something."

"He has nothing at all! A shirt and a pair of pantaloons! And a fur cap!"

Thus time passed until Thursday. And Thursday, at midnight, a large number of people entered Yanson's cell; a man with cloth epaulets said to him:

"Get ready! it is time to start."

Always with the same slowness and the same indolence Yanson dressed himself in all that he possessed, and tied his dirty shawl around his neck. While watching him dress, the man with the epaulets, who was smoking a cigarette, said to one of the assistants:

"How warm it is to-day! It is spring!"

Yanson's eyes closed; he was in a complete drowse. The guard shouted:

"Come, come! Make haste! You are going to sleep!"

Suddenly Yanson ceased to move.

"I must not be hanged," said he, with indolence.

He began to walk submissively, shrugging his shoulders. In the courtyard the moist spring air had a sudden effect upon him; his nose began to run; it was thawing; close by, drops of water were falling with a joyous sound. While the gendarmes were getting into the unlighted vehicle, bending over and rattling their swords, Yanson lazily passed his finger under his running nose, or arranged his badly-tied shawl.

IV

WE OF OREL

THE COURT that had tried Yanson sentenced to death at the same session Michael Goloubetz, known as Michka the Tzigane, a peasant of the department of Orel, district of Eletz. The last crime of which they accused him, with evidence in support of the charge, was robbery, followed by the assassination of three persons. As for his past, it was unknown. There were vague indications to warrant the belief that the Tzigane had taken part in a whole series of other murders. With absolute sincerity and frankness he termed himself a brigand, and overwhelmed with his irony those who, to follow the fashion, pompously styled themselves "expropriators"; his last crime he described willingly in all its details. But, at the slightest reference to the past, he answered:

"Go and ask the wind that blows over the fields!"

And, if they persisted in questioning him, the Tzigane assumed a dignified and serious air.

"We of Orel are all hot-heads, the fathers of all the robbers of the world," said he, in a sedate and judicial tone.

They had nicknamed him Tzigane because of his physiognomy and his thieving habits. He was thin and strangely dark; yellow spots outlined themselves upon his cheekbones which were as prominent as those of a Tartar. He had a way of rolling the whites of his eyes, that reminded one of a horse. His gaze was quick and keen, full of curiosity, terrifying. The things over which his swift glance passed seemed to lose something or other, and to become transformed by surrendering to him part of themselves. One hesitated to take a cigarette that he had looked at, as if it had already been in his mouth. His extraordinarily mobile nature made him seem now to coil and concentrate himself like a twisted handkerchief, now to scatter himself like a sheaf of sparks. He drank water almost by the pailful, like a horse.

When the judges questioned him, he raised his head quickly, and answered without hesitation, even with satisfaction:

"It is true!"

Sometimes, to lend emphasis, he rolled his "r's" vigorously.

Suddenly he jumped to his feet, and said to the presiding judge:

"Permit me to whistle?"

"Why?" exclaimed the judge, in astonishment.

"The witnesses say that I gave the signal to my comrades; I will show you how I did it. It is very interesting."

A little disconcerted, the judge granted the desired permission. The Tzigane quickly placed four fingers in his mouth, two of each hand; he rolled his eyes furiously. And the inanimate air of the court-room was rent by a truly savage whistle. There was everything in the piercing sound, partly human, partly animal; the mortal anguish of the victim, and the savage joy of the assassin; a threat, a call, and the tragic solitude, the darkness, of a rainy autumn night.

The judge shook his hand; with docility the Tzigane stopped. Like an artist who has just played a difficult air with assured success, he sat down, wiped his wet fingers on his cloak, and looked at the spectators with a satisfied air.

"What a brigand!" exclaimed one of the judges, rubbing his ear. But another, who had Tartar eyes, like the Tzigane's, was looking dreamily into the distance, over the brigand's head; he smiled, and replied:

"It was really interesting."

Without remorse, the judges sentenced the Tzigane to death.

"It is just!" said the Tzigane, when the sentence had been pronounced.

And, turning to a soldier of the guard, he added with an air of bravado:

"Well, let us be off, imbecile! And keep a good hold of your gun, lest I snatch it from you!"

The soldier looked at him seriously and timidly; he exchanged a glance with his comrade, and tested his weapon to see if it was in working order. The other did the same. And all the way to the prison it seemed to the soldiers that they did not walk, but flew; they were so absorbed by the condemned man that they were unconscious of the route, of the weather, and of themselves.

Like Yanson, Michka the Tzigane remained seventeen days in prison before being executed. And the seventeen days passed as rapidly as a single day, filled with a single thought, that of flight, of liberty, of life. The turbulent and incoercible spirit of the Tzigane, stifled by the walls, the gratings, and the opaque window through which nothing could be seen, employed all its force in setting Michka's brain on fire. As in a vapor of intoxication, bright but incomplete images whirled, clashed, and mingled in his head; they passed with a blinding and irresistible rapidity, and they all tended to the same end: flight, liberty, life. For entire hours, with nostrils distended like those of a horse, the Tzigane sniffed the air; it seemed to him that he inhaled the odor of hemp and flame, of dense smoke. Or else he turned in his cell like a top, examining the walls, feeling them with his fingers, measuring them, piercing the ceiling with his gaze, sawing the bars in his mind. His agitation was a source of torture to the soldier who watched him through the window; several times he threatened to fire on him.

During the night the Tzigane slept deeply, almost without stirring, in an invariable but living immobility, like a temporarily inactive spring. But, as soon as he jumped to his feet, he began again to plan, to grope, to study. His hands were always dry and hot. Sometimes his heart suddenly congealed, as if they had placed in his breast a new block of ice which did not melt, and which caused a continuous shiver to run over his skin. At these times his naturally dark complexion became darker still, taking on the blue-black shade of bronze. Then a queer tic seized him; he constantly licked his lips, as if he had eaten a dish that was much too sweet; then, with a hiss, and with set teeth, he spat upon the ground the saliva that had thus accumulated in his mouth. He left his words unfinished; his thoughts ran so fast that his tongue could no longer keep up with them.

One day the chief of the guards entered his cell, accompanied by a soldier. He squinted at the spittle with which the ground was spattered, and said rudely:

"See how he has dirtied his cell!"

The Tzigane replied quickly:

"And you, you ugly mug, you have soiled the whole earth, and I haven't said a word to you. Why do you annoy me?"

With the same rudeness the chief of the guards offered him the post of hangman. The Tzigane showed his teeth, and began to laugh:

"So they can find none! That's not bad! Go on then hanging people! Ah! Ah! There are necks and ropes, and nobody to do the hanging! My God, that's not bad."

"They will give your life as a reward!"

"I should say so: I could hardly play the hangman after I am dead!"

"Well, what do you say, yes or no?"

"And how do they hang here? They probably choke people secretly."

"No, they hang them to music!" retorted the chief.

"Imbecile! Of course there must be music . . . like this. . . ."

And he began to sing a captivating air.

"You have gone completely mad, my friend!" said the guard. "Come, speak seriously, what is your decision?"

The Tzigane showed his teeth.

"Are you in a hurry? Come back later, and I will tell you!"

And to the chaos of unfinished images which overwhelmed the Tzigane was added a new idea: how agreeable it would be to be the headsman! He clearly pictured to himself the square black with people, and the scaffold on which he, the Tzigane, walked back and forth, in a red shirt, with axe in hand. The sun illuminates the heads, plays gaily on the axe blade; everything is so joyous, so sumptuous, that even he whose head is to be cut off smiles. Behind the crowd are to be seen the carts and the noses of the horses; the peasants have come to town for the occasion. Still farther away fields. The Tzigane licked his lips, and spat upon the ground. Suddenly it seemed to him that his fur cap had just been pulled down over his mouth; everything became dark; he gasped for breath; and his heart changed into a block of ice, while little shivers ran through his body.

Twice more the chief came back; the Tzigane, showing his teeth again, answered:

"What a hurry you are in! Come back another time!"

Finally, one day, the gaoler cried to him, as he was passing by the window:

"You have lost your chance, my ill-favoured raven. They have found another."

"The devil take you! Go, be the hangman yourself!" replied the Tzigane. And he ceased to dream of the splendors of his trade.

But toward the end, the nearer drew the day of execution, the more intolerable became the impetuosity of the torn images. The Tzigane would have liked to wait, to halt, but the furious torrent carried him on, giving him no chance to get a hold on anything; for everything was

in a whirl. And his sleep became agitated; he had new
and shapeless visions, as badly squared as painted blocks,
and even more impetuous than his thoughts had been. It
was no longer a torrent, but a continual fall from an infinite
height, a whirling flight through the whole world of colors.
Formerly the Tzigane had worn only a mustache tolerably
well cared for; in prison he had been obliged to grow his
beard, which was short, black, and stubbly, giving him a
crazy look. There were moments, in fact, when the Tzigane
lost his mind. He turned about in his cell all unconscious
of his movements, continuing to feel for the rough and
uneven walls. And he always drank great quantities of
water, like a horse.

One evening, when they were lighting the lamps, the
Tzigane dropped on all fours in the middle of his cell, and
began to howl like a wolf. He did this very seriously, as
if performing an indispensable and important act. He
filled his lungs with air, and then expelled it slowly in a
prolonged and trembling howl. With knit brows, he listened
to himself attentively. The very trembling of the voice
seemed a little affected; he did not shout indistinctly: he
made each note in this wild beast's cry sound separately, full
of unspeakable suffering and terror.

Suddenly he stopped, and remained silent for a few
minutes, without getting up. He began to whisper, as if
speaking to the ground:

"Dear friends, good friends . . . dear friends . . . good
friends . . . have pit . . . friends! My friends!"

He said a word, and listened to it.

He jumped to his feet, and for a whole hour poured forth a steady stream of the worst curses.

"Go to the devil, you scoundrels!" he screamed, rolling his bloodshot eyes. "If I must be hanged, hang me, instead of ... Ah, you blackguards!"

The soldier on guard, as white as chalk, wept with anguish and fear; he pounded the door with the muzzle of his gun, and cried in a lamentable voice:

"I will shoot you! By God, do you hear? I will shoot you!"

But he did not dare to fire; they never fire on prisoners sentenced to death, except in case of revolt. And the Tzigane ground his teeth, swore, and spat. His brain, placed on the narrow frontier that separates life from death, crumbled like a lump of dried clay.

When they came, during the night, to take him to the gallows, he regained a little of his animation. His cheeks took on some color; in his eyes the usual strategy, a little savage, sparkled again, and he asked of one of the functionaries:

"Who will hang us? The new one? Is he accustomed to it yet?"

"You needn't disturb yourself about that," answered the personage thus appealed to.

"What? Not disturb myself! It is not Your Highness that is going to be hanged, but I! At least don't spare the soap on the slip-noose; the State pays for it!"

"I beg you to hold your tongue!"

"This fellow, you see, consumes all the soap in the prison;

see how his face shines," continued the Tzigane, pointing to the chief of the guards.

"Silence!"

"Don't spare the soap!"

Suddenly he began to laugh, and his legs became numb. Yet, when he arrived in the court-yard, he could still cry:

"Say, there! you fellows yonder, come forward with my carriage!"

V

"KISS HIM AND BE SILENT"

THE VERDICT against the five terrorists was pronounced in its final form and confirmed the same day. The condemned were not notified of the day of execution. But they foresaw that they would be hanged, according to custom, the same night, or, at the latest, the night following. When they were offered the opportunity of seeing their families the next day, they understood that the execution was fixed for Friday at daybreak.

Tanya Kovalchuk had no near relatives. She knew only of some distant relatives living in Little Russia, who probably knew nothing of the trial or the verdict. Musya and Werner, not having revealed their identity, did not insist on seeing any of their people. Only Sergey Golovin and Vasily Kashirin were to see their families. The thought of this approaching interview was frightful to both of them, but they could not make up their minds to refuse a final conversation, a last kiss.

Sergey Golovin thought sadly of this visit. He was fond of his father and mother; he had seen them very recently, and he was filled with terror at the thought of what was going to happen. The hanging itself, in all its monstrosity, in its disconcerting madness, outlined itself more readily in his imagination than these few short, incomprehensible minutes, that seemed apart from time, apart from life. What to do? What to say? The most simple and customary gestures—to shake hands, embrace, and say "How do you do, father?"—seemed to him frightful in their monstrous inhuman, insane insignificance.

After the verdict they did not put the condemned in the same cell, as Tanya expected them to do. All the morning, up to the time when he received his parents, Sergey Golovin walked back and forth in his cell, twisting his short beard, his features pitiably contracted. Sometimes he stopped suddenly, filled his lungs with air, and puffed like a swimmer who has remained too long under water. But, as he was in good health, and as his young life was solidly implanted within him, even in these minutes of atrocious suffering, the blood coursed under his skin, coloring his cheeks; his blue eyes preserved their usual brilliancy.

Everything went off better than Sergey expected; his father, Nicolas Sergiévitch Golovin, a retired colonel, was the first to enter the room where the visitors were received. Everything about him was white and of the same whiteness: face, hair, beard, hands. His old and well-brushed garment smelt of benzine; his epaulets seemed new. He entered with a firm and measured step, straightening himself up. Extending his dry, white hand, he said aloud:

"How do you do, Sergey?"

Behind him came the mother, with short steps; she wore a strange smile. But she too shook hands with her son, and repeated aloud:

"How do you do, my little Sergey?"

She kissed him and sat down without saying a word. She did not throw herself upon her son, she did not begin to weep or cry, as Sergey expected her to do. She kissed him and sat down without speaking. With a trembling hand she even smoothed the wrinkles in her black silk gown.

Sergey did not know that the colonel had spent the entire previous night in rehearsing this interview. "We must lighten the last moments of our son's life, and not make them more painful for him," the colonel had decided; and he had carefully weighed each phrase, each gesture, of the morrow's visit. But sometimes, in the course of the rehearsal, he became confused, he forgot what he had prepared himself to say, and he wept bitterly, sunk in the corner of his sofa. The next morning he had explained to his wife what she was to do.

"Above all, kiss him and be silent," he repeated. "You will be able to speak later, a little later; but, after kissing him, be silent. Do not speak immediately after kissing him, do you understand? Otherwise you will say what you should not."

"I understand, Nicholas Sergiévitch!" answered the mother, with tears.

"And do not weep! May God keep you from that! Do not weep! You will kill him if you weep, mother!"

"And why do you weep yourself?"

"Why should one not weep here with the rest of you? You must not weep, do you hear?"

"All right, Nicolas Sergiévitch."

They got into a cab and started off, silent, bent, old; they were plunged in their thoughts amid the gay roar of the city; it was the carnival season, and the streets were filled with a noisy crowd.

They sat down. The colonel assumed a suitable attitude, his right hand thrust in the front of his frock-coat. Sergey remained seated a moment; his look met his mother's wrinkled face; he rose suddenly.

"Sit down, my little Sergey!" begged the mother.

"Sit down, Sergey!" repeated the father.

They kept silence. The mother wore a strange smile.

"How many moves we have made in your behalf, Sergey! Your father . . ."

"It was useless, my little mother!"

The colonel said, firmly:

"We were in duty bound to do it that you might not think that your parents had abandoned you."

Again they became silent. They were afraid to utter a syllable, as if each word of the language had lost its proper meaning and now meant but one thing: death. Sergey looked at the neat little frock-coat smelling of benzine, and thought: "He has no orderly now; then he must have cleaned his coat himself. How is it that I have never seen him clean his coat? Probably he does it in the morning." Suddenly he asked:

"And my sister? Is she well?"

"Ninotchka knows nothing!" answered the mother, quickly.

But the colonel sternly interrupted her:

"What is the use of lying? She has read the newspaper . . . let Sergey know that . . . all . . . his own . . . have thought . . . and . . ."

Unable to continue, he stopped. Suddenly the mother's face contracted, her features became confused and wild. Her colorless eyes were madly distended; more and more she panted for breath.

"Se . . . Ser . . . Ser . . . Ser . . ." she repeated, without moving her lips; "Ser . . ."

"My little mother!"

The colonel took a step; trembling all over, without knowing how frightful he was in his corpse-like pallor, in his desperate and forced firmness, he said to his wife:

"Be silent! Do not torture him! Do not torture him! Do not torture him! He must die! Do not torture him!"

Frightened, she was silent already, and he continued to repeat, with his trembling hands pressed against his breast:

"Do not torture him!"

Then he took a step backward, and again thrust his hand into the front of his frock-coat; wearing an expression of forced calmness, he asked aloud, with pallid lips:

"When?"

"To-morrow morning," answered Sergey.

The mother looked at the ground, biting her lips, as if she heard nothing. And she seemed to continue to bite her lips as she let fall these simple words:

"Ninotchka told me to kiss you, my little Sergey!"

"Kiss her for me!" said the condemned man.

"Good! The Chvostofs send their salutations. . . ."

"Who are they? Ah! yes. . . ."

The colonel interrupted him:

"Well, we must start. Rise, mother, it is necessary!"

The two men lifted the swooning woman.

"Bid him farewell!" ordered the colonel. "Give him your blessing!"

She did everything that she was told. But, while giving her son a short kiss and making on his person the sign of the cross, she shook her head and repeated distractedly:

"No, it is not that! No, it is not that!"

"Adieu, Sergey!" said the father. They shook hands, and exchanged a short, but earnest, kiss.

"You . . ." began Sergey.

"Well?" asked the father, spasmodically.

"No, not like that. No, no! What shall I say?" repeated the mother, shaking her head.

She had sat down again, and was tottering.

"You . . ." resumed Sergey. Suddenly his face took on a lamentable expression, and he grimaced like a child, tears filling his eyes. Through their sparkling facets he saw beside him the pale face of his father, who was weeping also.

"Father, you are a strong man!"

"What do you say? What do you say?" said the bewildered colonel. Suddenly, as if completely broken, he fell with his head on his son's shoulder. And the two covered each other with ardent kisses, the father receiving them on his light hair, the prisoner on his cloak.

"And I?" asked suddenly a hoarse voice.

They looked: the mother was on her feet again, and, with her head thrown back, was watching them wrathfully, almost hatefully.

"What is the matter with you, mother?" cried the colonel.

"And I?" she repeated, shaking her head with an insane energy. "You embrace each other, and I? You are men, are you not? And I? and I? . . ."

"Mother!" and Sergey threw himself into her arms.

The last words of the colonel were:

"My blessing for your death, Sergey! Die with courage, like an officer!"

And they went away. . . . On returning to his cell Sergey lay upon his camp-bed, with face turned toward the wall that the soldiers might not see him, and wept a long time.

.   .   .   .

Vasily Kashirin's mother came alone to visit him. The father, a rich merchant, had refused to accompany her. When the old woman entered, Vasily was walking in his cell. In spite of the heat, he was trembling with cold. The conversation was short and painful.

"You ought not to have come, mother. Why should we two torment each other?"

"Why all this, Vasya? Why have you done this, my son? God! God!"

The old woman began to weep, drying her tears with her black silk neckerchief.

Accustomed as they were, his brothers and he, to treat their mother roughly, she being a simple woman who did not understand them, he stopped, and, in the midst of his shivering, said to her, harshly:

"That's it, I knew how it would be. You understand nothing, mama, nothing!"

"Very well, my son. What is the matter with you? Are you cold?"

"I am cold," answered Vasily, and he began to walk again, looking sidewise now and then at the old woman with the same air of irritation.

"You are cold, my son . . ."

"Ah! You speak of cold, but soon . . ." He made a gesture of desperation.

Again the mother began to sob.

"I said to your father: 'Go to see him, he is your son, your flesh; give him a last farewell.' He would not."

"The devil take him! He is not a father. All his life he has been a scoundrel. He remains one!"

"Yet, Vasya, he is your father. . . ."

And the old woman shook her head reproachfully.

It was ridiculous and terrible. This paltry and useless conversation engaged them when face to face with death. While almost weeping, so sad was the situation, Vasily cried out:

"Understand then, mother. They are going to hang me, to hang me! Do you understand, yes or no?"

"And why did you kill?" she cried.

"My God! What are you saying? Even the beasts have feelings. Am I your son or not?"

He sat down and wept. His mother wept also; but, in

their incapability of communicating in the same affection in order to face the terror of the approaching death, they wept cold tears that did not warm the heart.

"You ask me if I am your mother? You heap reproaches on me; and yet I have turned completely white these last few days."

"All right, all right, forgive me. Adieu! Embrace my brothers for me."

"Am I not your mother? Do I not suffer for you?"

At last she departed. She was weeping so that she could not see her way. And, the farther she got from the prison, the more abundant became her tears. She retraced her steps, losing herself in this city in which she was born, in which she had grown up, in which she had grown old. She entered a little abandoned garden, and sat down on a damp bench.

And suddenly she understood: to-morrow they would hang her son! She sprang to her feet, and tried to shout and run, but suddenly her head turned, and she sank to the earth. The path, white with frost, was wet and slippery; the old woman could not rise again. She rested her weight on her wrists, and then fell back again. The black neckerchief slipped from her head, uncovering her dirty gray hair. It seemed to her that she was celebrating her son's wedding. Yes, they had just married him, and she had drunk a little wine; she was slightly intoxicated.

"I cannot help myself! My God, I cannot help myself!"

And, with swinging head, she said to herself that she had drunk too much, and was crawling around on the wet ground, . . . but they gave her wine to drink, and wine again, and still more wine. And from her heart arose the laugh of the drunkard and the desire to abandon herself to a wild dance; . . . but they kept on lifting cups to her lips, one after another, one after another.

VI

THE HOURS FLY

IN THE fortress where the condemned terrorists were confined there was a steeple with an old clock. Every hour, every half-hour, every quarter of an hour, this clock struck in a tone of infinite sadness, like the distant and plaintive cry of birds of passage. In the daytime this odd and desolate music was lost in the noise of the city, of the broad and animated street that passed the fortress. The tramways rumbled, the shoes of the horses rattled, the trembling automobiles sounded their hoarse horns far into the distance. As the carnival was approaching, the peasants of the suburbs had come to town to earn some money as cab-drivers; the bells of the little Russian horses tinkled noisily. The conversations were gay, and had a flavor of intoxication, real holiday conversations. The weather harmonized with the occasion; the spring had brought a thaw, and the road was wet with dirty puddles. The trees on the squares had suddenly darkened. A slightly warm wind was blowing from the sea in copious moist puffs—a light, fresh air that seemed to have started on a joyous flight toward the infinite.

By night the street was silent under the brilliancy of the large electric suns. The immense fortress with its smooth walls was plunged in darkness and silence; a barrier of calm and shadow separated it from the ever-living city. Then they heard the striking of the hours, the slow, sad birth and death of a strange melody, foreign to the land. Like big drops of transparent glass, the hours and the minutes fell from an immeasurable height into a metallic basin that was vibrating gently. Sometimes they were like birds that passed.

Into the cells came, day and night, this single sound. It penetrated through the roof, through the thick stone walls; it alone broke the silence. Sometimes they forgot it, or did not hear it. Sometimes they awaited it with despair; they lived only by and for this sound, having learned to be distrustful of silence. The prison was reserved for criminals of note; its special, rigorous regulations were as rigid and sharp as the corners of the walls. If there is nobility in cruelty, then the solemn, deaf, dead silence that caught up every breath and every rustle was noble.

In this silence, penetrated by the desolate striking of the flying minutes, three men and two women, separated from the world, were awaiting the coming of the night, of the dawn, and of the execution; and each was preparing for it in his own fashion.

Throughout her life Tanya Kovalchuk had thought only of others, and now also it was for the comrades that she underwent suffering and torture. She pictured death to herself only because it threatened Sergey Golovin, Musya, and the others; but her thoughts did not dwell on the fact that she too would be executed.

As if to reward herself for the artificial firmness that she had shown before the judges, she wept for hours altogether. This is characteristic of old women who have suffered much. When it occurred to her that Sergey might be unprovided with tobacco, or that Werner possibly was deprived of the tea of which he was so fond—and this at the moment that they were about to die—she suffered perhaps as much as at the idea of the execution. The execution was something inevitable, even incidental, not worthy of consideration; but that an imprisoned man should be without tobacco on the very eve of his execution was an idea absolutely intolerable. Evoking the pleasant memories of their common life, she lamented over the interview between Sergey and his parents.

For Musya she felt a special pity. For a long time it had seemed to her, mistakenly, however that Musya was in love with Werner; she had beautiful and luminous dreams for their future. Before her arrest Musya wore a silver ring on which were engraved a skull and crossbones surrounded with a crown of thorns. Often Tanya Kovalchuk had looked at this ring sorrowfully, viewing it as a symbol of renunciation; half serious, half joking, she had asked Musya to take it off.

"No, Tanya, I will not give it to you. You will soon have another on your finger!"

Her comrades always thought that she would soon be married, which much offended her. She wanted no husband. And, as she recalled these conversations with Musya and reflected that Musya was indeed sacrificed, Tanya, full of motherly pity, felt the tears choking her. Every time the clock struck, she lifted her face, covered with tears, and listened, wondering how this plaintive and persistent summons of death was being received in the other cells.

VII

THERE IS NO DEATH

AND MUSYA was happy!

With arms folded behind her back, dressed in a prisoner's gown that was too large for her and that made her look like a youth wearing a borrowed costume, she walked back and forth in her cell, at a regular pace, never wearying. She had tucked up the long sleeves of her gown, and her thin and emaciated arms, the arms of a child, emerged from the flaring breadths like flower-stems from a coarse and unclean pitcher. The roughness of the stuff irritated the skin of her white and slender neck; sometimes, with her two hands, she released her throat, and felt cautiously for the spot where her skin was burning.

Musya walked with a long stride, and tried blushingly to justify to herself the fact that the finest of deaths, reserved hitherto for martyrs, had been assigned to her, so young, so humble, and who had done so little. It seemed to her that, in dying upon the scaffold, she was making a pretentious show that was in bad taste.

At her last interview with her lawyer she had asked him to procure poison for her, but immediately had given up the idea: would not people think that she was actuated by fear or by ostentation? Instead of dying modestly and unnoticed, would she not cause still further scandal? And she had added, quickly:

"No, no, it is useless!"

Now her sole desire was to explain, to prove, that she was not a heroine, that it was not a frightful thing to die, and that no one need pity her or worry on her account.

Musya sought excuses, pretexts of such a nature as to exalt her sacrifice and give it a real value, as if it had actually been called in question.

"In fact," she said to herself, "I am young; I might have lived for a long time. But . . ."

Just as the gleam of a candle is effaced by the radiance of the rising sun, youth and life seem to her dull and sombre beside the magnificent and luminous halo that is about to crown her modest person.

"Is it possible?" Musya asks herself, in great confusion. "Is it possible that I am worth anybody's tears?"

And she is seized with an unspeakable joy. There is no more doubt; she has been taken into the pale. She has a right to figure among the heroes who from all countries go to heaven through flames and executions. What serene peace, what infinite happiness! An immaterial being, she believes herself hovering in a divine light.

Of what else was Musya thinking? Of many things, since for her the thread of life was not severed by death but continued to unroll in a calm and regular fashion. She was thinking of her comrades, of those who at a distance were filled with anguish at the idea of her approaching execution, of those who nearer at hand would go with her to the gallows. She was astonished that Vasily should be a prey to terror, he who had always been brave. On Tuesday morning, when they had prepared themselves to kill, and then to die themselves, Tanya Kovalchuk had trembled with emotion; they had been obliged to send her away, whereas Vasily joked and laughed and moved about amid the bombs with so little caution that Werner had said to him severely:

"One should not play with death!"

Why, then, was Vasily afraid now? And this incomprehensible terror was so foreign to Musya's soul that she soon ceased to think about it and to inquire into its cause. Suddenly she felt a mad desire to see Sergey Golovin and laugh with him.

Perhaps too her thought was unwilling to dwell long on the same subject, resembling therein a light bird that hovers before infinite horizons, all space, the caressing and tender azure, being accessible to it. The hours continued to strike. Thoughts blended in this harmonious and distant symphony; fleeting images became a sort of music. It seemed to Musya that she was travelling on a broad and easy road in a quiet night; the carriage rode easily on its springs. All care had vanished; the tired body was dissolved in the darkness; joyous and weary, the thought peacefully created vivid images, and became intoxicated on their beauty. Musya recalled three comrades who had been hanged lately; their faces were illuminated and near, nearer than those of the living. . . . So in the morning one thinks gaily of the hospitable friends who will receive you in the evening with smiles on their lips.

At last Musya became weary from walking. She lay down

cautiously on the camp-bed and continued to dream, with half-closed eyes.

"Is this really death? My God, how beautiful it is! Or is it life? I do not know, I do not know! I am going to see and hear. . . ."

From the first days of her imprisonment she had been a prey to hallucinations. She had a very musical ear; her sense of hearing, sharpened by the silence, gathered in the slightest echoes of life; the footsteps of the sentinels in the corridor, the striking of the clock, the whispering of the wind over the zinc roof, the creaking of a lantern, all blended for her in a vast and mysterious symphony. At first the hallucinations frightened Musya, and she drove them away as morbid manifestations; then, perceiving that she was in good health and had no pathological symptoms, she ceased to resist.

But now she hears very plainly the sound of the military band. She opens her eyes in astonishment, and raises her head. Through the windows she sees the night; the clock strikes. "Again!" she thought, as she closed her eyes without disturbing herself. Again the music begins. Musya clearly distinguishes the steps of the soldiers as they turn the corner of the prison; a whole regiment is passing before her windows. The boots keep time to the music on the frozen ground; one! two! one! two! Sometimes a boot squeaks; a foot slips and then recovers itself. The music draws nearer; it is playing a noisy and stirring triumphal march which Musya does not know. There is probably some festival in the fortress.

The soldiers are under her windows, and the cell is filled

with joyous, regular, and harmonious sounds. A big brass trumpet emits false notes: it is not in time; now it is in advance, now it lags behind in a ridiculous fashion. Musya pictures to herself a little soldier playing this trumpet assiduously, and she laughs.

The regiment has passed; the sound of the footsteps grows fainter and fainter; one! two! one! two! In the distance the music becomes gayer and more beautiful. Several times more the trumpet sounds out of time, with its metallic, sonorous, and gay voice, and then all is quiet. Again the clock in the steeple strikes the hours.

New forms come and lean over her, surrounding her with transparent clouds and lifting her to a great height, where birds of prey are hovering. At left and right, above and below, everywhere birds are crying like heralds; they call, they warn. They spread their wings, and immensity sustains them. And on their inflated breasts that split the air is reflected the sparkling azure. The beating of Musya's heart becomes more and more regular, her respiration more and more calm and peaceful. She sleeps; her face is pale; her features are drawn; there are dark rings around her eyes. On her lips a smile. To-morrow, when the sun shall rise, this intelligent and fine face will be deformed by a grimace in which no trace of the human will be left; the brain will be inundated with thick blood; the glassy eyes will protrude from their orbits. But to-day Musya sleeps quietly, and smiles in her immortality.

Musya sleeps.

And the prison continues to live its special, blind, vigilant life, a sort of perpetual anxiety. They walk. They whisper.

A gun rings out. It seems as if someone cries out. Is this reality or hallucination?

The grating in the door lowers noiselessly. In the dark opening appears a sinister bearded face. For a long time the widely-opened eyes view with astonishment the sleeping Musya; then the face disappears as quietly as it came.

The bells in the steeple ring and sing interminably. One would say that the weary hours were climbing a high mountain toward midnight. The ascent grows more and more painful. They slip, fall back with a groan, and begin again to toil painfully toward the black summit.

There is a sound of footsteps. Whispering voices are heard. Already they are harnessing the horses to the sombre, unlighted vehicle.

VIII

DEATH EXISTS, AND LIFE ALSO

SERGEY GOLOVIN never thought of death. It seemed to him something incidental and foreign. He was robust, endowed with that serenity in the joy of living which causes all evil thoughts, all thoughts fatal to life, to disappear rapidly, leaving the organism intact. Just as, with him, physical wounds healed quickly, so all injuries to his soul were immediately nullified. He brought into all his acts, into his pleasures and into his preparations for crime, the same happy and tranquil gravity: everything in life was gay, everything was important, worthy of being well done.

And he did everything well; he sailed a boat admirably,

he was an excellent marksman. He was as faithful in friendship as in love, and had an unshakeable confidence in the "word of honor." His comrades declared laughingly that, if one who had been proved a spy should swear to Sergey that he was not a spy, Sergey would believe him and shake hands with him. A single fault: he thought himself a good singer, whereas he sang atrociously false, even in the case of revolutionary hymns. He got angry when they laughed at him.

"Either you are all asses, or else I am an ass!" he said in a serious and offended tone. And, after a moment's reflection, the comrades declared, in a tone quite as serious:

"It is you who are an ass. You show it in your voice!"

And, as is sometimes the case with worthy people, they loved him perhaps more for his eccentricities than for his virtues.

He thought so little of death, he feared it so little, that on the fatal morning, before leaving the dwelling of Tanya Kovalchuk, he alone had breakfasted with appetite, as usual. He had taken two glasses of tea, and eaten a whole two-cent loaf. Then, looking with sadness at Werner's untouched bread, he said to him:

"Why don't you eat? Eat; it is necessary to get strength!"

"I am not hungry."

"Well, I will eat your bread! Shall I?"

"What an appetite you have, Sergey!"

By way of reply, Sergey, with his mouth full, began to sing, in a false and hollow voice:

"A hostile wind is blowing o'er our heads."

After the arrest Sergey had a moment of sadness; the plot had been badly planned. But he said to himself: "Now there is something else that must be done well: to die." And his gaiety returned. On his second day in the fortress he began gymnastic exercises, according to the extremely rational system of a German named Müller, which interested him much. He undressed himself completely; and, to the amazement of the anxious sentinel, he went carefully through the eighteen prescribed exercises.

As a propagandist of the Müller system, it gave him much satisfaction to see the soldier follow his movements. Although he knew that he would get no answer, he said to the eye that appeared at the grating:

"That is the kind of thing that does you good, brother; that gives you strength! That is what they ought to make you do in the regiment," he added, in a gentle and persuasive voice, that he might not frighten the soldier, not suspecting that his guardian took him for a madman.

The fear of death showed itself in him progressively, seemingly by shocks: it seemed to him that someone was thumping him violently in the heart from below. Then the sensation disappeared, but came back a few hours later, each time more intense and prolonged. It was beginning already to take on the vague outlines of an unendurable anguish.

"Is it possible that I am afraid?" thought Sergey, in astonishment. "How stupid!"

It was not he who was afraid; it was his young, robust, and vigorous body, which neither the gymnastics of Müller nor the cold shower-baths could deceive. The stronger and fresher he became after his cold-water ablutions, the more acute and unendurable was his sensation of temporary fear. And it was in the morning, after his deep sleep and physical exercises, that this atrocious fear like something foreign appeared—exactly at the moment when formerly he had been particularly conscious of his strength and his joy in living. He noticed this, and said to himself:

"You are stupid, my friend. In order that the body may die more easily, it should be weakened, not fortified."

From that time he gave up his gymnastics and his massage. And, to explain this right-about-face, he cried to the soldier:

"Brother, the method is a good one. It is only for those who are going to be hanged that it is good for nothing."

In fact, he felt a sort of relief. He tried also to eat less in order to further weaken himself, but, in spite of the lack of air and exercise, his appetite remained excellent. Sergey could not resist it, and ate everything that they brought him. Then he resorted to a subterfuge; before sitting down to table, he poured half of his soup into his bucket. And this method succeeded; a great weariness, a vague numbness, took possession of him.

"I will teach you!" he said, threatening his body; and he caressed his softening muscles sadly.

But soon the body became accustomed to this régime and the fear of death appeared again, not in so acute a form, but as a vague sensation of nausea, still harder to bear. "It is because this lasts so long," thought Sergey. "If only I could sleep all the time until the day of execution!" He tried to sleep as much as possible. His first efforts were not altogether fruitless; then insomnia set in, accompanied with obsessing thoughts and, with these, a regret that he must part with life.

"Am I then afraid of it?" he asked himself, thinking of death. "It is the loss of life that I regret. Life is an admirable thing, whatever the pessimists may say. What would a pessimist say if they were to hang him? Ah! I regret to lose my life, I regret it much."

When he clearly understood that for him all was over, that he had before him only a few hours of empty waiting and then death, he had a queer feeling. It seemed to him that they had stripped him naked in an extraordinary fashion. Not only had they taken away his clothes, but also sun, air, sound and light, speech and the power of action. Death had not yet arrived, and yet life seemed already absent; he felt a strange sensation, sometimes incomprehensible, sometimes intelligible, but very subtle and mysterious.

"What is it then?" wondered Sergey, in his torment. "And I, where am I? I . . . What I?"

He examined himself attentively, with interest, beginning with his loose slippers, such as the prisoners wore, and stopping with his belly, over which hung his ample cloak. He began to walk back and forth in his cell, with arms apart, and continued to look at himself as a woman does when trying on a gown that is too long. He tried to turn his head: it turned. And what seemed to him a little terrifying was he himself, Sergey Golovin, who soon would be no more!

Everything became strange.

He tried to walk, and it seemed queer to him to walk.

He tried to sit down, and he was surprised that he could do so. He tried to drink water, and it seemed queer to him to drink, to swallow, to hold the goblet, to see his fingers, his trembling fingers. He began to cough, and thought: "How curious it is! I cough."

"What is the matter? Am I going mad?" he asked himself. "That would be the last straw, indeed!"

He wiped his brow, and this gesture seemed to him equally surprising. Then he fixed himself in a motionless posture, without breathing—for entire hours, it seemed to him, extinguishing all thought, holding his breath, avoiding all motion; for every thought was madness, every gesture an aberration. Time disappeared as if transformed into space, into a transparent space in which there was no air, into an immense place containing everything—land and life and men. And one could take in everything at a glance, to the very extremity, to the edge of the unknown gulf, to death. And it was not because he saw death that Sergey suffered, but because he saw life and death at the same time. A sacrilegious hand had lifted the curtain which from all eternity had hidden the mystery of life and the mystery of death; they had ceased to be mysterious, but they were no more comprehensible than truth written in a foreign language.

"And here we are back to Müller again!" he suddenly declared aloud, in a voice of deep conviction. He shook his head and began to laugh gaily, sincerely:

"Ah, my good Müller! My dear Müller! My worthy German! You are right, after all, Müller; as for me, brother Müller, I am only an ass!"

He quickly made the round of his cell; and, to the great astonishment of the soldier who was watching him through the grating, he entirely undressed and went through the eighteen exercises with scrupulous exactness. He bent and straightened up his young body which had grown a little thin; he stooped, inhaling and exhaling the air; he raised himself on tiptoe, and moved his arms and legs.

"Yes, but, you know, Müller, reasoned Sergey, throwing out his chest, his ribs outlining themselves plainly under his thin, distended skin—"you know, Müller, there is still a nineteenth exercise—suspension by the neck in a fixed position. And that is called hanging. Do you understand, Müller? They take a living man, Sergey Golovin, for example, they wrap him up like a doll, and they hang him by the neck until he is dead. It is stupid, Müller, but that is the way it is; one must be resigned!"

He leaned on his right side, and repeated:

"One must be resigned, Müller!"

IX

THE HORRIBLE SOLITUDE

UNDER THE same roof and to the same melodious chant of the different hours, separated from Sergey and from Musya by a few empty cells, but as isolated as if he alone had existed in the whole universe, the unhappy Vasily Kashirin was finishing his life in anguish and terror.

Covered with sweat, his shirt adhering to his body, his formerly curly hair now falling in straight locks, he went back and forth in his cell with the jerky and lamentable gait of one suffering atrociously with the toothache. He sat down for a moment, and then began to run again; then he rested his forehead against the wall, stopped, and looked about as if in search of a remedy. He had so changed that one might think that he possessed two different faces, one of which, the younger, had gone nobody knows where, to give place to the second, a terrible face, that seemed to have come from darkness.

Fear had shown itself suddenly to him, and had seized upon his person as an exclusive and sovereign mistress. On the fatal morning, when he was marching to certain death, he had played with it; but that evening, confined in his cell, he had been carried away and lashed by a wave of mad terror. As long as he had gone freely forward to meet danger and death, as long as he had held his fate in his own hands, however terrible it might be, he had appeared tranquil and even joyous, the small amount of shameful and decrepit fear that he had felt having disappeared in a consciousness of infinite liberty, in the firm and audacious affirmation of his intrepid will, leaving no trace behind. With an infernal machine strapped around his waist, he had transformed himself into an instrument of death, he had borrowed from the dynamite its cruel reason and its flashing and homicidal power. In the street, among the busy people preoccupied with their affairs and quickly dodging the tramcars and the cabs, it seemed to him as if he came from another and an unknown world, where there was no such thing as death or fear.

Suddenly a brutal, bewildering change had taken place. Vasily no longer went where he wanted to go, but was led where others wanted him to go. He no longer chose his place; they placed him in a stone cage and locked him in, as if he were a thing. He could no longer choose between life and death; they led him to death, certainly and inevitably. He who had been for a moment the incarnation of will, of life, and of force, had become a lamentable specimen of impotence; he was nothing but an animal destined for the slaughter. Whatever he might say, they would not listen; if he started to cry out, they would stuff a rag in his mouth; and, if he even tried to walk, they would take him away and hang him. If he resisted, if he struggled, if he lay down on the ground, they would be stronger than he; they would pick him up, they would tie him, and thus they would carry him to the gallows. And his imagination gave to the men charged with this execution, men like himself, the new, extraordinary, and terrifying aspect of unthinking automata, whom nothing in the world could stop, and who seized a man, overpowered him, hanged him, pulled him by the feet, cut the rope, put the body in a coffin, carried it away, and buried it.

From the first day of his imprisonment, people and life had transformed themselves for him into an unspeakably frightful world filled with mechanical dolls. Almost mad with fear, he tried to fancy to himself that these people had tongues and spoke, but he did not succeed. Their mouths opened, something like a sound came from them; then they separated with movements of their legs, and all was over. He was in the situation of a man who, left alone in a house at night, should see all things become animate, move, and assume over him an unlimited power; suddenly the wardrobe, the chair, the sofa, the writing-table would sit in judgment upon him. He would cry out, call for help, beg, and rove from room to room; and the things would speak to each other in their own tongue; and then the wardrobe, the chair, the sofa, and the writing-table would start to hang him, the other things looking on.

In the eyes of Vasily Kashirin, sentenced to be hanged, everything took on a puerile aspect; the cell, the grated door, the striking apparatus of the clock, the fortress with its carefully modelled ceilings, and, above, the mechanical doll equipped with a musket, who walked up and down in the corridor, and the other dolls who frightened him by looking through the grating and handing him his food without a word.

A man had disappeared from the world.

In court the presence of the comrades had brought Kashirin back to himself. Again for a moment he saw people; they were there, judging him, speaking the language of men, listening, and seeming to understand. But, when he saw his mother, he felt clearly, with the terror of a man who is going mad and he knows it, that this old woman in a black neckerchief was a simple mechanical doll. He was astonished at not having suspected it before, and at having awaited this visit as something infinitely sorrowful in its distressing gentleness. While forcing himself to speak, he thought with a shudder:

"My God! But it is a doll! A doll-mother! And yonder is a doll-soldier; at home there is a doll-father, and this is the doll Vasily Kashirin."

When the mother began to weep, Vasily again saw something human in her, but this disappeared with the first words that she uttered. With curiosity and terror he watched the tears flow from the doll's eyes.

When his fear became intolerable, Vasily Kashirin tried to pray. There remained with him only a bitter, detestable, and enervating rancor against all the religious principles upon which his youth had been nourished, in the house of his father, a large merchant. He had no faith. But one day, in his childhood, he had heard some words that had made an impression upon him and that remained surrounded forever with a gentle poesy. These words were:

"Joy of all the afflicted!"

Sometimes, in painful moments, he whispered, without praying, without even accounting to himself for what he was doing: "Joy of all the afflicted!" And then he suddenly felt relieved; he had a desire to approach someone who was dear to him and complain gently:

"Our life! . . . but is it really a life? Say, my dear, is it really a life?"

And then suddenly he felt himself ridiculous; he would have liked to bare his breast and ask someone to beat it.

He had spoken to no one, not even to his best comrades, of his "Joy of all the afflicted!" He seemed to know nothing of it himself, so deeply hidden was it in his soul. And he evoked it rarely, with precaution.

Now that the fear of unfathomable mystery which was rising before him completely covered him, as the water covers the plants on the bank when the tide is rising, he had a desire to pray. He wanted to fall upon his knees, but was seized with shame before the sentinel; so, with hands clasped upon his breast, he murmured in a low voice:

"Joy of all the afflicted!"

And he repeated with anxiety, in a tone of supplication:

"Joy of all the afflicted, descend into me, sustain me!"

Something moved softly. It seemed to him that a sorrowful and gentle force hovered in the distance and then vanished, without illuminating the shades of the agony. In the steeple the hour struck. The soldier yawned long and repeatedly.

"Joy of all the afflicted! You are silent! And you will say nothing to Vasily Kashirin!"

He wore an imploring smile, and waited. But in his soul there was the same void as around him. Useless and tormenting thoughts came to him; again he saw the lighted candles, the priest in his robe, the holy image painted on the wall, his father bending and straightening up again, praying and kneeling, casting furtive glances at Vasily to see if he too was praying or was simply amusing himself. And Kashirin was in still deeper anguish than before.

Everything disappeared.

His consciousness went out like the dying embers that one scatters on the hearth; it froze, like the body of a man just dead in which the heart is still warm while the hands and feet are already cold.

Vasily had a moment of wild terror when they came into his cell to get him. He did not even suspect that the hour of the execution had arrived; he simply saw the people and took fright, almost like a child.

"I will not do it again! I will not do it again!" he whispered, without being heard; and his lips became icy as he recoiled slowly toward the rear of his cell, just as in childhood he had tried to escape the punishments of his father.

"You will have to go . . ."

They talked, they walked around him, they gave him he knew not what. He closed his eyes, staggered, and began to prepare himself painfully. Undoubtedly he had recovered consciousness; he suddenly asked a cigarette of one of the officials, who amiably extended his cigarette case.

X

THE WALLS CRUMBLE

THE UNKNOWN, surnamed Werner, was a man fatigued by struggle. He had loved life, the theatre, society, art, literature, passionately. Endowed with an excellent memory, he spoke several languages perfectly. He was fond of dress, and had excellent manners. Of the whole group of terrorists he was the only one who was able to appear in society without risk of recognition.

For a long time already, and without his comrades having noticed it, he had entertained a profound contempt for men. More of a mathematician than a poet, ecstasy and inspiration had remained so far things unknown to him; at times he would look upon himself as a madman seeking to square the circle in seas of human blood. The enemy against which he daily struggled could not inspire him with respect; it was nothing but a compact network of stupidities, treasons, falsehoods, base deceits. The thing that had finally destroyed in him forever, it seemed to him, the desire to live, was his execution of a police-spy in obedience to the order of his party. He had killed him tranquilly, but at sight of this human countenance, inanimate, calm, but still false, pitiable in spite of everything, he suddenly lost his esteem for himself and his work. He considered himself as the most indifferent, the least interesting, of beings. Being a man of will, he did not leave his party; apparently he remained the same; but from that time there was something cold and terrifying in his eyes. He said nothing to anyone.

He possessed also a very rare quality: he knew not fear. He pitied those of his comrades who had this feeling, especially Vasily Kashirin. But his pity was cold, almost official.

Werner understood that the execution was not simply death, but also something more. In any case, he was determined to meet it calmly, to live until the end as if nothing had happened or would happen. Only in this way could he express the profoundest contempt for the execution and preserve his liberty of mind. In the courtroom—his comrades, although knowing well his cold and haughty intrepidity, perhaps would not have believed it themselves—he thought not of life or of death: he played in his mind a difficult game of chess, giving it his deepest and quietest attention. An excellent player, he had begun this game on the very day of his imprisonment, and he kept it up continually. And the verdict that condemned him did not displace a single piece on the invisible board.

The idea that he probably would not finish the game did not stop Werner. On the morning of the last day he began by correcting a plan that had failed the night before. With hands pressed between his knees, he sat a long time motionless; then he arose, and began to walk, reflecting. He had a gait of his own; the upper part of his body inclined a little forward, and he brought down his heels forcibly; even when the ground was dry, he left clear footprints behind him. He whistled softly a rather simple Italian melody, which helped him to reflect.

But now he was shrugging his shoulders and feeling his pulse. His heart beat fast, but tranquilly and regularly, with a sonorous force. Like a novice thrown into prison for the first time, he examined attentively the cell, the bolts, the chair screwed to the wall, and said to himself:

"Why have I such a sensation of joy, of liberty? Yes, of liberty; I think of to-morrow's execution, and it seems to me that it does not exist. I look at the walls, and they seem to me not to exist either. And I feel as free as if instead of being in prison, I had just come out of another cell in which I had been confined all my life."

Werner's hands began to tremble, a thing unknown to him. His thought became more and more vibrant. It seemed to him that tongues of fire were moving in his head, trying to escape from his brain to lighten the still obscure distance. Finally the flame darted forth, and the horizon was brilliantly illuminated.

The vague lassitude that had tortured Werner during the last two years had disappeared at the sight of death; his beautiful youth came back as he played. It was even something more than beautiful youth. With the astonishing clearness of mind that sometimes lifts man to the supreme heights of meditation, Werner saw suddenly both life and death; and the majesty of this new spectacle struck him. He seemed to be following a path as narrow as the edge of a blade, on the crest of the loftiest mountain. On one side he saw life, and on the other he saw death; and they were like two deep seas, sparkling and beautiful, melting into each other at the horizon in a single infinite extension.

"What is this, then? What a divine spectacle!" said he slowly.

He arose involuntarily and straightened up, as if in presence of the Supreme Being. And, annihilating the walls, annihilating space and time, by the force of his all-penetrating look, he cast his eyes into the depths of the life that he had quitted.

And life took on a new aspect. He no longer tried, as of old, to translate into words what he was; moreover, in the whole range of human language, still so poor and miserly, he found no words adequate. The paltry, dirty, and evil things that suggested to him contempt and sometimes even disgust at the sight of men had completely disappeared, just as, to people rising in a balloon, the mud and filth of the narrow streets become invisible and ugliness changes into beauty.

With an unconscious movement Werner walked toward the table and leaned upon it with his right arm. Haughty and authoritarian by nature, he had never been seen in a prouder, freer, and more imperious attitude; never had his face worn such a look, never had he so lifted up his head, for at no previous time had he been as free and powerful as now, in this prison, on the eve of execution, at the threshold of death.

In his illuminated eyes men wore a new aspect, an unknown beauty and charm. He hovered above time, and never had this humanity, which only the night before was howling like a wild beast in the forests, appeared to him so young. What had heretofore seemed to him terrible, unpardonable, and base became suddenly touching and naïve, just as we cherish in the child the awkwardness of its behaviour, the incoherent stammerings in which its unconscious genius glimmers, its laughable errors and blunders, its cruel bruises.

"My dear friend!"

Werner smiled suddenly, and his attitude lost its haughty and imposing force. Again he became the prisoner suffering in his narrow cell, weary of seeing a curious eye steadily fixed upon him through the door. He sat down, but not in his usual stiff position, and looked at the walls and the gratings with a weak and gentle smile such as his face had never worn. And something happened which had never happened to him before: he wept.

"My dear comrades!" he whispered, shedding bitter tears. "My dear comrades!"

What mysterious path had he followed to pass from a feeling of unlimited and haughty liberty to this passionate and moving pity? He did not know. Did he really pity his comrades, or did his tears hide something more passionate, something really greater? His heart, which had suddenly revived and reblossomed, could not tell him. Werner wept, and whispered:

"My dear comrades! My dear comrades!"

And in this man who wept, and who smiled through his

tears, no one—not the judges, or his comrades, or himself
—would have recognized the cold and haughty Werner,
skeptical and insolent.

XI

ON THE WAY TO THE GALLOWS

BEFORE GETTING into the vehicles, all five of the condemned
were gathered in a large cold room with an arched ceiling,
resembling an abandoned office or an unused reception-
room. They were permitted to talk with each other.

Only Tanya Kovalchuk took immediate advantage of the
permission. The others pressed in silence hands as cold as
ice or as hot as fire; dumb, trying to avoid each other's gaze,
they formed a confused and distracted group. Now that
they were reunited, they seemed to be ashamed of what they
had felt individually in the solitude. They were afraid to
look at each other, afraid to show the new, special, somewhat embarrassing thing that they felt or suspected in each
other.

Nevertheless, they did look, and, after a smile or two, all
found themselves at ease, as before; no change revealed itself, or, if something had happened, all had taken an equal
share in it, so that nothing special was noticeable in any one
of them. All talked and moved in a queer and jerky fashion,
impulsively, either too slowly or too quickly. Sometimes one
of them quickly repeated the same words, or else failed to
finish a phrase that he had begun or thought he had already

spoken. But nothing of all this did they notice. All blinkingly examined the familiar objects without recognizing them, like people who have suddenly taken off their glasses. They often turned around quickly, as if someone were calling them from the rear. But they did not notice this. The cheeks and ears of Musya and Tanya were burning. At first Sergey was a little pale; he soon recovered, and appeared as usual.

Vasily alone attracted attention. Even in such a group he was extraordinary and dreadful. Werner was moved, and said in a low voice to Musya, with deep anxiety:

"What is the matter with him, Musya? Is it possible that he has . . . ? Really, we must speak to him."

Vasily looked at Werner from a distance, as if he had not recognized him; then he lowered his eyes.

"But, Vasily, what is the matter with your hair? What is the matter with you? It is nothing, brother, it will soon be over! We must control ourselves! We really must!"

Vasily did not break the silence. But, when they had already concluded that he would say absolutely nothing, there came a hollow, tardy, terribly distant reply, such as the grave might give up after a long appeal:

"But there is nothing the matter with me. I am in control of myself!"

He repeated:

"I am in control of myself!"

Werner was delighted.

"Good, good! You are a brave fellow! All is well!"

But, when his eyes met the dark and heavy gaze of Vasily, he felt a momentary anguish, asking himself: "But whence does he look? whence does he speak?" In a tone of deep tenderness, he said:

"Vasily, do you hear? I love you much!"

"And I too, I love you much!" replied a tongue that moved painfully.

Suddenly Musya seized Werner by the arm, and, expressing her astonishment forcibly, like an actress on the stage, she said:

"Werner, what is the matter with you? You said: 'I love you'? You never said that to anyone before. And why is your face so sparkling and your voice so tender? What is it? What is it?"

And Werner, also in the manner of an actor dwelling upon his words, answered, as he pressed the young girl's hand:

"Yes, I love, now! Do not tell the others. I am ashamed of it, but I love my brothers passionately!"

Their eyes met and burst into flame: everything about them became extinct, just as all other lights pale in the fugitive flash of the lightning.

"Yes!" said Musya. "Yes, Werner!"

"Yes!" he answered. "Yes, Musya, yes!"

They had understood something and ratified it forever. With sparkling eyes and quick steps Werner moved on again in the direction of Sergey.

"Sergey!"

But it was Tanya Kovalchuk that answered. Full of joy, almost weeping with maternal pride, she pulled Sergey violently by the sleeve.

"Just listen, Werner! I weep on his account. I torment myself, and he, he does gymnastics!"

"The Müller system?" asked Werner, with a smile.

Sergey, somewhat confused, knit his brows.

"You do wrong to laugh, Werner! I have absolutely convinced myself . . ."

Everybody began to laugh. Gaining strength and firmness from their mutual communion, they gradually became again what they used to be; they did not notice it, and thought that they were always the same. Suddenly Werner stopped laughing; with perfect gravity he said to Sergey:

"You are right, Sergey! You are perfectly right!"

"Understand this then!" rejoined Sergey, satisfied. "Of course we . . ."

Just then they were asked to get into the vehicles. The officials even had the amiability to allow them to place themselves in their own fashion, in pairs. In general, they were very amiable with them, even too much so; were they trying to give evidence of a little humanity, or to show that they were not responsible for what was taking place and that everything was happening of itself? It is impossible to say, but all those taking part were pale.

"Go with him, Musya!" said Werner, pointing the young girl to Vasily, who stood motionless.

"I understand!" she answered, nodding her head. "And you?"

"I? Tanya will go with Sergey, you with Vasily. As for me, I shall be alone! What matters it? I can stand it, you know!"

When they had reached the courtyard, the damp and

slightly warm air fell softly upon their faces and eyes, cut their breathing, and penetrated their shivering bodies, purifying them. It was hard to believe that this stimulant was simply the wind, a spring wind, gentle and moist.

The astonishing spring night had a flavor of melted snow, of infinite space; it made the stones resound. Brisk and busy little drops of water fell rapidly, one after another, making a sonorous song. But, if one of them delayed a little or fell too soon, the song changed into a joyous splash, an animated confusion. Then a big drop fell heavily, and again the spring-like song began, rhythmical and sonorous. Above the city, higher than the walls of the fortress, was the pale halo formed by the electric lights.

Sergey Golovin heaved a deep sigh, and then held his breath, as if regretting to expel from his lungs air so pure and fresh.

"Have we had this fine weather long?" Werner inquired. "It is spring!"

"Only since yesterday!" they answered politely and promptly. "There have been many cold days."

One after another the black vehicles came up, took in two persons, and went away in the darkness, toward the spot where a lantern was swinging in the gateway. Around each vehicle were moving the gray outlines of soldiers; their horses' shoes resounded loudly; often the beasts slipped on the wet snow.

When Werner bent to get into the vehicle, a gendarme said to him, in a vague way:

"There is another in there who *goes* with you!"

Werner was astonished.

"Who *goes* where? Ah! Yes! Another one! Who is it?"

The soldier said nothing. In a dark corner something small and motionless, but alive, lay rolled up; an open eye shone under an oblique ray of the lantern. As he sat down, Werner brushed against a knee with his foot.

"Pardon me, comrade!"

There was no answer. Not until the vehicle had started did the man ask hesitatingly, in bad Russian:

"Who are you?"

"My name is Werner, sentenced to be hanged for an attempt upon the life of XX. And you?"

"I am Yanson. . . . I must not be hanged. . . ."

In two hours they would be face to face with the great mystery as yet unsolved; in two hours they would leave life for death; thither both were going, and yet they became acquainted. Life and death were marching simultaneously on two different planes, and to the very end, even in the most laughable and most stupid details, life remained life.

"What did you do, Yanson?"

"I stuck a knife into my boss. I stole money."

From the sound of his voice it seemed as if Yanson were asleep. Werner found his limp hand in the darkness, and pressed it. Yanson lazily withdrew it.

"You are afraid?" asked Werner.

"I do not want to be hanged."

They became silent. Again Werner found the Esthonian's hand, and pressed it tightly between his dry and burning palms. It remained motionless, but Yanson did not try again to release it.

They stifled in the cramped vehicle, whose musty smell mingled with the odors of the soldiers' uniform, of the muck-heap, and of wet leather. The breath of a young gendarme, redolent of garlic and bad tobacco, streamed continually into the face of Werner, who sat opposite. But the keen fresh air came in at the windows, and thanks to this the presence of spring was felt in the little moving box even more plainly than outside. The vehicle turned now to the right, now to the left; sometimes it seemed to turn around and go back. There were moments when it appeared to the prisoners as if they had been going in a circle for hours. At first the bluish electric light came in between the heavy lowered curtains; then suddenly, after a turn, darkness set in; it was from this that the travellers gathered that they reached the suburbs and were approaching the station of S——. Sometimes, at a sudden turn, Werner's bent and living knee brushed in a friendly way against the bent and living knee of the gendarme, and it was hard to believe in the approaching execution.

"Where are we going?" asked Yanson, suddenly. The continuous and prolonged shaking of the sombre vehicle gave him vertigo and a little nausea.

Werner answered, and pressed the Esthonian's hand more tightly than before. He would have liked to say specially friendly and kind words to this little sleeping man, whom already he loved more than anyone in the world.

"Dear friend! I think that you are in an uncomfortable position! Draw nearer to me!"

At first Yanson said nothing, but after a moment he replied:

"Thank you! I am comfortable! And you, they are going to hang you too?"

"Yes!" replied Werner, with an unlooked-for gaiety, almost laughing. He made a free-and-easy gesture, as if they were speaking of some futile and stupid prank that a band of affectionate practical jokers were trying to play upon them.

"You have a wife?" asked Yanson.

"No! A wife! I! No, I am alone!"

"So am I! I am alone."

Werner, too, was beginning to feel the vertigo. At times it seemed to him that he was on his way to some festivity. A queer thing; almost all those who were going to the execution had the same feeling; though a prey to fear and anguish, they rejoiced vaguely in the extraordinary thing that was about to happen. Reality became intoxicated on madness, and death, coupling with life, gave birth to phantoms.

"Here we are at last!" said Werner, gay and curious, when the vehicle stopped; and he leaped lightly to the ground. Not so with Yanson, who resisted, without saying a word, very lazily it seemed, and who refused to descend. He clung to the handle of the door; the gendarme loosened his weak fingers, and grasped his arm. Ivan caught at the corner, at the door, at the high wheel, but yielded at every intervention of the gendarme. He adhered to things rather than gripped them. And it was not necessary to use much force to loosen his grasp. In short, they prevailed over him.

As always at night, the station was dark, deserted, and inanimate. The passenger trains had already passed, and for the train that was waiting on the track for the prisoners there was no need of light or activity. Werner was seized with ennui. He was not afraid, he was not in distress, but he was bored; an immense, heavy, fatiguing ennui filled him with a desire to go away no matter where, lie down, and close his eyes. He stretched himself, and yawned repeatedly.

"If only they did these things more quickly!" said he, wearily.

Yanson said nothing, and shuddered.

When the condemned passed over the deserted platform surrounded with soldiers, on their way to the poorly-lighted railway carriages, Werner found himself placed beside Sergey Golovin. The latter designated something with his hand, and began to speak; his neighbor clearly understood only the word "lamp"; the rest of the phrase was lost in a weary and prolonged yawn.

"What did you say?" asked Werner, yawning also.

"The reflector . . . the lamp of the reflector is smoking," said Sergey.

Werner turned around. It was true; the glass shades were already black.

"Yes, it is smoking!"

Suddenly he thought: "What matters it to me whether the lamp is smoking, when . . . ?" Sergey undoubtedly had the same idea. He threw a quick glance at Werner, and turned away his head. But both stopped yawning.

All walked to the train without difficulty; Yanson alone had to be led. At first he stiffened his legs, and glued the soles of his feet to the platform; then he bent his knees.

The entire weight of his body fell upon the arms of the policemen; his legs dragged like those of a drunken man; and the toes of his boots ground against the wooden platform. With a thousand difficulties, but in silence, they lifted him into the railway-carriage.

Vasily Kashirin himself walked unsupported; unconsciously he imitated the movements of his comrades. After mounting the steps of the carriage, he drew back; a policeman took him by the elbow to sustain him. Then Vasily began to tremble violently and uttered a piercing cry, pushing away the policeman!

"Aie!"

"Vasily, what is the matter with you?" asked Werner, rushing toward him.

Vasily kept silence, shivering the while. The policeman, vexed and even chagrined, explained:

"I wanted to sustain him, and he—he . . ."

"Come, Vasily, I will sustain you," said Werner.

He tried to take his comrade's arm. But the latter repulsed him, and cried louder than ever.

"Vasily, it is I, Werner!"

"I know! Don't touch me! I want to walk alone!"

And, still trembling, he entered the carriage and sat down in a corner. Werner leaned toward Musya, and asked in a low voice, designating Vasily with his eyes:

"Well, how are things with him?"

"Badly!" answered Musya, in a whisper. "He is already dead. Tell me, Werner, does death really exist?"

"I don't know, Musya; but I think not!" answered Werner in a serious and thoughtful tone.

"That is what I thought! And he? I suffered on his account during the whole ride; it seemed to me that I was travelling beside a dead man."

"I don't know, Musya. Perhaps death still exists for some. Later it will not exist at all. For me, for instance, death has existed, but now it exists no more."

The slightly pallid cheeks of Musya reddened.

"It has existed for you, Werner? For you?"

"Yes, but no more. As for you!"

They heard a sound at the door of the railway carriage; Michka the Tzigane entered spitting, breathing noisily, and making a racket with his boot-heels. He glanced about him, and stopped short.

"There is no room left, officer!" he declared to the fatigued and irritated policeman. "See to it that I travel comfortably, otherwise I will not go with you! Rather hang me right here, to the lamp-post! Oh, the scoundrels, what a carriage they have given me! Do you call this a carriage? The devil's guts, yes, but not a carriage!"

But suddenly he lowered his head, stretched out his neck, and advanced towards the other prisoners. From the frame of his bushy hair and beard his black eyes shot a savage, sharp, and rather crazy look.

"Oh, my God!" he cried; "so this is where we are! How do you do, sir!"

He sat down opposite Werner, holding out his hand; then, with a wink, he leaned over and swiftly passed his hand across his companion's neck:

"You too? Eh?"

"Yes!" smiled Werner.

"All?"

"All!"

"Oh! oh!" said the Tzigane, showing his teeth. He examined the other prisoners with a swift glance, which nevertheless dwelt longest on Musya and Yanson.

"On account of the Minister?"

"Yes. And you?"

"Oh, sir, my case is quite another story. I am not so distinguished! I, sir, am a brigand, an assassin. That makes no difference, sir; move up a little to make room for me; it is not my fault that they have put me in your company! In the other world there will be room for all."

He took the measure of all the prisoners with a watchful, distrustful, and savage gaze. But they looked at him without a word, seriously and even with evident compassion. Again he showed his teeth, and slapped Werner several times on the knee.

"So that is how it is, sir! As they say in the song:

" 'Take care to make no sound, O forest of green oaks!' "

"Why do you call me sir, when all of us . . ."

"You are right!" acquiesced the Tzigane, with satisfaction. "Why should you be sir, since you are to be hanged beside me? There sits the real sir!"

He pointed his finger at the silent policeman.

"And your comrade yonder, he doesn't seem to be enjoying himself hugely!" he added, looking at Vasily. "Say there, you are afraid?"

"No!" answered a tongue that moved with difficulty.

"Well, then, don't be so disturbed; there is nothing to

be ashamed of. It is only dogs that wag their tails and show their teeth when they are going to be hanged; you are a man. And this marionette, who is he? He certainly is not one of your crowd?"

His eyes danced incessantly; constantly, with a hissing sound, he spat out his abundant and sweetish saliva. Yanson, doubled up motionless in a corner, slightly shook the ears of his bald fur cap, but said nothing. Werner answered for him.

"He killed his employer."

"My God!" exclaimed the Tzigane, in astonishment. "How is it that they permit such birds as that to kill people?"

For a moment he looked at Musya stealthily; then suddenly he turned, and fixed his straight and piercing gaze upon her.

"Miss! Say there, Miss! what is the matter with you? Your cheeks are pink, and you are laughing! Look, she is really laughing! Look! Look!" And he seized Werner's knee with his hooked fingers.

Blushing and somewhat confused, Musya squarely returned the gaze of the attentive and savage eyes that questioned her. All kept silence.

The little cars bounced speedily along the narrow track. At every turn or grade-crossing the whistle blew, the engineer being afraid of crushing somebody. Was it not atrocious to think that so much care and effort, in short all human activity, was being expended in taking men to be hanged? The maddest thing in the world was being done with an air of simplicity and reasonableness. Cars were running; people were sitting in them as usual, travelling as people ordinarily travel. Then there would be a halt as usual: "Five minutes' stop."

And then would come death—eternity—the great mystery.

XII

THE ARRIVAL

The train advanced rapidly.

Sergey Golovin remembered to have spent the summer, some years before, in a little country-house along this very line. He had often travelled the road by day and by night, and knew it well. Closing his eyes, he could fancy himself returning by the last train, after staying out late at night with friends.

"I shall arrive soon," thought he, straightening up: and his eyes met the dark grated window. Around him nothing stirred. Only the Tzigane kept on spitting, and his eyes ran the length of the car, seeming to touch the doors and the soldiers.

"It is cold," said Vasily Kashirin between his thin lips, which seemed frozen.

Tanya Kovalchuk bestirred herself in a maternal fashion: "Here's a very warm kerchief to wrap around your . . ."

"Neck?" asked Sergey, and he was frightened by his own question.

"What matters it, Vasya? Take it."

"Wrap yourself up. You will be warmer," added Werner. He turned to Yanson, and asked him tenderly:

"And aren't you cold, too?"

"Werner, perhaps he wants to smoke. Comrade, do you want to smoke?" asked Musya. "We have some tobacco."

"Yes, I want to."

"Give him a cigarette, Sergey," said Werner.

But Sergey was already holding out his cigarette-case.

And all began to watch tenderly Yanson's clumsy fingers as they took the cigarette and struck the match, and the little curl of bluish smoke that issued from his mouth.

"Thank you," said Yanson. "It is good."

"How queer it is," said Sergey.

"How queer what is?" asked Werner.

"The cigarette," answered Sergey, unwilling to say all that he thought.

Yanson held the cigarette between his pale and living fingers. With astonishment he looked at it. And all fixed their gaze on this tiny bit of paper, on this little curl of smoke rising from the gray ashes.

The cigarette went out.

"It is out," said Tanya.

"Yes, it is out."

"The devil take it!" said Werner, looking anxiously at Yanson, whose hand, holding the cigarette, hung as if dead. Suddenly the Tzigane turned, placed his face close to Werner's, and, looking into the whites of his eyes, whispered:

"Suppose, sir, we were to attack the soldiers of the convoy? What do you think about it?"

"No," answered Werner.

"Why? It is better to die fighting. I will strike a blow, they strike back, and I shall die without noticing it."

"No, it is not necessary," said Werner. And he turned to Yanson:

"Why don't you smoke?"

Yanson's dried-up face wrinkled pitifully, as if someone had pulled the threads that moved the creases in his face. As in a nightmare, Yanson sobbed in a colorless voice, shedding no tears:

"I can't smoke. Ah! Ah! Ah! I must not be hanged. Ah! Ah! Ah!"

Everybody turned toward him. Tanya, weeping copiously, stroked his arms and readjusted his fur cap.

"My dear, my friend, don't cry, my friend! My poor friend!"

Suddenly the cars bumped into one another and began to slow up. The prisoners rose, but immediately sat down again.

"Here we are," said Sergey.

It was as if all the air had suddenly been pumped out of the car. It became difficult to breathe. Their swollen hearts became heavy in their breasts, rose to their throats, beat desperately and their blood, in its terror, seemed to revolt. Their eyes looked at the trembling floor, their ears listened to the slowly-turning wheels, which began to turn more slowly still, and gently stopped.

The train halted.

The prisoners were plunged into a strange stupor. They did not suffer. They seemed to live an unconscious life. Their corporeal being was absent; only its phantom moved about, voiceless but speaking, silent but walking. They went out. They arranged themselves in pairs, breathing in the fresh air of the woods. Like one in a dream, Yanson struggled awkwardly: they dragged him from the car.

"Are we to go on foot?" asked someone, almost gaily.

"It isn't far," answered a careless voice.

Without a word they advanced into the forest, along a damp and muddy road. Their feet slipped and sank into the snow, and their hands sometimes clung involuntarily to those of their comrades. Breathing with difficulty the soldiers marched in single file, on either side of the prisoners. An irritated voice complained:

"Could they not have cleared the road? It is difficult to advance."

A deferential voice answered:

"It was cleaned, Your Honour, but it is thawing. There is nothing to be done."

The prisoners began to recover their consciousness. Now they seemed to grasp the idea: "It is true, they could not clean the roads"; now it became obscured again, and there remained only the sense of smell, which perceived with singular keenness the strong and healthy odor of the forest; and now again all became very clear and comprehensible, the forest, and the night, and the road . . . and the certainty that very soon, in a minute, implacable death would lay its hands upon them. And little by little a whispering began:

"It is almost four o'clock."

"I told you so. We started too early."

"The sun rises at five."

"That's right, at five: we should have waited."

They halted in the twilight. Near by, behind the trees, whose huge shadows were waving on the ground, swung silently two lanterns. There the gallows had been erected.

"I have lost one of my rubbers," said Sergey.

"Well?" asked Werner, not understanding.

"I have lost it. I am cold."

"Where is Vasily?"

"I don't know. There he is."

Vasily was standing close by them, gloomy and motionless.

"Where is Musya?"

"Here I am. Is that you, Werner?"

They looked at each other, their eyes avoiding the silent and terrible significant swaying of the lanterns. At the left the thin forest seemed to be growing lighter. And beyond, something vast and gray and flat appeared, whence came a moist breeze.

"That is the sea," said Sergey, sucking in the damp air. "That is the sea."

Musya answered by a line from the song:

> "My love as broad as is the sea."

"What did you say, Musya?"

> "The shores of life cannot contain
> My love as broad as is the sea."

" 'My love as broad as is the sea,' " repeated Sergey, pensively.

" 'My love as broad as is the sea,' " echoed Werner. And suddenly he exclaimed in astonishment:

"Musya, my little Musya, how young you still are!"

Just then, close to Werner's ear, sounded the breathless and passionate voice of the Tzigane:

"Sir, sir, look at the forest. My God! What is all that? And yonder! The lanterns! My God, is that the scaffold?"

Werner looked at him. The convulsed features of the unfortunate man were frightful to see.

"We must say our farewells," said Tanya.

"Wait! They still have to read the sentence. Where is Yanson?"

Yanson lay stretched in the snow, surrounded by people. A strong smell of ammonia filled the air around him.

"Well, doctor, will you soon be through?" asked someone, impatiently.

"It's nothing. A fainting fit. Rub his ears with snow. He is better already. You can read."

The light of a dark lantern fell upon the paper and the ungloved white hands. Both paper and hands trembled. The voice also.

"Gentlemen, perhaps it is better not to read. You all know the sentence."

"Do not read!" answered Werner for all; and the light immediately went out.

The condemned refused also the services of the priest. Said the Tzigane:

"No nonsense, father; you will forgive me, they will hang me."

The broad dark silhouette of the priest took a few steps backward and disappeared. The day was breaking. The snow became whiter, the faces of the condemned darker, and the forest barer and sadder.

"Gentlemen, you will go in pairs, choosing your companion. But I beg you to make haste."

Werner pointed to Yanson, who now was standing again, sustained by two soldiers.

"I will go with him. You, Sergey, take Vasily. You g first."

"All right."

"I am going with you, Musya," said Tanya. "Come, let us kiss each other!"

Quickly they kissed all round. The Tzigane kissed forcibly; they felt his teeth. Yanson kissed gently and softly, with mouth half open. He did not seem to understand what he was doing. When Sergey and Kashirin had taken a few steps, the latter stopped suddenly, and in a loud voice, which seemed strange and unfamiliar, shouted:

"Good-bye, comrades."

"Good-bye, comrade," they answered him.

The two started off again. All was quiet. The lanterns behind the trees became motionless. They expected to hear a cry, a voice, some sound or other, but there as here all was calm.

"Oh! My God!" exclaimed someone hoarsely.

They turned around: it was Tzigane, crying desperately:

"They are going to hang us."

He struggled, clutching the air with his hands, and cried again:

"God! Am I to be hanged alone? My God!"

His convulsive hands gripped the hands of Werner, and he continued:

"Sir, my dear sir, my good sir. You will come with me, won't you?"

Werner, his face drawn with sorrow, answered:

"I cannot; I am with Yanson."

"Oh! My God! then I shall be alone. Why? Why?"

Musya took a step toward him, and said softly:

"I will go with you."

The Tzigane drew back, and fixed his big swollen eyes upon her:

"Will you?"

"Yes."

"But you are so little! You are not afraid of me? No, I don't want you to. I will go alone."

"But I am not afraid of you."

The Tzigane grinned.

"Don't you know that I am a brigand? And you are willing to go with me? Think a moment. I shall not be angry if you refuse."

Musya was silent. And in the faint light of the dawn her face seemed to take on a luminous and mystic pallor. Suddenly she advanced rapidly toward the Tzigane, and, taking his head in her hands, kissed him vigorously. He took her by the shoulders, put her away a little, and then kissed her loudly on her cheeks and eyes.

The soldier nearest them stopped, opened his hands, and let his gun fall. But he did not stoop to pick it up. He stood still for a moment, then turned suddenly, and began to walk into the forest.

"Where are you going?" shouted his comrade, in a frightened voice. "Stay!"

But the other painfully endeavored to advance. Suddenly he clutched the air with his hands, and fell, face downward.

"Milksop, pick up your gun, or I will pick it up for you," cried the Tzigane, firmly. "You don't know your duty. Have you never seen a man die?"

Again the lantern swung. The turn of Werner and Yanson had come.

"Good-bye, sir!" said the Tzigane, in a loud voice. "We shall meet again in the other world. When you see me there, don't turn away from me."

"Good-bye!"

"I must not be hanged," said Yanson again, in a faint voice.

But Werner grasped his hand, and Yanson took a few steps. Then he was seen to sink into the snow. They bent over him, lifted him up, and carried him, while he weakly struggled in the soldiers' arms.

And again the yellow lanterns became motionless.

"And I, Musya? Am I then to go alone?" said Tanya, sadly. "We have lived together, and now . . ."

"Tanya, my good Tanya!"

The Tzigane hotly interrupted, holding Musya as if he feared that they might tear her from him.

"Miss," he cried, "you are able to go alone. You have a pure soul. You can go alone where you like. But I cannot. I am a bandit. I cannot go alone. 'Where are you going?' they will say to me, 'you who have killed, you who have stolen?' For I have stolen horses, too, Miss. And with her I shall be as if I were with an innocent child. Do you understand?"

"Yes, I understand. Go on then! Let me kiss you once more, Musya."

"Kiss each other! Kiss each other!" said the Tzigane. "You are women. You must say good-bye to each other."

Then came the turn of Musya and the Tzigane. The

woman walked carefully, her feet slipping, lifting her skirts by force of habit. Holding her with a strong hand, and feeling the ground with his foot, the man accompanied her to death. The lights became motionless. Around Tanya all was tranquil again, and solitary. The soldiers, gray in the dawn's pale light, were silent.

"I am left alone," said Tanya. And she sighed. "Sergey is dead, Werner and Vasily are dead. And Musya is dying. I am alone. Soldiers, my little soldiers, you see, I am alone, alone . . ."

The sun appeared above the sea. . . .

They placed the bodies in boxes, and started off with them. With elongated necks, bulging eyes, and blue tongues protruding from their mouths, the dead retraced the road by which, living, they had come.

And the snow was still soft, and the air of the forest was still pure and balmy.

On the white road lay the black rubber that Sergey had lost. . . .

Thus it was that men greeted the rising sun.

THE RED LAUGH

———— ♦♦♦ ————

By L. N. Andreyev

PART I

FRAGMENT I

. . . HORROR and madness.

I felt it for the first time as we were marching along the road—marching incessantly for ten hours without stopping, never diminishing our step, never waiting to pick up those that had fallen, but leaving them to the enemy, that was moving behind us in a compact mass only three or four hours later effacing the marks of our feet by their own.

It was very sultry. I do not know how many degrees there were—120°, 140°, or more— I only know that the heat was incessant, hopelessly even and profound. The sun was so enormous, so fiery and terrible, that it seemed as if the earth had drawn nearer to it and would soon be burnt up altogether in its merciless rays. Our eyes had ceased to look. The small shrunk pupil, as small as a poppy-seed, sought in vain for darkness under the closed eyelid; the sun pierced the thin covering and penetrated into the tortured brain in a blood-red glow. But, nevertheless, it was better so: with closed eyelids, and for a long time, perhaps for several

437

hours, I walked along with my eyes shut, hearing the multitude moving around me: the heavy, uneven tread of many feet, men's and horses', the grinding of iron wheels, crushing the small stones, somebody's deep strained breathing and the dry smacking of parched lips. But I heard no word. All were silent, as if an army of dumb people were moving, and when anyone fell down, he fell in silence; others stumbled against his body, fell down and rose mutely, and, without turning their heads, marched on, as though these dumb men were also blind and deaf. I stumbled and fell several times and then involuntarily opened my eyes, and all that I saw seemed a wild fiction, the terrible raving of a mad world. The air vibrated at a white-hot temperature, the stones seemed to be trembling silently, ready to flow, and in the distance, at a curve of the road, the files of men, guns and horses seemed detached from the earth, and trembled like a mass of jelly in their onward progress, and it seemed to me that they were not living people that I saw before me, but an army of incorporate shadows.

The enormous, near, terrible sun lit up thousands of tiny blinding suns on every gun-barrel and metal plate, and these suns, as fiery-white and sharp as the white-hot points of the bayonets, crept into your eyes from every side. And the consuming, burning heat penetrated into your body— into your very bones and brain—and at times it seemed to me that it was not a head that swayed upon my shoulders, but a strange and extraordinary globe, heavy and light, belonging to somebody else, and horrible.

And then—then I suddenly remembered my home: a corner of my room, a scrap of light-blue wall-paper, and a dusty untouched water-bottle on my table—on my table, which has one leg shorter than the others, and had a small piece of paper folded under it. While in the next room— and I cannot see them—are my wife and little son. If I had had the power to cry out, I would have done so—so wonderful was this simple and peaceful picture—the scrap of light-blue wall-paper and dusty untouched water-bottle. I know that I stood still and lifted up my arms, but somebody gave me a push from behind, and I quickly moved on, thrusting the crowd aside, and hastening whither I knew not, but feeling now neither heat nor fatigue. And I marched on thus for a long time through the endless mute files, past red sunburnt necks, almost touching the helplessly lowered hot bayonets, when suddenly the thought of what I was doing, whither I was hastening, stopped me. I turned aside in the same hasty way, forced my way to the open, clambered across a gulley and sat down on a stone in a preoccupied manner, as if that rough hot stone was the aim of all my strivings.

And then I felt it for the first time. I clearly perceived that all these people, marching silently on in the glaring sun, torpid from fatigue and heat, swaying and falling— that they were all mad. They did not know whither they were going, they did not know what that sun was for, they did not know anything. It was not heads that they had on their shoulders, but strange and terrible globes. There— I saw a man in the same plight as I, pushing his way hurriedly through the rows and falling down; there—another, and a third. Suddenly a horse's head appeared above the throng with bloodshot and senseless eyes and a wide-open grinning mouth, that only hinted at a terrible unearthly cry; this head appeared, fell down, and for an instant the crowd stopped, growing denser in that spot; I could hear hoarse, hollow voices, then a shot, and again the silent end- less march continued.

An hour passed as I sat on that stone, but the multitude still moved on past me, and the air and earth and the dis- tant phantom-like ranks trembled as before. And again the burning heat pierced my body and I forgot what for an instant I had pictured to myself; and the multitudes moved on past me, but I did not know who they were. An hour ago I was alone on the stone, but now I was surrounded by a group of grey people; some lying motionless, perhaps dead; others were sitting up and staring vacantly at those passing by. Some had guns and resembled soldiers; others were stripped almost naked, and the skin on their bodies was so livid, that one did not care to look at it. Not far from me someone was lying with his bared back upturned.

One could see by the unconcerned manner in which he had buried his face in the sharp burning sand, by the white- ness of the palm of his upturned hand, that he was dead, but his back was as red as if he were alive, and only a slight yellowish tinge, such as one sees on smoked meat, spoke of death. I wanted to move away from him, but I had not the strength, and, tottering from weakness, I con- tinued looking at the endless phantom-like swaying files of men. By the condition of my head I knew that I should soon have a sunstroke too, but I awaited it calmly, as in a dream, where death seems only a stage on the path of wonderful and confused visions.

And I saw a soldier part from the crowd and direct his steps in a decided manner towards us. For an instant I lost sight of him in a ditch, but when he reappeared and moved on towards us, his gait was unsteady, and in his endeavors to control his restlessly tossing body, one felt he was using his last strength. He was coming so straight upon me that I grew frightened and, breaking through the heavy torpor that enveloped my brain, I asked: "What do you want?"

He stopped short, as if it was only a word that he was waiting for, and stood before me, enormous, bearded, in a torn shirt. He had no gun, his trousers hung only by one button, and through a slit in them one could see his white body. He flung his arms and legs about and he was visibly trying to control them, but could not; the instant he brought his arms together, they fell apart again.

"What is the matter? You had better sit down," I said.

But he continued standing, vainly trying to gather himself together, and stared at me in silence. Involuntarily I got up from the stone and, tottering, looked into his eyes —and saw an abyss of horror and insanity in them. Everybody's pupils were shrunk—but his had dilated and covered his whole eye: what a sea of fire he must have seen through those enormous black windows! Maybe I had only imagined it, maybe in his look there was only death—but, no, I was not mistaken—in those black, bottomless pupils, surrounded by a narrow orange-colored rim, like a bird's eye, there was more than death, more than the horror of death. "Go away!" I cried falling back. "Go away!" And as if he was only waiting for a word, enormous, disorderly and mute as before, he suddenly fell down upon me, knocking me over.

With a shudder I freed my legs from under him, jumped up and longed to run—somewhere away from men into the sunlit, unpeopled and quivering distance, when suddenly, on the left-hand side, a cannon boomed forth from a hill-top, and directly after it two others, like an echo. And somewhere above our heads a shell flew past with a gladsome, many-voiced scr-e-e-ch and howl.

We were outflanked.

The murderous heat, fear and fatigue disappeared instantly. My thoughts cleared, my mind grew clear and sharp, and when I ran up, out of breath, to the files of men drawing up, I saw serene, almost joyous faces, heard hoarse, but loud voices, orders, jokes. The sun seemed to have drawn itself up higher so as not to be in the way, and had grown dim and still—and again a shell, like a witch, cut the air with a gladsome scr-e-e-ch.

I came up. . . .

FRAGMENT II

. . . .NEARLY all the horses and men. The same in the eighth battery. In our twelfth battery, towards the end of the third day, there remained only three guns—all the others being disabled—six men and one officer, myself. We had neither slept nor eaten for twenty hours; for three days and nights a Satanic roar and howl enveloped us in a cloud of insanity, isolated us from the earth, the sky and ourselves—and we, the living, wandered about like lunatics. The dead—they lay still, while we moved about doing our duty, talking and laughing, and we were—like lunatics. All our movements were quick and certain, our orders clear, the execution of them precise, but if you had suddenly asked any one of us who we were, undoubtedly we should not have been able to find an answer in our troubled brain. As in a dream all faces seemed familiar, and all that was going on seemed quite familiar and natural—as if it had happened before; but when I looked closely at any face or gun, or began listening to the din, I was struck by the novelty and endless mystery of everything. Night approached imperceptibly, and before we had time to notice it and wonder where it had come from, the sun was again burning above our heads. And only from those who came to our battery we learnt that it was the third day of the battle that was dawning, and instantly forgot it again: to us it appeared as one endless day without any beginning, sometimes dark, sometimes bright, but always incomprehensible and blind. And nobody was afraid of death, for nobody understood what death was.

On the third or fourth night—I do not remember which —I lay down for a minute behind the breastwork, and, as soon as I shut my eyes, the same familiar and extraordinary picture stood before them: the scrap of light-blue wall-paper and the dusty untouched water-bottle on my table. While in the next room—and I could not see them—were my wife and little son. But this time a lamp with a green shade was burning on the table, so it must have been evening or night. The picture stood motionless, and I contemplated it very calmly and attentively for a long time, letting my eyes rest on the light reflected in the crystal of the water-bottle, and on the wall-paper, and wondered why my son was not asleep: for it was night and time for him to go to bed. Then

I again began examining the wall-paper: every spiral, silvery flower, square and line—and never imagined that I knew my room so well. Now and then I opened my eyes and saw the black sky with beautiful fiery stripes upon it, then shut them again and saw once more the wall-paper, the bright water-bottle, and wondered why my son was not asleep, for it was night and time for him to go to bed. Once a shell burst not far from me, making my legs give a jerk, and somebody cried out loudly, louder than the bursting of the shell, and I said to myself: "Somebody is killed," but I did not get up and did not tear my eyes away from the light-blue wall-paper and the water-bottle.

Afterwards I got up, moved about, gave orders, looked at the men's faces, trained the guns, and kept on wondering why my son was not asleep. Once I asked the sergeant, and he explained it to me at length with great detail, and we kept nodding our heads. And he laughed, and his left eye-brow kept twitching, while his eye winked cunningly at somebody behind us. Behind us were somebody's feet—and nothing more.

By this time it was quite light, when suddenly there fell a drop of rain. Rain—just the same as at home, the most ordinary little drops of rain. But it was so sudden and out of place, and we were so afraid of getting wet, that we left our guns, stopped firing, and tried to find shelter any-where we could.

The sergeant with whom I had only just been speaking got under the gun-carriage and dozed off, although he might have been crushed any minute; the stout artilleryman, for some reason or other, began undressing a corpse, while I began running about the battery in search of something—a cloak or an umbrella. And the same instant over the whole enormous area, where the rain-cloud had burst, a wonderful stillness fell. A belated shrapnel-shot shrieked and burst, and everything grew still—so still that one could hear the stout artilleryman panting, and the drops of rain splashing upon the stones and guns. And this soft and continuous sound, that reminded one of autumn—the smell of the moist earth and the stillness—seemed to tear the bloody, savage nightmare asunder for an instant; and when I glanced at the wet, glistening gun it unexpectedly reminded me of something dear and peaceful—my childhood, or perhaps my first love. But in the distance a gun boomed forth particularly loud, and the spell of the momentary lull disappeared; the men began coming out of their hiding-places as suddenly as they had hid themselves; a gun roared, then another, and once again the weary brain was enveloped by bloody, indissoluble gloom. And nobody noticed when the rain stopped. I only remember seeing the water rolling off the fat, sunken yellow face of the killed artilleryman; so I supposed it rained for rather a long time. . . .

. . . . Before me stood a young volunteer holding his hand to his cap and reporting to me that the general wanted us to retain our position for only two hours more, when we should be relieved. I was wondering why my son was not in bed, and answered that I could hold on as much as he wished. But suddenly I became interested in the young man's face, probably because of its unusual and striking pallor. I never saw anything whiter than that face: even the dead have more colour than that young, beardless face had. I suppose he became terrified on his way to us, and could not recover himself; and in holding his hands to his cap he was only making an effort to drive away his mad fear by a simple and habitual gesture.

"Are you afraid?" I asked, touching his elbow. But his elbow seemed as if made of wood, and he only smiled and remained silent. Better to say, his lips alone were twitching into a smile, while his eyes were full of youth and terror only—nothing more.

"Are you afraid?" I repeated kindly. His lips twitched, trying to frame a word, and the same instant there happened something incomprehensible, monstrous and supernatural. I felt a draught of warm air upon my right cheek that made me sway—that is all—while before my eyes, in place of the white face, there was something short, blunt and red, and out of it the blood was gushing as out of an uncorked bottle, such as is drawn on badly executed signboards. And that short red and flowing "something" still seemed to be smiling a sort of smile, a toothless laugh—a red laugh.

I recognised it—that red laugh. I had been searching for it, and I had found it—that red laugh. Now I understood what there was in all those mutilated, torn, strange bodies. It was a red laugh. It was in the sky, it was in the sun, and soon it was going to overspread the whole earth—that red laugh!

While they, with precision and calmness, like lunatics. . . .

FRAGMENT III

THEY say there are a great number of madmen in our army as well as in the enemy's. Four lunatic wards have been opened. When I was on the staff our adjutant showed me. . . .

FRAGMENT IV

. . . COILED round like snakes. He saw the wire, chopped through at one end, cut the air and coil itself round three soldiers. The barbs tore their uniforms and stuck into their bodies, and, shrieking, the soldiers spun round in frenzy, two of them dragging the third, who was already dead, after them. Then only one remained alive, and he tried to push the two that were dead away from him; but they trailed after him, whirling and rolling over each other and over him; and suddenly all three became motionless.

He told me that no less than two thousand men were lost at that one wire entanglement. While they were hacking at the wire and getting entangled in its serpentine coils, they were pelted by an incessant rain of balls and grapeshot. He assured me it was very terrifying, and if only they had known in which direction to run, that attack would have ended in a panic flight. But ten or twelve continuous lines of wire and the struggle with it, a whole labyrinth of pitfalls with stakes driven in at the bottom, had muddled them so, that they were quite incapable of defining the direction of escape.

Some, like men blind, fell into the funnel-shaped pits, and hung upon the sharp stakes, pierced through the stomach, twitching convulsively and dancing like toy clowns; they were crushed down by fresh bodies, and soon the whole pit filled to the edges, and presented a writhing mass of bleeding bodies, dead and living. Hands thrust themselves out of it in all directions, the fingers working convulsively, catching at everything; and those who once got caught in that trap could not get back again: hundreds of fingers, strong and blind, like the claws of a lobster, gripped them firmly by the legs, caught at their clothes, threw them down upon themselves, gouged out their eyes and throttled them. Many seemed as if they were intoxicated, and ran straight at the wire, got caught in it, and remained shrieking, until a bullet finished them.

Generally speaking, they all seemed like people intoxicated: some swore dreadfully, others laughed when the wire caught them by the arm or leg and died there and then. He himself, although he had had nothing to eat or drink since the morning, felt very queer. His head swam, and there were moments when the feeling of terror in him changed to wild rapture, and from rapture again to terror. When somebody struck up a song at his side, he caught up the tune, and soon a whole unanimous chorus broke forth. He did not remember what they sang, only that it was lively in a dancing strain. Yes, they sang, while all around them was red with blood. The very sky seemed to be red, and one could have thought that a catastrophe had overwhelmed the universe—a strange disappearance of colors: the light-blue and green and other habitual peaceful colors had disappeared, while the sun blazed forth in a red flare-light.

"The red laugh," said I.

But he did not understand.

"Yes, and they laughed, as I told you before, like people intoxicated. Perhaps they even danced. There was something of the sort. At least the movements of those three resembled dancing."

He remembers distinctly, when he was shot through the chest and fell, his legs twitched for some time until he lost consciousness, as if he were dancing to music. And at the present moment, when he thinks of that attack, a strange feeling comes over him: partly fear and partly the desire to experience it all over again.

"And get another ball in your chest?" asked I.

"There now, why should I get a ball each time? But it would not be half so bad, old boy, to get a medal for bravery."

He was lying on his back with a waxen face, sharp nose, prominent cheek-bones and sunken eyes. He was lying looking like a corpse and dreaming of a medal! Mortification had already set in; he had a high temperature, and in three days' time he was to be thrown into the grave to join the dead; nevertheless he lay smiling dreamingly and talking about a medal.

"Have you telegraphed your mother?" I asked.

He glanced at me with terror, animosity and anger, and did not answer. I was silent, and then the groans and ravings of the wounded became audible. But when I rose to go, he caught my hand in his hot, but still strong one, and fixed his sunken burning eyes upon me in a lost and distressed way.

"What does it all mean, ay? What does it all mean?"

asked he in a frightened and persistent manner, pulling at my hand.

"What?"

"Everything . . . in general. Now, she is waiting for me. But I cannot. My country—is it possible to make her understand, what my country means?"

"The red laugh," answered I.

"Ah! you are always joking, but I am serious. It is indispensable to explain it; but is it possible to make her understand? If you only knew what she says in her letters! —what she writes. And you know her words—are greyhaired. And you—" he looked curiously at my head, pointed his finger and suddenly breaking into a laugh said: "Why, you have grown bald. Have you noticed it?"

"There are no looking-glasses here."

"Many have grown bald and grey. Look here, give me a looking-glass. Give me one! I feel white hair growing out of my head. Give me a looking-glass!" He became delirious, crying and shouting out, and I left the hospital.

That same evening we got up an entertainment—a sad and strange entertainment, at which, amongst the guests, the shadows of the dead assisted. We decided to gather in the evening and have tea, as if we were at home, at a picnic. We got a samovar, we even got a lemon and glasses, and established ourselves under a tree, as if we were at home, at a picnic. Our companions arrived noisily in twos and threes, talking, joking and full of gleeful expectation—but soon grew silent, and avoided looking at each other, for there was something fearful in this meeting of spared men. In tatters, dirty, itching, as if we were covered by a dreadful ringworm, with hair neglected, thin and worn, having lost all familiar and habitual aspect, we seemed to see each other for the first time as we gathered round the samovar, and seeing each other, we grew terrified. In vain I looked for a familiar face in this group of disconcerted men—I could not find one. These men, restless, hasty and jerky in their movements, starting at every sound, constantly looking for something behind their backs, trying to fill up that mysterious void into which they were too terrified to look, by superfluous gesticulations—were new, strange men, whom I did not know. And their voices sounded different, articulating the words with difficulty in jerks, easily passing into angry shouts or senseless irrepressible laughter at the slightest provocation. And everything around us was strange to us. The tree was strange, and the sunset strange, and the water strange, with a peculiar taste and smell, as if we had left the earth and entered into a new world together with the dead —a world of mysterious phenomena and ominous sombre shadows. The sunset was yellow and cold; black, unillumined, motionless clouds hung heavily over it, while the earth under it was black, and our faces in that ill-omened light seemed yellow, like the faces of the dead. We all sat watching the samovar, but it went out, its sides reflecting the yellowishness and menace of the sunset, and it seemed also an unfamiliar, dead and incomprehensible object.

"Where are we?" asked somebody, and uneasiness and fear sounded in his voice. Somebody sighed; somebody convulsively cracked his fingers; somebody laughed; somebody jumped up and began walking quickly round the table. These last days one could often meet with such men, who were always walking hastily, almost running, at times strangely silent, at times mumbling something in an uncanny way.

"At the war," answered he who had laughed, and again burst into a hollow, lingering laugh, as if something was choking him.

"What is he laughing at?" asked somebody indignantly. "Look here, stop it!"

The other choked once more, gave a titter and stopped obediently.

It was growing dark, the cloud seemed to be settling down on the earth, and we could with difficulty distinguish each other's yellow phantom-like faces. Somebody asked,—

"And where is Fatty-legs?"

"Fatty-legs" we called a fellow-officer, who, being short, wore enormous water-tight boots.

"He was here just now. Fatty-legs, where are you?"

"Fatty-legs, don't hide. We can smell your boots."

Everybody laughed, but their laugh was interrupted by a rough, indignant voice that sounded out of the darkness:

"Stop that! Are you not ashamed? Fatty-legs was killed this morning reconnoitring."

"He was here just now. It must be a mistake."

"You imagined it. Heigh-ho! you there, behind the samovar, cut me a slice of lemon."

"And me!"

"And me!"

"The lemon is finished."

"How is that, boys?" sounded a gentle, hurt voice, full

of distress and almost crying; "why, I only came for the sake of the lemon."

The other again burst into a hollow and lingering laugh, and nobody checked him. But he soon stopped. He gave a snigger, and was silent. Somebody said:

"To-morrow we begin the advance on the enemy."

But several voices cried out angrily:

"Nonsense, advance on the enemy, indeed!"

"But you know yourself——"

"Shut up. As if we cannot talk of something else."

The sunset faded. The cloud lifted, and it seemed to grow lighter; the faces became more familiar, and he, who kept circling round us, grew calmer and sat down.

"I wonder what it's like at home now?" asked he vaguely, and in his voice there sounded a guilty smile.

And once again all became terrible, incomprehensible and strange—so intensely so that we were filled with horror, almost to the verge of losing consciousness. And we all began talking and shouting at the same time, bustling about, moving our glasses, touching each other's shoulders, hands, knees—and all at once became silent, giving way before the incomprehensible.

"At home?" cried somebody out of the darkness. His voice was hoarse and quivering with emotion, fear and hatred. And some of the words would not come out, as if he had forgotten how to say them.

"At home? What home? Why, is there home anywhere? Don't interrupt me or else I shall fire. At home I used to take a bath every day—can you understand?—a bath with water—water up to the very edges. While now—I do not even wash my face every day. My head is covered with scurf, and my whole body itches and over it crawl, crawl . . . I am going mad from dirt, while you talk of—home! I am like an animal, I despise myself, I cannot recognise myself and death is not at all terrifying. You tear my brain with your shrapnel-shots. Aim at what you will, all hit my brain—and you can speak of—home. What home? Streets, windows, people, but I would not go into the street now for anything. I should be ashamed to. You brought a samovar here, but I was ashamed to look at it."

The other laughed again. Somebody called out:

"D—n it all! I shall go home."

"Home?"

"You don't understand what duty is!"

"Home? Listen! he wants to go home!"

There was a burst of laughter and of painful shouts—and again all became silent—giving way before the incomprehensible. And then not only I, but every one of us felt *that*. It was coming towards us out of those dark, mysterious and strange fields; it was rising from out of those obscure dark ravines, where, maybe, the forgotten and lost among the stones were still dying; it was flowing from the strange, unfamiliar sky. We stood around the dying-out samovar in silence, losing consciousness from horror, while an enormous, shapeless shadow that had arisen above the world, looked down upon us from the sky with a steady and silent gaze. Suddenly, quite close to us, probably at the Commanders' house, music burst forth, and the frenzied, joyous, loud sounds seemed to flash out into the night and stillness. The band played with frenzied mirth and defiance, hurriedly, discordantly, too loudly, and too joyously, and one could feel that those who were playing, and those who were listening, saw as we did, that same enormous, shapeless shadow, risen above the world. And it was clear the player on the trumpet carried in himself, in his very brain and ears, that same enormous dumb shadow. The abrupt and broken sound tossed about, jumping and running away from the others, quivering with horror and insanity in its lonesomeness. And the other sounds seemed to be looking round at it, so clumsily they ran, stumbling, falling, and again rising in a disorderly crowd—too loud, too joyous, too close to the black ravines, where most probably the forgotten and lost among the boulders were still dying.

And we stood for a long time around the cold samovar and were silent.

FRAGMENT V

. . . I was already asleep when the doctor roused me by pushing me cautiously. I woke, and jumping up, cried out, as we all did when anybody wakened us, and rushed to the entrance of our tent. But the doctor held me firmly by the arm, excusing himself:

"I frightened you, forgive me. I know you want to sleep . . ."

"Five days and nights . . ." I muttered, dozing off. I fell asleep and slept, as it seemed to me for a long time, when the doctor again began speaking, poking me cautiously in the ribs and legs.

"But it is very urgent. Dear fellow, please—it is so pres

ing. I keep thinking . . . I cannot . . . I keep thinking, that some of the wounded were left . . ."

"What wounded? Why, you were bringing them in the whole day long. Leave me in peace. It is not fair—I have not slept for five days!"

"Dear boy, don't be angry," muttered the doctor, awkwardly putting my cap on my head; "everybody is asleep, it's impossible to rouse anybody. I've got hold of an engine and seven carriages, but we're in want of men. I understand. . . . Dear fellow, I implore you. Everybody is asleep and everybody refuses. I'm afraid of falling asleep myself. I don't remember when I slept last. I believe I'm beginning to have hallucinations. There's a dear fellow, put down your feet, just one—there—there. . . ."

The doctor was pale and tottering, and one could see that if he were only to lie down for an instant he would fall asleep and remain so without waking for several days running. My legs sank under me, and I am certain I fell asleep as I walked—so suddenly and unexpectedly appeared before us a row of black outlines—the engine and carriages. Near them, scarcely distinguishable in the darkness, some men were wandering about slowly and silently. There was not a single light either on the engine or carriages, and only the shut ash-box threw a dim reddish light on to the rails.

"What is this?" asked I, stepping back.

"Why, we are going in the train. Have you forgotten? We are going in the train," muttered the doctor.

The night was chilly and he was trembling from cold, and as I looked at him I felt the same rapid tickling shiver all over my body.

"D—n you!" I cried loudly. "Just as if you couldn't have taken somebody else."

"Hush! please, hush!" and the doctor caught me by the arm. Somebody out of the darkness said:

"If you were to fire a volley from all the guns, nobody would stir. They are all asleep. One could go up and bind them all. Just now I passed quite close to the sentry. He looked at me and did not say a word, never stirred. I suppose he was asleep too. It's a wonder he does not fall down."

He who spoke yawned and his clothes rustled, evidently he was stretching himself. I leaned against the side of the carriage, intending to climb up—and was instantly overcome by sleep. Somebody lifted me up from behind and laid me down, while I began pushing him away with my feet, without knowing why, and again I fell asleep, hearing as in a dream fragments of a conversation:

"At the seventh verst."

"Have you forgotten the lanterns?"

"No, he won't go."

"Give them here. Back a little. That's it."

The carriages were jerking backwards and forwards, something was rattling. And gradually, because of all these sounds and because I was lying comfortably and quietly, sleep deserted me. But the doctor was sound asleep, and when I took him by the hand it was like the hand of a corpse, heavy and limp. The train was now moving slowly and cautiously, shaking slightly, as if groping its way. The student acting as hospital orderly lighted the candle in the lantern, lighting up the walls and the black aperture of the entrance, and said angrily:

"D—n it! Much they need us by this time. But you had better wake him, before he falls into a sound sleep, for then you won't be able to do anything with him. I know by myself."

We roused the doctor and he sat up, rolling his eyes vacantly. He tried to lie down again, but we did not let him.

"It would be good to have a drop of vodka now," said the student.

We drank a mouthful of brandy, and all sleepiness disappeared entirely. The big black square of the door began to grow pink, then red—somewhere from behind the hills appeared an enormous mute flare of a conflagration as if the sun was rising in the middle of the night.

"It's far away. About twenty versts."

"I feel cold," said the doctor, snapping his teeth.

The student looked out of the door and beckoned me to come up to him. I looked out: at different points of the horizon motionless flares of similar conflagration stood out in a mute row: as if dozens of suns were rising simultaneously. And now the darkness was not so great. The distant hills were growing more densely black, sharply outlined against the sky in a broken and wavy contour, while in the foreground all was flooded with a red soft glow, silent and motionless. I glanced at the student; his face was tinged by the same red fantastic color of blood, that had changed itself into air and light.

"Are there many wounded?" asked I.

He waved his hand.

"A great many madmen. More so than wounded."

"Real madmen?"

"What others can there be?"

He was looking at me, and his eyes wore the same fixed, wild expression, full of cold horror, that the soldier's had, who died of sunstroke.

"Stop that," said I, turning away.

"The doctor is mad also. Just look at him."

The doctor had not heard. He was sitting cross-legged, like a Turk, swaying to and fro, soundlessly moving his lips and finger-tips. And in his gaze there was the same fixed, stupefied, blunt, stricken expression.

"I feel cold," said he, and smiled.

"Hang you all!" cried I, moving away into a corner of the carriage. "What did you call me up for?"

Nobody answered. The student stood gazing out at the mute spreading glow, and the back of his head with its curly hair was youthful; and when I looked at him, I do not know why, but I kept picturing to myself a delicate woman's hand passing through that hair. And this image was so unpleasant, that a feeling of hatred sprang up in my breast, and I could not look at him without a feeling of loathing.

"How old are you?" I asked, but he did not turn his head and did not answer.

The doctor kept on rocking himself.

"I feel cold."

"When I think," said the student, without turning round. "when I think that there are streets, houses, a University . . ."

He broke off, as if he had said all and was silent. Suddenly the train stopped almost instantaneously, making me knock myself against the wall, and voices were to be heard. We jumped out. In front of the very engine upon the rails lay something, a not very large lump, out of which a leg was projecting.

"Wounded?"

"No, dead. The head is torn off. Say what you will, but I will light the head-light. Otherwise we shall be crushing somebody."

The lump with the protruding leg was thrown aside; for an instant the leg lifted itself up, as if it wanted to run through the air, and all disappeared in a black ditch. The head-light was lit and the engine instantly grew black.

"Listen!" whispered somebody, full of silent terror.

How was it that we had not heard it before? From everywhere—the exact place could not be defined—a groan, unbroken and scraping, wonderfully calm in its breadth, and even indifferent, as it seemed, was borne upon us. We had heard many cries and groans, but this resembled none of those heard before. On the dim reddish surface our eyes could perceive nothing, and therefore the very earth and sky, lit up by a never-rising sun, seemed to be groaning.

"The fifth verst," said the engine-driver.

"That is where it comes from," and the doctor pointed forwards. The student shuddered, and slowly turned towards us.

"What is it? It's terrible to listen to!"

"Let's move on."

We walked along in front of the engine, throwing a dense shadow upon the rails, but it was not black but of a dim red color, lit up by the soft motionless flares, that stood out mutely at the different points of the black sky. And with each step we made, that wild unearthly groan, that had no visible source, grew ominously, as if it was the red air, the very earth and sky, that were groaning. In its ceaselessness and strange indifference it recalled at times the noise of grasshoppers in a meadow—the ceaseless noise of grasshoppers in a meadow on a warm summer day. And we came upon dead bodies oftener and oftener. We examined them rapidly, and threw them off the rails—those indifferent, calm, limp bodies, that left dark oily stains where the blood had soaked into the earth where they had lain. At first we counted them, but soon got muddled, and ceased. They were many—too many for that ominous night, that breathed cold and groans from each fibre of its being.

"What does it mean?" cried the doctor, and threatened somebody with his fist. "Just listen . . ."

We were nearing the sixth verst, and the groans were growing distinct and sharp, and we could almost feel the distorted mouths, from which those terrible sounds were issuing.

We looked anxiously into the rosy gloom, so deceitful in its fantastic light, when suddenly, almost at our feet, beside the rails, somebody gave a loud, calling, crying groan. We found him instantly, that wounded man, whose face seemed to consist only of two eyes, so big they appeared, when the light of the lantern fell on his face. He stopped groaning, and rested his eyes on each of us and our lanterns in turn, and in his glance there was a mad joy at seeing men and lights—and a mad fear that all would disappear like a vision. Perhaps he had seen men with lanterns bending over him many times, but they had always disappeared in a bloody confused nightmare.

We moved on, and almost instantly stumbled against two more wounded, one lying on the rails, the other groaning in a ditch. As we were picking them up, the doctor, trembling with anger, said to me: "Well?" and turned away. Several steps farther on we met a man wounded slightly, who was walking alone, supporting one arm with the other. He was walking with his head thrown back, straight towards us, but seemed not to notice us, when we drew aside to let him pass. I believe he did not see us. He stopped for an instant near the engine, turned aside, and went past the train.

"You had better get in!" cried the doctor, but he did not answer.

These were the first that we found, and they horrified us. But later on we came upon them oftener and oftener along the rails or near them, and the whole field, lit up by the motionless red flare of the conflagrations, began stirring as if it were alive, breaking out into loud cries, wails, curses and groans. All those dark mounds stirred and crawled about like half-dead lobsters let out of a basket, with outspread legs, scarcely resembling men in their broken, unconscious movements and ponderous immobility. Some were mute and obedient, others groaned, wailed, swore and showed such a passionate hate towards us who were saving them, as if *we* had brought about that bloody, indifferent night, and been the cause of all those terrible wounds and their loneliness amidst the night and dead bodies.

The train was full, and our clothes were saturated with blood, as if we had stood for a long time under a rain of blood, while the wounded were still being brought in, and the field, come to life, was stirring wildly as before.

Some of the wounded crawled up themselves, some walked up tottering and falling. One soldier almost ran up to us. His face was smashed, and only one eye remained, burning wildly and terribly, and he was almost naked, as if he had come from the bath-room. Pushing me aside, he caught sight of the doctor, and rapidly seized him by the chest with his left hand.

"I'll smash your snout!" he cried, shaking the doctor, and added slowly and mordantly a coarse oath. "I'll smash your snouts, you rabble!"

The doctor broke away from the soldier, and advancing towards him, cried chokingly:

"I will have you court-martialled, you scoundrel! To prison with you! You're hindering my work! Scoundrel! Brute!"

We pulled them apart, but the soldier kept on crying out for a long time: "Rabble! I'll smash your snout!"

I was beginning to get exhausted, and went a little way off to have a smoke and rest a bit. The blood, dried to my hands, covered them like a pair of black gloves, making it difficult for me to bend my fingers, so that I kept dropping my cigarettes and matches. And when I succeeded in lighting my cigarette, the tobacco smoke struck me as novel and strange, with quite a peculiar taste, the like of which I never experienced before or after. Just then the ambulance student with whom I had travelled came up to me, and it seemed to me as if I had met with him several years back, but where I could not remember. His tread was firm as if he were marching, and he was staring through me at something farther on and higher up.

"And they are sleeping," said he, as it seemed, quite calmly.

I flew in a rage, as if the reproach was addressed to me.

"You forget, that they fought like lions for ten days."

"And they are sleeping," he repeated, looking through me and higher up. Then he stooped down to me and shaking his finger, continued in the same dry and calm way: "I will tell you—I will tell you . . ."

"What?"

He stooped still lower towards me, shaking his finger meaningly, and kept repeating the words as if they expressed a completed idea:

"I will tell you—I will tell you. Tell them . . ." And still looking at me in the same severe way, he shook his finger once more, then took out his revolver and shot himself in the temple. And this did not surprise or terrify me in the least. Putting my cigarette in the left hand, I felt his wound with my fingers, and went back to the train.

"The student has shot himself. I believe he is still alive," said I to the doctor. The latter caught hold of his head and groaned.

"D—n him! . . . There is no room. There, that one will go and shoot himself, too, soon. And I give you my word of honor," cried he, angrily and menacingly, "I will do the same! Yes! And let me beg you—just walk back. There is no room. You can lodge a complaint against me if you like."

And he turned away, still shouting, while I went up to the other who was about to commit suicide. He was an ambulance man, and also, I believe, a student. He stood, pressing his forehead against the wall of the carriage, and his shoulders shook with sobs.

"Stop!" said I, touching his quivering shoulder. But he did not turn round or answer, and continued crying. And the back of his head was youthful, like the other student's, and as terrifying, and he stood in an absurd manner with his legs spread out like a person drunk, who is sick; and his neck was covered with blood; probably he had clutched it with his own hands.

"Well?" said I, impatiently.

He pushed himself away from the carriage and, stooping like old man, with his head bent down, he went away into the darkness away from all of us. I do not know why, but I followed him, and we walked along for a long time away from the carriages. I believe he was crying, and a feeling of distress stole over me, and I wanted to cry too.

"Stop!" I cried, standing still.

But he walked on, moving his feet ponderously, bent down, looking like an old man with his narrow shoulders and shuffling gait. And soon he disappeared in the reddish haze, that resembled light and yet lit nothing. And I remained alone. To the left of me a row of dim lights floated past—it was the train. I was alone—amidst the dead and dying. How many more remained? Near me all was still and dead, but farther on the field was stirring, as if it were alive—or so it seemed to me in my loneliness. But the moan did not grow less. It spread along the earth—high-pitched, hopeless, like the cry of a child or the yelping of thousands of cast-away puppies, starving and cold. Like a sharp, endless, icy needle it pierced your brain and slowly moved backwards and forwards—backwards and forwards. . . .

FRAGMENT VI

. . . THEY were our own men. During the strange confusion of all movements that reigned in both armies, our own and the enemy's, during the last month, frustrating all orders and plans, we were sure it was the enemy that was approaching us, namely, the 4th corps. And everything was ready for an attack, when somebody clearly discerned our uniforms, and ten minutes later our guess had become a calm and happy certainty: they were our own men. They apparently had recognized us too: they advanced quite calmly, and that calm motion seemed to express the same happy smile of an unexpected meeting.

And when they began firing, we did not understand for some time what it meant, and still continued smiling—under a hail of shrapnel and bullets, that poured down upon us, snatching away at one stroke hundreds of men. Somebody cried out by mistake and—I clearly remember—we all saw that it was the enemy, that it was his uniform and not ours, and instantly answered the fire. About fifteen minutes after the beginning of that strange engagement both my legs were torn off, and I recovered consciousness in the hospital after the amputation.

I asked how the battle had ended, and received an evasive, reassuring answer, by which I could understand that we had been beaten; and afterwards, legless as I was, I was overcome by joy at the thought that now I would be sent home, that I was alive—alive for a long time to come, alive for ever. And only a week later I learnt some particulars, that once more filled me with doubts and a new, unexperienced feeling of terror. Yes, I believe they were our own men after all—and it was with one of our shells, fired out of one of our guns by one of our men, that my legs had been torn off. And nobody could explain how it had happened. Something occurred, something darkened our vision, and two regiments, belonging to the same army, facing each other at a distance of one verst, had been destroying each other for a whole hour in the full conviction that it was the enemy they had before them. Later on the incident was remembered and spoken of reluctantly in half-words and—what is most surprising of all—one could feel that many of the speakers did not admit the mistake even then. That is to say, they admitted it, but thought that it had occurred later on, that in the beginning they really had the enemy before them, but that he disappeared somewhere during the general fray, leaving us in the range of our own shells. Some spoke of it openly, giving precise explanations, which seemed to them plausible and clear. Up to this very minute I cannot say for certain how the strange blunder began, as I saw with equal clearness first our red uniforms and then their orange-colored ones. And somehow very soon everybody forgot about the incident, forgot about it to such an extent that it was spoken of as a real battle and in that sense many accounts were written and sent to the papers in all good faith; I read them when I was back home. At first the public's attitude towards us, the wounded in that engagement, was rather strange—we seemed to be less pitied than those wounded in other battles, but soon even that disappeared too. And only new facts, similar to the one just described, and a case in the enemy's army, when two detachments actually destroyed each other almost entirely, having come to a hand-to-hand fight during the night—gives me the right to think that a mistake did occur.

Our doctor, the one that did the amputation, a lean, bony old man, tainted with tobacco smoke and carbolic acid, everlastingly smiling at something through his yellowish-grey thin mustache, said to me, winking his eye:

"You're in luck to be going home. There's something wrong here."

"What is it?"

"Something's going wrong. In our time it was simpler."

He had taken part in the last European war almost a quarter of a century back and often referred to it with pleasure. But this war he did not understand, and, as I noticed, feared it.

"Yes, there's something wrong," sighed he, and frowned, disappearing in a cloud of tobacco smoke. "I would leave too, if I could."

And bending over me he whispered through his yellow smoked mustache:

"A time will come when nobody will be able to go away from here. Yes, neither I nor anybody," and in his old eyes, so close to me, I saw the same fixed, dull, stricken expression. And something terrible, unbearable, resembling the fall of thousands of buildings, darted through my head, and growing cold from terror, I whispered:

"The red laugh."

And he was the first to understand me. He hastily nodded his head and repeated:

"Yes. The red laugh."

He sat down quite close to me and looking round began whispering rapidly, in a senile way, wagging his sharp, grey little beard.

"You are leaving soon, and I will tell you. Did you ever see a fight in an asylum? No? Well, I saw one. And they fought like sane people. You understand—like sane people." He significantly repeated the last phrase several times.

"Well, and what of that?" asked I, also in a whisper, full of terror.

"Nothing. Like sane people."

"The red laugh," said I.

"They were separated by water being poured over them."

I remembered the rain that had frightened us so, and got angry.

"You are mad, doctor!"

"Not more than you. Not more than you in any case."

He hugged his sharp old knees and chuckled; and, looking at me over his shoulder and still with the echo of that unexpected painful laugh on his parched lips, he winked at me slyly several times, as if we two knew something very funny, that nobody else knew. Then with the solemnity of a professor of black magic giving a conjuring performance, he lifted his arm and, lowering it slowly, carefully touched with two fingers that part of the blanket under which my legs would have been, if they had not been cut off.

"And do you understand this?" he asked mysteriously.

Then, in the same solemn and significant manner, he waved his hand towards the row of beds on which the wounded were lying, and repeated:

"And can you explain this?"

"The wounded?" said I. "The wounded?"

"The wounded," repeated he, like an echo. "The wounded. Legless and armless, with pierced sides, smashed-in chests and torn-out eyes. You understand it? I am very glad. So I suppose you will understand this also?"

With an agility, quite unexpected for his age, he flung himself down and stood on his hands, balancing his legs in the air. His white working clothes turned down, his face grew purple and, looking at me fixedly with a strange upturned gaze, he threw at me with difficulty a few broken words:

"And this . . . do you . . . also . . . understand?"

"Stop!" whispered I in terror, "or else I will cry out."

He turned over into a natural position, sat down again near my bed, and, taking breath, remarked instinctively:

"And nobody can understand it."

"Yesterday they were firing again."

"Yes, they were firing yesterday and the day before," said he, nodding his head affirmatively.

"I want to go home!" said I in distress. "Doctor, dear fellow, I want to go home. I cannot remain here any longer. At times I cannot bring myself to believe that I have a home, where it is so good."

He was thinking of something and did not answer, and I began to cry.

"My God, I have no legs. I used to love my bicycle so, to walk and run, and now I have no legs. I used to danc: my boy on the right foot and he laughed, and now . . . Curse you all! What shall I go home for? I am only thirty . . . Curse you all!"

And I sobbed and sobbed, as I thought of my dear legs, my fleet, strong legs. Who took them away from me, who dared to take them away!

"Listen," said the doctor, looking aside. "Yesterday I saw a mad soldier that came to us. An enemy's soldier. He was stripped almost naked, beaten and scratched and hungry as an animal, his hair was unkempt, as ours is, and he resembled a savage, primitive man or monkey. He waved his arms about, made grimaces, sang and shouted and wanted to fight. He was fed and driven out again—into the open country. Where could we have kept him? Days and nights they wander about the hills, backwards and forwards in all directions, keeping to no path, having no aim or resting-place, all in tatters like ominous phantoms. They wave their arms, laugh, shout and sing, and when they come across anybody they begin to fight, or maybe, without noticing each other, pass by. What do they eat? Probably nothing, or, maybe, they feed on the dead bodies together with the beasts, together with those fat wild dogs, that fight in the hills and yelp the whole night long. At night they gather about the fires like monstrous moths or birds awakened by a storm, and you need only light a fire to have in less than half-an-hour a dozen noisy, tattered wild shapes, resembling chilled monkeys, gathering around it. Sometimes they are fired at by mistake, sometimes on purpose, for they make you lose all patience with their unintelligible, terrifying cries. . . . ."

"I want to go home!" cried I, shutting my ears.

But new terrible words, sounding hollow and phantom-like, as if they were passing through a layer of wadding, kept hammering at my brain.

"They are many. They die by hundreds in the precipices and pitfalls, that are made for sound and clever men, in the remnants of the barbed wire and on the stakes they take part in the regular battles and fight like heroes—always in the foremost ranks, always undaunted, but often turn against their own men. I like them. At present I am only beginning to go mad, and that is why I am sitting and talking to you, but when my senses leave me entirely, I will go out into the open country—I will go out into the open country, and I will give a call—I will give a call, I will gather those grave ones, those knights-errant, around me, and declare war to the whole world. We will enter the towns and villages in a joyous crowd, with music and songs, leaving in our wake a trail of red, in which everything will whirl and dance like fire. Those that remain alive will join us, and our brave army will grow like an avalanche, and will cleanse the whole world. Who said that one must not kill, burn or rob? . . ."

He was shouting now, that mad doctor, and seemed to have awakened by his cries the slumbering pain of all those around him with their ripped-open chests and sides, torn-out eyes and cut-off legs. The ward filled with a broad, rasping, crying groan, and from all sides pale, yellow, exhausted faces, some eyeless, some so monstrously mutilated that it seemed as if they had returned from hell turned toward us. And they groaned and listened, and a black shapeless shadow, risen up from the earth, peeped in cautiously through the open door, while the mad doctor went on shouting, stretching out his arms.

"Who said one must not kill, burn, or rob? We will kill and burn and rob. We, a joyous careless band of braves, we will destroy all; their buildings, universities and museums, and merry as children, full of fiery laughter, we will dance on the ruins. I will proclaim the madhouse our fatherland; all those that have not gone mad—our enemies and madmen; and when I, great, unconquerable and joyous, will begin to reign over the whole world, its sole lord and master, what a glad laugh will ring over the whole universe."

"The red laugh!" cried I, interrupting him. "Help! Again I hear the red laugh!"

"Friends!" continued the doctor, addressing himself to the groaning, mutilated shadows. "Friends! we shall have a red moon and a red sun, and the animals will have a merry red coat, and we will skin all those that are too white—that are too white. . . . You have not tasted blood? It is slightly sticky and slightly warm, but it is red, and has such a merry red laugh! . . ."

FRAGMENT VII

. . . It was godless and unlawful. The Red Cross is respected by the whole world, as a thing sacred, and they saw that it was a train full of harmless wounded and not soldiers, and they ought to have warned us of the mine. The poor fellows, they were dreaming of home. . . .

FRAGMENT VIII

. . . AROUND a samovar, around a real samovar, out of which the steam was rising as out of an engine—the glass on the lamp had even grown dim, there was so much steam. And the cups were the same, blue outside and white inside, very pretty little cups, a wedding present. My wife's sister gave them—she is a very kind and good woman.

"Is it possible they are all whole?" asked I, incredulously, mixing the sugar in my glass with a clean silver spoon.

"One was broken," said my wife, absently; she was holding the tap open just then and the water was running out easily and prettily.

I laughed.

"What's it about?" asked my brother.

"Oh, nothing. Wheel me into the study just once more. You may as well trouble yourself for the sake of a hero. You idled away your time while I was away, but now that is over, I'll bring you to order," and I began singing, as a joke of course—"My friends, we're bravely hurrying towards the foe . . ."

They understood the joke and smiled, only my wife did not lift up her face, she was wiping the cups with a clean embroidered cloth. And in the study I saw once again the light-blue wall-paper, a lamp with a green shade and a table with a water-bottle upon it. And it was a little dusty.

"Pour me some water out of this," ordered I, merrily.

"But you've just had tea."

"That doesn't matter, pour me out some. And you," said I to my wife, "take our son, and go into the next room for a minute. Please."

And I drank the water with delight in small sips, while my wife and son were in the next room, and I could not see them.

"That's all right. Now come here. But why is he not in bed by this time?"

"He is so glad you have come home. Darling, go to your father."

But the child began to cry and hid himself at his mother's feet.

"Why is he crying?" asked I, in perplexity, and looked around, "why are you all so pale and silent, following me like shadows?"

My brother burst into a loud laugh and said, "We are not silent."

And my sister said, "We are talking the whole time."

"I will go and see about the supper," said my mother, and hurriedly left the room.

"Yes, you are silent," I repeated, with sudden conviction. "Since morning I have not heard a word from you; I am the only one who chats, laughs, and makes merry. Are you not glad to see me then? And why do you all avoid looking at me? Have I changed so? Yes, I am changed. But I do not see any looking-glasses about. Have you put them all away? Give me a looking-glass."

"I will bring you one directly," answered my wife, and did not come back for a long time, and the looking-glass was brought by the maid. I looked into it, and—I had seen myself before in the train, at the station—it was the same face, grown older a little, but the most ordinary face. While they, I believe, expected me to cry out and faint—so glad were they when I asked calmly—

"What is there so unusual in me?"

Laughing louder and louder, my sister left the room hurriedly, and my brother said with calm assurance: "Yes, you have not changed much, only grown slightly bald."

"You can be thankful that my head is not broken," answered I, unconcernedly. "But where do they all disappear? —first one, then another. Wheel me about the rooms, please. What a comfortable armchair, it does not make the slightest sound. How much did it cost? You bet I won't spare the money; I will buy myself such a pair of legs, better ... My bicycle!"

It was hanging on the wall, quite new, only the tires were limp for want of pumping. A tiny bit of mud had dried to the tire of the back wheel—the last time I had ridden it. My brother was silent and did not move my chair, and I understood his silence and irresoluteness.

"Only four officers remained alive in our regiment," said I, surlily. "I am very lucky. . . . You can take it for yourself—take it away to-morrow."

"All right, I will take it," agreed my brother submissively. "Yes, you are lucky. Half of the town is in mourning. While legs—that is really . . ."

"Of course I am not a postman."

My brother stopped suddenly and asked—"But why does your head shake?"

"That's nothing. The doctor said it will pass."

"And your hands too?"

"Yes, yes. And my hands too. It will all pass. Wheel me on, please. I am tired of remaining still."

They upset me, those discontented people, but my gladness returned to me when they began making my bed; a real bed, a handsome bed, that I had bought just before our wedding four years ago. They spread a clean sheet, then they shook the pillows and turned down the blanket; while I watched the solemn proceedings, my eyes were full of tears with laughing.

"And now undress me and put me to bed," said I to my wife. "How good it is!"

"This minute, dear."

"Quicker!"

"This minute, dear."

"Why; what are you doing?"

"This minute, dear."

She was standing behind my back, near the toilet table, and I vainly tried to turn my head so as to see her. And suddenly she gave a cry, such a cry as one hears only at the war——

"What does it all mean?"

She rushed towards me, put her arms round me, and fell down, hiding her head near the stumps of my cut-off legs, from which she turned away with horror, and again pressed herself against them, kissing them, and crying——

"What have you become? Why, you are only thirty years

old. You were young and handsome. What does it all mean? How cruel men are. What is it for? For whom is it necessary? You, my gentle, poor darling, darling. . . ."

At her cry they all ran up—my mother, sister, nurse—and they all began crying and saying something or other, and fell at my feet wailing. While on the threshold stood my brother, pale, terribly pale, with a trembling jaw, and cried out in a high-pitched voice——

"I shall go mad with you all. I shall go mad!"

While my mother grovelled at my chair and had not the strength to cry, but only gasped, beating her head against the wheels. And there stood the clean bed with the well-shaken pillows and turned-down blanket, the same bed that I bought just before our wedding four years ago. . . .

FRAGMENT IX

. . . I was sitting in a warm bath, while my brother was pacing up and down the small room in a troubled manner, sitting down, getting up again, catching hold of the soap and towel, bringing them close up to his short-sighted eyes and again putting them back in their places. At last he stood up with his face to the wall and picking at the plaster with his finger, continued hotly:

"Judge for yourself: one cannot teach people mercy, sense, logic—teach them to act consciously for tens and hundreds of years running with impunity. And, in particular, to act consciously. One can become merciless, lose all sensitiveness, get accustomed to blood and tears and pain—for instance butchers, and some doctors and officers do, but how can one renounce truth, after one has learnt to know it? In my opinion it is impossible. I was taught from infancy not to torture animals and be compassionate; all the books that I have read told me the same, and I am painfully sorry for all those that suffer at your cursed war. But time passes, and I am beginning to get accustomed to all those deaths, sufferings and all this blood; I feel that I am getting less sensitive, less responsive in my everyday life and respond only to great stimulants, but I cannot get accustomed to *war;* my brain refuses to understand and explain a thing that is senseless in its basis. Millions of people gather at one place and, giving their actions order and regularity, kill each other, and it hurts everybody equally, and all are unhappy—what is it if not madness?" My brother turned round and looked at me inquiringly with his shortsighted, artless eyes.

"The red laugh," said I merrily, splashing about.

"I will tell you the truth," and my brother put his cold hand trustingly on my shoulder, but quickly pulled it back, as if he was frightened at its being naked and wet. "I will tell you the truth; I am very much afraid of going mad. I cannot understand what is happening. I cannot understand it, and it is dreadful. If only anybody could explain it to me, but nobody can. You were at the front, you saw it all—explain it to me."

"Deuce take you," answered I jokingly, splashing about.

"There, and you too," said my brother sadly. "Nobody is capable of helping me. It's dreadful. And I am beginning to lose all understanding of what is permissible and what is not, what has sense and what is senseless. If I were to seize you suddenly by the throat, at first gently, as if caressing you, and then firmly, and strangle you, what would that be?"

"You are talking nonsense. Nobody does such things."

My brother rubbed his cold hands, smiled softly, and continued:

"When you were away there were nights when I did not sleep, could not sleep, and strange ideas entered my head—to take a hatchet, for instance, and go and kill everybody—mother, sister, the servants, our dog. Of course they were only fancies, and I would never do so."

"I should hope not," smiled I, splashing about.

"Then again, I am afraid of knives, of all that is sharp and shining; it seems to me that if I were to take up a knife I should certainly kill somebody with it. Now, is it not true—why should I not plunge it into somebody, if it were sharp enough?"

"The argument is sufficient. What a queer fellow you are, brother! Just open the hot-water tap."

My brother opened the tap, let in some hot water, and continued:

"Then, again, I am afraid of crowds—of men, when many of them gather together. When of an evening I hear a noise in the street—a loud shout, for instance—I start and believe that . . . a massacre has begun. When several men stand together, and I cannot hear what they are talking about, it seems to me that they will suddenly cry out, fall upon each other, and blood will flow. And you know"—he bent mysteriously towards my ear—"the papers are full of murders—strange murders. It is all nonsense that there are as many brains as there are men; mankind has only one intellect, and it is beginning to get muddled. Just feel my head, how hot it is. It is on fire. And sometimes it gets cold, and everything freezes in it, grows benumbed, and changes into a terrible deadlike piece of ice. I must go mad; don't laugh, brother. I must go mad. A quarter of an hour has passed, it's time for you to get out of your bath."

"A little bit more. Just a minute."

It was so good to be sitting again in that bath and listening to the well-known voice, without reflecting upon the words, and to see all the familiar, simple and ordinary things around me: the brass, slightly-green tap, the walls, with the familiar pattern, and all the photographic outfit laid out in order upon the shelves. I would take up photography again, take simple, peaceful landscapes and portraits of my son walking, laughing and playing. One could do that without legs. And I would take up my writing again— about clever books, the progress of human thought, beauty, and peace.

"Ho, ho, ho!" roared I, splashing about.

"What is the matter with you?" asked my brother, growing pale and full of fear.

"Nothing. I am glad to be home."

He smiled at me as one smiles at a child or on one younger than oneself, although I was three years older than he, and grew thoughtful, like a grown-up person or an old man who has great, burdensome old thoughts.

"Where can one fly to?" he asked, shrugging his shoulders. "Every day, at about the same hour, the papers close the circuit, and all mankind gets a shock. This simultaneousness of feelings, tears, thoughts, sufferings and horror deprives me of all stay, and I am like a chip of wood tossing about on the waves, or a bit of dust in a whirlwind.

I am forcibly torn away from all that is habitual, and there is one terrible moment every morning, when I seem to hang in the air over the black abyss of insanity. And I shall fall into it, I must fall into it. You don't know all, brother. You don't read the papers, and much is held back from you—you don't know all, brother."

I took all his words for rather a gloomy joke—the usual attitude towards all those who, being touched by insanity, have an inkling of the insanity of war, and gave us a warning. I considered it as a joke, as if I had forgotten for the moment, while I was splashing about in the hot water, all that I had seen over there. "Well, let them hold things back from me, but I must get out of the bath, anyway," said I lightly, and my brother smiled and called my man, and together they lifted me out of my bath and dressed me. Afterwards I had some fragrant tea, which I drank out of my cut-glass tumbler, and said to myself that life was worth living even without a pair of legs; and then they wheeled me into the study up to my table and I prepared for work.

Before the war I was on the staff of a journal reviewing foreign literature, and now, disposed within my reach, lay a heap of those dear, sweet books in yellow, blue and brown covers. My joy was so great, my delight so profound, that I could not make up my mind to begin reading them, and I merely fingered the books, passing my hand caressingly over them. I felt a smile spread over my face, most probably a very silly smile, but I could not keep it back, as I contemplated admiringly the type, the vignettes, the severe beautiful simplicity of the drawings. How much thought and sense of beauty there was in them all! How many people had to work and search, how much talent and taste were needed to bring forth that letter, for instance, so simple and elegant, so clever, harmonious and eloquent in its interlaced lines.

"And now I must set to work," said I, seriously, full of respect for work.

And I took up my pen to write the heading and, like a frog tied to a string, my hand began plunging about the paper. The pen stuck into the paper, scratched it, jerked about, slipped irresistibly aside, and brought forth hideous lines, broken, crooked, devoid of all sense. And I did not cry out or move, I grew cold and still as the approaching terrible truth dawned upon me; while my hand danced over the brightly illuminated paper, and each finger shook in such hopeless, living, insane horror, as if they, those fingers, were still at the front and saw the conflagrations and blood, and heard the groans and cries of indescribable pain. They had detached themselves from me, those madly quivering fingers, they were alive, they had become ears and eyes; and, growing cold from horror, without the strength to move or cry out, I watched their wild dance over the clean, bright white page.

And all was quiet. They thought I was working, and had shut all the doors, so as not to interrupt me by any sound—and I was alone in the room, deprived of the power of moving, obediently watching my shaking hands.

"It's nothing," said I aloud, and in the stillness and loneliness of the study my voice sounded hollow and nasty like the voice of a madman. "It is nothing. I will dictate. Why,

Milton was blind when he wrote his *Paradise Regained*. I can think, and that is the chief thing, in fact it is all."

And I began inventing a long clever phrase about the blind Milton, but the words got confused, fell away as out of a rotten printing frame, and when I came to the end of the phrase I had forgotten the beginning. Then I tried to remember what made me begin, and why I was inventing that strange senseless phrase about Milton, and could not.

"Paradise Regained, Paradise Regained," I repeated, and could not understand what it meant.

And then I saw that I often forgot very many things, that I had become strangely absent-minded, and confused familiar faces; that I forgot words even in a simple conversation, and sometimes, remembering a word, I could not understand its meaning. And I clearly pictured to myself my daily existence. A strange short day, cut off like my legs, with empty mysterious spaces, long hours of unconsciousness or apathy, about which I could remember nothing.

I wanted to call my wife, but could not remember her name—and this did not surprise or frighten me. Softly I whispered:

"Wife!"

The incoherent, unusual word sounded softly and died away without bringing any response. And all was quiet. They were afraid of disturbing me at my work by any careless sound, and all was quiet—a perfect study for a savant —cosy, quiet, disposing one to meditation and creative energy. "Dear ones, how solicitous they are of me!" I thought tenderly.

. . . And inspiration, sacred inspiration, came to me. The sun burst forth in my head, and its burning creative rays darted over the whole world, dropping flowers and songs— flowers and songs. And I wrote on through the whole night, feeling no exhaustion, but soaring freely on the wings of mighty, sacred inspiration. I was writing something great —something immortal—flowers and songs—flowers and songs. . . .

PART II

FRAGMENT X

. . . HAPPILY he died last week on Friday. I say "happily," and repeat that my brother's death was a great blessing to him. A cripple with no legs, palsied, with a smitten soul, he was terrible and piteous in his senseless creative ecstasy. Ever since that night he wrote for two months, without leaving his chair, refusing all food, weeping and scolding whenever we wheeled him away from his table even for a short time. He moved his dry pen over the paper with wonderful rapidity, throwing aside page after page, and kept on writing and writing. Sleep deserted him, and only twice did we succeed in putting him to bed for a few hours, thanks to a strong narcotic; but, later, even a narcotic was powerless to conquer his senseless creative ecstasy. At his order the curtains were kept drawn over all the windows the whole day long and the lamp was allowed to burn, giv.

ing the illusion of night, while he wrote on, smoking one cigarette after another. Apparently he was happy, and I never happened to meet any healthy person with such an inspired face—the face of a prophet or of a great poet. He became extremely emaciated, with the waxen transparency of a corpse or of an ascetic, and his hair grew quite grey; he began his senseless work a comparatively young man, but finished it an old one. Sometimes he hurried on his work, writing more than usual, and his pen would stick into the pages and break, but he never noticed it; at such times one durst not touch him, for at the slightest contact he was overtaken by fits of tears and laughter; but sometimes, very rarely, he rested blissfully from his work and talked to me affably, each time asking the same questions: Who was I, what was my name, and since when had I taken up literature.

And then he would condescendingly tell, always using the same words, what an absurd fright he had had at the thought that he had lost his memory and was incapable of work, and how splendidly he had refuted the insane supposition there and then by beginning his great immortal work about the flowers and songs.

"Of course I do not count upon being recognized by my contemporaries," he would say proudly and unassumingly at the same time, putting his trembling hand on the heap of empty sheets, "but the future—the future—will understand my idea."

He never once remembered the war or his wife and son; the mirage of his endless work engrossed his attention so undividedly that it is doubtful whether he was conscious of anything else. One could walk and talk in his presence —he noticed nothing, and not for an instant did his face lose its expression of terrible tension and inspiration. In the stillness of the night, when everybody was asleep and he alone wove untiringly the endless thread of insanity, he seemed terrible, and only his mother and I ventured to approach him. Once I tried to give him a pencil instead of his dry pen, thinking that perhaps he really wrote something, but on the paper there remained only hideous lines, broken, crooked, devoid of any sense. And he died in the night at his work. I knew my brother well, and his insanity did not come as a surprise to me; the passionate dream of work that filled all his letters from the war and was the stay of his life after his return, had to come into inevitable collision with the impotence of his exhausted, tortured brain, and bring about the catastrophe. And I believe that I have succeeded in reconstructing with sufficient accuracy the successive feelings that brought him to the end during that fatal night. Generally speaking, all that I have written down concerning the war is founded upon the words of my dead brother, often so confused and incoherent; only a few separate episodes were burnt into his brain so deeply and indelibly that I could cite the very words that he used in telling me them. I loved him, and his death weighs upon me like a stone, oppressing my brain by its senselessness. It has added one more loop to the incomprehensible that envelops my head like a web, and has drawn it tight. The whole family has left for the country on a visit to some relatives, and I am alone in the house—the house that my brother loved so. The servants have been paid off, and only

the porter from the next door comes every morning to light
the fires, while the rest of the time I am alone, and resemble a fly caught between two window-frames,* plunging
about and knocking myself against a transparent but insur-
mountable obstacle. And I feel, I know, that I shall never
leave the house. Now, when I am alone, the war possesses
me wholly and stands before me like an inscrutable mystery,
like a terrible spirit, to which I can give no form. I give it
all sorts of shapes: of a headless skeleton on horseback, of a
shapeless shadow, born in a black thundercloud mutely
enveloping the earth, but not one of them can give me an
answer and extinguish the cold, constant, blunt horror that
possesses me.

I do not understand war, and I must go mad, like my
brother, like the hundreds of men that are sent back from
there. And this does not terrify me. The loss of reason
seems to me honorable, like the death of a sentry at his
post. By the expectancy, the slow and infallible approach
of madness, the instantaneous feeling of something enormous falling into an abyss, the unbearable pain of tortured
thought. . . . My heart has grown benumbed, it is dead,
and there is no new life for it, but thought is still alive—
still struggling, once mighty as Samson, but now helpless
and weak as a child—and, I am sorry for my poor thought.
There are moments when I cannot endure the torture of
those iron clasps that are compressing my brain; I feel an
irrepressible longing to run out into the street, into the
market-place, where there are people and cry out:

* In Russia the windows have double panes during the winter for the
purpose of keeping out the cold.—Trans.

"Stop the war this instant—or else . . ."

But what "else" is there? Are there any words that can make them come to their senses? Words, in answer to which one cannot find just such other loud and lying words? Or must I fall upon my knees before them and burst into tears? But then, hundreds of thousands are making the earth resound with their weeping, but does that change anything? Or, perhaps, kill myself before them all? Kill myself! Thousands are dying every day, but does that change anything?

And when I feel my impotence, I am seized with rage— the rage of war, which I hate. Like the doctor, I long to burn down their houses with all their treasures, their wives and children; to poison the water which they drink; to raise all the killed from their graves and throw the corpses into their unclean houses on to their beds. Let them sleep with them as with their wives or mistresses!

Oh, if only I were the Devil! I would transplant all the horrors that hell exhales on to their earth. I would become the lord of all their dreams, and, when they cross their children with a smile before falling asleep, I would rise up before them a black vision. . . . Yes, I must go mad—only let it come quicker—let it come quicker. . . .

FRAGMENT XI

. . . PRISONERS, a group of trembling, terrified men. When they were led out of the train the crowd gave a roar— the roar of an enormous savage dog, whose chain is too short and not strong enough. The crowd gave a roar and was silent, breathing deeply, while they advanced in a compact group with their hands in their pockets, smiling with their white lips as if currying favour, and stepping out in such a manner as if somebody was just going to strike them with a long stick under their knees from behind. But one of them walked at a short distance from the others, calm, serious, without a smile, and when my eyes met his black ones I saw bare open hatred in them. I saw clearly that he despised me and thought me capable of anything; if I were to begin killing him, unarmed as he was, he would not have cried out or tried to defend or right himself—he considered me capable of anything.

I ran along together with the crowd, to meet his gaze once more, and only succeeded as they were entering a house. He went in the last, letting his companions pass before him, and glanced at me once more. And then I saw such pain, such an abyss of horror and insanity in his big black eyes, as if I had looked into the most wretched soul on earth.

"Who is that with the eyes?" I asked of a soldier of the escort.

"An officer—a madman. There are many such."

"What is his name?"

"He does not say. And his countrymen don't know him. A stranger they picked up. He has been saved from hanging himself once already, but what is there to be done!" . . . and the soldier made a vague gesture and disappeared in the door.

And now, this evening I am thinking of him. He is alone amidst the enemy, who, in his opinion, are capable of doing anything with him, and his own people do not know him.

He keeps silence and waits patiently for the moment when he will be able to go out of this world altogether. I do not believe that he is mad, and he is no coward; he was the only one who held himself with dignity in that group of trembling, terrified men, whom apparently he does not regard as his own people. What is he thinking about? What a depth of despair must be in the soul of that man, who, dying, does not wish to name himself. Why give his name? He has done with life and men, he has grasped their real value and notices none around him, either his own people or strangers, shout, rage and threaten as they will. I made inquiries about him. He was taken in the last terrible battle during which several tens of thousands of men lost their lives and he showed no resistance when he was being taken prisoner: he was unarmed for some reason or other, and when the soldier, not having noticed it, struck him with his sword he did not get up or try to act in self-defence. But the wound, unhappily for him, was a slight one.

But, maybe, he is really mad? The soldier said there were many such. . . .

FRAGMENT XII

. . . It is beginning. When I entered my brother's study yesterday evening he was sitting in his armchair at his table heaped with books. The hallucination disappeared the moment I lighted a candle, but for a long time I could not bring myself to sit down in the armchair that he had occupied. At first it was terrifying—the empty rooms in which one was constantly hearing rustlings and crackings were the cause of this dread, but afterwards I even liked it—better he than somebody else. Nevertheless, I did not leave the armchair the whole evening; it seemed to me that if I were to get up he would instantly sit down in my place. And I left the room very quickly without looking round. The lamps ought to have been lit in all the rooms, but was it worth while? It would have been perhaps worse if I had seen anything by lamp-light—as it was, there was still room for doubt.

To-day I entered with a candle and there was nobody in the armchair. Evidently it must have been only a shadow. Again I went to the station—I go there every morning now —and saw a whole carriage full of our mad soldiers. It was not opened, but shunted on to another line, and I had time to see several faces through the windows. They were terrible, especially one. Fearfully drawn, the colour of a lemon, with an open black mouth and fixed eyes, it was so like a mask of horror that I could not tear my eyes away from it. And it stared at me, the whole of it, and was motionless, and glided past together with the moving carriage, just as motionless, without the slightest change, never transferring its gaze for an instant. If it were to appear before me this minute in that dark door, I do not believe I should be able to hold out. I made inquiries: there were twenty-two men. The infection is spreading. The papers are hushing up something and, I believe, there is something wrong in our town too. Black, closely-shut carriages have made their appearance—I counted six during one day in different parts of the town. I suppose I shall also go off in one of them one of these days.

And the papers clamour for fresh troops and more blood

every day, and I am beginning to understand less and less what it all means. Yesterday I read an article full of suspicion, stating that there were many spies and traitors amongst the people, warning us to be cautious and mindful, and that the wrath of the people would not fail to find out the guilty. What guilty, and guilty of what? As I was returning from the station in the tram, I heard a strange conversation, I suppose in reference to the same article.

"They ought to be all hung without any trial," said one, looking scrutinisingly at me and all the passengers. "Traitors ought to be hung, yes."

"Without any mercy," confirmed the other. "They've been shown mercy enough!"

I jumped out of the tram. The war was making everybody shed tears, and they were crying too—why, what did it mean? A bloody mist seemed to have enveloped the earth, hiding it from our gaze, and I was beginning to think that the moment of the universal catastrophe was approaching. The red laugh that my brother saw. The madness was coming from over there, from those bloody burnt-out fields, and I felt its cold breath in the air. I am a strong man and have none of those illnesses that corrupt the body, bringing in their train the corruption of the brain also, but I see the infection catching me, and half of my thoughts belong to me no longer. It is worse than the plague and its horrors. One can hide from the plague, take measures, but how can one hide from all-penetrating thought, that knows neither distances nor obstacles?

In the daytime I can still fight against it, but during the night I become, as everybody else does, the slave of my

dreams—and my dreams are terrible and full of madness. . . .

FRAGMENT XIII

. . . UNIVERSAL mob-fights, senseless and sanguinary. The
slightest provocation gives rise to the most savage club-
law, knives, stones, logs of wood coming into action, and
it is all the same who is being killed—red blood asks to be
let loose, and flows willingly and plentifully.

There were six of them, all peasants, and they were
being led by three soldiers with loaded guns. In their quaint
peasant's dress, simple and primitive like a savage's, with
their quaint countenances, that seemed as if made of clay
and adorned with felted wool instead of hair, in the streets
of a rich town, under the escort of disciplined soldiers—
they resembled slaves of the antique world. They were
being led off to the war, and they moved along in obedience to the bayonets as innocent and dull as cattle led to the
slaughter-house. In front walked a youth, tall, beardless,
with a long goose neck, at the end of which was a motionless little head. His whole body was bent forward like a
switch, and he stared at the ground under his feet as fixedly
as if his gaze penetrated into the very depths of the earth.
The last in the group was a man of small stature, bearded
and middle-aged; he had no desire of resistance, and there
was no thought in his eyes, but the earth attracted his feet,
gripped them tightly, not letting them loose, and he advanced with his body thrown back, as if struggling against
a strong wind. And at each step the soldier gave him a push
with the butt-end of his rifle, and one leg, tearing itself from

the earth, convulsively thrust itself forward, while the other still stuck tightly. The faces of the soldiers were weary and angry, and evidently they had been marching so for a long time; one felt they were tired and indifferent as to how they carried their guns and how they marched, keeping no step, with their feet turned in like countrymen. The senseless, lingering and silent resistance—of the peasants, seemed to have dimmed their disciplined brains, and they had ceased to understand where they were going and what their goal was.

"Where are you leading them to?" I asked of one of the soldiers. He started, glanced at me, and in the keen flash of his eyes I felt the bayonet as distinctly as if it were already at my breast.

"Go away!" said the soldier; "go away, or else . . ."

The middle-aged man took advantage of the moment and ran away; he ran with a light trot up to the iron railings of the boulevard and sat down on his heels, as if he were hiding. No animal would have acted so stupidly, so senselessly. But the soldier became savage. I saw him go close up to him, stoop down and, thrusting his gun into the left hand, strike something soft and flat with the right one. And then again. A crowd was gathering. Laughter and shouts were heard. . . .

FRAGMENT XIV

. . . IN THE eleventh row of stalls. Somebody's arms were pressing closely against me on my right- and left-hand side, while far around me in the semi-darkness stuck out motionless heads, tinged with red from the lights upon the stage. And gradually the mass of people, confined in that narrow space, filled me with horror. Everybody was silent, listening to what was being said on the stage or, perhaps, thinking out his own thoughts, but as they were many they were more audible, for all their silence, than the loud voices of the actors. They were coughing, blowing their noses, making a noise with their feet and clothes, and I could distinctly hear their deep, uneven breathing, that was heating the air. They were terrible, for each of them could become a corpse, and they all had senseless brains. In the calmness of those well-brushed heads, resting upon white, stiff collars, I felt a hurricane of madness ready to burst every second.

My hands grew cold as I thought how many and how terrible they were, and how far away I was from the entrance. They were calm, but what if I were to cry out "Fire!" . . . And full of terror, I experienced a painfully passionate desire, of which I cannot think without my hands growing cold and moist. Who could hinder me from crying out—yes, standing up, turning round and crying out: "Fire! Save yourselves—fire!"

A convulsive wave of madness would overwhelm their still limbs. They would jump up, yelling and howling like animals; they would forget that they had wives, sisters, mothers, and would begin casting themselves about like men stricken with sudden blindness, in their madness throttling each other with their white fingers fragrant with scent. The light would be turned on, and somebody with an ashen face would appear upon the stage, shouting that all was in order and that there was no fire, and the music, trembling and halting, would begin playing something wildly merry—but they would be deaf to everything—they would be throttling, trampling, and beating the heads of the women, demolishing their ingenious, cunning headdress. They would tear at each other's ears, bite off each other's noses, and tear the very clothes off each other's bodies, feeling no shame, for they would be mad. Their sensitive, delicate, beautiful, adorable women would scream and writhe helplessly at their feet, clasping their knees, still believing in their generosity—while they would beat them viciously upon their beautiful upturned faces, trying to force their way towards the entrance. For men are always murderers, and their calmness and generosity is the calmness of a well-fed animal, that knows itself out of danger.

And when, having made corpses of half their number, they would gather at the entrance in a trembling, tattered group of shamefaced animals, with a false smile upon their lips, I would go on the stage and say with a laugh:

"It has all happened because you killed my brother." Yes, I would say with a laugh: "It has all happened because you killed my brother."

I must have whispered something aloud, for my neighbor on the right-hand side moved angrily in his chair and said:

"Hush! You are interrupting."

I felt merry and wanted to play a joke. Assuming a warning severe expression, I stooped towards him.

"What is it?" he asked suspiciously. "Why do you look at me so?"

"Hush, I implore you," whispered I with my lips. "Do

you not perceive a smell of burning? There is a fire in the theatre."

He had enough power of will and good sense not to cry out. His face grew pale, his eyes starting out of their sockets and almost protruding over his cheeks, enormous as bladders, but he did not cry out. He rose quietly and, without even thanking me, walked totteringly towards the entrance, convulsively keeping back his steps. He was afraid of the others guessing about the fire and preventing him getting away—him, the only one worthy of being saved.

I felt disgusted and left the theatre also; besides I did not want to make known my *incognito* too soon. In the street I looked towards that part of the sky where the war was raging; everything was calm, and the night clouds, yellow from the lights of the town, were slowly and calmly drifting past.

"Perhaps it is only a dream, and there is no war?" thought I, deceived by the stillness of the sky and town.

But a boy sprang out from behind a corner, crying joyously:

"A terrible battle. Enormous losses. Buy a list of telegrams—night telegrams!"

I read it by the light of the street lamp. Four thousand dead. In the theatre, I should say, there were not more than one thousand. And the whole way home I kept repeating—"Four thousand dead."

Now I am afraid of returning to my empty house. When I put my key into the lock and look at the dumb, flat door, I can feel all its dark empty rooms behind it, which, however, the next minute, a man in a hat would pass through, looking furtively around him. I know the way well, but on the stairs I begin lighting match after match, until I find a candle. I never enter my brother's study, and it is locked with all that it contains. And I sleep in the dining-room, whither I have shifted altogether; there I feel calmer, for the air seems to have still retained the traces of talking and laughing, and the merry clang of dishes. Sometimes I distinctly hear the scraping of a dry pen—and when I lie down on my bed . . .

FRAGMENT XV

. . . That absurd and terrible dream. It seemed as if the skull had been taken off my brain and, bared and unprotected, it submissively and greedily imbibed all the horrors of those bloody and senseless days. I was lying curled up, occupying only five feet of space, while my thought embraced the whole world. I saw with the eyes of all mankind, and listened with its ears; I died with the killed, sorrowed and wept with all that were wounded and left behind, and, when blood flowed out of anybody's body, I felt the pain of the wound and suffered. Even all that had not happened and was far away, I saw as clearly as if it had happened and was close by, and there was no end to the sufferings of my bared brain.

Those children, those innocent little children. I saw them in the street playing at war and chasing each other, and one of them was already crying in a high-pitched, childish voice—and something shrank within me from horror and

disgust. And I went home; night came on—and in fiery
dreams, resembling midnight conflagrations, those innocent
little children changed into a band of child-murderers.

Something was ominously burning in a broad red glare,
and in the smoke there swarmed monstrous, misshapen
children, with heads of grown-up murderers. They were
jumping lightly and nimbly, like young goats at play, and
were breathing with difficulty, like sick people. Their
mouths, resembling the jaws of toads or frogs, opened
widely and convulsively; behind the transparent skin of
their naked bodies the red blood was coursing angrily—
and they were killing each other at play. They were the
most terrible of all that I had seen, for they were little and
could penetrate everywhere.

I was looking out of the window and one of the little
ones noticed me, smiled, and with his eyes asked me to let
him in.

"I want to go to you," he said.

"You will kill me."

"I want to go to you," he said, growing suddenly pale,
and began scrambling up the white wall like a rat—just like
a hungry rat. He kept losing his footing, and squealed and
darted about the wall with such rapidity that I could not
follow his impetuous, sudden movements.

"He can crawl in under the door," said I to myself with
horror, and as if he had guessed my thoughts, he grew thin
and long and, waving the end of his tail rapidly, he crawled
into the dark crack under the front door. But I had time
to hide myself under the blanket, and heard him searching

for me in the dark rooms, cautiously stepping along with his tiny bare foot. He approached my room very slowly, stopping now and then, and at last entered it; but I did not hear any sound, either rustle or movement, for a long time, as if there was nobody near my bed. And then somebody's little hand began lifting up the edge of the coverlet, and I could feel the cold air of the room upon my face and chest. I held the blanket tightly, but it persisted in lifting itself up on all sides; and all of a sudden my feet became so cold, as if I had dipped them into water. Now they are lying unprotected in the chill darkness of the room, and he was looking at them.

In the yard, behind the house, a dog barked and was silent, and I heard the trail of the chain as it went into its kennel. But he still watched my naked feet and kept silence; I knew he was there by the unendurable horror that was binding me like death with a stony, sepulchral immobility. If I could have cried out, I would have awakened the whole town, the whole world, but my voice was dead within me, and I lay submissive and motionless, feeling the little cold hands moving over my body and nearing my throat.

"I cannot!" I groaned, gasping and waking up for an instant, I saw the vigilant darkness of the night, mysterious and living, and again I believe I fell asleep. . . .

"Don't fear," said my brother, sitting down upon my bed, and the bed creaked, so heavy was he—dead. "Never fear, you see it is a dream. You only imagine that you were being strangled, while in reality you are asleep in the dark rooms, where there is not a soul, and I am in my study writing. Nobody understood what I wrote about, and you derided me as one insane, but now I will tell you the truth. I am writing about the red laugh. Do you see it?"

Something enormous, red and bloody, was standing before me, laughing a toothless laugh.

"That is the red laugh. When the earth goes mad, it begins to laugh like that. You know, the earth has gone mad. There are no more flowers or songs on it; it has become round, smooth and red like a scalped head. Do you see it?"

"Yes, I see it. It is laughing."

"Look what its brain is like. It is red, like bloody porridge, and is muddled."

"It is crying out."

"It is in pain. It has no flowers or songs. And now— let me lie down upon you."

"You are heavy and I am afraid."

"We, the dead, lie down on the living. Do you feel warm?"

"Yes."

"Are you comfortable?"

"I am dying."

"Awake and cry out. Awake and cry out. I am going away. . . ."

FRAGMENT XVI

. . . To-DAY is the eighth day of the battle. It began last Friday, and Saturday, Sunday, Monday, Tuesday, Wednesday and Thursday have passed—and Friday has come again and is gone—and it is still going on. Both armies, hundreds of thousands of men, are standing in front of each other, never flinching, sending explosive, crashing projectiles without stopping, and every instant living men are turned into corpses. The roar and incessant vibration of the air has made the very sky shudder and gather black thunder-clouds above their heads—while they continue to stand in front of each other, never flinching and still killing each other. If a man does not sleep for three nights, he becomes ill and loses his memory, but they have not slept for a whole week, and are all mad. That is why they feel no pain, do not retreat, and go on fighting until they have killed all to the last man. They say that some of the detach-ments came to the end of their ammunition, but still they fought on, using their fists and stones, and biting each other like dogs. If the remnants of those regiments return home, they will have canine teeth like wolves—but they will not return, they have gone mad and die, every man of them. They have gone mad. Everything is muddled in their heads, and they cease to understand anything! If they were to be turned round suddenly and sharply, they would begin firing at their own men, thinking that they were firing at the enemy.

Strange rumours—strange rumours that are told in a whisper, those repeating them turning white from horror and dreadful forebodings. Brother, brother, listen what is being told of the red laugh! They say phantom regiments have appeared, large bands of shadows, the exact copy of living men. At night, when the men forget themselves for an instant in sleep, or in the thick of the day's fight, when the bright day itself seems a phantom, they suddenly appear, firing out of phantom guns, filling the air with phantom noises; and men, living but insane men, astounded by the suddenness of the attack, fight to the death against the phantom enemy, go mad from horror, become grey in an instant and die. The phantoms disappear as suddenly as they appear, and all becomes still, while the earth is strewn with fresh mutilated bodies. Who killed them? You know, brother, who killed them. When there is a lull between two battles and the enemy is far off, suddenly in the darkness of the night there resounds a solitary, frightened shot. And all jump up and begin firing into the darkness, into the silent dumb darkness, for a long time, for whole hours. Whom do they see there? Whose terrible, silent shape, full of horror and madness appears before them? You know, brother, and I know, but men do not know yet, but they have a foreboding, and ask, turning pale: "Why are there so many madmen? Before there never used to be so many."

"Before there never used to be so many madmen," they say, turning pale, trying to believe that now it is as before, and that the universal violence done to the brains of humanity would have no effect upon their weak little intellects.

"Why, men fought before and always have fought, and nothing of the sort happened. Strife is a law of nature," they say with conviction and calmness, growing pale, nevertheless, seeking for the doctor with their eyes, and calling out hurriedly: "Water, quick, a glass of water!"

They would willingly become idiots, those people, only not to feel their intellect reeling and their reason succumbing in the hopeless combat with insanity.

In those days, when men over there were constantly being turned into corpses, I could find no peace, and sought the society of my fellow-men; and I heard many conversations and saw many false smiling faces, that asserted that the war was far off and in no way concerned them. But much oftener I met naked, frank horror, hopeless, bitter tears and frenzied cries of despair, when the great Mind itself cried out of man its last prayer, its last curse, with all the intensity of its power:

"Whenever will the senseless carnage end?"

At the home of some friends, whom I had not seen for a long time, perhaps several years, I unexpectedly met a mad officer, invalided from the war. He was a school fellow of mine, but I did not recognise him: if he had lain for a year in his grave, he would have returned more like himself than he was then. His hair was grey and his face quite white, his features were but little changed—but he was always silent, and seemed to be listening to something, and this stamped upon his face a look of such formidable remoteness, such indifference to all around him, that it was fearful to talk to him. His relatives were told he went mad in the following circumstances: they were in the reserve, while the neighboring regiment was ordered to make a bayonet charge. The men rushed shouting "Hurrah" so loudly as almost to drown the noise of the cannon—and suddenly the guns ceased firing, the "Hurrah" ceased also, and a sepulchral stillness ensued: they had run up to the enemy and were charging him with their bayonets. And his reason succumbed to that stillness.

Now he is calm when people make a noise around him, talk and shout, he listens and waits; but if only there is a moment's silence, he catches hold of his head, rushes up to the wall or against the furniture, and falls down in a fit resembling epilepsy. He has many relations, and they take turns and surround him with sound, but there remain the nights, long solitary nights—but here his father, a grey-haired old man, slightly wandering in his mind too, helped. He hung the walls of his son's room with loudly ticking clocks, that constantly struck the hour at different times, and at present he is arranging a wheel, resembling an incessantly going rattle. None of them lose hope that he will recover, as he is only twenty-seven, and their house is even gay. He is dressed very cleanly—not in his uniform—great care is taken of his appearance, and he is even handsome with his white hair, young, thoughtful face and well-bred, slow, tired movements.

When I was told all, I went up and kissed his hand, his white, languid hand, which will never more be lifted for a blow—and this did not seem to surprise anybody very much. Only his young sister smiled at me with her eyes, and afterwards showed me such attention that it seemed as if I were her betrothed and she loved me more than anybody in the world. She showed me such attention that I very nearly told her about my dark empty rooms, in which I was worse than alone—miserable heart, that never loses hope. . . . And she managed it so that we remained alone.

"How pale you are and what dark rings you have under

your eyes," she said kindly. "Are you ill? Are you grieving for your brother?"

"I am grieving for everybody. And I do not feel well."

"I know why you kissed my brother's hand. They did not understand. Because he is mad, yes?"

"Yes, because he is mad."

She grew thoughtful and looked very much like her brother, only younger.

"And will you," she stopped and blushed, but did not lower her eyes, "will you let me kiss your hand?"

I kneeled before her and said: "Bless me."

She paled slightly, drew back and whispered with her lips:

"I do not believe."

"And I also."

For an instant her hand touched my head, and the instant was gone.

"Do you know," she said, "I am leaving for the war?"

"Go! But you will not be able to bear it."

"I do not know. But they need help, the same as you or my brother. It is not their fault. Will you remember me?"

"Yes. And you?"

"And I will remember you too. Good-bye!"

"Good-bye for ever!"

And I grew calm and felt happier, as if I had passed through the most terrible that there is in death and madness. And yesterday, for the first time, I entered my house calmly without any fear, and opened my brother's study and sat for a long time at his table. And when in the night I suddenly awoke as if from a push, and heard the scraping of the dry pen upon the paper, I was not frightened, but thought to myself, almost with a smile:

"Work on, brother, work on! Your pen is not dry, it is steeped in living human blood. Let your paper seem empty —in its ominous emptiness it is more eloquent of war and reason than all that is written by the most clever men. Work on, brother, work on!"

. . . And this morning I read that the battle is still raging, and again I was possessed with a dread fear and a feeling of something falling upon my brain. It is coming, it is here; it is already standing upon the threshold of these empty, light rooms. Remember, remember me, dear girl; I am going mad. Thirty thousand dead, thirty thousand dead! . . .

FRAGMENT XVII

. . . A FIGHT is going on in the town. There are dark and dreadful rumours. . . .

FRAGMENT XVIII

THIS morning, looking through the endless list of killed in the newspaper, I saw a familiar name; my sister's affianced husband, an officer called for military service at the same time as my dead brother, was killed. And, an hour later, the postman handed me a letter addressed to my brother, and I recognized the handwriting of the deceased on the envelope: the dead was writing to the dead. But still it was better so than the dead writing to the living. A mother was pointed out to me who kept receiving letters from her son for a whole month after she had read of his terrible death in the papers: he had been torn to pieces by a shell. He was a fond son, and each letter was full of endearing and encouraging words and youthful, naïve hopes of happiness. He was dead, but wrote of life with a fearful accuracy every day, and the mother ceased to believe in his death; and when a day passed without any letter, then a second and third, and the endless silence of death ensued, she took a large old-fashioned revolver belonging to her son in both hands, and shot herself in the breast. I believe she survived, but I am not sure; I never heard.

I looked at the envelope for a long time, and thought: He held it in his hands, he bought it somewhere, he gave the money to pay for it, and his servant went to fetch it from some shop; he sealed and perhaps posted it himself. Then the wheel of the complex machine called "post" came into action, and the letter glided past forest, fields and towns, passing from hand to hand, but rushing infallibly towards its destination. He put on his boots that last morn-ing, while it went gliding on; he was killed, but it glided on; he was thrown into a pit and covered up with dead bodies and earth, while it still glided on past forests, fields and towns, a living phantom in a grey stamped envelope. And now I was holding it in my hands.

Here are the contents of the letter. It was written with a pencil on scraps of paper, and was not finished: some-thing interfered.

". . . Only now do I understand the great joy of war, the ancient, primitive delight of killing man—clever, schem-ing, artful man, immeasurably more interesting than the most ravenous animal. To be ever taking life is as good ᴀs playing at lawn-tennis with planets and stars. Poor friend, what a pity you are not with us, but are constrained to weary away your time amidst an unleavened daily existence! In the atmosphere of death you would have found all that your restless, noble heart yearned for. A bloody feast—what truth there is in this somewhat hackneyed comparison! We go about up to our knees in blood, and this red wine, as my jolly men call it in jest, makes our heads swim. To drink the blood of one's enemy is not at all such a stupid custom as we think: they knew what they were doing. . . .

". . . The crows are cawing. Do you hear, the crows are cawing. From whence have they all gathered? The sky is black with them; they settle down beside us, having lost all fear, and follow us everywhere; and we are always underneath them, like under a black lace sunshade or a moving tree with black leaves. One of them approached quite close to my face and wanted to peck at it: he thought, most probably, that I was dead. The crows are cawing, and this troubles me a little. From whence have they all gathered? . . .

". . . Yesterday we stabbed them all sleeping. We approached stealthily, scarcely touching the ground with our feet, as if we were stalking wild ducks. We stole up to them so skilfully and cautiously that we did not touch a corpse and did not scare one single crow. We stole up like shadows, and the night hid us. I killed the sentry myself— knocked him down and strangled him with my hands, so as not to let him cry out. You understand: the slightest sound, ᴀnd all would have been lost. But he did not cry out; he had no time, I believe, even to guess that he was being killed.

"They were all sleeping around the smouldering fires—sleeping peacefully, as if they were at home in their beds. We hacked about us for more than an hour, and only a few had time to awake before they received their death-blow. They howled, and of course begged for mercy. They used their teeth. One bit off a finger on my left hand, with which I was incautiously holding his head. He bit off my finger, but I twisted his head clean off: how do you think —are we quits? How they did not all wake up I cannot imagine. One could hear their bones crackling and their bodies being hacked. Afterwards we stripped all naked and divided their clothes amongst ourselves. My friend, don't get angry over a joke. With your susceptibility you will say this savours of marauding, but then we are almost naked ourselves; our clothes are quite worn-out. I have been wearing a woman's jacket for a long time, and resemble more a . . . than an officer of a victorious army. By the bye, you are, I believe, married, and it is not quite right for you to read such things. But . . . you understand? Women. D—n it, I am young, and thirst for love! Stop a minute: I believe it was you who was engaged to be married? It was you, was it not, who showed me the portrait of a young girl and told me she was your promised bride?—and there was something sad, something very sad and mournful underneath it. And you cried. That was a long time ago, and I remember it but confusedly; there is no time for softness at war. And you cried. What did you cry about? What was there written that was as sad and mournful as a drooping flower?

And you kept crying and crying. . . . Were you not ashamed, an officer, to cry?

". . . The crows are cawing. Do you hear, friend, the crows are cawing. What do they want?"

Further on the pencil-written lines were effaced and it was impossible to decipher the signature. And strange to say the dead man called forth no compassion in me. I distinctly pictured to myself his face, in which all was soft and delicate as a woman's: the color of his cheeks, the clearness and morning freshness of the eyes, the beard so bushy and soft, that a woman could almost have adorned herself with it. He liked books, flowers and music, feared all that was coarse, and wrote poetry—my brother, as a critic, declared that he wrote very good poetry. And I could not connect all that I knew and remembered of him with the cawing crows, bloody carnage and death.

. . . The crows are cawing. . . .

And suddenly for one mad, unutterably happy instant, I clearly saw that all was a lie and that there was no war. There were no killed, no corpses, there was no anguish of reeling, helpless thought. I was sleeping on my back and seeing a dream, as I used to in my childhood: the silent dread rooms, devastated by death and terror, and myself with a wild letter in my hand. My brother was living, and they were all sitting at the tea-table, and I could hear the noise of the crockery.

. . . The crows are cawing. . . .

No, it is but true. Unhappy earth, it is true. The crows are cawing. It is not the invention of an idle scribbler, aiming at cheap effects, or of a madman, who has lost his senses. The crows are cawing. Where is my brother? He was noble-hearted and gentle and wished no one evil. Where is he? I am asking you, you cursed murderers. I am asking you, you cursed murderers, crows sitting on carrion, wretched, imbecile animals, before the whole world. For you are animals. What did you kill my brother for? If you had a face, I would give you a blow upon it, but you have no face, you have only the snout of a wild beast. You pretend that you are men, but I see claws under your gloves and the flat skull of an animal under your hat; hidden beneath your clever conversation I hear insanity rattling its rusty chains. And with all the power of my grief, my anguish and dishonored thought—I curse you, you wretched, imbecile animals!

FRAGMENT THE LAST

". . . WE LOOK to you for the regeneration of human life!"

So shouted a speaker, holding on with difficulty to a small pillar, balancing himself with his arms, and waving a flag with a large inscription half-hidden in its folds: "Down with the war!"

"You, who are young, you, whose lives are only just beginning, save yourselves and the future generations from this horror, from this madness. It is unbearable, our eyes are drowned with blood. The sky is falling upon us, the earth is giving way under our feet. Kind people . . ."

The crowd was buzzing enigmatically and the voice of the speaker was drowned at times in the living threatening noise.

". . . Suppose I am mad, but I am speaking the truth.

My father and brother are rotting over there like carrion.
Make bonfires, dig pits and destroy, bury all your arms. De-
molish all the barracks, and strip all the men of their bright
clothes of madness, tear them off. One cannot bear it. . . ."
Men are dying . . ."

Somebody very tall gave him a blow and knocked him
off the pillar; the flag rose once again and fell. I had no
time to see the face of the man who struck him, as instantly
everything turned into a nightmare. Everything became
commotion, became agitated and howled; stones and logs of
wood went flying through the air, fists, which were beating
somebody, appeared above the heads. The crowd, like a
living, roaring wave, lifted me up, carried me along several
steps and threw me violently against a fence, then carried
me back and away somewhere, and at last pressed me
against a high pile of wood, that inclined forwards, threatening to fall down upon somebody's head. Something
crackled and rattled against the beams in rapid dry succession; an instant's stillness—and again a roar burst forth,
enormous, open-mouthed, terrible in its overwhelming
power. And then the dry rapid crackling was heard again
and somebody fell down near me with the blood flowing
out of a red hole where his eye had been. And a heavy log
of wood came whirling through the air and struck me in
the face, and I fell down and began crawling, whither I
knew not, amidst the trampling feet, and came to a open
space. Then I climbed over some fences, breaking all my
nails, clambered up piles of wood; one pile fell to pieces
under me and I fell amidst a cataract of thumping logs; at
last I succeeded with difficulty in getting out of a closed-in

space—while behind me all crashed, roared, howled and crackled, trying to overtake me. A bell was ringing somewhere; something fell with a thundering crash, as if it were a five-story house. The twilight seemed to have stopped still, keeping back the night, and the roar of shots, as if steeped in red, had driven away the darkness. Jumping over the last fence I found myself in a narrow, crooked lane resembling a corridor, between two obscure walls, and began running. I ran for a long time, but the lane seemed to have no outlet; it was terminated by a wall, behind which piles of wood and scaffolding rose up black against the sky. And again I climbed over the mobile, shifting piles, falling into pits, where all was still and smelt of damp wood, getting out of them again into the open, not daring to look back, for I knew quite well what was happening by the dull reddish color that tinged the black beams and made them look like murdered giants. My smashed face had stopped bleeding and felt numbed and strange, like a mask of plaster; and the pain had almost quite disappeared. I believe I fainted and lost consciousness in one of the black holes into which I had fallen, but I am not certain whether I only imagined it or was it really so, as I can remember myself only running.

I rushed about the unfamiliar streets, which had no lamps, past the black death-like houses for a long time, unable to find my way out of the dumb labyrinth. I ought to have stopped and looked around me to define the necessary direction, but it was impossible to do so: the still distant din and howl was following at my heels and gradually overtaking me; sometimes, at a sudden turning, it struck me in the face red and enveloped in clouds of livid, curling smoke, and then I turned back and rushed on until it was at my back once more. At one corner I saw a strip of light, that disappeared at my approach: it was a shop that was being hastily closed. I caught a glimpse of the counter and a barrel through a wide chink, but suddenly all became enveloped in a silent, crouching gloom. Not far from the shop I met a man, who was running towards me, and we almost collided in the darkness, stopping short at the distance of two steps from each other. I do not know who he was: I only saw the dark blue alert outline.

"Are you coming from over there?" he asked.

"Yes."

"And where are you running to?"

"Home."

"Ah! Home?"

He was silent for an instant and suddenly flung himself upon me, trying to bring me to the ground, and his cold fingers searched hungrily for my throat, but got entangled in my clothes. I bit his hand, loosened myself from his grip and set off running through the deserted streets with him after me, stamping loudly with his boots, for a long time. Then he stopped—I suppose the bite hurt him.

I do not know how I hit upon my street. It had no lamps either, and the houses had not a single light, as if they were dead, and I would have run past without recognising it, if I had not by chance lifted my eyes and seen my house. But I hesitated for some time: the house in which I had lived for so many years seemed to me unfamiliar in that strange dead street, in which my loud breathing awakened an extraordinary and mournful echo. Then I was seized with a sudden wild terror at the thought that I had lost my key when I fell, and I found it with difficulty, although it was there all the time in the pocket of my coat. And when I turned the lock the echo repeated the sound so loudly and extraordinarily, as if all the doors of those dead houses in the whole street had opened simultaneously.

... At first I hid myself in the cellar, but it was terrible and dull down there, and something began darting before my eyes, so I quietly stole into the rooms. Groping my way in the dark, I locked all the doors and after a short meditation decided to barricade them with the furniture, but the sound of the furniture being moved was terribly loud in the empty rooms and terrified me. "I shall await death thus. It's all the same," I decided. There was some water, very warm water in the water-jug, and I washed my face in the dark and wiped it with a sheet. The parts that were smashed galled and smarted much, and I felt a desire to look at myself in the looking-glass. I lit a match—and in its uneven, faint light there glanced at me from out of the darkness something so hideous and terrible that I hastily threw the match upon the floor. I believe my nose was broken. "It makes no difference now," said I to myself. "Nobody will mind."

And I felt gay. With strange grimaces and contortions of the body, as if I were personating a thief on the stage, I went into the larder and began searching for food. I clearly saw the unsuitableness of all my grimaces, but it pleased me so. And I ate with the same contortions, pretending that I was very hungry.

But the darkness and quiet frightened me. I opened the window into the yard and began listening. At first, probably as the traffic had ceased, all seemed to me to be quite still. And I heard no shots. But soon I clearly distinguished a distant din of voices: shouts, the crash of something falling, a laugh. The sounds grew louder perceptibly. I looked at the sky; it was livid and sweeping past rapidly. And the coach-house opposite me, and the paving of the streets, and the dog's kennel, all were tinged with the same reddish glare, I called the dog softly—

"Neptune!"

But nothing stirred in the kennel, and near it I distinguished in the livid light a shining piece of broken chain. The distant cries and noise of something falling kept on growing, and I shut the window.

"They are coming here!" I said to myself, and began looking for some place to hide myself. I opened the stoves, fumbled at the grate, opened the cupboards, but they would not do. I made the round of all the rooms, excepting the study, into which I did not want to look. I knew he was sitting in his armchair at his table, heaped with books, and this was unpleasant to me at that moment.

Gradually it began to appear that I was not alone: around me people were silently moving about in the darkness. They almost touched me, and once somebody's breath sent a cold thrill through the back of my head.

"Who is there?" I asked in a whisper, but nobody answered.

And when I moved on they followed me, silent and terrible. I knew that it was only a hallucination because I was ill and apparently feverish, but I could not conquer my fear, from which I was trembling all over as if I had the ague. I felt my head: it was hot as if on fire.

"I had better go there," said I to myself. "He is one of my own people after all."

He was sitting in his armchair at the table, heaped with books, and did not disappear as he did the last time, but remained seated. The reddish light was making its way through the red drawn curtains into the room, but did not light up anything, and he was scarcely visible. I sat down at a distance from him on the couch and waited. All was still in the room, while from outside the even buzzing noise, the crash of something falling and disjointed cries were borne in upon us. And they were nearing us. The livid light became brighter and brighter, and I could distinguish him in his armchair—his black, iron-like profile, outlined by a narrow stripe of red.

"Brother!" I said.

But he kept silence, immobile and black, like a monument. A board cracked in the next room and suddenly all became so extraordinarily still, as it is where there are many dead. All the sounds died away and the livid light itself assumed a scarcely perceptible shade of deathliness and stillness and became motionless and a little dim. I thought the stillness was coming from my brother and told him so.

"No, it is not from me," he answered. "Look out of the window."

I pulled the curtains aside and staggered back.

"So that's what it is!" said I.

"Call my wife; she has not seen that yet," ordered my brother.

She was sitting in the dining-room sewing something and, seeing my face, rose obediently, stuck her needle into her work and followed me. I pulled back the curtains from all the windows and the livid light flowed in through the broad openings unhindered, but somehow did not make the room any lighter: it was just as dark and only the big red squares of the windows burned brightly.

We went up to the window. Before the house there stretched an even, fiery red sky, without a single cloud, star or sun, and ended at the horizon, while below it lay just such an even dark red field, and it was covered with dead bodies. All the corpses were naked and lay with their legs towards us, so that we could only see their feet and triangular heads. And all was still; apparently they were all dead, and there were no wounded left behind in that endless field.

"Their number is growing," said my brother.

He was standing at the window also, and all were there: my mother, sister and everybody that lived in the house. I could not distinguish their faces, and could recognise them only by their voices.

"It only seems so," said my sister.

"No, it's true. Just look."

And, truly, there seemed to be more bodies. We looked attentively for the reason and found it: at the side of a corpse, where there was a free space, a fresh corpse suddenly appeared; apparently the earth was throwing them up. And all the unoccupied spaces filled rapidly, and the earth grew lighter from the light pink bodies, that were lying side by side with their feet towards us. And the room grew lighter, filled with a light pink dead light.

"Look, there is not enough room for them," said my brother.

And my mother answered:

"There is one here already."

We looked round: behind us on the floor lay a naked, light pink body with its head thrown back. And instantly at its side there appeared a second, and a third. And the earth threw them up one after the other, and soon the orderly rows of light pink dead bodies filled all the rooms.

"They are in the nursery too," said the nurse. "I saw them."

"We must go away," said my sister.

"But we cannot pass," said my brother.

"Look!"

And sure enough, they were lying close together, arm to arm, and their naked feet were touching us. And suddenly they stirred and swayed and rose up in the same orderly rows: the earth was throwing up new bodies, and they were lifting the first ones upwards.

"They will smother us!" said I. "Let us save ourselves through the window."

"We cannot!" cried my brother. "We cannot! Look what is there!"

. . . Behind the window, in a livid, motionless light stood the Red Laugh.

THE GENTLEMAN FROM
SAN FRANCISCO

By Ivan Bunin

Alas, alas, that great city Babylon,
that mighty city!
THE APOCALYPSE

THE GENTLEMAN from San Francisco—neither at Naples nor at Capri had anyone remembered his name—was journeying to the Old World for two full years, with wife and daughter, wholly for recreation.

He felt firmly assured that he had every right to take a rest, pleasure, in a prolonged and comfortable journey, and other things besides. For such an assurance he had the good reason, that, in the first place, he was rich, and that, in the second, in spite of his fifty-eight years, he was only just taking his first plunge into life. Before this he had not lived but merely existed—to be sure, not so badly, but none the less putting all his hopes in the future. He had laboured diligently—the coolies, whom he had employed by the thousands, knew well what this meant!—and at last he saw that much had been achieved, that he was now equal to those he had at one time appointed as his models, and he decided to give himself a well-earned rest. It was a custom among his kind of people to begin the enjoyment of life with a journey to Europe, to India, to Egypt. He proposed to follow their example. Before all, of course, he desired to reward himself for his years of hard toil; nevertheless, he was happy also for his wife's and daughter's sakes. His wife had never been distinguished for any particular susceptibility to fresh impressions, but then all elderly American women are ardent travellers. As for his daughter, a girl no longer young and somewhat ailing, the journey would do her positive good: to say nothing of the benefits her health would derive, was there not always the likelihood of happy encounters during journeys? While travelling one may indeed, at times, sit at the same table with a multi-millionaire, or enjoy looking at frescoes in his company.

The itinerary planned by the gentleman from San Francisco was an extensive one. In December and January he hoped to enjoy the sun of Southern Italy, the monuments of antiquity, the *tarantella,* the serenades of strolling singers, and another thing for which men of his age have a peculiar relish: the love of young Neopolitan women, conferred—let us admit—not with wholly disinterested motives; he planned to spend the Carnival in Nice, in Monto Carlo, toward which the most select society gravitated at this season—that society upon which all the blessings of civilization depend: not alone the cut of the smoking jacket, but also the stability of thrones, and the declaration of wars, and the welfare of hotels—where some devote themselves with ardour to automobile and sail races, others to roulette, while a third group engages in what is called flirting; a fourth in shoot-

ing pigeons which, emerging from their shelters, gracefully
soar upward above emerald-green lawns, against the background of a sea of the colour of forget-me-nots, only in the
next instant to strike the ground as crumpled little shapes
of white. The beginning of March he wanted to devote to
Florence; on the eve of the Passion of Our Lord to arrive
at Rome, in order to hear the *Miserere* there; his plans also
included Venice, and Paris, and bull-fights in Seville, and·
sea-bathing in the British Isles, and Athens, and Constanti-
nople, and Palestine, and Egypt, and even Japan—naturally,
on the return journey . . . And everything went splendidly
at first.

It was the end of November; almost to Gibraltar itself the
ship proceeded now through an icy mist, now through a
storm with wet snow; but it sailed on unperturbed and even
without rolling; the passengers on the steamer were many,
and all of them persons of consequence; the ship—the famous *Atlantis*—resembled the most expensive of European
hotels, with all conveniences; an all-night bar, Turkish
baths, a newspaper of its own,—and life upon it flowed in
accordance with a splendid system of regulations: the passengers rose early, to the sound of bugles, sharply reverberating through the passages at the yet dark hour when day
was so slowly and reluctantly dawning above the gray-green
watery desert, ponderously restless in the mist. They put
on their flannel pyjamas, drank coffee, chocolate, cocoa;
then they reclined in marble bath-tubs, performed exercises,
awakening an appetite and a sense of well-being, attended
to their daily toilet and went to breakfast. Until eleven they
were supposed to promenade the decks lustily, breathing in

the cool freshness of the ocean, or to play at shuffleboard and other games for a renewed stimulation of the appetite; and at eleven, to seek refreshment in bouillon and sandwiches; after which they read their newspaper with pleasure and calmly awaited lunch, a meal even more nourishing and varied than the breakfast; the following two hours were dedicated to repose; all the decks were then arranged with *chaises longues,* upon which the travellers reclined, covered up with plaid rugs, contemplating the cloudy sky and the foaming billows flashing by beyond the rail, or else gently drowsing. At five o'clock, enlivened and refreshed, they were served with strong fragrant tea and pastries; at seven, the bugle call announced dinner, consisting of nine courses. . . . At this point the gentleman from San Francisco, greatly cheered, would hurry to his magnificent *cabin de luxe,* to dress.

In the evening the tiers of the *Atlantis* gaped through the dusk as with fiery, countless eyes, and a great multitude of servants worked with especial feverishness in the kitchens, sculleries, and wine vaults. The ocean, heaving on the other side of the walls, was terrifying, but none gave it a thought, firmly believing it under the sway of the captain,—a red-haired man of monstrous bulk and ponderousness, always seeming sleepy, resembling, in his uniform frock-coat, with its golden chevrons, an enormous idol; it was only very rarely that he left his mysterious quarters to appear in public. A siren on the forecastle howled ceaselessly in hellish sullenness and whined in frenzied malice, but not many of the diners heard the siren,—it was drowned by the strains of a splendid stringed orchestra, playing exquisitely and without pause in the two-tiered hall, decorated with marble, its floors covered with velvet rugs; festively flooded with the lights of crystal lustres and gilded *girandoles,* filled to capacity with diamond-bedecked ladies in *décolleté* and men in smoking jackets, graceful waiters and deferential *maîtres d'hôtel,*—among whom one, who took orders for wines exclusively, even walked about with a chain around his neck, like a lord mayor. A smoking jacket and perfect linen made the gentleman from San Francisco appear very much younger. Spare, not tall, awkwardly but strongly built, groomed until he shone and moderately animated, he sat in the aureate-pearly refulgence of this palatial room, at a table with a bottle of amber Johannesberg, with countless goblets, small and large, of the thinnest glass, with a fragrant bouquet of curly hyacinths. There was something Mongolian about his yellowish face with clipped silvery moustache; his large teeth gleamed with gold fillings; his stalwart, bald head glistened like old ivory. Rich, yet in keeping with her years, was the attire of his wife,—a big, broad, calm woman; elaborate, yet light and diaphanous, with an innocent frankness, was that of his daughter,—a girl innocently frank, tall, slender, with magnificent hair, exquisitely dressed, with breath aromatic from violet cachous and with the tenderest of tiny moles about her lips and between her shoulder blades, slightly powdered. . . .

The dinner went on for two whole hours; after dinner there was dancing in the ball-room, during which the men, —the gentleman from San Francisco among their number, of course,—with their feet cocked up, decided, upon the basis of the latest political and stock-exchange news, the destinies of nations, smoking Havana cigars and drinking *liqueurs* until their faces were flushed, while seated in the bar, where the waiters were Negroes in red jackets, the whites of their eyes resembling peeled, hard-boiled eggs. The ocean, with a dull roar, was moving in black mountains on the other side of the wall; the snow-gale whistled fiercely through the soaked rigging; the whole ship quivered as it mastered both the gale and the mountains, sundering to either side, as though with a plough, their shifting masses, which again and again boiled up and flung themselves high, with tails of foam; the siren, stifled by the fog, was moaning with a deathly anguish; the lookouts up in their crow's-nest froze with the cold and grew dazed from straining their attention beyond their strength. Akin to the grim sultry depths of the infernal regions, akin to their ultimate, their ninth circle, was the womb of the steamer, below the water line,—that womb where dully gurgled the gigantic furnaces, devouring with their fiery maws mountains of hard coal, cast into them by men stripped to the waist, purple from the flames, and with smarting, filthy sweat pouring over them; while here, in the bar, men threw their legs over the arms of their chairs with never a care, sipping cognac and *liqueurs,* and were wafted among clouds of spicy smoke as they indulged in refined conversation; in the ball-room everything was radiant with light and warmth and joy; couples were now whirling in waltzes, now swaying in the tango,—and the music insistently, in some delectably-shameless melancholy, supplicated always of one, always of the same thing. . . . There was an ambassador among this brilliant throng,—a lean, modest little

old man; there was a rich man,—clean-shaven, lanky, of in-
determinate years, and with the appearance of a prelate, in
an old-fashioned frock-coat; there was a well-known Span-
ish writer; there was a world-celebrated beauty, already just
the very least trifle faded and of an unenviable morality;
there was an exquisite couple in love with each other, whom
all watched with curiosity and whose happiness was uncon-
cealed: *he* danced only with *her;* sang—and with great
ability—only to *her* accompaniment; everything they did
was carried out so charmingly; and only the captain knew
that this pair was hired by Lloyd's to play at love for good
money, and that they had been sailing for a long time, now
on one ship, now on another.

At Gibraltar everybody was gladdened by the sun,—it
seemed like early spring; a new passenger, whose person
aroused the general interest, made his appearance on board
the *Atlantis*,—he was the hereditary prince of a certain Asi-
atic kingdom, travelling incognito; a little man who somehow seemed to be all made of wood, even though he was
agile in his movements; broad of face, with narrow eyes, in
gold-rimmed spectacles; a trifle unpleasant owing to the
fact that his skin showed through his coarse black moustache like that of a corpse; on the whole, however, he was
charming, simple, and modest. On the Mediterranean Sea
there was a whiff of winter again; the billows ran high,
were as multi-coloured as the tail of a peacock, and had
snowy-white crests, due, in spite of the sparklingly bright
sun and perfectly clear sky, to a *tramontana,* a chill northern wind from beyond the mountains, that was joyously
and madly rushing to meet the ship. . . . Then, on the sec-

ond day, the sky began to pale, the horizon became covered with mist, land was nearing; Ischia, Capri appeared; through the binoculars, Naples—lumps of sugar strewn at the foot of some dove-coloured mass—could be seen; while over it and this dove-coloured object were visible the ridges of distant mountains, vaguely glimmering with the dead whiteness of snow. There was a great number of people on deck; many of the ladies and gentlemen had already put on short, light fur coats, with the fur outside; Chinese boys, patient and always speaking in a whisper, bow-legged striplings with pitch-black queues reaching to their heels and with eyelashes as long and thick as those of young girls, were already dragging, little by little, sundry plaids, canes, and portmanteaux and grips of alligator hide toward the companion-ways. . . . The daughter of the gentleman from San Francisco was standing beside the prince, who had been, by a happy chance, presented to her yesterday evening, and she pretended to be looking intently into the distance, in a direction he was pointing out to her, telling, explaining something or other to her, hurriedly and quietly. On account of his height he seemed a boy by contrast with others,—he was odd and not at all prepossessing of person, with his spectacles, his bowler, his English great coat, while his scanty moustache looked just as if it were of horse-hair, and the swarthy, thin skin seemed to be drawn tightly over his face, and somehow had the appearance of being lacquered,—but the young girl was listening to him, without understanding, in her perturbation, what he was saying; her heart was thumping from an incomprehensible rapture in his presence and from pride that he was speaking with her, and not some one else; everything about him that was different from others,—his lean hands, his clear skin, under which flowed the ancient blood of kings, even his wholly unpretentious, yet somehow singularly neat, European dress, —everything held a secret, inexplicable charm, evoked a feeling of amorousness. As for the gentleman from San Francisco himself,—he, in a high silk hat, in gray spats over patent-leather shoes, kept on glancing at the famous beauty, who was standing beside him,—a tall blonde of striking figure, with eyes painted in the latest Parisian fashion; she was holding a diminutive, hunched-up, mangy lap dog on a silver chain and was chattering to it without pause. And the daughter, in some vague embarrassment, tried not to notice her father.

Like all Americans of means, he was very generous while travelling, and, like all of them, believed in the full sincerity and good-will of those who brought him food and drink with such solicitude, who served him from morn till night, anticipating his slightest wish; of those who guarded his cleanliness and rest, lugged his things around, summoned porters for him, delivered his trunks to hotels. Thus had it been everywhere, thus had it been on the ship, and thus it had to be in Naples as well. Naples grew, and drew nearer; the musicians, the brass of their instruments flashing, had already clustered upon the deck, and suddenly deafened everybody with the triumphant strains of a march; the gigantic captain, in his full-dress uniform, appeared upon his stage, and, like a gracious pagan god, waved his hand amiably to the passengers,—and to the gentleman from San Francisco it seemed that it was for him alone that the march so beloved by proud America was thundering, that it was he whom the captain was felicitating upon a safe arrival. And every other passenger felt similarly about himself—or herself. And when the *Atlantis* finally entered the harbour, heaved to at the wharf with her many-tiered mass, black with people, and the gang-planks clattered down,— what a multitude of porters and their helpers in caps with gold braid, what a multitude of different *commissionaires,* whistling gamins, and strapping ragamuffins with packets of coloured postal cards in their hands, made a rush toward the gentleman from San Francisco, with offers of their services! And he smiled, with a kindly contemptuousness, at these ragamuffins, as he went toward the automobile of precisely that hotel where there was a likelihood of the prince's stopping. He drawled through his teeth, now in English, now in Italian:

"Go away! *Via!"*

Life at Naples at once assumed its wonted, ordered routine: in the early morning, breakfast in the gloomy dining-room with its damp draught from windows opening on some sort of a stony little garden. The sky was overcast, holding out little promise, and there was the usual crowd of guides at the door of the vestibule; then came the first smiles of a warm, rosy sun. From the high hanging balcony Vesuvius came into view, enveloped to its foot by radiant morning mists, and the silver-and-pearl eddies on the surface of the Bay, and the delicate contour of Capri against the horizon. One could see tiny burros, harnessed in twos to little carts, running down below over the quay, sticky with mire, and detachments of diminutive soldiers, march-

ing somewhere to lively and exhilarating music. Next came
the procession to the waiting automobile and the slow progress through populous, narrow, and damp corridors of
streets, between tall, many-windowed houses; the inspection
of lifelessly-clean museums, evenly and pleasantly, yet
bleakly, lighted, seemingly illuminated by snow; or of cool
churches, smelling of wax, which everywhere and always
contain the same things; a majestic portal, screened by a
heavy curtain of leather, and inside,—empty vastness, silence, quiescent tiny flames of a seven-branched candle-stick
glowing redly in the distant depths, on an altar bedecked
with laces; a solitary old woman among the dark wooden
pews; slippery tombstones underfoot; and someone's "De-
scent from the Cross,"—it goes without saying, a celebrated
one. At one o'clock there was luncheon upon the mountain
of San Martino, where, toward noon, not a few people of
the very first quality gathered, and where the daughter of
the gentleman from San Francisco had once almost fainted
away for joy, because she thought she saw the prince sitting
in the hall, although she already knew through the newspapers that he had left for a temporary stay at Rome. At five
came tea at the hotel, in the showy salon, so cosy with its
rugs and flaming fireplaces; and after that it was already
time to prepare for dinner,—and once more came the
mighty clamour of the gong reverberating through the
hotel; once more the moving queues of ladies in *décolleté,*
rustling in their silks upon the staircases and reflected in all
the mirrors; once more the palatial dining-room, widely
and hospitably opened, and the red jackets of the musicians
upon their platform, and the black cluster of waiters about

the *maître d'hôtel,* who, with inordinate skill, was ladling some sort of thick, reddish soup into plates. . . . The dinners, as everywhere else, were the crowning glory of each day; the guests dressed for them as for a party, and these dinners were so abundant in edibles, and wines, and mineral waters, and sweets, and fruits, that toward eleven o'clock at night the chambermaids were distributing through all the rooms rubber bags with hot water to warm the stomachs.

As it happened, the December of that year proved to be not a wholly successful one for Naples; the porters grew confused when one talked with them of the weather, and merely shrugged their shoulders guiltily, muttering that they could not recall such a year,—although it was not the first year that they had been forced to mutter this, and to base their statement on that "something terrible is happening everywhere"; there were unheard of storms and torrents of rain on the Riviera; there was snow in Athens; Etna was also all snowed over and was aglow at night; tourists were fleeing from Palermo in all directions, to escape from the cold. The morning sun deceived the Neapolitans every day that winter: toward noon the sky became gray and a fine rain began falling, but grew heavier and colder all the time; then the palms near the entrance of the hotel glistened as though they were of tin, the town seemed especially dirty and cramped, the museums curiously alike; the cigar stumps of the corpulent cabmen, whose rubber coats flapped in the wind like wings, seemed to have an insufferable stench, while the energetic snapping of their whips over their scrawny-necked nags was patently false; the foot-gear of the *signori* sweeping the rails of the tramways seemed horrible; the women, splashing through the mud, their black-haired heads bared to the rain, appeared hideously short-legged; as for the dampness, and the stench of putrid fish from the sea foaming at the quay,—there was nothing to be said. The gentleman and the lady from San Francisco began quarreling in the morning; their daughter either walked about pale, with a headache, or, coming to life again, went into raptures over everything, and was, at times both charming and beautiful: beautiful were those tender and complex emotions which had been awakened within her by meeting that unsightly man through whose veins flowed uncommon blood; for, after all is said and done, perhaps it is of no actual importance just what it is, precisely, that awakens a maiden's soul,—whether it be money, or fame, or illustrious ancestry. . . . Everybody asserted that things were quite different in Sorrento, in Capri, —there it was both warmer and sunnier, and the lemons were in blossom, and the customs were more honest, and the wine was better. And so the family from San Francisco resolved to set out with all its trunks to Capri, and, after seeing it all, after treading the stones where the palace of Tiberius had once stood, after visiting the faery-like caverns of the Blue Grotto, and hearing the bag-pipers of Abruzzi, who for a whole month preceding Christmas wander over the island and sing the praises of the Virgin Mary, they meant to settle in Sorrento.

On the day of departure,—a most memorable one for the family from San Francisco!—there was no early morning sun. A heavy fog hid Vesuvius to the very base; this gray fog spread low over the leaden swell of the sea that was lost to the eye at a distance of a half a mile. Capri was quite invisible,—as if there had never been such an island in the world. And the tiny steamer that set out for it was so tossed from side to side that the family from San Francisco was laid prostrate upon the divans in the sorry general cabin of this tiny steamer, their feet wrapped up in plaid rugs, and their eyes closed. The mother suffered,—so she thought,— more than anybody; she was overcome by sea-sickness several times; it seemed to her that she was dying, while the stewardess, who always ran up to her with a small basin, —she had been, for many years, day in and day out, rolling on these waves, in sultry weather and in cold, and yet was still tireless and kind to everybody,—merely laughed. The daughter was dreadfully pale and held a slice of lemon between her teeth; now she could not have been comforted even by the hope of a chance meeting with the prince at Sorrento, where he intended to be about Christmas. The father, who was lying on his back, in roomy overcoat and large cap, never opened his jaws all the way over; his face had grown darker and his moustache whiter, and his head ached dreadfully: during the last days, thanks to the bad weather, he had been drinking too heavily of evenings, and had too much admired the "living pictures" in the haunts of manufactured libertinage. But the rain kept on lashing against the jarring windows, the water from them running down on the divans; the wind, howling, bent the masts, and at times, aided by the onslaught of a wave, careened the little steamer entirely to one side, and then something in the hold would roll with a rumble. During the stops at

Castellamare, at Sorrento, things were a trifle more bearable, but even then the rocking was fearful,—the shore, with all its cliffs, gardens, pine-groves, its pink and white hotels and hazy mountains clad in wavy greenery, swayed up and down as if on a swing; boats bumped up against the sides of the ship; sailors and steerage passengers were shouting fiercely; somewhere, as if it had been crushed, a baby was wailing and smothering; a raw wind was blowing in at the door; and, from a swaying boat with the flag of the Hotel Royal, a lisping gamin was screaming, luring travellers: "Kgoya-al! Hôtel Kgoya-al! . . ." And the gentleman from San Francisco, feeling himself to be incredibly old,—which was as it should be,—was already thinking with sadness and loathing of all these Royals, Splendids, Excelsiors, and of these greedy, insignificant little men, reeking of garlic, called Italians. Once, having opened his eyes and raised himself from the divan, he saw, underneath the craggy barrier on the shore, a cluster of stone hovels mouldy through and through, stuck one on top of another near the very edge of the water, near boats, near all sorts of rags, tins, and brown nets,—hovels so wretched, that, at the recollection this was the very Italy he had come here to enjoy, he felt despair. . . . Finally, at twilight, the dark mass of the island began to draw near, seemingly bored through and through by little red lights near its base; the wind became softer, warmer, more fragrant; over the abating waves, as opalescent as black oil, golden serpents flowed from the lanterns on the wharf. . . . Then came the sudden rumble of the anchor, and it fell with a splash into the water; the savage shouts of the boatmen, vying with one another, floated in from all quarters,—and at once the heart grew lighter, the lamps in the general cabin shone more brightly, a desire arose to eat, to drink, to smoke, to be stirring. . . . Ten minutes later the family from San Francisco had descended into a large boat; within fifteen minutes it had set foot upon the stones of the wharf, and had then got into a bright little railway car and to its buzzing started the ascent of the slope, amid the stakes of the vineyards, half-crumbled stone enclosures, and wet, gnarled orange trees, some of them under coverings of straw,—trees with thick, glossy foliage, aglimmer with the orange fruits; all these objects were sliding downward, past the open windows of the little car, toward the base of the mountain. . . . Sweetly smells the earth of Italy after rain, and her every island has its own, its especial aroma!

On this evening the island of Capri was damp and dark. But now for an instant it came into life; lights sprang up here and there, as always on the steamer's arrival. At the top of the mountain, where stood the station of the *funicular,* there was another throng of those whose duty it was to receive fittingly the gentleman from San Francisco. There were other arrivals, but they merited no attention,—several Russians, who had settled in Capri,—absent-minded because of their bookish meditations, unkempt, bearded, spectacled, the collars of their old frayed overcoats turned up; and a group of long-legged, long-necked, round-headed German youths in Tyrolean costumes, with canvas knapsacks slung over their shoulders; these stood in no need of anybody's services, feeling themselves at home everywhere, and knowing how to practise the strictest economies. The gentleman from San Francisco, on the other hand, who was calmly keeping aloof from both the one group and the other, was immediately observed. He and his ladies were promptly helped out, some men running ahead of him to show him the way. Again he was surrounded by urchins, and by those stalwart Caprian wives who bear on their heads the portmanteaux and trunks of respectable travellers. The wooden pattens of these women clattered over a little square, which seemed to belong to some opera, an electric globe swaying above it in the damp wind. The rabble of urchins burst into sharp, bird-like whistles,—and, as if on a stage, the gentleman from San Francisco proceeded in their midst toward some mediæval arch underneath houses that had become merged into one mass, beyond which a little echoing street,—with the tuft of a palm above flat roofs on its left, and with blue stars in the black sky overhead,—led slopingly to the now visible grand entrance of the hotel, all agleam with light. . . . And again it seemed that it was in honour of the guests from San Francisco that this damp little town of stone on a craggy little island of the Mediterranean Sea had come to life, that it was they who had made the proprietor of the hotel so happy and affable, that it was only for them that the Chinese gong began to sound the summons to dinner through all the stories of the hotel, the instant they had set foot in the vestibule.

The proprietor, a young man of courtly elegance, who had met them with a polite and exquisite bow, for a minute dumbfounded the gentleman from San Francisco. After a glance at him, the gentleman from San Francisco suddenly remembered that just the night before, among the confusion of numerous images which had beset him in his sleep, he had seen precisely this gentleman,—just like him, down to the least detail: in the same sort of frock with rounded skirts, and with the same pomaded and painstakingly combed head. Startled, he almost paused. But since, from long, long before, there was not even a mustard seed of any sort of so-called mystical emotions left in his soul, his astonishment was dimmed the same instant; as he proceeded through a corridor of the hotel, he spoke jestingly to his wife and daughter of this strange coincidence of dream and reality. And only his daughter glanced at him with alarm at that moment: her heart suddenly contracted from sadness, from a feeling of their loneliness upon this dark alien island,—a feeling so strong that she almost burst into tears. Nevertheless, she said nothing of her feelings to her father, —as always.

An exalted personage—Rais XVII—who had been visiting Capri, had just taken his departure. And now the guests from San Francisco were conducted to the same apartments that he had occupied. To them was assigned the ablest and handsomest chambermaid, a Belgian, whose waist was slenderly and firmly corseted, and whose tiny starched cap looked like a scalloped crown; also, the best-looking and most dignified of flunkies, a fiery-eyed Sicilian, black as coal; and the nimblest of bell-boys, the short and stout Luigi,—a fellow who was very fond of a joke, and who had served many masters in his time. And a minute later there was a slight tap at the door of the room of the gentleman from San Francisco,—the French *maître d'hôtel* had come to find out if the newly arrived guests would dine, and, in event of an answer in the affirmative,—of which, of course, there was no doubt,—to inform them that the *carte de jour* consisted of crawfish, roast beef, asparagus, pheasants, and so forth. The floor was still rocking under the gentleman from San Francisco,—so badly had the atrocious little Italian steamer tossed him about,—but, without hurrying, with his own hands, although somewhat awkwardly from being unaccustomed to such things, he shut a window that had banged when the *maître d'hôtel* had entered and had let in the odours of the distant kitchen and of the wet flowers in the garden, and with a lingering deliberateness replied that they would dine, that their table must be placed as far as possible from the door, at the other end of the dining-room, that they woud drink local wine and champagne,—moderately dry and only slightly chilled. The *maître d'hôtel* approved every word of his, in most varied intonations, having, in any case, but one significance,—that there was never a doubt, nor could there possibly be any, about the correctness of the wishes of the gentleman from San Francisco, and that everything would be carried out with precision. In conclusion he inclined his head, and asked deferentially:

"Will that be all, sir?"

And, having received in answer a leisurely "Yes," he added that the *tarantella* would be danced in the vestibule to-night,—the dancers would be Carmella and Giuseppe, known to all Italy, and to "the entire world of tourists."

"I have seen her on post cards," said the gentleman from San Francisco in a wholly inexpressive voice. "As for this Giuseppe,—is he her husband?"

"Her cousin, sir," answered the *maître d'hôtel*.

And, after a brief pause, during which he appeared to be considering something, the gentleman from San Francisco dismissed him with a nod.

And then he once more began his preparations, as if for a wedding ceremony: he turned on all the electric lights, filling all the mirrors with reflections of light and glitter, of furniture and opened trunks; he began shaving and washing, ringing the bell every minute, while other impatient rings from his wife's and daughter's rooms sounded through the entire corridor and interrupted his. And Luigi, in his red apron, was rushing forward to answer the bell, with an agility peculiar to many stout men, not omitting grimaces of horror that made the chambermaids, running by with glazed porcelain pails in their hands, laugh till they cried. He knocked on the door with his knuckles, and asked with an assumed timidity, with a deference which verged on idiocy:

"*Ha sonato, signore?*"

And from the other side of the door came an unhurried grating voice, humiliatingly polite:

"Yes, come in. . . ."

What were the thoughts, what were the emotions of the gentleman from San Francisco on this evening, that was to be of such significance to him? He felt nothing exceptional, —for the trouble in this world is just that everything is apparently all too simple! And even if he had sensed within his soul that something was impending, he would, nevertheless, have thought that this thing would not occur for some time to come,—in any case, not immediately. Besides that, like everyone who has experienced the rocking of a ship, he wanted very much to eat, was looking forward to the first spoonful of soup, the first mouthful of wine, and performed the usual routine of dressing, even with a certain degree of exhilaration that left no time for reflections.

After shaving and washing himself, after inserting several artificial teeth properly, he remained standing before a mirror, while he wetted the remnants of his thick, pearly-gray hair and plastered it down around his swarthy yellow skull, with brushes set in silver; drew a suit of cream-coloured silk underwear over his strong old body, beginning to be full at the waist from excesses in food, and put on silk socks and dancing slippers on his shrivelled, splayed feet; sitting down, he put in order his black trousers, drawn high by black silk braces, as well as his snowy-white shirt, with the bosom bulging out; put the links through the glossy cuffs, and began the agonizing manipulation of the collar-button underneath the stiffly starched collar. The floor was still swaying beneath him, the tips of his fingers pained him greatly, the collar-button at times nipped hard the flabby skin in the hollow under his Adam's-apple, but he was persistent and at last, his eyes glittering from the exertion, his face all livid from the collar that was choking his throat,—a collar far too tight,—he did succeed in accomplishing his task, and sat down in exhaustion in front of the pier glass. He was reflected in it from head to foot, a reflection that was repeated in all the other mirrors.

"Oh, this is dreadful!" he muttered, lowering his strong bald head, and without trying to understand, without considering, just what, precisely, was dreadful; then, with an accustomed and attentive glance, he inspected his stubby fingers, with gouty hardenings at the joints, and his convex nails of an almond colour, and repeated, with conviction: "This is dreadful. . . ."

At this point the second gong, sonorously, as in some pagan temple, dinned through the entire house. And, getting up quickly from his seat, the gentleman from San Francisco drew his collar still tighter with the necktie and his stomach by means of the low-cut vest, put on his smoking-jacket, arranged his cuffs, surveyed himself once more in the mirror. . . . This Carmella, swarthy, with eyes which she knew well how to use tellingly, resembling a mulatto woman, clad in a dress of many colours, with the colour of orange predominant, must dance exceptionally, he imagined. And, stepping briskly out of his room and walking over the carpet to the next one,—his wife's—he asked loudly, if they would be ready soon.

"In five minutes, Dad!" a girl's voice, ringing and by now gay, responded from the other side of the door.

"Very well," said the gentleman from San Francisco.

And, leisurely, he walked through red-carpeted corridors and down staircases, in quest of the reading room. The servants he met stood aside and hugged the wall to let him pass, but he kept on his way as though he had never even noticed them. And old woman who was late for dinner, already stooping, with milky hair but *décolleté* in a light-gray gown of silk, was hurrying with all her might, but drolly, in a hen-like manner, and he easily outstripped her. Near the glass doors of the dining-room, where all the guests had already assembled, and were beginning their dinner, he stopped before a little table piled with boxes of cigars and Egyptian cigarettes, took a large Manila cigar, and flung three *lire* upon the little table. Walking on the terrace, he glanced, in passing, through the open window; out of the darkness he felt a breath of the balmy air upon him, thought he saw the tip of an ancient palm. Its gigantic fronds seemed to reach out across the stars. He heard the distant, measured din of the sea. . . . In the reading room, —snug, quiet, and illuminated only above the tables, some gray-haired German was standing, rustling the newspapers, —unkempt, resembling Ibsen, in round silver spectacles and with mad, astonished eyes. After scrutinizing him coldly, the gentleman from San Francisco sat down in a deep leather chair in a corner near a green-shaded lamp, put on his *pince nez,* twitching his head because his collar was choking him, and hid himself completely behind the newspaper. He rapidly ran through the headlines of certain items, read a few lines about the never-ceasing Balkan war, with an accustomed gesture turned the newspaper over,— when suddenly the lines flared up before him with a glassy glare, his neck became taut, his eyes bulged out, the *pince nez* flew off his nose. . . . He lunged forward, tried to swallow some air,—and made a wild hoarse sound; his lower jaw sank, lighting up his entire mouth with the reflection of the gold fillings; his head dropped back on his shoulder and began to sway; the bosom of his shirt bulged out like a basket,—and his whole body, squirming, his heels catching the carpet, slid downward to the floor, desperately struggling with someone.

Had the German not been in the reading room, the hotel attendants would have managed, quickly and adroitly, to hush up this dreadful occurrence; instantly, through back passages, seizing him by the head and feet, they would have rushed off the gentleman from San Francisco as far away as possible,—and not a soul among the guests would have found out what he had been up to. But the German had dashed out of the reading room with a scream,—he had aroused the entire house, the entire dining-room. And many jumped up from their meal, overturning their chairs; many, paling, ran toward the reading room. "What—what has happened?" was heard in all languages,—and no one gave a sensible answer, no one comprehended anything, since even to this day men are amazed most of all by death, and will not, in any circumstances, believe in it. The proprietor dashed from one guest to another, trying to detain those who were running away and to pacify them with hasty assurances that this was just a trifling occurrence, a slight fainting spell of a certain gentleman from San Francisco. . . . No one listened to him; many had seen the flunkeys and corridor attendants tearing the necktie, the vest, and the rumpled smoking-jacket off this gentleman, and even, for some reason or other, the dancing slippers off his splayed feet, clad in black silk. He was still struggling. He was still obdurately wrestling with death; he absolutey refused to yield to her, who had so unexpectedly and inconsiderately fallen upon him. His head was swaying, he rattled hoarsely, like one with his throat cut; his eyes had rolled up, like a drunkard's. . . . When he was hurriedly carried in and laid upon a bed in room Number Forty-three,—the smallest, the poorest, the dampest and the coldest, situated at the end of the bottom corridor,—his daughter ran in, with her hair down, in a little dressing-gown that had flown open, her bosom, raised up by the corset, uncovered; then his wife, big and ponderous, already dressed for dinner,—her mouth rounded in terror. . . . But by now he had ceased even wagging his head.

A quarter of an hour later everything in the hotel had assumed a semblance of order. Nevertheless, the evening was irreparably spoiled. Some guests, returning to the dining-room, finished their dinner, but in silence, with aggrieved faces, while the proprietor would approach now one group, now another, shrugging his shoulders in polite yet impotent irritation, feeling himself guilty without guilt, assuring everybody that he understood very well "how unpleasant all this was," and pledging his word that he would take "all measures within his power" to remove this unpleasantness. The *tarantella* had to be called off, all superfluous electric lights were extinguished, the majority of the guests withdrew into the bar, and it became so quiet that one heard distinctly the ticking of the clock in the vestibule, whose sole occupant was a parrot, dully muttering something, fussing in his cage before going to sleep, contriving to doze off at last with one claw ludicrously stretched up to the upper perch. . . . The gentleman from San Francisco was lying upon a cheap iron bed, under coarse woolen blankets, upon which the dull light of a single bulb beat down from the ceiling. An ice-bag was askew on his moist and cold forehead. The livid face, already dead, was gradually growing cold; the hoarse rattling, expelled from the open mouth, illuminated by the reflection of gold, was growing fainter. This was no longer the gentleman from

San Francisco rattling,—he no longer existed,—but some other. His wife, his daughter, the doctor and the servants were standing, gazing at him dully. Suddenly, that which they awaited and feared was consummated,—the rattling ceased abruptly. And slowly, slowly, before the eyes of all, a pallor suffused the face of the man who had died, and his features seemed to grow finer, to become irradiated with a beauty which had been rightfully his in the long ago. . . .

The proprietor entered. *"Già è morto,"* said the doctor to him in a whisper. The proprietor, with dispassionate face, shrugged his shoulders. The wife, down whose cheeks the tears were quietly coursing, walked up to him and timidly said that the deceased ought now to be carried to his own room.

"Oh, no, madam," hastily, correctly, but now without any amiability and not in English, but in French, retorted the proprietor, who was not at all interested now in such trifling sums as the arrivals from San Francisco might leave in his coffers. "That is absolutely impossible, madam," he said, and added in explanation that he valued the apartments occupied by them very much; that, were he to carry out her wishes, everybody in Capri would know it and the tourists would shun those apartments.

The young woman, who had been all this time gazing at him strangely, sat down on a chair, and, pressing a hand-kerchief to her mouth, burst into sobs. The wife dried her tears immediately, her face flaring up. She adopted a louder tone, making demands in her own language, and still in-credulous of the fact that all respect for them had been completely lost. The proprietor, with polite dignity, cut her short: if madam was not pleased with the customs of the hotel, he would not venture to detain her; and he firmly announced that the body must be gotten away this very day, at dawn, that the police had already been notified, and one of the police officers would be here very soon and would carry out all the necessary formalities. Was it possible to secure even a common coffin in Capri?—madam asked. Regrettably, no,—it was beyond possibility, and no one would be able to make one in time. It would be necessary to have recourse to something else. . . . He had a suggestion. —English soda water came in large and long boxes. . . . It was possible to knock the partitions out of such a box. . . .

At night the whole hotel slept. The window in room Number Forty-three was opened,—it gave out upon a corner of the garden where, near a high stone wall with broken glass upon its crest, a consumptive banana tree was growing; the electric light was switched off; the key was turned in the door, and everybody went away. The dead man remained in the darkness,—the blue stars looked down upon him from the sky, a cricket with a pensive insouciance began his song in the wall. . . . In the dimly lit corridor two chambermaids were seated on a window sill, at some darning. Luigi, in slippers, entered with a pile of clothing in his arms.

"*Pronto?*" he asked solicitously, in an audible whisper, indicating with his eyes the fearsome door at the end of the corridor. And, he waved his hand airily in that direction. . . . "*Partenza!*" he called out in a whisper, as though he were speeding a train, the usual phrase used in Italian depots at the departure of trains,—and the chambermaids, choking with silent laughter, let their heads sink on each other's shoulder.

Thereupon, hopping softly, he ran up to the very door, gave it the merest tap, and, inclining his head to one side, in a low voice, asked with the utmost deference:

"Ha sonato, signore?"

And, squeezing his throat, thrusting out his lower jaw, in a grating voice, slowly and sadly, he answered his own question, in English, as though from the other side of the door:

"Yes, come in. . . ."

And at dawn, when it had become light beyond the window of room Number Forty-three, and a humid wind had begun to rustle the tattered leaves of the banana tree; when the blue sky of morning had lifted and spread out over the Island of Capri, and the pure and clear-cut summit of Monte Solaro had grown golden against the sun that was rising beyond the distant blue mountains of Italy; when the stone masons, who were repairing the tourists' paths on the island, had set out to work,—a long box that had formerly been used for soda water was brought to room Number Forty-three. Soon it became very heavy, and was pressing hard against the knees of the junior porter, who bore it off briskly on a one horse cab over the white paved highway that was sinuously winding over the slopes of Capri, among the stone walls and the vineyards, ever downwards, to the sea itself. The cabby, a puny little man with reddened eyes, in an old jacket with short sleeves and in much-worn shoes, was suffering the after effects of drink,—he had spent the whole night long in playing with dice in a *tratoria,* and kept on lashing his sturdy little horse, rigged out in Sicilian fashion, with all sorts of little bells livelily jingling upon the bridle with its tufts of coloured wool, and upon the brass points of its high pad; with a yard-long feather stuck in its cropped forelock,—a feather that shook as the horse ran. The cabby kept silent; he was oppressed by his shiftlessness, his vices,—by the circumstance that he had, that night, lost to the last mite all those coppers with which his pockets had been filled. But the morning was fresh; in air such as this, with the sea all around, under the morning sky, the after effects of drink quickly evaporate, and a man is soon restored to a care-free mood, and the cabby was furthermore consoled by that unexpected windfall, conferred upon him by some gentleman from San Francisco, whose lifeless head was bobbing from side to side in the box at his back. . . . The little steamer,—a beetle lying far down below, against the tender and vivid deep-blue with which the Bay of Naples is so densely and highly flooded,—was already blowing its final whistles, that reverberated loudly all over the island, whose every bend, every ridge, every stone, was as distinctly visible from every point as if there were absolutely no such thing as atmosphere. Near the wharf the junior porter was joined by the senior, who was speeding with the daughter and wife of the gentleman from San Francisco in his automobile,—they were pale, with eyes hollow from tears and a sleepless night. And ten minutes later the little steamer was again noisily making its way through the water, again running toward Sorrento, toward Castellamare, carrying away from Capri, for all time, the family from San

Francisco. . . . And again peace and quiet reigned upon the island.

Upon this island, two thousand years ago, had lived a man who had become completely enmeshed in his cruel and foul deeds, who had for some reason seized the power over millions of people in his hands, and who, having himself lost his head at the senselessness of this power and from the fear of death by assassination by some one, lurking round the corner, had committed cruelties beyond all measure,—and humankind has remembered him for all time; and those who, in their collusion, just as incomprehensively and, in substance, just as cruelly as he, reign at present in power over this world, gather from all over the earth to gaze upon the ruins of that stone villa where he had dwelt on one of the steepest ascents of the island. On this marvellous morning all those who had come to Capri for just this purpose were still sleeping in the hotels, although, toward the entrances, were already being led little mouse-gray burros with red saddles, upon which, after awaking and sating themselves with food, Americans and Germans, men and women, young and old, would again ponderously clamber up the steep paths this day, and after whom would again run the old Caprian beggar women, with sticks in their gnarled hands,—would run over stony paths, and always up-hill, up to the very summit of Mount Tiberio. Comforted by the knowledge that the dead old man from San Francisco, who had likewise been planning to go with them but instead of that had only frightened them with a reminder of death, had already been shipped off to Naples, the travellers slept on heavily, and the quiet of the island was still undisturbed, the shops in the town were still shut. The market place in the little square alone was carrying on traffic,—in fish and greens; and the people there were all simple folk, among whom, without anything to do, as always, was standing Lorenzo the boatman, famous all over Italy,—a tall old man, a care-free rake and a handsome fellow, who had served more than once as a model to many artists; he had brought, and had already sold for a trifle, two lobsters that he had caught that night and which were already rustling in the apron of the cook of that very hotel where the family from San Francisco had passed the night, and now he could afford to stand in calm idleness even until the evening, looking about him with a kingly bearing, consciously and flauntingly picturesque with his tatters, clay pipe, and a red woolen *beretta* drooping over one ear.

And, along the precipices of Monte Solaro, upon the ancient Phœnician road, hewn out of the crags, down its stone steps, two mountaineers of Abruzzi were descending from Anacapri. One had bag-pipes under his leathern mantle,—a large bag made from the skin of a she-goat, with two pipes; the other had something in the nature of wooden Pan's-reeds. They went on,—and all the land, joyous, lovely, sun-swept, spread out below them: the stony humps of the island, which was lying almost in its entirety at their feet; and that faery-like deep-blue in which it was afloat; and the shining morning vapours over the sea, toward the east, under the blinding sun, that was now beating down hotly, rising ever higher and higher; and, still in their morning vagueness, the mistily blue massive outlines of Italy, of her mountains near and far, whose beauty human speech is impotent to express. . . . Half way down the pipers slackened their pace: over the path, within a grotto in the craggy side of Monte Solaro, all bright in the sun, all bathed in its warmth and glow, in snowy-white raiment of gypsum, and in a royal crown, golden-rusty from inclement weathers, stood the Mother of God, meek and gracious, her orbs lifted up to heaven, to the eternal and happy abodes of Her thrice-blessed Son. The pipers bared their heads, put their reeds to their lips,—and there poured forth their naïve and humbly-jubilant praises to the sun, to the morning, to Her, the Immaculate Intercessor for all those who suffer in this evil and beautiful world, and to Him Who had been born of Her womb in a cavern at Bethlehem, in a poor shepherd's shelter in the distant land of Judæa. . . .

Meanwhile, the body of the dead old man from San Francisco was returning to its home, to a grave on the shores of the New World. Having gone through many humiliations, through much human neglect, having wandered for a week from one port warehouse to another, it had finally gotten once more on board that same famous ship upon which but lately, with so much deference, he had been borne to the Old World. But now he was already being concealed from the quick,—he was lowered in his tarred coffin deep into the black hold. And once more the ship was sailing on and on upon its long sea voyage. By night it sailed past the Island of Capri, and, to one watching them from the island, there was something sad about the ships' lights, slowly disappearing over the dark sea. But, upon the ship itself, in its brilliant *salons* resplendent with lustres and marble, there was, as usual, a crowded ball that night.

There was a ball on the second night, and also on the third,—again in the midst of a raging snow gale, whirling over an ocean booming like a burial mass, and rolling in mountains arrayed in mourning by the silvery foam. The innumerable fiery eyes of the ship were barely visible, because of the snow, to the Devil watching from the crags of Gibraltar, from the stony gateway of two worlds, the ship receding into the night and the snow gale. The Devil was as enormous as a cliff, but even more enormous was the ship, many-tiered, many-funnelled, created by the pride of the New Man with an ancient heart. The snow gale smote upon its rigging and wide-throated funnels, white from the snow, but the ship was steadfast, firm, majestic—and terrifying. Upon its topmost deck were reared, in their solitude among the snowy whirlwinds, those snug, dimly lighted chambers where, plunged in a light and uneasy slumber, was its ponderous guide who resembled a pagan idol, reigning over the whole ship. He heard the pained howlings and the ferocious squealings of the storm-stifled siren, but comforted himself by the proximity of that which, in the final summing up, was incomprehensible even to himself, that which was on the other side of his wall: that large cabin, which had the appearance of being armoured, and was being constantly filled by the mysterious rumbling, quivering, and crisp sputtering of blue flames, flaring up and exploding around the pale-faced operator with a metal half-hoop upon his head. In the very depths, in the submerged womb of the *Atlantis,* were the thirty-thousand-pound masses of boilers and of all sorts of other machinery —dully glittering with steel, hissing out steam and exuding oil and boiling water,—of that kitchen, made red hot from infernal furnaces underneath, wherein was brewing the motion of the ship. Forces, fearful in their concentration, were bubbling, were being transmitted to its very keel, into an endlessly long dungeon, into a tunnel, illuminated by electricity, wherein slowly, with an inexorableness that was crushing to the human soul, was revolving within its oily couch the gigantic shaft, exactly like a living monster that had stretched itself out in this tunnel.

Meanwhile, amidship the *Atlantis,* its warm and luxurious cabins, its dining halls and ball-rooms, poured forth radiance and joyousness, were humming with the voices of a well-dressed gathering, were fragrant with fresh flowers, and the strains of the stringed orchestra were their song. And again excruciatingly coiled and at intervals feverishly came together among this throng, among this glitter of lights, silks, diamonds and bared feminine shoulders, the pliant pair of hired lovers: the sinfully modest, very pretty young woman, with eyelashes cast down, with a chaste coiffure, and the well-built young man, with black hair that seemed to be pasted on, with his face pale from powder, shod in the most elegant of patent-leather foot-gear, clad in a tight-fitting dress coat with long tails,—a handsome man who resembled a huge leech. And one knew that, already for a long time, this pair had grown weary of languishing dissemblingly in their blissful torment to the sounds of the shamelessly sad music,—nor that far, far below, at the bottom of the black hold, stood a tarred coffin, neighbouring on the gloomy, sultry depths of the ship that was ponderously overcoming the darkness, the ocean, the gale. . . .

1915.